MW00755802

# ADAM & EVE

Also by Sena Jeter Naslund

*Abundance, A Novel of Marie Antoinette*

*Four Spirits*

*Ahab's Wife or, The Star-Gazer*

*The Disobedience of Water*

*The Animal Way to Love*

*Sherlock in Love*

*Ice Skating at the North Pole*

# ADAM & EVE

*Sena Jeter Naslund*

wm

WILLIAM MORROW

*An Imprint of* HarperCollins*Publishers*

This book is a work of fiction. References to real people, events, establishments, organizations, or locales are intended only to provide a sense of authenticity, and are used fictitiously. All other characters, and all incidents and dialogue, are drawn from the author's imagination and are not to be construed as real.



FIRST EDITION

*Designed and illustrated by Lisa Stokes*

Library of Congress Cataloging-in-Publication Data has been applied for.

ISBN 978-0-06-157927-1

10 11 12 13 14 OV/RRD 10 9 8 7 6 5 4 3 2 1

To the memory of

James Michael Callaghan

Move him into the sun—

Gently its touch awoke him once,

At home, whispering of fields unsown.

Always it woke him, even in France,

Until this morning and this snow.

If anything might rouse him now

The kind old sun will know.

Think how it wakes the seeds—

Woke, once, the clays of a cold star.

Are limbs so dear-achieved, are sides

Full-nerved,—still warm,—too hard to stir?

Was it for this the clay grew tall?

—O what made fatuous sunbeams toil

To break earth's sleep at all?

—Wilfred Owen

# CONTENTS

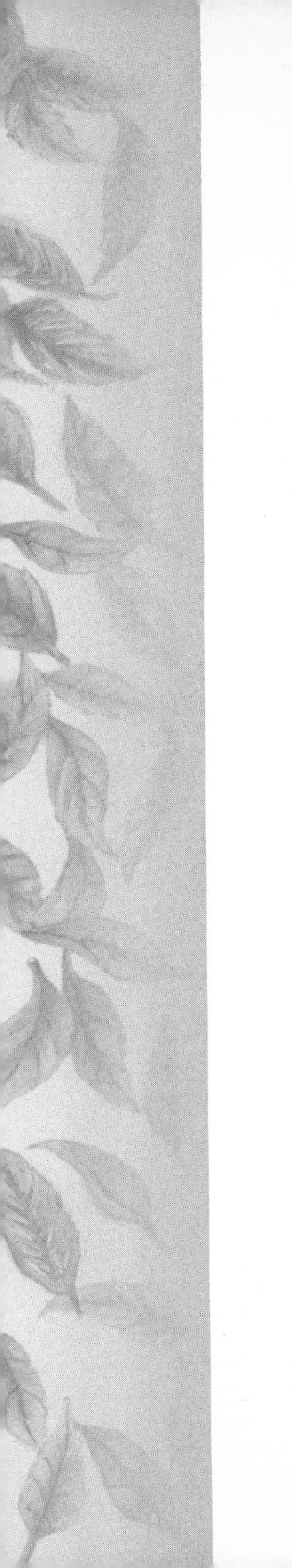

# PART ONE

# WHEN THE PIANO FALLS

A NUDE COUPLE is standing in the shade of a small, leafy tree. The quality of the filtered light on their bare skin attracts me, and I stand with them to enjoy the dappled shade. Through pinholes formed where leaves cross, the sunlight creates globules of brightness on the grass. My bare toes nudge inside one of those softly defined orbs, but then I remember to look up.

From the sky, at the rate of 32.2 feet per second per second, a grand piano is hurtling down like a huge black bird of prey over our upturned faces. In that moment is a beginning and an end, alpha and omega, Genesis and Revelation.

Because we always ask, like any logical child, "Yes, but what came before the beginning and after the end?" I start with the year 2017, three years before I fell into Adam's world and lived with him in the shade of an apple tree.

The instant before the piano fell, from a block away, I saw only a curiosity in the Amsterdam sky: a grand piano, aloft. To the beat of my rapidly moving feet, the words of the White Rabbit—"I'm late, I'm late, for a very important date"—played through my mind from *Alice in Wonderland.* My date was with my beloved husband, Thom Bergmann, an astrophysicist of international reputation. My name was and is Lucy Bergmann, and I was scheduled to join him and his colleagues for lunch. An imaginative, playful group for all their dedication to science, they'd named themselves collectively ELF—Extraterrestrial Life Focus. Using spectroscopy, they analyzed light from distant reaches of the universe to determine if the spectra had been emitted by biomolecules. My husband and his colleagues were searching for the atomic structure of amino acids, essential to life as we know it on Earth.

Not that I had anything to contribute to their scientific inquiry; I merely represented the curiosity of an ordinary, somewhat bright human being. Nonetheless, I knew something that none of them knew. I knew something that my husband had confided to me that morning in our hotel room. Because I had faith in my husband and believed what he told me, I knew a secret to which no person in the history of humankind had been privy. In an effort to contain my extraordinary excitement, I forced myself to watch the ascent of the piano as I hurried past the tall seventeenth-century Dutch houses on Prince Street toward the Blue Tulip Café.

That fine day in Amsterdam, in the spring of 2017, I thought it strange that the body of the delicate, expensive instrument was not dressed in a quilted case tailored to fit its unique shape. Darkly gleaming above the trees, the grand piano's ebony-colored sides flashed back the fresh late-morning sunlight, but the three pedals hanging under the keyboard had been fitted with socks of green felt. To protect the piano cabinet from the abrasive cables of the sling at points of contact, plump red cushions had been placed between the twisted wire and the polished wood. Someone who lived on the top floor must have been in a great hurry to have a piano delivered.

My husband had been talking about buying just such a handsome grand. Like many people gifted in mathematics, Thom was also a fine musician.

As I walked down Prince Street, I speculated that the piano was being lifted up the outside of the narrow Dutch house because the interior stairs twirled their way up too tightly to accommodate the passage of so massive an instrument. Almost three centuries earlier, the clever Dutch had anticipated the installation problem posed by furniture too grand for their interior stairs yet essential to their egos as testaments of bourgeois magnificence. During the construction of these multistoried, substantial homes, their builders usually had a hook permanently implanted outside at the apex of the ornate, arched facade of each house. By means of a pulley attached to the hook, large and heavy furnishings could be raised by laborious degrees outside the building to even the highest level.

At the top of this particular Dutch house was a high, large window, subdivided into many small panes, and it had been flung wide from its side hinges, like an open arm, to welcome the huge piano. I tried to see if the glass of the mullioned window was wavy at the bottom of each pane, but my eyesight was not acute enough to detect such an irregularity in glass at that height and distance. I knew glass behaves rather like a slow-flowing liquid; over time, gravity drags its molecules downward. I touched my own just-beginning-to-sag jawline and thought how gravity was beginning to do its work on me, at age thirty-nine.

That Amsterdam day four years ago, I was not only excited but also upset. I had spent the morning of our arrival from the States by visiting the Anne Frank House. The remnants of Anne's innocence—sepia photographs of movie stars pinned to her bedroom wall—and the horror of what had been done by the Nazis screamed that the world I called home was too terrible a place to abide.

A line from Handel's *Messiah* haunted me: "But who may abide the day of His coming?" In a scrambled way, I thought of Hitler as a kind of Antichrist, and of course millions of people did not abide the day of his coming. Some people—Muslim thinkers—have said that Western civilization ended with all that preceded and comprised the conducting of World War II. Some say that in our beginning are the seeds of our ending, but I believe, more optimistically, that in our endings are new beginnings.

Of course I would not attempt to talk with Thom about the Anne Frank House or the Nazi atrocities until after luncheon, when we were alone. Although I had left the orthodoxy of the Christian religion long ago, I had been *spiritually* moved, and that was what I wanted to discuss with Thom. I knew the profoundly disturbing Anne Frank House was sacred to the human spirit.

To try to settle myself (my *self*, not just my nerves, teetering between my stunned wonder at Thom's scientific discovery and the horror of human willingness to kill fellow humans), I had walked an extra block before I started down Prince Street toward the Blue Tulip. I suppose that decision to take the time, despite being late, to soothe my agitation into a smoother coherence saved my life.

Thinking of the Holocaust, I remembered when my fifth-grade class had visited the Lorraine Motel in Memphis. My school friend Janet Stimson had pointed at the balcony and said, "Murder. That's what happened here. Real murder." Despite Janet's words, I had been unable to grasp that reality—the assassination of Martin Luther King Jr. in my hometown. That morning in Amsterdam, at the Anne Frank House, I had felt the edges of murder. Like a thin sizzle crossing from ear to ear, real murder seemed to skewer my mind.

And yes, because of the reality of mass murder, I *wanted* Thom to buy himself a grand piano. I would tell him that much at lunch—just lean over and whisper in his ear. "You don't have to perform in Carnegie Hall," I would whisper, "to deserve to play on a concert grand." Painfully, I wondered as I walked what childish ditties Anne Frank might have sung when she was five or six. At that age she had been a friend of Thom's mother. Playing tea party, the little girls had lifted thin Dresden cups and saucers over a toy table to their dolls. Equally innocent, one had lived a full life, married, had a brilliant son, and one had not.

Perhaps, I mused as I walked—*You're late, you're late, for a very important date*—Thom and I might have a child: a daughter named Sarah Anne, for Thom's mother and Anne Frank. Late thirties was by no means too late to have a child.

A dark-skinned man wearing a loosely wrapped white turban leaned over the high windowsill and looked down to check the progress of the piano's ascent. He might have been from India or Africa. I wondered if Martin Luther King Jr. had visited Africa, the continent of his ancestors and of all our ancestors for that matter, if science is to be believed, before he met death on the balcony of the Lorraine Motel. I had the impulse to wave at the man, up there, but decided distraction would be unwelcome. His face seemed carved and soberly set. In the interior of my heart, I gave a discreet little wave. He reached out to touch the cable, almost as though he were twanging a single vertical string of a bass fiddle.

The piano continued to mount the sky. Strangely, it didn't stop at the high open window, though the man reached out his dark arms through the space to guide it in. The piano continued to rise till the metal loop at the top of its sling slammed against the pulley—I heard the clangor of the collision. Held tightly against the pulley, the naked piano swung wildly. Suddenly the three cables broke apart at the top, opened, and released the expensive instrument and the three red cushions that had been protecting its glossy finish from the sling.

As the huge black piano fell a little crookedly, its lid opened out, flapped slowly like the single stiff wing of a monstrous bird. The protective felt socks dropped away, and sunlight transmogrified the pedals into the brass talons of a stooping bird of prey.

I began to run. Still running, I heard the impact of the instrument, heard how it broke in jangled discord and the terrified screams of people close by. I ran harder. Approaching the door of the café, I gasped first with relief to see our friend Gabriel Plum lying beside the wrecked piano on the cobblestones. Stretched out, unhurt, he held Thom's eyeglasses with the thick black plastic frame in his hand and seemed to be studying the pavement through one of the lenses. Then I saw a pool of blood seeping from underneath the golden struts and snarled strings, the scattered keys and felted hammers of the shattered piano.

"Thom!" I screamed. My knees buckled, and I would have fallen but felt under my elbow the supporting male hand of some stranger who muttered in an unknown tongue the word *Igtiyal!*

Three years later, I would learn that this Arabic word meant "murder."

The day of Thom's death, I felt myself disintegrating, turning into dust, into nothing.

---

Earlier that morning, after Thom and I got up, Thom had taken his computer flash drive, which I called the memory stick, though the term usually applies to a device for cameras, from around his own neck and lowered the black silk cord over my head. It was a familiar ritual for the first morning after our arrival for a conference in a foreign country. During the scientific meetings, I would venture out mostly on my own; Thom's flash drive was a talisman, a love token, and a reminder that he was with me on my rambles. Without fail, I would return the memory stick to him at a shared meal just before he spoke at the conference.

That fateful day in our Amsterdam hotel, as he positioned the cord and its pendant around my neck, he said, "The keys to the kingdom." Smiling fondly at me, he gave the titanium case of his flash drive a little pat against my breastbone.

Adjusting the stick so that it hung concealed inside my silk blouse between my breasts, I smiled to recall that as a child in Memphis I had sometimes worn the key to my grandmother's home on a string around my neck.

"The keys to which kingdom?" I asked Thom.

"The inhabited universe."

"Only that?" I teased.

"Let me show you, Ms. Smarty," he said.

Drawing shut the hotel's blackout curtains, he turned morning into night. By lamplight, his large adept hands moved automatically among the utilitarian instruments of his profession: a small projector, his computer, a connecting cable. When he retrieved the flash drive, cupping it in his hand, he remarked, "Already warm," kissed it, and winked at me. Then he inserted the device into a port on the computer and turned off the table lamp.

In the darkness over our heads appeared a dazzling star-studded sky, clouded occasionally with reddish-pinkish zones.

"Behold," he said dramatically. Then he spoke in his normal, soft voice, full of intimacy. "The reddish clouds indicate a statistical reality—where extraterrestrial life is most likely to be found."

So many reddish areas! My knees felt wobbly. The tints of thin red and purple—sunset colors, dawn colors—looked like veils dropped here and there over the vast array of stars.

"How do you know?" I asked.

"Spectroscopic analysis—new methods—for detecting the presence of biomolecules in deep space. Other life is very far away, but it exists."

*Like heaven, but where?* I wanted to ask. Cloudy wisps of colors represented various biomolecules—pink, magenta, lavender, orange, a waver of green. Overlapping and combining in some places, the colors veiled the swirls of galaxies, stars, and golden intergalactic dust.

"It's gorgeous," I said, and my voice trembled. "You represent statistical reality as gorgeous." I was moved by his graphic, the way works of art sometimes move me in their ability to combine truth and beauty. Sometimes the paintings of my patients moved me that way—I was an art therapist at University Hospital in Iowa City.

"I suppose we're hardwired to see creation as beautiful," he replied.

In one reddish area, a drop of pure crimson, red as blood, caught my eye. I pointed and said, "It's throbbing."

"Growing larger, actually," he said.

As the dot enlarged, it lost its circularity and took on the point and lobes of a valentine. I realized I was seeing a love note from Thom emerge from the universe. The dot had become a heart. Hubris! I thought, but I was amused and pleased, too. In a red arch across the night sky I saw letters emerging. A message: "A Valentine to all the Lucys of the Universe." I felt embarrassed, giddy, and terribly in love.

"Oh, Thom!" I said. "You're not going to show this at the meeting. It's too much!"

"No," he said. "Not this part."

Then he made the sun rise. The stars on the ceiling dimmed, and finally the letters faded away into artificial dawn. While Thom opened the curtains to admit the real world of a busy Dutch morning, he mentioned that the flash drive held his backup data and the programs for interpreting it. "Much of it's also on the printout in my briefcase—the part I'm ready to present at the meeting." He unplugged the drive from the computer and placed its cord around my neck again. "But you'll bring me the memory stick, like always?" In the early days of our travels I had wondered why Thom wanted to risk the possibility that perhaps I would be delayed, through no fault of my own. Then this gesture of trust—in me, in good luck—became a ritual of our faith in each other. Again he patted the titanium case against my heart. "I won't show ELF my love letter," he answered.

As he bent to kiss my forehead, he remarked, "I'm not ready to tell them yet."

"Tell them what?"

"It's more than statistical probability. The place marked by pure red—that's it."

"What do you mean?" I felt blood suffuse my face, while my body flooded with fear.

"It's there. The red dot marks the place. It's there. Some form of extraterrestrial life."

I was stunned. It was as though I were seeing an alien in Thom. Then came an impulse to throw my arms around him, to recover my Thom with a barrage of kisses all over his face, his head, his neck. Instead, I kissed him once, slowly and tenderly on the mouth.

"Gabriel Plum called last night," Thom said quietly.

Gabriel was British, very dry and rational, a dear enough friend so that sometimes we called him "Sherlock" to tease him. Part of the Geneva group, he was enthusiastic about finding planets.

Thom went on, "Some fundamentalist group feels threatened by our search for extraterrestrial life." My husband spoke the sentence thoughtfully; it wasn't his style to ridicule anybody. "They contacted Gabriel."

"You've told Gabriel? The red dot?"

"Before showing you? Not on my life." He smiled at me. "But we communicate. He knows my methods for analyzing the data. He knows a discovery is imminent."

"When will you announce it? At the meeting? At lunch?"

"All the amino acids are there, in the spectra. It's life. I'm sure of it."

"But?" I could feel his hesitation.

Thom glanced away from me. He studied the carpet in our hotel room. He seemed embarrassed. "You know Gabriel is looking for planets."

"We've found thousands," I said.

"They're sterile. Gabriel wants them to be sterile."

"Why?"

"He wants us to be the only ones. Earth is God's chosen place. Where he sent his Son, in Gabriel's belief."

"But Gabriel was your student, years ago. He wants ELF to succeed." I took off the memory stick. "I don't want to wear it, Thom. It's too important."

He shrugged. Then he tapped his head. "It's all in here. I could do it again if I needed to."

"Yes, but how long would it take?"

"A few years. The programs are on the drive, too, the ones that make sense of the data."

I heard the enthusiasm in Thom's voice. Next he would offer to show me the programs, but I'd seen programs before—a jungle of numbers, tedious ones strewn with symbols, full of repetition. I had no training or ability to read them.

"I want to prepare people for the news. They aren't ready. It's too big. It will affect everything about our identity, about being human."

I knew myself to be shaken in a hair-raising way. "It's an earthquake of an idea," I agreed. "A tsunami." I squelched the impulse to ask him again, Have you really found life in space? Real life?

"I've invited an anthropologist, a Franco-Egyptian, to talk to them about the social and moral impact of scientific discoveries. He'll come to lunch. Remember Einstein's letter to President Roosevelt?"

"What would a discovery of extraterrestrial life mean to people?"

"Different things, of course. Fundamentalists in any religion are literalists. They take the words of their scriptures to be true in a literal sense, not evocative, not symbolic, not sometimes mysterious and incomprehensible, not reflective of the historic moment when they were written. Beyond their literalist interpretations, they're cocky enough to think they believe they have access to the mind of God."

"What did Gabriel want you to do?"

Thom kissed first one cheek and then the other. " 'Consider the repercussions,' was all Gabriel said. Adam was created in God's image. If extraterrestrial life looks like green mold, then so must their god, I suppose."

"I thought Adam was made of mud."

"From the dust of the soil—*adamah,* in Hebrew—hence Adam. But made in the image of God."

"Maybe polytheism is a better belief," I said provocatively. "I always thought monotheism was an arrogant idea designed to serve repressive political goals. We ought to go back to the Greeks—the Egyptians! Over to India! Dozens, hundreds, maybe thousands of gods."

After remarking that those cultures certainly had had their own forms of political oppression, Thom added, "Think how the discovery that the sun did not travel around the earth influenced our concept of our cosmic importance."

"Why does Gabriel engage in extraterrestrial research if he doesn't want to find life on any of the new planets?"

"Sometimes one does research to prove an idea is wrong."

Squinting in the bathroom mirror the way he always did, Thom made his usual effort to part his curly hair with a small fine-toothed comb. "Twenty-twenty could be the scientists' Year of Clear Vision," he replied. "Let's hope we're ready by then. Today I'll just talk about refinements in the methods of spectroscopy." Amused at the prospect of seeing clearly, Thom turned to regard me through his own thick lenses. He slid his glasses to the end of his nose. "Remember, a president of the United States thought the rights of his God would be violated by stem cell research."

In five minutes I knew those loose brown curls, increasingly tinged with gray, would be all over Thom's head again in sweet disarray. He was a large man and strong; I thought he was aging just as gracefully as he did everything else.

I replied, "I'll just meet you inside the Blue Tulip, right?"

When I explained how I planned to spend the morning at the house where the Frank family had hidden, Thom reminded me that his mother had known Anne Frank when they were both young children.

"I remember," I said.

"Sometimes," he said soberly, "I think we should achieve peace on earth before we deal with extraterrestrial life. It would be a sign that we're ready. Fission and fusion, the bombs, came too soon."

I felt a surge of love for Thom. He was a scientist who cared about human life, about politics, about culture. But I said, "Thom, I feel frightened. I don't think I should wear the memory stick."

"It's safer on you than on me. I could be kidnapped." He smiled.

"So could I. And what should I do if—"

"If I keeled over from a heart attack?"

"If anything?"

"Well, wait for a sign. Wait till your heart tells you it's time, till you see clearly. Consult Gabriel if you want to."

The conversation was too spooky. We both stopped. *Dazzled*. My mind was dazzled by the magnitude of Thom's discovery. He bent down, and I stretched up. Tenderly, we exchanged our last kiss.

More than twenty years earlier, in 1995, I had been a better-than-fair high school classical musician, but upon graduation I renounced playing the viola; I knew I was already nearing the limits of my musical talent, though not of my intellectual curiosity about my own mind or the minds of others. The last year in high school I read psychology on my own and insisted on taking the standardized exam for graduating college psychology majors. I scored well. In selecting a college from among several offering nice scholarships, I told my grandmother, "I want to be in the *middle* of the country," and I somewhat capriciously chose Iowa as the heart of the Midwest, though I considered Chicago. Three weeks after my arrival in Iowa City, I met Thom at an orchestral rehearsal held in the Union at the University of Iowa. Despite having aborted my own musical career, in my loneliness I had been drawn toward the familiar scene of rehearsal.

At the rehearsal I became irritated when the conductor had the violin and viola soloists skip over the unaccompanied duet section of the Mozart *Sinfo-*

*nia*. The conductor was depriving me and the rest of the rehearsal audience of hearing one of the best parts. I was mad at myself, too, for feeling desolate and missing my friends, especially Janet Stimson, and my grandmother, with whom I lived. (When I was nine, my parents had gone, as missionaries, to live in Japan.) Partly just because I wanted to have contact with somebody, I remarked crossly to the man sitting near but not next to me, "Haven't they left out the cadenza?"

The man looked startled. He had a large head and wore thick glasses. His hair was curly and soft. "I don't know," he answered quietly. "I'm not familiar with this piece." He turned back to the orchestra. In profile his nose and lips were large—suitable for his large head, I decided. The black temple piece of his thick glasses gleamed silvery in the mellow houselights. I forgot him.

No, after the music had been poignant in the way only Mozart could conceive, I glanced at my neighbor and noticed the quality of his attention. He wore the expression of one who could be moved by beauty. Then I forgot him.

Until, in a pause in the rehearsal, he blew his large nose into the neat white square of a folded cloth handkerchief. As a girl, I had learned to iron by ironing my grandfather's similar 100 percent cotton white handkerchiefs, but my rehearsal neighbor wasn't old. Older than I, but not old. Probably a doctoral student.

When I stood to go back to my dorm room, he smiled at me. It was the most purely welcoming smile I had ever seen—free of all intent but sheer friendliness.

"So they left out the cadenza?" he asked.

"A cadenza from eighteenth-century music characteristically ends with trills," I answered. "We heard the trills, but no cadenza. I'm an old viola player."

He looked at me quizzically. "Old?" Then he grinned. "Which high school do you go to?"

I knew I looked young: my hair was in two braids. I'm sure I flushed. "I'm a student at the university. From Memphis. Are you a graduate student?"

"I'm an associate professor in the physics department."

We had both misjudged each other. I laughed, and he smiled.

He waited, and then with unexpected sophistication I realized what I must say if the conversation was to continue. I must exempt myself from being a student in his department.

"I'm a psychology major," I said.

"A junior?" he asked, still smiling, and I knew he needed to guess my age.

"I'm a freshman," I answered, "but they accepted me as a psych major because I aced the advanced test in psychology on the Graduate Record Exam." It had been difficult to get permission to take the GRE; most high school students took the SAT.

"Did you?" He was obviously pleased for me. Perhaps he was pleased with me.

"I'm eighteen," I added. "I bet you waited too late to get a ticket to the performance. Like me." Suddenly my confidence faltered, and I relied on stereotype. "A typical absentminded professor?"

"Actually," he answered, "I do have a ticket. I just like coming to dress rehearsals. It's more relaxed."

"I procrastinated," I confessed. "I meant to get a ticket."

"I always get two. Usually the second one goes to waste. Maybe you'd like to have it?"

"Yes," I said. "Thank you."

As he handed over the ticket, he remarked, "The two seats are together."

"Of course," I answered, though I hadn't thought that far ahead.

He grinned more broadly, amused at both of us. "I'm forty-one."

The next day before the concert, I walked to the inexpensive beauty school near the campus and asked for a student stylist who could do an updo with curls. "With wings over the tops of the ears," I added. For the first time, I wanted to be transformed from a big child into a young woman. Entranced with studies, teachers, and a few good friends, throughout high school, I'd never dated anyone.

While the stylist combed through my hair, I avoided my reflection in the mirror by mentally reviewing the appearance of the physics professor—his steep, rather forbidding forehead, the thick lenses of his glasses—what did he want to see through those glasses? Big black frames. I realized I didn't know his name. A physicist—someone who wanted to understand the physical world in mathematical terms—*$E=mc^2$: Energy equals mass times the speed of light squared.* A physicist was someone whose inquiry concerned the basic nature of the physical world. Probably he didn't consider psychology to be much of a science, but I wanted to understand the *immaterial* realm—what *were* thought and feeling? What did being human mean?

"Did you bring a clip?" the hairstylist asked.

"No."

"That's okay. I can just pin it."

I enjoyed tipping back my head and fitting my neck against the rounded curve of the big sink. My grandmother always said, "I love going to the beauty parlor—the shampoo." I relaxed into the warm water flowing through my hair, the impersonal fingertips of the stylist pushing into my scalp and against the bone of my skull; I enjoyed considering how my brain was just beyond the stylist's touch. Shampoo provided a time to wander effortlessly through one's sense of self. How smoothly awareness moved from impression to thought to thought! What to make of it all? What did it mean to think? Even to see?

Sitting in the stylist's chair before the glass, I passively watched how the shaping of my hair was changing the meaning of my face, my future.

On the way back to my dorm on Iowa Avenue, I paused in front of a shop window and immediately decided to buy a white eyelet dress, Edwardian, with a long skirt and a long overblouse. As we shifted hangers along the rack of dresses to find the right size, the dress clerk said to me, "Your hair is lovely. Just add earrings—sky blue. I have some."

That night, I came to the crowded concert hall only a few minutes early. I was afraid I wouldn't have anything interesting to say to the professor if we had a lot of time to fill. From a distance, I paused to notice how the professor was shifting nervously in his seat as he waited.

He glanced at his watch; he tucked his chin down and studied his diagonally striped tie; he pulled down the cuffs of his white dress shirt. He wore large midnight blue glass cuff links, arched like two blue-tending-toward-black marbles. He had dressed up, too. He shuffled his feet; he pushed his thick glasses up onto the bridge of his nose. When he saw me at the end of the aisle, he grinned. Happy that I had come, he was at ease with himself again.

As I stepped sideways across the knees of those already seated, he stood up, stretched out his hand to shake hands with me, to welcome me, and said, "My name is Thom Bergmann."

"I'm Lucy," I answered, not bothering with my last name, for in the loveliness of the moment, I felt sure my name, too, would someday be Bergmann.

Each year of marriage seemed better than the one before. I grew up, really, within the safe boundaries of a loving marriage. My study of psychology and my deep-rooted interest in the importance of aesthetic expression led to my career as an art therapist for those who suffer a range of mental disorders. Thom went on to be promoted to professor in his department, then to occupy the Van Allen–Bergmann Chair. Coincidentally the hyphenated chair was named for Gustav Bergmann, an eminent professor of ontology and the philosophy of science who happened to be a distant relative of my Thom Bergmann. Eventually Thom became known internationally for his work in spectroscopy, and we traveled the world together because of his lectures and scientific connections.

I still believe the piano crashing into the Amsterdam pavement crushed the best brain in astrophysics in the world—my husband, my gallant lover.

In a few years, with war in the Middle East seeming like an immutable fact of life, my path would take me back among the scientists. At the same time, another story—one I would come to know as well as my own—another connection that would redirect my life, had its genesis.

# 2020: THE GATHERING OF THE DUST

ONE MORNING in Mesopotamia the strong Middle Eastern sun sought to warm the lifeless body of a nude man lying diagonally, like a slash, across an almost flat, bare riverbank. Vulnerable and exposed, he lay on his back on moist, sandy clay. His heels rested in the scarcely moving shallow water of the river. No life stirred in him, but he was not a corpse. To any who looked down and saw him from the sky, the beautifully formed young man would have been a puzzle piece. However, for a time there was no other to look down on his perfect, helpless flesh. A puff of fog hovered over his body for a moment before dissipating in the strong light.

It was the heat of the sun, the discomfort of it, that first caused Adam to stir to consciousness. He wanted relief. While he lay on his back in the mud on the sandy, moist riverbank, the sun of the Middle East baked him till he knew he was done. That was the first thing he knew, even before he opened his eyes, that he was too hot to stay as he was—in the oven, so to speak. He was done.

A cooling breeze passed over him, and he was washed by the coolness, the need of which had awakened him, though his eyes remained closed. The gentle energy of wafting breezes entered his nostrils, and the moving air tunneled its way as though it had volition through his nose, down his throat, and into his lungs. What had been outside him, and refreshing to him, was now gently invading him. When the breeze moved within him, he believed he was One with what was Beyond him because It had freely visited him. He sucked air into himself and was blessed with life.

As Adam lay on his back, he both felt and heard his breathing—the in and out of it—and he heard also, beyond the quietly flowing river, the sound of not too distant surf, with its own rhythm of coming in and going out. *The sea,* he named that sound, though he had yet to see it.

He knew his parts before he knew the wholeness of his being. There was something that thumped at the center of him. From the inside of his body beneath the bone of his chest, he felt its drumming.

Feeling—touch—was the first sense to awaken fully.

He folded the lobe of one ear and pressed it against the canal that led into his head, that passage to the interior, and listened. He listened patiently. Adam waited. Then he heard it—faintly at first, and then strong and regular, the drumbeats from the interior. Reverently, he placed both hands over his heart.

His feet stirred restlessly. The gentle caress of barely flowing water on his heels was not enough. His whole body wanted caressing, and like any baby, he wanted it *now.* If that was not possible, perhaps he could address that area of his body that seemed to be the origin of longing.

(Not his solemn heart!)

Something boisterous and frolicking, something mischievous and needy, something goatish with grapes in its hair, something laughing, and ready to dance on cloven silver hoofs! That part!

With first one hand and then the other, he reached for the part of his body that called without words to his hands: *Ease me!* Rolling from his back onto his side, Adam curled his body like the letter C so that he might know himself. And Adam touched himself till he was satisfied.

And Adam slept. He dreamed of vast watery heaving; he envisioned it as a mighty bosom ready to pillow the entirety of himself. Adam was, above all, a dreamer.

When Adam awoke and parted the lids of his eyes, he saw the fringe of his own lashes, both the top and the bottom. They frightened him, for he had an intuitive dread of the legs of spiders. 'Twas fear that caused his brain to jump. When electricity of very low but important voltage passed from one cell to another, the world beyond his own eyelashes flashed into being.

Thus Adam achieved through fear the sense called sight.

Noiseless, bright beyond belief! Banglike, but silent: behold: the visual world!

Adam looked and there was light.

He felt his heart beating, running, trying to leap beyond the confines of his chest, trying to squeeze itself out through the less solid spaces between the ribs. To leave that cage of self, to be a part, a true part of Out There! That was his frantic heart's desire.

Before him, the world hung flat as a painted window shade. It hung before him like an Impressionist's canvas—Renoir, Monet—all a-shimmer with color, but initially the world was without form or meaning. Patches of color: blue shimmered against small red dashes, leaving his eyeballs vibrating; green rested against blue and gave him peace and comfort. And what color was he?

Adam lifted his finger into his line of sight, and he saw that he was blue. Or that his hands, at least, were splotched and streaked with blue.

And why not? he thought. (It was his first fully formed sentence: *And why not?*) Surely I am born of the heavens, and why should I not be as blue as they are? And as sweet? Am I not as sweet as that heavenly hue? Thus began Adam's meditations on his own nature, but contemplation did not last long.

Though Adam was of adult size and had the body of a thirty-year-old man—undeniably—this was the first day of his life, and so he *was* but a babe. Lacking experience, or the consciousness of experience, he did not yet know the world into which he had come miraculously or by design. The baby in Adam watched his toes wiggle, but he quickly felt such playfulness lacked dignity, and he ceased. English words bubbled out of his mouth, though his syllables were ill formed and sounded like babble. Adam babbled on, not trying to make any sense but, like any baby and some poets, delighting simply in the music of his human voice.

A whistle mingled with the watery murmurings, yet it was more penetrating, a descant over woodwinds. I must know! Adam thought. Even before he could turn to look, the idea that he must know what was around him—the source of that noise—mutated into the idea that he must know *everything.* Scientist! He carried that possibility. Or philosopher. Poet, painter, lover, husband, father?

To locate the origin of the whistle, Adam surveyed the trees set back from the water. At this time, Eden-by-the-Sea had many varieties of trees living together in harmony. Here, certainly, were the palm trees, who were not only friendly within their genus—the date palm conversing happily with the coconut palms, the royal ones with the plebeian—but reached out with their fronds to the nearby oaks and tickled their thick and fissured bark, while the mighty oaks playfully peppered acorns into the boughs of the Norway spruce, which, in turn, seductively rubbed the dark striations encircling the white bark of the birches, some as thick as your waist, others as slender as your wrist. Chinese elms lived there, too, and pecan trees grew nearby, with their beautifully smooth-shelled, still-green nuts bunched in clusters. A grove of redwoods soared to celestial heights, begging to be worshiped in and of themselves for their ascendancy. So as not to be shaded out, the fruit trees and fruiting vines did stand away a bit from the more overwhelming forest, giving one another a courteous amount of space, apple from peach, peach from pomegranate, persimmon, scuppernong, etc.

It was among the trees of the fruit orchard that Adam saw a flash of color—red—and for a moment he thought that apples had the gift of flight, but then he saw that there were not only plants in the world but also animals, and here came a bird, who could whistle and fly. It was covered with feathers, and they were red. Quickly Adam checked his forearms to see if he were feathered, but he found that he was not. Nonetheless, he immediately wished he could fly.

And so desire (more intangible than lust) was born in his human breast.

The cardinal swooped toward Adam but came to rest on the prong of a piece of driftwood that the sea had deposited on the shore. Almost the length of a recumbent Adam, the driftwood propped itself on the shore, its gray feet still in the lapping waves. Adam wanted the bird—never mind the graceful driftwood or the unending ocean. He called out something poetic about how the bird was kin to his heart, but the bird could not understand his babble.

Lacking feathers, Adam could not fly to the bird, but he could crawl. He reached out with one hand, and it sank a bit into wetter sand; he moved the opposite knee forward. Repeating the motion provided locomotion, but Adam paused. He noted his handprint in the sand: the shape of it, four fringy fingers and an off-sprout of a thumb. He took proprietary note of the form he had created in the sand and said that it was good.

Though he had manly, well-sculpted muscles, Adam had not used them, and they were weak. He sat back on his heels and haunches to rest. A bird with long legs was wading in the foam of the surf—a beautiful bird, blue like himself, but with graceful drooping, curving feathers, a great blue heron, and Adam determined to stand up, for after all *he* had two legs like the birds, even if he lacked their wings.

Adam stumbled uncertainly on toddler legs toward the cardinal, but then the beaked red featherball flew away.

Adam wept.

He sat down in the moving water and rested his head on the knee of the gray driftwood. With his cheek against the smooth wood, he wondered about its story—where had it been, and how long had it floated in the water? The need for narrative began to gnaw its way outward from the deep convolutions of his brain. He felt a certain sympathy for the driftwood with its sinuous silvery curves—how time or wear had defined its grain.

At that moment, a larger wave broke over Adam's chest and head with a good hard smack. The wave knocked him backward, then withdrew itself into the sea with a large, rude sucking sound. Adam was amazed. The arabesque of driftwood, almost as big as himself, had been washed back out to sea.

Should he try to pursue it? No. He remembered how the bird had flown away.

He formulated an idea that had something of the ring of truth to it, though he had no idea whether his maxim was true or not: when something leaves you, do not try to reclaim it.

The color of the sky began to change on one side. Perhaps he had learned enough. The sky became pinker, then redder. Adam wondered if he himself would change color. As far as he could tell by examining his hands, he was the same blue hue, but the light was disappearing.

The sun was powerful and did as it pleased: it slid right down the slope of sky and into the water. And the world grew darker.

It was the evening of Adam's first day.

He was lonely. As the daylight drained from the sky, he was almost afraid.

Perhaps it was the nature of things that he was to have only one day. As the world darkened, would he slip back into the clay whence he came?

Forgetting how to walk, Adam crawled back through the water to the shore. If he were to dissolve in the twilight, he thought, if his flesh were to become again a part of the earth, he would have liked to make another handprint, to leave his mark behind. Perhaps a latter-day Adam would see his sign.

Resolutely, he spread his fingers and pressed his hand into the yielding sand. Because the sand was wet but not sloppy, it retained the form of his hand when he withdrew it. How well this lonely vacant print represented the reality of his palpable hand. Slowly, the mold of his hand filled up with water. Reflecting something of the scant light, his liquid palm print glimmered in the sand.

Leaving his work to fend for itself, Adam crawled to a slope of sand. To sleep, he lay curled on his side, his cheek pillowed by both his hands pressed together, palm to palm. But then one hand strayed to his hair. There he found a seam of dried blood. Perhaps he had been struck? Perhaps he had had a fall followed by a hard landing. Sleepy, Adam nestled against the dune, where the dry sand offered lingering warmth of the sun to its visitor's bare back.

Adam's eyelids fluttered down. He recalled how the redbird's wings had closed when it settled on the prong of driftwood.

Suddenly Adam awoke to look for more animals but saw none. He appeared alone upon an earth devoid of living creatures, save himself. Then the darkness parted her lips and smiled at him—the crescent moon rode above the black bosom of the sea.

Thus Adam's first day closed, but in his innocence he hoped to see another.

# A LIFE IN RAMALLAH

EYAD BIN BAGEN had been a Greek Orthodox Christian and a star physics student at Birzeit University near Ramallah until a chirpy classmate from Las Vegas asked him just exactly where the Virgin Mary had gone when she had ascended into heaven, bodily. Eyad had also studied English, so he tried as best he could to explain in her language that her question was irrelevant. Then she mocked him in competent Arabic and said heaven was someplace or it was no place and had no ontological status in reality. She had chosen to speak to him just while the muezzin intoned the Muslim call to prayer from his station high above the street. Eyad saw she was insolent, arrogant, blasphemous, and very pretty.

When he opened his mouth to rebuke her, to his own amazement, he, too, sang out the Muslim call to prayer, which he had heard and ignored all his Christian life. He could not have been more startled than if a dove had flown out of his lips. While his mouth hung open in an elongated O, she laughed in his face. In what language did she laugh? Filled with confusion and rage, Eyad could feel his hands tingle with the desire to strangle her, and he wished he were taller and stronger.

Instead, he turned away from her so quickly he spun out of one of his sandals. Where could he go but toward the mosque? While he crossed the pavement, he could feel her eyes scorning his straight back, his slight stature, and the limp in his gait caused by having to walk with one bare foot and one shod.

"Oedipus," she shrieked after him, braying her knowledge like a donkey. So she had studied ancient Greek literature. So had he. The prophecy was that a man wearing only one sandal would kill his father and marry his mother. Let it be, Eyad bin Bagen thought in his fury: I will kill the religion of my father and mother, as though the idea were a translation of Sophocles' Greek.

Eyad stalked onto the porch of the mosque, removed the remaining sandal, entered the holy place, and knelt toward Mecca, though he had no prayer rug. He banged his forehead directly against the floor until he began to leave a stamp on the stone with his blood.

"Comrade," the very tall young man next to him whispered. He had risen and was holding out his own rug to Eyad bin Bagen. And he was smiling: no teeth showing, just a simple curve of lips below friendly dark eyes. To Eyad's surprise, the towering young man turned and left.

For a few moments Eyad continued his devotion. Then he realized he wanted more than anything to see the softness in his brother comrade's eyes. When he arose and returned to the porch, the other young man was waiting for him, holding both of Eyad's sandals in his hand. "I have seen you at university," he said. "You are the number one physics student."

"I'm changing to mathematics," Eyad answered.

"Why?"

"It's a purer world. It has no reference to physical realities."

"I think this is the first time you are coming to the mosque? You are an Arab, but you have worshipped with the Greeks."

"The Muslims do not pretend that God is man, or that God was born of a human woman."

"There is no God but God," the student replied, and smiled. Eyad focused again on the sweet curve of his friend's smile spreading across his face and recalled that the tall student was majoring in English. "Romi is my name," he said.

—

The two remained friends for thirty years. While Eyad admired Romi's forgiving nature and his goodwill toward all people, Eyad did not share his friend's temperament. Romi married, and his wife bore seven children. He became a beloved teacher of high school English and a man with many friends, the second dearest of whom was Eyad.

In mid-September of 2001, Eyad made a pilgrimage to Mecca and took Romi's next-to-oldest son with him during a time when checkpoints had made it so difficult for students and faculty to reach the university that many courses were suspended, including the course in nonlinear algebra that Eyad taught. Eyad had not married, but he had become a highly regarded professor in mathematics, though he was considering resigning so that he might spend all his time with the Holy Book. He told Romi that a renowned English mathematician, Isaac Newton, had regarded his greatest work to be a commentary on the book of Daniel.

One day, coming out of a date shop, Eyad saw the woman, his classmate, who had laughed at him for believing that the mother of Lord Jesus had ascended directly to heaven. Of course the scoffer had grown older, too; he had heard years ago that she had married a Persian and lived in Isfahan, but here she was, entering the date store in Ramallah, wearing loose slacks and a green tunic, her hair uncovered. Quickly Eyad drew out the blade he always kept at hand and cut a smile on her cheek.

"Now I have given you a second mouth," he said quickly in a low voice. "Make it smile, if you can. Laugh long."

Eyad ran without limping into the crowd, and no one knew him from any other man. No drop of blood had spotted his robe, and he had dropped the razor, its mission complete.

"Life is a closed circle," he told his friend Romi that night at dinner. His friend said nothing, but nodded. Romi provided many sweet foods for his friend to enjoy—sugared almonds, honeyed dates, candied oranges—but he could not sweeten his friend's bitter mood, and Romi remained ignorant of its cause. For his part, all that evening Eyad felt his eyes shifting from the upturned corners of Romi's smile to the satisfyingly smooth cheek of Romi's pleasant wife.

After Eyad went home, full of bitter satisfaction, a knock came on his door. A holy man, an imam, stood there and said he was aware of Eyad's devotion to the faith. "You are a man of action," he said. "There is an American woman who wears an amulet. She is coming to Egypt; her husband was an astrophysicist. The amulet is a piece for a computer; it contains blasphemous information about life beyond the stars."

"The Quran speaks of no such evidence," Eyad answered.

"People are easily misled. It is never for us to know the mind of God, blessed be his holy name. The truth is everlasting. There is no God but God, and Muhammad is his prophet."

To these statements, Eyad nodded assent.

"Our resources are immense," the imam went on. "We watch many people who interest us. You are one of them. We have a mission for you."

"In whose name do you speak?"

"Perpetuity."

"Give me a sign," Eyad asked, but joy coursed through his body like a river that knows its origin and its destination.

With the tip of his finger, the visitor traced a smile on his own cheek, but he did not smile.

Eyad could not resist telling his old friend Romi, the master of English, that he had been chosen as a protector of the faith, in perpetuity.

"I have no quarrel with the other religions," Romi said.

"You don't understand. It is in concert with the Jews and even the Christians that we will act."

"Almost I wish that you had not told me," Romi said, but he put his arm affectionately around the shoulder of his second-best friend.

# PASSAGE TO EGYPT

IN THE THREE years following my husband's death, I never slid Thom's memory stick into my computer, but I kept the memento as a tangible object, a pendant hanging on the black silk cord between my breasts. Although I promptly turned over Thom's briefcase and printouts to the scientists, their work using spectroscopy to locate extraterrestrial life scarcely progressed after his death. As Thom and I had agreed in those last moments we spent together, I kept to myself not only his words to me, writ large on the face of the universe, but also the existence of the small red dot—that collapsed valentine, that drop of Thom's blood.

In those years while the nations warred in the Middle East and parts of Asia, I lived in a depression, a deep crevice. Certainly I received no sign from within my own gloom or from the state of the nations that I should reveal the secret of extraterrestrial life. The idea of that distant life seemed unreal, the emblem of a trauma I needed to bury. Yet I always wore the memory stick.

After Thom's death, I moved from Iowa City to New York City to a new position as an art therapist. When I was with my clients, my attention was absorbed to a great extent by the patients' paintings and sculptures—their work as a whole and all its parts. I rejoiced in their achievements. That they could create—begin, develop, and finish something! Wasn't that the very template of sanity? At least of continuity, which was one of the hallmarks of sanity.

Only once in the presence of a patient did I have a mental lapse: of a patient's white-and-gray rendering of the hospital cafeteria, I had involuntarily thought, "The Garden of Grief," and I said, "It's a wonderful garden," when I had intended to say it was a wonderful *painting*. Rendered in neutral tones of ash and char, the painting had been the opposite of a wonderful, colorful garden, but I found consoling beauty in its vision. Another time—not with the patients—at a bookstore near Lincoln Center, I had looked at the array of appealing book covers and said, "What beautiful flowers." Was *displacement* what I was after? A displacement from extended grief? Moving my work from Iowa City to New York had helped me leave some portion of sorrow behind. Not enough.

A new international symposium—in Egypt—had been organized to honor Thom, and I agreed to travel to Cairo to greet the group. I was glad to go, glad to have a mission, a new direction, a small but new duty to perform. I wore the memory stick like a shield over my heart.

After traveling alone from New York to Paris, I joined one of the scientists whom I've already mentioned in passing, our old friend Gabriel Plum the Sherlockian Brit, for the second half of the journey from Paris to Cairo. From the moment I hugged him at Charles de Gaulle, I found his tweedy aroma to be unexpectedly comforting. I'd always liked Gabriel, how a certain warmth and wit shone through his dry manner. Once aloft, we chatted brightly, then settled into moments of pleasant silence, as only old friends can do. From the window of the huge jet, I was admiring the ruggedness below of the mountains forming the spine of northern Italy when Gabriel leaned over and said quietly but with a certain British briskness, "I say, Lucy, suppose we get married one day?"

I burst into laughter, thinking he was making an old-friend joke.

Unperturbed, he went on. "Why not? We've known each other forever."

A tremor of grief wobbled my chin, and I bit my lower lip.

With smooth aplomb, Gabriel transitioned into a question. "Could you fly a plane this size? What's the biggest airplane you ever flew?"

"Corporate jet," I answered. "And you?" It pleased me to remember that Gabriel was also fascinated with flying. "What are you flying these days?" Since I'd moved from Iowa to New York, I hadn't flown much.

"Yes," Gabriel answered; he sighed. "Nothing hot, the new Cessna." He reached over and squeezed my knee. "For all your playing of Penelope," he said kindly, "Thom is a Ulysses who will never come home."

What I liked about Gabriel—he seemed as articulate and debonair as Tony Blair, the British prime minister who sent his troops to Iraq. Gabriel was more cynical, though.

Yet he had made me laugh. That spontaneous burst had let some daylight into my dark world.

On the difficult first day in Cairo, though I was exhausted from travel, I was scheduled to speak a few words of welcome to the symposium convened to continue Thom's work. Arriving a bit late, I walked straight to the podium. From just the corner of my eye, I caught the peripheral movement of the Egyptian host—a drapery of white robes—rising in a gesture of respect. The other scientists remained seated; they knew me well: an ordinary wife of a revered man. Determinedly, I grasped the edges of the speaker's stand. As I looked at the ELF team, I realized again that Thom was not only absent but dead; I pressed his memory stick—my talisman—against my breastbone to give me courage to speak into that void. Should I give the memory stick to them? Make a grand splash? There had been no sign. No revelation had occurred on the road to Now.

"Because this is the year 2020," I said to them. Then stopped. My voice brought to mind an antique china doll, plain and white—the type called a "Frozen Charlotte"—its face crazed with minute cracks in the glaze. I was breaking up. I tried to fight down my grief, but my mind reached forward in my prepared remarks to grasp their closing sentences: "'Twenty-twenty,' Thom used to say to me, 'might be the Year of Clear Vision.' May you prove him right." Then I mumbled, mortified by my naked emotion before the scientists, "Thank you for coming to this ancient land to pursue new truths, in Thom's name."

To supportive applause, I left the symposium quickly and entered the hallway. My hand closed convulsively over my talisman, but I considered jerking it off. I have never understood anger directed at a person who has died, but in that moment I felt a flash of hot anger at Thom for deserting me.

Just behind my shoulder as I hurried down the corridor, I heard the Egyptian host, Pierre Saad, padding along almost noiselessly in his soft sandals behind me. "Mrs. Bergmann," he called quietly. I hesitated.

"Mrs. Bergmann, I am so sorry. Please wait."

I stopped but, ashamed, I could not bring myself to meet his eyes. Three years after Thom's death, I should not have made a public display of frozen grief. With bowed head, I stared at the weave of the Egyptian's white robe, hanging straight down like a choir robe. In a flash, I remembered how I had pulled off my Methodist robe in children's choir and—to my parents' horror—refused anymore to sing praises to God, after my grandfather's death.

"We should not have asked you to do something so difficult." His accented English seemed as softly padded as the sound of his footfalls. "It is entirely my fault." His voice was too sympathetic; I could not look up at him without dissolving in tears.

Focusing on his sandal straps and on the square-trimmed brown-pink toenail of the big toe on one foot, I whispered, "I need to leave here."

"Of course." His voice modulated into formula: "I completely understand, and I am so very sorry that you are upset." Suddenly, in a new rush of emotion, he asked urgently, "But where will you go?"

"Nag Hammadi," I answered automatically. It was just a name, a place Thom and I had wanted to visit because ancient scrolls pertaining to the gospels had been found close to that Egyptian village. Those pages, as well as the death of my grandfather, had played a role in my rejection of the standard model of Christianity, the ardent faith of my parents.

"There, then," the faceless foreign voice continued, apparently satisfied. "Nag Hammadi. We have a museum there now. I hope we will meet again." He turned away to rejoin the symposium.

That night in Cairo—after grief had risen up like a floating stone in my throat, then sunk again—Gabriel and I shared a drink in the Marriott, a hotel with a largely foreign clientele, certainly non-Muslim. The hotel management maintained special permission to set up a bar to sell liquor. The hotel also hosted a gambling casino, which Egyptians were forbidden by Islamic law even to enter. I felt grateful to Gabriel for choosing a liberated hotel. While I was by no means an alcoholic—at least in my own opinion—I had noticed that a private glass of sherry at bedtime did a lot to ameliorate my chronic sadness.

Over drinks, Gabriel encouraged me to take a cruise-and-camp riverboat tour while he participated in the scientific meeting. Tilting my sociable martini glass toward him, I said, "There *is* a balm in Gilead, thank God." Wishing that the cone-shaped glass was a cylinder holding three times as much of the potent alcohol, I savored its flavor as I swallowed. I wondered if Gabriel had anticipated I would have a minor meltdown at the opening meeting, that I would need recuperation.

He had already researched the tour: a flight to Luxor to see the temple ruins, a Nile cruise with stops along the way—another flight to the Aswan dam—the gigantic stone figures of Abu Simbel—and a return to Luxor, where he would join me.

"Time in Egypt," he said, swirling his Manhattan, "casts a very long shadow. When I'm in this country, I always think how short our human lives are. It's depressing. Think how many of us it would require to lie end-to-end to take us back to the time of Moses."

The mixture of fatigue and gin allowed me to blurt out, "Moses. You believe in the biblical Moses, and I'm not religious." Had he actually proposed that we marry? I remembered glancing down at the bony mountains of northern Italy. "What makes you think we could get over our differences about religion?"

"I'm a gentleman," he answered, wryly smiling. "And an Anglican. We don't ever need to talk about our religious beliefs." He glanced up and down my body in a way too intentionally obvious to be offensive. "You might even enjoy High Church ceremony once every few years. At Christmas, perhaps." He tilted his head, his expression both shrewd and puckish.

For a moment I remembered that Thom had worried that Gabriel's faith might be threatened by the discovery of extraterrestrial life. I recalled the profound repercussions of Copernicus's astounding notion that Earth was not the center of the universe. Yet the church had survived.

I laughed. "I hate to admit it, but I do like the ceremony sometimes." On the heels of laughter, I fought down hysteria, my engulfing grief for Thom, who happily celebrated Christmas and Hanukkah. "Religion is always a quest," Thom had said, though he was not religious. "Stop questing and know you've become a fossil."

"I'm not as dedicated to endless research as Thom was, bless him," Gabriel went on in his casual, friendly way. "But if we were married, we could travel constantly. Where would you like to go with me?"

"Russia. I loved Tolstoy's novels. *Anna Karenina.*"

"The Russian *Madame Bovary.*"

"Their authors murdered them, don't you think?" I asked.

He ignored the question. "What about *War and Peace*? What about Dostoyevsky?"

"*Anna K.* is a better novel than *War and Peace*. The characters are more complex. But Dostoyevsky—he's too extreme for my taste, a fanatic."

"Quite right," Gabriel answered pleasantly. "At least our literary tastes are compatible. Another day we'll check off art. Matisse but not Picasso, I presume. Whatever made you become an art therapist?"

"Another night," I said.

"I look forward to it," he answered, taking the hint, but he hesitated. He bowed his head, then leaned toward me and touched just with the tip of his finger the cord around my neck. "What's this?" Carefully he pulled on the silk cord till the memory stick emerged from under my blouse. "Thom's flash drive? I wondered what became of it."

"It's comforting," I replied, feeling invaded.

"It could be useful, scientifically," he speculated. "Thom always used his flash drive at the end of a presentation. It was where he kept his latest thoughts, his grand summary. He always had a grand summary at the end of these big meetings. Did you know that? A moment when he drew all the data together, gave it his own brilliant spin, and made his next new insight seem inevitable."

He stopped and looked at me too hopefully.

"I gave you his briefcase. All his notes," I said. "The memory stick is for me." I began to feel irritated, a little vulnerable.

"But you've removed your wedding ring."

I said nothing.

When Gabriel bowed his head and seemed chagrined, I remarked, "Did you say there was *camping* on this tour?"

He lifted his face, and his eyes twinkled in their wry and engaging way. "On the edge of the Sahara. The tents each have a small solar-powered air conditioner."

Then, because I had not heard the terms of math uttered for three years, I asked impulsively, "Tell me again, the equation for elliptical orbits."

"*X* squared over *a* squared plus *y* squared over *b* squared equals one," he said, as I watched his lips speak the notation describing the orbit. Then he leaned forward, kissed me lightly on the mouth, and named a tour agency I could contact.

In the morning I made arrangements to travel and felt glad to escape the scientists. I told Gabriel good-bye in the lobby of the Marriott, though he offered to accompany me to the Cairo airport. When I saw that he wanted to kiss me farewell, I averted my eyes. I'd had enough of kissing. When I looked at him again, he had resumed an expression of friendly amusement. That afternoon I flew to Luxor, as Gabriel suggested, to take a cruise on the Upper Nile. I was glad to be traveling into the mythic past.

When I settled into the gray, wooden-slat lounging chair on the top deck of the cruise boat, I felt my entire body relax. Beyond the banks of the Nile, the landscape blazed like a mirror. I found it more comfortable to gaze down into the flowing river.

In my hometown of Memphis, Tennessee, the Lower Mississippi lay to the south, while the Upper Mississippi had its headwaters in Minnesota, but in Egypt the Lower Nile fanned out in a delta to the north before emptying its waters into the Mediterranean, and the Upper Nile had its roots deep in the heart of Africa. My gaze followed a north-flowing bubble on the river. "Where are you going, and where have you been?" I muttered to the waters of the Nile surrounding the boat. Hadn't I learned to ask those questions from a nursery rhyme while sitting in my grandmother's lap? Unlike the muddy Mississippi, the Nile was a ribbon of glorious blue.

The water seemed to reply to me with a question I both wanted and needed to hear: *Where are* you *going?* it asked. And my answer: *Nag Hammadi,* though I knew it was not a stop on the tour itinerary.

It was at Nag Hammadi that the outcast books of the New Testament had been found in 1945. Learning of the existence of those rejected gospels had broken the spine of my belief in the Bible as a canon of sacred texts. Sylvia, an elderly neighbor who was also a professor of comparative religions, had enlightened me. "Robbed you!" my mother had said. "Buddha! Enlightenment! You're nine years old! What can you possibly know of enlightenment? 'I am the Light of the World.' Who said that? Do you know who said that?" My skepticism about a God defined as both good and all-powerful began with my grandfather's cancer and death and my grandmother's heartrending grief, though it did not break her faith.

"The name Lucy derives from the word for light," neighbor Sylvia had said. She kissed me on the forehead. "Even a child can pursue enlightenment."

To ensure the safety of tourists from fundamentalist Muslim terrorist attacks on busloads of Western foreigners, heavily armed military guards stood at the perimeter of every attraction: at the Great Pyramids of Giza, at the Sphinx, at the Valley of the Kings, at the High Dam. At one of the attractions, I looked up, saw the ubiquitous soldier with a machine gun at the highest point, and remarked to a fellow traveler that his presence was reassuring. "Not entirely," the man replied. "The government obviously considers us to be at risk."

I rather liked the idea of being at risk. It made me feel more alert.

—

The first night we camped, I stretched my body so that it completely filled the cot. That night I enjoyed something like a sense of largesse—maybe it was just my body's response to the smooth clean sheet below and the pleasant soft whiteness above. I smoothed the sheets with open palms. Egyptian long-staple cotton, I thought happily, and a space that was all mine. In Memphis, beside the Mississippi, farmers had grown huge fields of cotton.

And when was the last time I had felt exceptionally brave and strong? Independent? In my friendship with other girls, especially Janet Stimson when we were about eleven and rode the city bus to the public library. The crown of childhood had come the year before college, when I had studied psychology on my own as a high school senior and then scored well on the psychology test for college graduates. Before Iowa.

It was not the *remembrance* of things past that I wanted, but their recovery. And not of *things* but of the natural self I once embodied. Suddenly I was glad to be alone, and I felt like a smart, young girl again, full of power, back before Thom entered my life.

I fingered the memory stick and took it off, for the night. Restless, I got up and went outside to view the Egyptian night sky. From the dazzle of stars in the dark, I picked out constellations. Had Thom really found out there a planet or planets that hosted life? Not among any of those tiny lights visible to me. Beyond that. Did those beings have eyes, and did they look this way and imagine us, bare forked creatures?

In the morning, I lifted the tent window flap and squinted at the world outside. Mercilessly the morning sun had filled the world with painful brightness. Other small tents were spaced around me. How to take life by the hand and sally forth?

Another night when the setting sun, swollen like the belly of a pregnant woman, slid down behind the peak of the obelisk at Luxor, I wished someone were there to see it with me—a man to whom I would say, with some satisfaction, that the Arabic word for sun was feminine. I pronounced the word for sun and thought of how I might spell it in the Roman alphabet: *sham su*?

If that imagined man were Gabriel, he would laugh and call me "smarty pants" for my effort with Arabic. Likely, he would also pinch my cheek in a paternal way. Gabriel was ten years older than I was, but then Thom had been twenty-three years older. I was glad that Thom had gotten to live as long as he had, though he had not made it to sixty. Unthinkable really, that I myself should ever arrive at age sixty.

Marry Gabriel Plum? Why not? I had known him since graduate school days in Iowa City. He had come there to study the Van Allen radiation belts. He had known Thom. Perhaps Thom had saved Gabriel's life by pushing him out of harm's way as the piano hurtled downward. I thought bitterly of the unbearable, premature relief I had felt seeing Gabriel lying on the pavement, clear of the shattered piano.

Did I want to move on with my life? Or did I want to move backward, to childhood, to a time before loss and grief? Both, of course.

When I looked at the broken columns and damaged images of temple ruins, I only felt how broken and damaged I was. It was only as I stared at the waters of the Nile that I felt any peace. A river can be like a great life-supporting artery flowing through the body of a country. The Mississippi, the Nile, the Thames, the Seine, the Danube, the Rhine, the Amazon, the Ganges, and the Yangtze. Such a river is an artery with its own pulse. Such a river is its own heart as well as that of the land it parts and nourishes. I wished for such a conduit of life to flow through me and enliven all my parts. Or some ocean to rock and lave me. A tour of ruins, however noble or ambitious, was not enough.

After a week with the tour group, I decided to strike out on my own. When the guide said, "I am forbidden to allow you to leave the group," I replied, "I state in this letter that I have left without obtaining your permission." Then I turned and walked away, carrying only my small suitcase with me. If they wanted to transport my other baggage for me, let them. I could not say what possessed me to do such a thing—to follow a mere name: *Nag Hammadi*. It was a whim, an impulse. No, it was part of a desire to be free. I wanted to test myself as an independent woman.

## *IGTIYAL!*

AMONG THE NAG HAMMADI texts—sometimes called the Gnostic gospels—was one purported to be written by Mary Magdalene, an actual disciple and possible lover of Jesus; another, the repressed Gospel of Thomas, had been construed as stressing the humanity rather than the divinity of Jesus. These religious texts took their name from the place on the Upper Nile—Nag Hammadi—where they had been found in 1945.

Considering myself to be fairly well informed as a teen—at least I *wanted* to be well informed, to know, to study, to see with my own eyes—I wondered why so few people seemed to have even heard anything about books excluded from the biblical canon, let alone considered their content. Since the revelation by neighbor Sylvia, I was amazed at how few religious people wanted to know how the canon had been formed. Held sacred by my evangelical parents and most of the people I knew, the Bible was inviolate, as though it had no history. But mere men had struggled for intellectual ascendancy in establishing what was sacred, and they had eliminated those books with alternative views. An array of gospels had been boiled down to the standard four included in the New Testament.

"Skepticism is a path," my retired neighbor the dear old professor had cautioned, "not a destination."

Of Tennyson's poem *In Memoriam*, written against the loss of his friend Arthur Hallam, Sylvia told me T. S. Eliot had said it was a great poem not for the quality of its faith but for the quality of its doubt.

Before I entered the information center at Nag Hammadi, I noticed an alabaster many-mouthed fountain, a large, bubbling jar positioned at the center of the entrance plaza. The fountain referenced the actual man-size jar containing the suppressed gospels that had been buried in the sand near Nag Hammadi, hidden for fifteen centuries. The bubbling fountain jar, fashioned from mottled alabaster, seemed both stately and droll. In response to its figure, I had a dizzy impulse to say, "How do you do?" Perhaps I did speak. I noticed a brown man wearing a loosely wrapped turban gazing curiously at me. His eyes were dark as dates, but menacing. Because of the heat, I hurried toward the information center.

The ferociously air-conditioned, beautifully modern structure provided a great relief from the Egyptian oven. From the bottom of a framed picture of the current president-dictator cascaded a ladder of translations of the word *Welcome*.

"Thank you," I said out loud to the dictator and wondered if I were losing my mind.

From the place where I stood, thirteen spokes projected outward in a semicircle, one for each of the Nag Hammadi gospels, like rays from a half-risen sun. Each ray displayed along its walls a series of the individual pages with translations from that gospel. Even before I began to read, my feet protested the hard granite floors. No one likes to read standing up; even at the Louvre the short placards beside famous paintings are always read with impatience.

Dutifully, I explored the extensive display, starting with the Gospel of Philip, Nag Hammadi Codex II. I read, "God is a dyer," that "good dyes, true dyes" dissolved into the fabrics dipped into them. So it is with heat, I thought: when I am plunged into heat, it becomes part of me and I of it.

The Gospel of Philip suggested that Adam and Eve were originally one androgynous figure. I wanted to drink to the idea. *Let Adam and Eve absorb one another,* I amended. But most of the Gospel of Philip was about the Christian era, not Genesis. I studied the Willis Barnstone English versification of Philip's meditation on names:

> Father, son, holy spirit, life, light, resurrection, church.
> *These words are not real. They are unreal*
> *but refer to the real, and are heard in the world.*
> *They fool us. If those names were in the eternal realm,*
> *they would never be heard on earth.*
> *They were not assigned to us here.*
> *Their end dwells in the eternal realm.*

I, too, believed in the ineffable. As an art therapist, I believed that the hand that draws inner realities is the friend of the anguished soul. A picture can evoke what cannot be said. But what would I myself do without language? Without Freud, without neighbor Sylvia? Without explanation? Philip in early Christian times had an answer, disregarding any shame at contradicting himself. He conceded, "Truth made names in the world; without words we cannot think." I added, *But to weigh any word as solid gold is a snare and delusion. Admire language as we admire pyrite, for its lovely glitter.*

I walked on through the display to read a hilarious idea from the early days of Christendom: "Some people are afraid they will ascend from death naked." This expression of anxious modesty had been written probably in the third century, in Greek, perhaps in the land of Syria, and, I read, it had come down as a Coptic translation found in Egypt. But had not certain sincere, God-drenched nineteenth-century American sects made for themselves ascension robes to avoid just that problem of nakedness? For how many centuries would people languish in their foolishness?

My globed and sagging grandmother had often emerged stark naked from our only bathroom looking like the prehistoric Venus of Willendorf as she shuffled her bare, lumpy flesh to her bedroom for clothes. "Too steamy to dress in there," she sometimes explained. Thom had liked to sleep half nude in a thin T-shirt, but I had said, laughing, that if I slept entirely in the nude (the way he liked) then he had to, too. Yet, in the morning, he often was wearing a T-shirt, grinning like a bad boy. "Gray curls above, gray curls below," I teased when he emerged from the sheets. I always added the exclamation, "Beautiful!" Had Thom ever said a cross or unkind word in his life? Not that I could remember. Not to me. Our life had been full of hard work, for both of us, but it had been paradise.

Perhaps because of its name, I felt most interested in the Gospel of Thomas and walked to that display. A good Jew, my own Thomas had regarded Jesus as a teacher, a prophet—as did the respectful Muslims who had created the Nag Hammadi exhibition.

While surveying the Swedish translation for familiar cognates, I realized that a man standing nearby was looking steadfastly at me. For a moment, I continued to consider the enlarged page exhibited before me—it was hand-lettered onto tawny "aged" papyrus. Then, because he still stared, I took a deep breath of the cooled, delicious air and turned to encounter the gaze of a middle-aged Arab with golden eyes. Though suspended between crutches, he took three quick steps toward me. I must have looked frightened, because he immediately not only turned away from me but also hobbled toward the exit and out of the building.

Half an hour later, I was ready to exit, but at the open door the heat of the desert drove me back. I retreated to a restroom and took off my bra and underpants and stuffed them in my small suitcase. My long skirt wrapped around me twice and fastened securely with a tie. I was perfectly decent. When I left the information center, the outdoor brightness of the Middle Eastern sun surprised me again—a sun more blinding than illuminating. But I felt freer and cooler. No one could really study the meaning of texts while standing before a display case, I grumbled to myself. I felt vaguely disappointed with my pilgrimage.

While I had been inside, protestors from the Christian religious right had convened to march in a tight, pointless circle around the jar fountain; their placards read: "Beware the Lies of the So-Called Gospels!" "Trust the True Bible," "COUNTERFEIT!" "Beware the Snares of SATAN!" Though these

Christian fundamentalists were marching peacefully, all the signs were printed in bloodred. They were like an inexorable clock in their circumambulation. I walked through their circle to approach the fountain. The bronze placard inset beside the jar fountain was inscribed in Arabic, German, and English, and it identified the sculptor as a woman. I was pleased.

The fountain was only a year old, installed in the year 2019. Water bubbled, sometimes seeped, from apertures piercing the alabaster of the fountain jar, one opening for each of the thirteen books the actual ancient jar had contained. The meticulous sculptor had gone to the trouble of examining the site of the discovered stone jar and had reproduced that slope here as the base for the fountain.

I envisioned the moment in 1945 when just the lip of the mouth of the original jar had made its way to the surface after having been buried for some fifteen hundred years. It was as though the jar had wanted to speak. Chasing a goat, perhaps, a peasant boy had stubbed his toe against the curved protrusion.

Beside me, someone female said, "It makes one wonder, doesn't it, how many other stone jars lie buried in the sand and rocks, all of them with suppressed messages?"

Turning, I saw a young Middle Eastern woman; she had spoken confident English with an American accent. Her black hair—uncovered, tucked behind her ear on one side—hung loosely almost to her shoulders. She had perched her black-framed sunglasses on top of her dark hair, like a headband. The young woman—perhaps twenty-five—was tall and pretty, unpretentious.

"No," I answered slowly. "I wasn't thinking that. I was just admiring the fountain."

"Do you like it?" she asked. "Aesthetically?" A smile still hovered around her lips, but instead of looking at me, she was gazing fondly at the fountain.

"Very much," I answered.

"I'm glad," she answered. "I made it." She pointed to the bronze plaque. "I am Arielle Saad. I believe you know my father."

"No," I said again, but I suddenly felt better than I had for a long time—interested and eager. The circle of protestors had removed themselves to flank the entrance to the museum.

"My father's name is Pierre Saad; he knew your husband."

I realized that the Egyptian woman's father had been the host for the symposium. "I'm sorry to have missed getting acquainted with your father," I said.

"Perhaps you'd like to talk with him now?" Arielle Saad suggested. "I could take you to him. Only a three-minute walk from here."

I took a breath. "So you are a sculptor?" I said evasively.

"Yes," Arielle answered. "And a pilot, as you are."

I drew back. How would this young woman know that fact about me?

Arielle laughed. Perfectly at ease, she added, "I've frightened you. I'm sorry. We have a favor to ask of you, but my father can explain it better than I can."

"A favor? Couldn't he come here?"

"Here we are watched. Soldiers with telescopic lenses—don't look—are on the tops of all these buildings."

"You think he would be shot?"

"They use the lens, binoculars, too, to read lips."

"Perhaps they are reading our lips," I suggested shrewdly.

"I made this fountain. Why shouldn't I come here to admire my work?" she asked. "Notice I'm facing the desert." She seemed not only composed but happy with our conversation. Yes, Arielle Saad stood with her back to the two brown-clad guards high up on the structure of the information center.

"Where is your father?"

"He is in the back part of a house that tourists visit, one that sells figures carved from camel bone and also essential oils, Egyptian-woven carpets, objects for tourists. Follow me." She lowered her sunglasses and strode away.

For a moment I hesitated. Arielle Saad? She did not look back as she stepped into the deep shade of a narrow street. I looked around. Three soldiers were dispersing the sign-carrying protestors from the tourist attraction. I began to follow Arielle Saad.

It was not easy to keep the young woman in sight. Walking quickly, Arielle turned the stucco corner of a thick-walled building. A man with a donkey steered his onion cart to one side so she could pass. She had to skirt a large hairy lump of a camel sitting in the narrow street and chewing its cud. The smell of animal hair pervaded the passage. Glancing back, to try to memorize the return route, I saw soldiers arresting some Egyptian men in turbans. Veiled women looked at me curiously and quickly glanced away. After my next hurried turn, I looked back again. Ahead, Arielle had disappeared. I concluded the young woman must have turned down another narrow street. As I rounded a stuccoed corner, a film of sweat veiled my skin.

Ah! My guide had paused in the blue arched doorway of a white building. She had lowered her dark glasses, but she smiled slightly at me. Arielle looked a bit like old photos of Jackie Onassis, but younger, more confident, browner, of course. A man passed by, leading a billy goat, its horns tipped with red balls. While I hurried toward my guide, Arielle extended her hand, palm up, beckoning.

"Come speak with my father."

I stepped inside. Though the floor was made of packed dirt, paradoxically it seemed clean; the room was painted a vibrant turquoise blue throughout. Its walls were lined with mud-brick benches, like buttresses, against the wall. The benches were wide enough to serve as beds and were covered in places with woven mats, orange and red. No one was inside the turquoise room.

"Back here," Arielle encouraged.

Passing an open, waist-high square formed of white-painted mud bricks, I glanced down into it. The enclosure sank below the surface of the floor—a pit for small crocodiles, each about as long as my forearm. One baby croc stood up in a corner with an open pink mouth, full of sharp teeth.

"You can buy one." Arielle tossed back the sentence over her shoulder.

"What for?"

"For dinner," Arielle answered. She shrugged. "For a pet. For a wallet."

We pushed aside a curtain into a room with chalk-white walls and ceiling. Under the high, vaulted ceiling a lone man with drooping head sat dozing at a wooden table. A wooden crutch, with a sponge-padded shoulder rest, slanted against the table, and on the rough table rested a book bound in black leather. Like so many objects I had seen in Egypt, the old-fashioned crutch suggested American items discarded many decades earlier.

The man lifted his sleepy eyes, but he did not rise. "Enchanté," he said.

His eyes were golden. "Je m'appelle Pierre Saad." He seemed to be still asleep, speaking from a dream.

"I'm Lucy Bergmann," I said firmly. "We spoke briefly in Cairo. I believe you knew my husband."

"Only a little," he answered. His accent was like a fragrance—sandalwood; it had wafted my way before. "I knew of Thom Bergmann. . . . I knew his voice," he murmured, his lips barely moving.

Suddenly he became fully awake. "Before Professor Bergmann's unfortunate death, we had spoken several times on the telephone."

"I'm sorry; I didn't feel up to conversation in Cairo." I remembered Pierre Saad's concern, his kindness. Trying to be polite, I stammered, "I . . . I appreciate your sympathy."

"But you are better now?" He smiled. "Your journey on the Nile has soothed you?"

I felt embarrassed. "You wanted to speak with me. A favor?"

"Yes." He merely gazed at me. Now he was fully alert—a stranger, but my having watched him return by degrees to consciousness had enveloped us in an aura of intimacy. A hypnotic spell. His eyes were the color of wet sand, tawny like a lion's eyes, and he was comely in a manner that seemed some mixture of French and Egyptian. His beard—gray at the edges—was trimmed in the typical Arabic manner. Without hurry, he returned my gaze.

Finally he opened the book before him, looked at me again, and recited: "'In the beginning God created the heaven and the earth.' You know these words?"

"The first verse of the first chapter of Genesis, King James version." I felt uncomfortable, but I remembered he was an anthropologist—surely not some sort of hybrid guru.

He asked, "And do you believe them? Do you believe these words of Genesis that give us Adam and Eve?"

"I'm not religious," I answered. It was a relief to establish my footing with him.

"Who wrote those words?"

"I don't know," I answered. "Probably no one knows. Some ancient scribe."

"I know who wrote them."

A shudder ran through me. Was he mad? What kind of trap had I walked into? I looked to Arielle for connection. Off to one side, the young woman stood perfectly still, regarding her father with her luminous brown eyes flecked with gold. In spite of her physical presence, she had absented herself from our exchange.

"You wished to ask a favor of me," I gently reminded him. I recognized my tone of voice: it was the neutral, nonthreatening, noncolluding voice I used when speaking to the mental patients who had come for art therapy.

"You came here to learn more about the Nag Hammadi texts," he said. "But we have found a new text, here in Egypt, not about Jesus. A newly discovered text but older than the ones found in 1945. Our codex of 2020, these pages, place the book of Genesis in a new context. They refer to the genesis of Genesis. *Malheureusement*—unfortunately—their existence is known to certain religious fundamentalists who would like to destroy them."

"Right-wing Christians," I said, readily enough.

"Yes, and—"

"Literalist Jews," I added.

"And?"

"Muslim extremists," Arielle put in. "I myself am a Muslim, but not a fundamentalist."

"And your father?" I asked her.

"Objective. An anthropologist."

"And you want . . . ?" I asked Pierre Saad.

Time seemed to be suspended in the cool silence of the white room under its high, vaulted ceiling while I waited to learn what he wanted of me. I felt defined by the walls, chalk white but bright. Blank. A fly lit on the sponge shoulder cushion of the crutch. Even our flies are here, I thought. Suddenly I felt very American—practical, normal.

"We hope that you will allow me to fly you back to Cairo," Arielle said. "We have a little plane for you there—my father's plane. Quite old but in good condition."

"And then, from Cairo, we would like for you to smuggle this new manuscript, this precious, irreplaceable codex, out of Egypt," Pierre Saad continued. "To fly safely, which means circuitously, ultimately to the south of France. To the area of the ancient cave paintings, between Lascaux and Chauvet. I am the resident cultural anthropologist there at the complex, and I will be waiting for you."

"Egypt herself has been hospitable to ancient scrolls. Don't they belong here?"

"The Nag Hammadi scrolls," he explained, "impinge only on the question of the divinity of Jesus. They are old news—discovered in 1945; everyone who wishes to learn about them has had the opportunity to do so. Christianity continues virtually untouched by the implications of the Gnostic Gospels. On the other hand, the Genesis story is sacred to not just one but three major monotheistic religions. There is a small secret group, members of three religions, who want to destroy the codex. Perpetuity, they name themselves."

"How do they know of the existence of this codex?"

"The Muslim wing watches me because I once wrote a book they found to be anathema. I thought I was careful when the codex fell into my hands, but somehow they know. I'm spied upon. My daughter and I were very thoroughly searched when we exited the country a year ago."

"And Perpetuity?" I asked. "How do you know this name?"

I seemed to hear other people in the turquoise room, with the crocodiles. Pierre and Arielle were growing restless with my questions. But Pierre continued to speak in the same quiet way.

"I have an old friend. Someone I studied English with when I was a child. He is the friend of a friend who tried to recruit him for Perpetuity, but his friendship with me has the deeper root." Pierre sighed. "As I said, the codex I have is about the genesis of Genesis. Only in the matter of annihilating this manuscript do the members of this small secret group cooperate with one another in any way. Usually they struggle for political power, but the perpetual war in the Middle East is only the beginning. The more reasonable, more imaginative leaders of each religion, but also their followers, even the uneducated, must be made to understand the common origins of the three religions. Their similarities."

He paused, staring at me with his flat, tawny eyes, as though he would force his ideas into my mind. He thrust his body toward me as he continued, "If the Jews, the Christians, the Muslims, learn nothing new about their own origins—the mutual origin of their religions—we will have another world war. There will not be enough humanists or people of simple reason to stop them. Each faith will call it a Holy War, and the carnage, the bloodshed, of the medieval Crusades and the more recent European Holocaust will pale in comparison."

What memory gave me was the image of Thom's spreading blood, the curled tips of his lifeless fingers extending from beneath the wreckage of the grand piano. Killed absurdly not by a terrorist bomb but by a musical instrument, a vehicle of beauty. I tasted dust in my mouth.

"And there are other factions." Pierre Saad paused again. His eyes were like the eyes of a lazy African lion tracking a small female gazelle but waiting for the lioness to do the work. The lion's mane fluttered in a slight breeze. Again, I felt mesmerized—and afraid. Strangely alive.

"Perhaps even within your country," Pierre Saad continued in a calm, even voice, "those who believe in the literal truth of the Bible will rise up against the community of scientists. *Scientist* will become a more inflammatory term than *communiste*."

"We know what you wear around your neck," Arielle said.

I bunched my fingertips nervously against Thom's memory stick.

Pierre continued. "There are as many who would like to block his work—the discovery of extraterrestrial life, sure to come in the near future—as those who would block my work, which is to illumine the origins of our beliefs. The enemies of this codex are those who would shroud the past, our origins, our art, our sacred *poetry*, with their ignorance. Perpetuity is the enemy of both science and history."

Perhaps I had made the wrong decision not to give Thom's flash drive to ELF or to Gabriel.

"Where is this manuscript?" I asked.

Pierre Saad threw back his head; his nose cut the air like a scimitar; he seemed to gaze into the distance, but he said with pure trust and friendliness,

"Of course the manuscript is here." He pointed to a dark, heavy case—a compact, misshapen squarish case of a musical instrument—near the wall. "'*Ceci n'est pas une pipe*,'" he said, shrugging his shoulders in the Gallic manner.

"It's not a pipe?" I asked, incredulous.

"Of course not. I was merely quoting Magritte about his painting of his tobacco pipe. I mean it is not a French horn, or even the case of a French horn. It only *looks* like a French horn case. It is a specially prepared case containing very ancient writing."

"What is your hope for this manuscript?" I asked.

"That, once translated and made public, these words, the implications of these ancient words, will defuse the fanaticism, the literalism, of three religions."

The man who had begun to seem impressively cosmopolitan and sophisticated now seemed astonishingly naive. But I liked him better.

"Can you trust me, Lucy?" he asked.

Too soon, I thought. You ask too soon.

"Will you help us?" Arielle asked.

"You have the eyes of a predator," I said to him.

"No, no," he said, shaking his head sadly. "It is not true." Then he turned and looked directly into my eyes. "Look again," he said. And he held my gaze. "Here in the East, often you must look twice—or more—to see the truth."

There was candor in his expression. I saw the same kindness I had heard in his voice, outside the symposium room, when I could not bring myself to meet his eyes. And now, in his golden gaze, I saw hope—his faith in me—ardent hope.

"Yes," I said simply. "I will help you."

Why did I agree? Because they needed me? Because I liked them—father and daughter? Because like my parents I wanted to define myself with a mission? I did regard religious rigidity as a growing global danger.

As one, the three of us took a breath, then gently laughed away our tension. If the codex concealed in the retrofitted French horn case would cause people—Christians, Jews, and Muslims—to find unity in reading Genesis less literally, then I was all for it.

—

When I asked about the crutches, one leaning against the table, the other against the white wall, Pierre drew up his robe a bit and stuck out his foot, coffined in a heavy plaster cast. "A simple accident," he said. He wiggled his brown toes sticking out from the cutaway end of the cast. I actually recognized the square cut of the nail on his big toe, now rather more dusty than in Cairo. "After we spoke in Cairo, you left, but I could not let you go, after all. I hurried to the stairwell—you had taken the elevator—and in my haste I tripped on my sandal and broke my leg."

I expressed my regret at his mishap, but I wondered if the explanation was true. I asked suspiciously, "Why do you choose to ask me for help?"

"From your husband, I knew something of your temperament."

"And you are a pilot," Arielle said. "Perpetuity would like to have the flash drive as well as the codex."

"And you are"—Pierre paused as though searching his mind for the whole truth—"available. You are *at hand*, as the English say."

"As though sent to us by Allah," Arielle added happily.

"Even your name," her father hurried on, "is strangely appropriate for your role."

"What do you mean?"

"Lucy is the name the paleontologists gave to the female fossil found at the Olduvai Gorge, south of us, in the heart of Africa. Actually, the gorge should be called the Oldupi—the scientists misheard the native pronunciation. In any case, for a long time Lucy was the oldest of all the fossils that had been found, the mother of us all. Lucy—your name—Lucy is the evolutionist's Eve."

"How old was she?" I felt suddenly diminished, shrunken.

"Lucy lived about two and a half million years ago."

I smiled. "I believe she was named for a Beatles song, 'Lucy in the Sky with Diamonds.'"

Arielle moved closer and asked, "Beatles?"

"You know," I said gently. "Four pop musicians, from Liverpool. John Lennon?"

Instantly distressed, Arielle blurted, "John Lennon?" Then she covered her mouth with her hand and softly said something that sounded like *"Igtiyal."* For just a moment, she looked frightened, but I asked for no explanation.

"We'll meet again in France, God willing," Pierre Saad said softly. He handed me a card that affirmed his affiliation with Lascaux.

"May we not open the instrument case?" I asked. "I'd like to see the codex." Suppose he was asking me unwittingly to smuggle drugs—germs, a bomb?

"I alone have the key. I have already mailed it to myself in France."

"You would not have us break the lock," Arielle said. "It would be very difficult to do."

During the pause that followed, I shifted my gaze back and forth between the father and daughter.

Finally Pierre said, "Either you trust, or you do not."

Carrying the heavy French horn case, I walked with Arielle back into the turquoise anteroom, now filled with people examining wares displayed on the benchlike beds. How silently they had assembled! Their skin color, dress, and hair bespoke the far-flung fullness of the world. Tourists, like myself, whom chance had thrown together for a brief moment. It's just a tour bus, I thought. Their presence just means a tour bus has arrived. Utterly silent, isolate, the unreal people examined small figures carved from bone. None of them gave the slightest attention to the truncated chimney full of crocodiles.

As we two women passed through the streets of the village, Arielle explained, "I will fly you to Cairo to an abandoned airfield and show you the old plane that belongs to my father. You will like the little plane. Of course you will fly east at low altitude to avoid the war and the radar. The plane has a medical symbol on its belly. No one will shoot at you from below."

"I'm game," I repeated, almost panting. Having shorter legs than Arielle, I had to hustle to keep up with her.

"Good," Arielle replied. "Do you want me to carry the horn case?"

"No. I've got it." I rather enjoyed feeling the weight of responsibility.

Like a bird suddenly spreading one wing, the young woman opened out an arm to enclose my shoulders. I had seen such a gesture on a temple wall at Abu Simbel: a guardian figure—Isis, her lifted wing carved into stone. As Arielle squeezed the cap of my shoulder, I felt a frightening strength in her grip.

I had seen such a gesture when the black piano lifted its wing.

Our flight from Luxor to Cairo provided little opportunity for extended conversation. Once seated in the Cessna, Arielle put on her headphones and said simply, "I must concentrate on the flying. I am not so experienced a pilot as you, and this is a rental."

Despite my pilot's disclaimer, I never felt the least doubt about the young woman's competence. Her hands were quick and sure, and she was entirely focused on her work. Or was she simply a splendid actor, pretending to be focused on piloting to avoid conversation? Doubts and questions flooded my mind. It was comforting to follow the blue thread of the Nile, off to the left. As we began our descent, the river was lost in the smog-smudged sprawl of Cairo.

Arielle set the plane down with perfect grace. Removing her headphones, she said, "We need to hurry."

While we walked rapidly over the tarmac of the small, almost deserted airport east of Cairo, I inquired of Arielle about her mother.

*"Igtiyal!"* Arielle replied. Her voice seemed tightly controlled.

"That word again!" I exclaimed. It roused me like a long-ignored alarm bell. "What does it mean?"

"*Igtiyal* is the Arabic word for murder. My mother was murdered by extremists who hated my father's anthropological approach to Islam. I was a little girl then."

"I'm sorry," I answered. So Arielle, like myself, had known sudden loss. I put my arm around her and touched her shoulder.

"We have no time now," she said. "Papa and I will tell you about her death when you bring the codex to Lascaux."

My mind swung again to the image of Thom's blood, red as horror. From beneath the shattered piano, the pool had enlarged steadily, its advancing edge a smooth curve. Before I had fainted, someone with a foreign accent—Egyptian, I now recognized—had said the word *igtiyal*. And now I knew: it meant murder. Someone had labeled Thom's terrible accident, his death, as murder. My heart pumped fear and denial.

There was the promised plane—very old and small. Something left behind by Americans after World War II. From the PA series—Piper Aircraft—a PA-11.

"Ah!" I gasped as soon as I saw it. Not just satisfied, in a moment of recognition I felt shocked into happiness. I had learned to fly in just such an airplane.

I knew all about it.

Quickly Arielle said to me, "My father is so trusting, he did not think to tell you. The case is not only locked but also sealed against impact and water. An attempt to open the case might violate the integrity of the seal. Now hurry! Go!"

As quietly as I could, I said, "I need to run the flight check."

"There's no time. I did it myself. I did it this morning!"

Her eyes pleaded for trust; against all my training and better judgment, I gave in to her. So quickly she seemed a member of my family!

# THE DRAGON'S NECK

WHEN ADAM AWOKE in the burning morning sunlight, alone and naked, he asked himself, What do you really know about anything? Stealthy as a serpent, memory began to crawl through the convolutions of his brain.

*Burn me! Burn them!* he had prayed to the Middle Eastern sun, while he lay naked, his hands bound behind his back, flat on his stomach on the searing metal of their truck bed. They had put a pair of nylon women's underpants over his head as they raped him over and over, and he knew that the underwear was meant to be an unbearable humiliation, revenge for something that happened to someone they might have known in the past, but the panties reminded Adam of underwear hung in the sunshine behind the ranch house at home on a gleaming wire clothesline, his mother's underwear, part of an intimate family array—his father's undershorts, his own, and in diminishing sizes all those of his younger brothers. The nylon panties placed over his head by his torturers had comforted him. As he had looked through one leg opening straight at the sun, his chin bouncing on the metal bed of the eastward-moving truck, he had prayed backward to the setting sun to kill him quickly. Them, too.

Adam had given up on God and asked the sun for mercy and vengeance.

Finally one of the soldiers had sent him into oblivion by crashing the butt of his rifle against the side of his head. They must have dumped him into the road. Yes, his body remembered how it curled before he hit the hard-packed sand—how they lifted his feet up and over his head and he spiraled out of the open-ended truck. They must have cut the ropes that bound his hands before they hurled him out.

That must have happened some days ago, because now he was healing. His body had been blue with bruises. Before they tied his wrists together, they had stamped on his fingers and hands with their heavy boots, but now his flesh was almost pink again, and he could flex his fingers, curl them inward into a fist.

Yesterday, he remembered, he had flattened and pressed his hand into the sand. Yesterday he had awakened into a holy sheen of light as though for the first time, and the day had blessed and restored him. He had been refashioned and born again in Eden.

But what else had happened in his life before yesterday had occurred?

He remembered more from the recent past: a large, hairy monkey had come from nowhere. After they tumbled him onto the hard sand and left him, a large, hairy monkey with a child's face had given him water and roughly forced fruit into his mouth, then something raw and bloody. But now he was waking up alone.

And now he must claim his mind as his own. Now he must kneel in the sand and beg for God's forgiveness. Adam knew that in his pain he had no longer believed in the Invisible, although he had survived. God had saved Adam anyway. He had blasphemed in praying to the sun, but he knew it was the hand of God that intervened and cushioned the blow from the rifle butt so that it damaged but failed to shatter his skull. And God must have put the idea into their heads to throw Adam out, just as He had made the whale cough up Jonah onto dry land, when Jonah's punishment was complete. And perhaps God was making his torturers feel ashamed of what they had done to him—six young men dressed like sand in swirls of tan, gray-green, splotches of brown. They wore clothes borrowed or stolen from those who had been dressed once just like himself.

Now God was making Adam new, and He would come in the evening and walk and talk with him, as was described in the book of Genesis. Here was the beautiful world: palm trees and trees of all possible and impossible kinds and a river. When he turned his head, he saw a sea with blue water dancing in the sunlight. Clouds hanging over water. An ocean transplanted from another geography to delight his eye.

The sun stood in the sky, a gleaming disk too bright to hold color of any name. God's shield. Perhaps it was a new sun, risen as it was in a different place—a new place, a new time, and he himself a new creation. In the state hospital in Idaho, on the stationary bike facing east, long ago Adam had sometimes pedaled hard to pull up the sun. They had not known then what he was doing. There was a translucent, almost invisible thread connecting the sprocket of the bicycle to the sun. With the action of his legs, he had made the sun rise, reeling it up so that they would all benefit from its heat and light. Adam's morning job had been to wind up the sun while it spread its wings like a golden bird rising from its nest behind the eastern mountains.

Now they could serve his bowl of hot oatmeal.

But the hospital had vanished. All the walls were gone. The large window through which he liked to look at the parklike grounds and at the Northern Rockies beyond the treetops had vanished. Not even the window frame was left hanging in the air. Here was a new world, much more simple; not even the long, narrow white tables in the cafeteria were here, and the short little round stools that could tilt up under the tables, the better to mop the floor—which he himself had often done, pretending with the gray water and the mop head to be making a swirling painting of marvelous colors.

The bad part was that he was hungry. Then he remembered the cherry orchard at home, and the orchard he knew was here, magically full of every fruit he had ever wanted to eat.

Walking beside the river, he looked for the spot on the bank where he had lain when the sun first woke him. He looked for yesterday but could not find the seam in the air that would allow him to slip backward in time. A scuffed place on the sandy bank might be where he had lain, the round of his heels resting in the slow swirl of water. He felt proud of himself, rising up from that. Where had God gone? Adam wondered, then remembered that it was His habit to walk in the garden, the orchard, in the cool of the day. It was only morning now.

Impulsively, Adam splashed into the river, then paused to feel its friendly water flowing all around him. The current parted for him, encircling the calves of his legs. He lifted his knees high and splashed his foot down playfully. *Not like the soldiers' boots. Up and down like a fence-post-driving machine. No!* His bare sole slapped the water playfully and made it squirt in all directions in a shower of round clear stones. He would walk through water, just like Jesus had walked *on* water in the old days, but now those days were yet to come, weren't they? He must live down all the days, all the days of all the books of the Bible from Genesis to Malachi, before Jesus came.

In college, he had read the words of an ancient seer who had said that time was like a river, this river, and you could never step in the same river twice, for it had flowed away.

But he was still young. He stood still in the water and regarded the beautiful, almost tropical place surrounding him. His land. So must his own father have looked long ago at the waiting land in Idaho and claimed it for his own. His father had been younger even, fully a man before he left his teens. But thirty, Adam thought, his own age, was not very old, not anymore—not more than a third of one's life. Hadn't Jesus been just thirty when he started his career? Adam walked out of the river. And Muhammad had been forty before his first revelation came.

In the war, Adam remembered he himself had killed a boy, more handsome than himself, who had died pronouncing the words *Ahl-lah, Ahl-lah,* with a bubble of blood on his lips. He had not pronounced the words the way an American would have done, but they were understandable enough, though distorted.

He remembered what it was like before he was captured—himself and the others moving over the desert, their uniforms the color of moving sand, and how they would sometimes come to an oasis. He remembered the first green-and-dun oasis he had seen, and how it seemed enchanted. Beyond the trunks of the palms spread the shallow pool of the oasis waters. The oasis had been deserted. Animal footprints led down to the shining glaze of water. He and his buddies had all run to the sky-blue pool. He remembered the surprised look on the face of a furry gray donkey as they thundered past.

When the soldiers walked into the shallow pool, their feet had found people under the water. Sometimes the cloth of their robes floated up to the surface, supported by trapped air or rising gas. Yes, those were not smooth rocks out there but ballooning pouches of wet cloth risen to the surface and also the backs of heads, wet black hair glistening blue-black in the sunlight. When he and his friends left the water, all the troops had done so stepping backward, trying to retrace their steps.

Among the buildings of the oasis, they saw that the liquid splashing into stone fountains was the color of watered blood. No one could bring himself or herself to drink the pink-tinted water in that place. Beside a red granite basin stood a young American woman in uniform, her thin blond hair cropped short, sunburn on her high cheekbones, a skinny neck, her thin cracked lips forming words: "I want to go home," she said over and over, her blue eyes covered with a second lens of tears.

The U.S. Army had had to airlift to the oasis great tanks of water dangling from trios of helicopters.

But all of that had happened before yesterday, before when God had created Adam anew.

After the hospital at home in Idaho he had gotten well, too. Well enough in his mind so they wanted him as a soldier. Next came the time of war, which he would will and had willed himself never to remember, though at times, like images of the oasis, the war might drift back to him. With his left hand, Adam caressed his index finger on his right hand—the trigger finger, its muscle still grotesquely enlarged. He didn't want that time. He wanted Now and Here: those apples, and even juicier fruit, the tangerines. They had poisoned the water of the oasis, but here they wouldn't have poisoned the fruit. That would take too long. They would have had to inject each separate fruit, using a hypodermic needle. That wasn't reasonable. The globed fruit bounced back the morning light, and the fruit of many colors shone like small lanterns in the orchard.

Here there were fuzzy-sided peaches that he wanted, and the slick-sided purple plums. Both peaches and plums had a cleft, or a seam, in one place, a cleft such as a woman might have between her legs.

His entire body rigid with desire, Adam walked slowly among the trees of the bountiful orchard but would not allow himself to pluck a single fruit. Because of the tension in all his limbs, it was difficult to take a step. He must punish himself. *Catatonic, catatonia*—where had he heard those words? Then he remembered that God had said not to eat apples, hadn't He? Adam reached up and plucked a tangerine from among green leaves. It was easy for his hand to obey his will, once he had decided what to do, what to choose.

With his strong thumbnail, he easily broke through the dimpled skin of the tangerine. He loved the compliant way the peeling yielded to the leverage of his prying thumbnail. When he tore off a patch of the rind, he turned it over and saw that the underside of the bright orange peel was white and pithy. Through the window he had torn from its side, Adam saw a round of plump crescents. He removed a cluster of those little purses and took it into his mouth. With his molars, he gently squeezed and then enjoyed the pleasure of the sweet gush of flavor onto his tongue.

That night God came to Adam as a breeze.

In the cool of the evening, when Adam moved among the rough, crisscrossed trunks of the royal palms, scaly trees planted in rows like the sugarbeet fields of Idaho, God kept pace with Adam by moving quietly and tenderly in the row next to him. At one point, Adam reached out his right arm through the spaced trees to offer his hand, which God caressed with the breath of His passing.

When Adam stopped, God gently lifted the back of Adam's hand to His own lips and kissed Adam's knuckles. In a whisper, God murmured a blessing, "Peace." He walked away, diagonally across the rows of palm trees. Perhaps God's slanted path intersected other Adams in the field of palms as they also walked forward down their rows, and perhaps He walked with each of them awhile. Finally God left the garden to cross the boundary river toward another place. Adam could hear His distant feet lifting the water, so still were the quiet and the cool of the evening.

Alone, Adam sank to his knees; he crossed his arms and leaned them against the coarse diamonds of the trunk of a royal palm. He placed his forehead against his crossed forearms and sang aloud part of a hymn he had loved as a boy of six, his family having come into town for church and sociability:

*When we've been there*
*Ten thousand years*
*Bright shin-ing as the sun*

*We've no-o less days*
*To sing God's praise*
*Than when we first begun.*

Yet here, in Eden, there was no *we*. No Eve knelt or stood beside him with open hymnal to sing God's praise. Adam was entirely alone. He stood up, placed the palms of his hands on each side of the rough waist of the palm tree, and squeezed, trembling with intensity, as though he could squeeze her out of the trunk of the tree. If God enjoyed a hymn of praise, He'd no less trouble hearing the silent cry of Adam's heart. With the brute force of his powerful rancher's hands, Adam squeezed the tree trunk, scaly as a dragon's neck, and begged God to send him Eve.

Till it yielded up a dryad, he would strangle the tree trunk.

# A LIFE IN SAN ANTONIO

SAM B. HOUSTON. That would be Sam Ben Houston, or S. B. Houston, or Son-of-a-Bitch Houston back when he was a drunk. He had celebrated his fortieth birthday with the biggest bender of his life, after which somebody shoveled him into a taxi and sent him to San Antonio General. As he ebbed in and out of consciousness, he could have sworn that his wife came back like a good angel and told him it wasn't his fault he'd taught her to be a big girl who liked the taste of beer, and it wasn't his fault the alcohol had eaten the calcium out of her bones and teeth, and their child had had fetal alcohol syndrome and was someone who needed an institution. And it wasn't his fault about the recreational drugs either or that she had wrecked the car, dead drunk. *Come on to heaven with me,* she whispered, fanning him with her snow-white feathery wings.

That was in the past. That was way before Perpetuity got hold of him and made him into somebody smart and important and damn-near rich, too.

But before Perpetuity, there was AA and Jesus. And that was what saved him after Susan died in the wreck. Almost dead drunk himself, he had stood unbalanced on the edge of a high red rock cliff, and Jesus had grabbed the middle of the back of his belt and pulled him away from the abyss.

These days Sam B. Houston was an expensively dressed businessman who taught Sunday school. He was an expert on the Second Coming, the Rapture, the End of the World, and the last book of the Bible, Revelation. He knew that before Jesus could come again, the Jews must return to their homeland. He was helping to make it come to pass. His church supported Jewish settlers. Mr. Houston had escorted both young Christians and uncommitted teens to the Holy Land to increase their awareness of how little time was left for repentance. While he was there, he had been approached by a Jewish member of Perpetuity.

People were always trying to debunk God's Word. Treat it like damn literature or tribal history. They'd tried with Jesus; they'd tried to make out like he was a man, like any man. Sex and all. Now the evolutionists were after God the Creator.

As a souvenir, Perpetuity gave Sam Houston the most expensive holster and six-shooter you could darn well imagine.

He was a great shot, too.

There was some sort of papers found in Egypt, and they wanted him to get hold of them. The scientists were out to rewrite Genesis.

In early spring, 2020, back home, Sam Houston sat on a rock far from the city, though he was still wearing his business clothes. He hadn't had a drink in seven years. It was time for the rattlesnakes to come out and sun themselves. When they did, he'd pop off their heads. Here came two big guys so long they just kept pouring and pouring out of the rock crack. Sam B. squinted his eyes, took aim, and squeezed the trigger.

"Get thee behind me, Satan!" he said, his voice suffused with venom.

Soon they were going to send him to the Holy Land again, or thereabouts.

# AIRPLANE!

BEFORE TAKEOFF, I put on the ancient leather gloves and a leather bombardier's jacket with a ratty fur collar left in the Cub—clothes doubtlessly belonging to Pierre Saad. As I flew—over Egypt, eastward over the elbow of the Mediterranean, over Lebanon, and northeast—I rejoiced at being in the pilot's seat again. My eyes passed fondly over the simple instrumentation as though I were surveying the eyes of trusting children: the tachometer, the pressure and temperature gauges, the altimeter with its two clocklike hands, the airspeed indicator, the bubble compass. While it was too big for me, I was glad to have the antique leather helmet's protection from the wind. Piloting the Cub was like flying in a sieve.

Twice, since Cairo, I had been able to spot small informal runways as indicated on my flight plan. I had been able to land the plane and refuel without arousing even a murmur of suspicion, but the magical third port indicated in the flight plan refused to appear. I checked the handheld global positioning device for reassurance. When I looked down, all I saw was the shadow of my own small plane as it undulated over the crowns of acacia trees.

Under my plane slid a changing topography, sometimes of undulating green, sometimes a sandy dun flatness. High overhead a tiny jet zipped across a blue hole in a masklike cloud. Not all the way across. Within the circumference of the eyehole, the glint of silver suddenly burst into a few sharp, red splinters, the way a tiny blood vessel sometimes hemorrhages into the human eye.

There's death, I thought: death for a pilot beyond the clouds, a man or woman who was as real as I was riding in the cockpit of the ancient Piper Cub. As real as Thom had been. *Igtiyal?* My heart had contorted even before I learned its translation.

*Igtiyal?* How could Thom's death have possibly been murder? If Thom had been murdered, did someone want to murder me, too? The idea was preposterous. Totally harmless, I wasn't worth murdering. Why swat a bumbling, stumbling bee out of the air?

The warplanes were miles overhead, and they cast no shadows. But exactly where was I? Anxiety would have been a reasonable response to my uncertainty, but instead I felt almost lighthearted—strangely free. Perhaps I didn't care what happened to me. Since Thom's death, I had occasionally had such moments of disregard for my own life. It pleased me that Pierre Saad's Piper Cub was nearly identical to the one in which I had learned to fly. "Fly me back to childhood," I whispered to it. "Let me try again."

I had been eleven years old when I called my grandmother on the telephone to ask permission to fly with Mr. Stimson in his latest toy. Sandwiched exactly between his daughters aged ten and twelve, I had been closest friend to both Janet and her younger sister Margarita. Being sandwiched between them alleviated the loneliness of being an only child whose parents were missionaries in Japan.

Their father was a large fleshy man with red hair. Once when he was washing his car, I saw that his milk-white back had been plowed by a big bullet. He had fought in Vietnam. It gave me a rather optimistic view of war: if you came home from it with a big scar on your back, you got to be the fascinating father of the two most wonderful girls in the world.

The first time I came home from school with Janet (we were in the same grade because I had been double-promoted), Mr. Stimson had asked me what my IQ was. Though I knew such questions were considered impolite, I felt flattered that he was curious. When I told him, he remarked admiringly, "You're even smarter than I am." I had felt smugly glad (for his sake) that he had the intelligence to look at me with new appreciation. After that I was always welcome at the Stimsons', and when opportunities for fun came up for the Stimson girls, I was often included. After Mr. Stimson took me up in the Piper Cub, he taught me to fly it.

"Yes," my grandmother had said, when queried over Cheerios. "It would be good for you to learn to fly. I don't want you to end up like me." My grandmother was referring to the fact that she herself had never learned to drive a car. "Who knows what people will need to be able to do in the future?"

When I asked Janet and Margarita if they were excited about learning to fly, they had answered with one voice, "We don't want to. We're not going to."

I could hear their voices again, while I piloted the Piper Cub over the Middle East, as clearly as I could hear my grandmother. Janet had added, "Mother doesn't want us to." Over breakfast, my grandmother had only cautioned, "Pay attention and be careful."

I noted the oil temperature gauge had slightly passed the normal range, 170°F–180°F, but the air over the desert was quite hot, which could account for an abnormal reading.

Biting down on the fingertip of the glove, I pulled my hand free. I wanted to touch my talisman, the metal case of Thom's memory stick. Fumbling into the leather jacket, from inside my shirt, I retrieved the pendant. As soon as I touched it, I relived how Thom had lowered the black cord over my head that last morning together. How he had remarked on its warmth. It was warm now, from my body. Stroking the smooth metal casing between my thumb and forefinger, I listened to the comforting low hum of the little plane's engine. *Murder? Thom murdered?* I tightened my whole hand around Thom's best gift to me. Actually, it still belonged to him. I had just been entrusted with it—like the manuscript. While the codex was a capsule from the past, the flash drive pointed to the future. Did I hold the location of extraterrestrial life within my hand?

If Thom had been murdered, surely it was my duty to find out why, and by whom? Perpetuity?

The sound of the engine seemed to transpose up a half step. The temperature had passed 200°.

Once again I traced the shape of the memory stick, rounded at both ends and only as long as the last joint of my thumb. In 2017, Thom and I had thought it to be wonderfully miniaturized. Now, only three years later, such devices were only as big as the *nail* of my thumb. "Buttons," they were called.

Such a strange item. All it could do was remember—but not think.

Thom was dead. All I could do was remember him. What if he had been murdered instead of accidentally killed—so ironically, by a falling piano? Would he be any less dead, if he had been murdered?

The compass reading changed abruptly. Perhaps a magnetic deviation—an iron deposit underground. Far above the Piper Cub, the mask and its empty blue eyeholes had sailed east.

I flew over what may have once been an oil refinery. Now it was a pile of ashes. The rims of seven huge holding tanks had been reduced to rusted curves of cut metal. Then the land beneath became sandy—desertlike, gray and tan.

Below, there was still no sign of a third airport hacked out of the wilderness, though a third airport was noted in my flight plan, and then a change of planes. Below me scrubby grass gave way to a wave of trees.

To go forward, to reclaim my own life, did I need to know? Had Thom been murdered? *Igtiyal?*

As soon as I had left Memphis for college in Iowa, I met Thom, who was as tender and sympathetic as any mother, as strong and reliable as the best of fathers, and who regarded me as a desirable adult.

"If you're undecided about having children," Grandmother had managed to whisper when she was very ill, "I mean if it's a fifty-fifty proposition—not if you're sure you don't want to—go ahead and do it, for my sake." But I had hesitated to do anything to unbalance the happy equilibrium of marriage and work.

—

In the layer between the fighter zone and the green earth, my craft moved steadily forward—was this what it meant to be lost? Just moving along? And *was* I lost? Maybe I was locally lost; globally, I and the small plane were someplace over Mesopotamia. The dial of the fuel gauge indicated I could make it to Baghdad if I had to. Was I lost or free? I realized the battery in the GPS had failed.

When the Piper Cub engine began to emit a persistent grinding sound, the peril of the moment seized me. The engine was struggling. Plenty of fuel, but the temperature gauge read 218°F. Between 220° and 230° the engine would seize up. The metal parts would stick together, and the propeller would stop turning.

As the plane lost altitude, the acacia canopy rose up at me like aggressive heads of broccoli. To the left side stood a surprising group of very tall trees—redwoods?—rising over the other vegetation like cathedral spires over a medieval village. Redwoods? Here? Ahead a break in the greenery was doubtlessly caused by a river. To try to gain altitude, I turned the nose of the plane down a little so the wings would hit the air at the right angle for lift. It's counterintuitive to point the nose down when you're falling, but it speeds the airflow over the wings, lowering the air pressure. The maneuver can result in lift. There, there! I had a moment of lift, but the propeller stopped dead. I was gliding, not falling. Yes, there was a river with a broad, bare embankment. I tried to pull the lever to dump the gasoline, but it was rusted shut.

When I looked down, I saw a huge worm lying on the bank of the river—no, surely a man. In a brief flash, I envisioned Thom's body, clothed but mangled, lying under the snarl of piano wires and gilded struts. This man seemed to lie on his side, naked, alone on the bare bank.

My plane was stepping down and down through the air. If I was going down, I must try to save the codex. I saw Arielle's brown eyes, her father's golden gaze. Still holding half a tank of fuel, likely the Cub would burn after impact. The codex would be safer if it went down separately. I pulled the hard case onto my lap. I raised the unlocked lever of the door, then shuffled the heavily reinforced case outside. Instantly, the French horn case dropped toward the green of the treetops.

The trees themselves disappeared. Ahead, waves glittered like a field of diamonds—prismatic, silver, gold. Unless I was wildly off course, there was no sea in this location, yet *there* was a sea and a sandy shore! How could an ocean, sparkling like the streets of paradise, lie ahead? The presence of soft blue water, as blue as the sky? I tried to angle the plane to land on the beach—a gust lifted us for a moment, airspeed sixty miles per hour, and I sailed, I sailed, now the sea was parallel to the plane—I wouldn't plunge into the water. If only I could float on air forever, on and on, half a mile, good wings, good wings, but sinking, finally sinking. If only my speed might drop to forty—not an impossible landing at all. The tip of the right wing gouged into the sand—a sudden drop with too much torque for a pancake landing—then the beginning of a grand loop of cartwheeling, the fuel tank rupturing, while the good seat belt held—

Impact, and my vision sheeted with blood, the greedy crackle of flames.

# IN THE GARDEN

OVER HIS SHOULDER, God whispered to Adam on the breeze, *I have set you down not in Idaho, not in a Wilderness of mountains, but in a Garden. And this time you are like unto the first Adam to whom I gave the power to name the animals.*

Adam knew that all the animals were inside himself. They lived in his head, and they were small enough to curl up inside the convolutions of his brain, even the elephant and the giraffe. He would have liked to draw them.

In the small space between his skull and his brain, insects buzzed, cicadas and locusts. Grasshoppers such as might eat up all the wheat whirred and jumped within his synapses, but none of them gave him pain—not even the lion whose roar blasted from his ears into the waiting air.

Only what was that gnawing—not in his mind—in his body, close to his heart? *Name the animal you harbor in your heart!* God commanded.

"Fox!" Adam shrieked, and high in the trees the cherries trembled on their stems. God intensified their color and gave their smooth cheeks a sheen.

Then Adam remembered the sharp teeth of the fox and how it had been, long ago, in Idaho.

He was ten, and in the fifth grade he read the story of the Spartan boy, who lived near ancient Athens, who had stolen a fox. Ashamed of himself, the boy hid the fox under his garment and felt the animal's fur nestled against his own skin covering his ribs. But the fox was hungry, and he was a wild thing. Even when teeth sharp as needles pierced his skin, the Spartan boy, ashamed of his theft, did not cry out, for he was also ashamed of the resentment that he held against his harsh father. Yes, Adam had hidden rebellion in his heart without confessing his feelings. Quietly, the fox bit and chewed and swallowed the boy's flesh and neatly nursed his blood so that on the outside the boy's robe remained pristine white. Finally, the Spartan boy slumped dead in his desk, and only then, when they pulled aside the folds of his clothing, did anyone see the smiling fox sitting under the arch of the boy's ribs.

Adam had loved the truth of the story and its undeniable vividness even more than he admired the boy's fortitude, and he took the schoolbook home and read it aloud to his mother at the kitchen table.

When he finished reading the story, he had asked, "Don't you feel like that sometimes, Mother?"

She went to the window over the sink and looked out over the ranch.

"Yes," she said. "We're so alone here. Sometimes I feel that something is eating my heart and that honor requires that I hide it from everyone, especially your father."

Like my drawings of the girls and their sacred parts, he had thought. His hands scurried under his thighs because they remembered the doubled-up belt smiting his knuckles.

So his mother had understood the world as he did: sometimes the heart must be hidden, and the impulses of the hand as well. But she had let his father put him away. Eight years later, his mother who understood him had let his father take Adam to the hospital and leave him there—not nineteen years old—with the shock machine.

Alone in the Garden, Adam's heart ached for companionship. *We're so alone here,* his mother's words echoed on the breeze in the Garden. He watched a noisy, low-flying bird, a stiff-winged dragon with a red cross on its belly, sail over. The monster coughed and sputtered, and Adam named it *airplane,* for it was his assignment to name every beast that crept on the earth, or swam in the water, or flew through the air. In the air, the bird laid an egg. It was a black egg, strangely warped, and it fell straight down, fast, while the bird flew on.

The pain of his loneliness roared in Adam's brain, and all the animals in his head wanted out at once. As he crossed the sunny meadow, the grass brushing the sides of his bare feet was dry and warm. An Arctic hare, white and unusually large, hopped away from him. He passed clusters of grazing animals—eland, wildebeest, and Thompson's gazelle. Only one lifted his head to note Adam's passing; gratefully, Adam met the eyes of the animal. At the base of a magnolia tree, he found a small reservoir of water. Cradled between the tree roots, it reflected the blue of the sky; Adam leaned his face over the still water.

There he was: a single, scythelike curl on his forehead, and he remembered when he was six years old and his mother had made him a Superman outfit to wear to a Halloween party at the church in town. Really his costume was a too-tight pair of blue knit pajamas, but she had sewn a large red *S* on his chest, and tied a piece of red sheet over his shoulders for a cape.

At the party, he had leaped over chairs and shouted, "Faster than a speeding bullet." Later he had asked Evelyn, his mother, "What *is* a tall building? *How* tall are they?" She told him skyscrapers were like a church steeple or a grain silo, or taller—better. She had added, "Perhaps someday you will build tall buildings, or have an office in one or live in New York City." But that was not what he wanted. *Skyscraper*—how he loved the word. He wanted to *be* one. Perfect and powerful. He wanted to be the whole structure.

As he regarded his reflection in the small pool trapped between the roots of the magnolia, he saw that he still resembled Superman, only now his bare shoulders were heavily muscled, his jaw was more square. In the water mirror, he saw his hair was metallic blue-black—but there beside him—another face! It was the large monkey that had found him dumped out of the truck in the desert. Like the good Samaritan, the monkey had fed him: first fruit and then bloody, uncooked meat. Though Adam stood up and looked around for his friend, he saw no one. Had a friend followed him into Eden?

Again, he knelt down on all fours and looked at his reflection. Now only a spray of stiff magnolia leaves appeared beside his own cheek, and he wondered if the monkey might have been in the tree. He turned his head to look up, but he saw only the branches and the flickering of leaves, slick green on one side and soft buff on the other. Beyond that, the pale vacancy of the sky.

God had whispered on the breeze, *I have set you down in a Garden.* Even an animal would ease the isolation—an ape, a fox.

*Fox!* He howled and beat the animal in his chest with his fist.

# FOR THE BEAUTY OF THE EARTH

WHEN I STRUGGLED from the burning Piper Cub, I was on fire.

With more determination than I had ever felt before, I stumbled toward the water till my knees buckled. I folded at the waist, and my face bowed into the sand. I heard the snapping of the flames on my back. The fur collar around the back of the leather jacket was burning, and I willed myself to rise, to stumble forward again toward the waves. I would fall into the water, then I would roll. The water would save me. Staggering toward the sea, I yanked off the jacket, but my unsteady legs gave way again.

Twisting myself, I rolled over the sand toward the surf. Though I thought to extinguish the flames by crushing them with my body, the rolling wrapped me in so much pain that I knew I would lose consciousness to escape it. My long skirt came untied and fell away. My blouse and my back were burning. I rose onto all fours and determined to crawl, but I stopped to rip away my blouse. My alertness was waxing and waning.

When I smelled my hair burning, I tried to yank it out. The seared skin of my naked back screamed. Though I collapsed forward, I drove my fingers down into the wet sand and pulled my body toward the water. Once more. Again I pulled and lunged forward. A wave broke over my outstretched hands and my forearms, over my forehead and face, finally—yes—dousing my back.

When the water receded, I gasped for breath and made myself roll sideways despite the pain. Sharp sand embedded itself into my burned back. Completely nude, I rolled into the water, turned faceup, and knew that I had killed the fire in my hair. The water was shallow, stunningly cold, divinely welcome to the burn on my back. For the briefest of respites, I floated on my back and registered the presence of the sky.

Remembering that the plane would surely explode, I rolled over and swam two strokes downward. When my hands met with slush, I knew I was now entirely submerged. Holding my breath under the water, I shoved my fingertips into the sandy bottom. I determined to stay attached there, moving my legs against the water only enough to keep my body anchored. Perhaps a foot of ocean covered me. If I turned over and sat up, surely I would be able to breathe—but not yet.

Finally, through the water, the muffled sound of explosion reached my ears.

I waited underwater as long as I could, then rolled over. When the skin of my buttocks found the unstable bottom, I realized anew that I had discarded or lost all that I wore—except Thom's memory stick. I held it tightly. Had Thom given me a fireproof cord? The watertight, fireproof titanium case still hung from its black silk cord around my neck. I sat up, gasped for breath, and opened my eyes again.

The Piper Cub sat in a wigwam tangle of metal; its green-painted canvas was scorched brown and black. A bit of feeble and harmless flame continued to lick at the wreckage. A few jagged metal scraps of the exploded gas tank lay on the beach. I knew I was hurt, burned across my back and scalp, but for the moment I felt nothing but relief. And triumph. I was alive. Lucky.

*Remember your name is Lucy, and Lucy is part of the word* lucky. *It's always lucky just to be alive*. Words my grandmother once said to me.

I sat in the water and surveyed my situation. What I saw around me seemed cut from the fabric of pure simplicity—blue sky, green sea. Unspeakably beautiful. More: my eyes glorified the sandy yellow neutrality of the beach. Cloud billows without motion hung in the blue. *Lucky merely to be alive.*

Green water incessantly rocking like the sublime comfort of Grandmother's soft sway. *Lucky.*

For a brief moment relief and beauty held pain at bay before their power dissolved. As though I and the plane were falling again, I saw an endless sea of bubbling green treetops rushing toward me. I heard again the desperate coughing of the little plane. *No:* I was sitting in the sea, not far from shore, coughing. Like a struck gong, my body rang with pain.

*Think,* my mind commanded itself.

Up there, from the air, I had seen someone, a man who might help me. Or I him. Like something discarded, he had lain on the riverbank.

*Go on,* inner voices commanded.

*You know you can bear anything.*

Where had I heard such voices? They seemed the voices of Thom's parents—Thom, who was dead—his parents' voices speaking from Auschwitz and Treblinka.

I must ignore the twisted wreckage of my plane. The pale beach was a blessing I must claim. I stood up in the shallow, blue-green water and took a step toward shore. I remembered the word *Lascaux*. A man named Pierre Saad had entrusted me with ancient, irreplaceable pages relevant to the book of Genesis, which I had thrown out the airplane door. The pain of the burn slammed against my back, and I staggered.

I shifted my feet in the slushy underwater sand to recalibrate my balance. Somehow I would reclaim the codex. My hand enclosed the memory stick.

# A LIFE IN WEST JERUSALEM

THE MAN BORN as Jacob ben Ezra was an identical twin; so identical were he and his slightly younger brother that no teacher could tell them apart, and often they even succeeded in deceiving their mother. Their mother said they had knocked at the gate to the world at just the same moment, but Jacob had elbowed his way past his slightly smaller brother and so became the firstborn. Because the younger one, who was not smaller, had thicker hair on his head, he was named Esau. When they started school—two merry black-haired, brown-eyed, bright little boys—their mother tousled their hair, felt the difference, and realized that by this comparative method she would always have a way to distinguish who was who. She shared this secret with no one, not even her pious husband.

In temperament the boys seemed quite different. Esau shared his father's interest in scriptures and memorized them with great exactness; he could recite the entirety of the book of Genesis by the time he was eight, and Exodus and Psalms, though he found the meaning of poetry more slippery than prose, by age ten. In this way, he earned his father's special protection. Jacob's interests were more scientific: he observed the world with focused curiosity, and when he had classified the plants and bugs of the neighborhood, he lifted his eyes to the heavens and learned about the stars of the constellations over West Jerusalem and to identify the planets. He liked math.

Jacob had one other passion discovered quite by accident: he overheard a portion of an Easter service held by touring Methodists with an American singing "Jerusalem, the Golden." Never had Jacob heard such stirring music and beautiful tones. And this was his place, his home, celebrated in the song. The man's voice itself was like a golden trumpet. The melody soared, yet it had a martial beat to it that made the boy want to march, then soar. Like a fanfare in the middle of the piece—*do, sol, me, do*—the music spanned a rapid octave; the notes climbed like quick feet mounting the golden steps to heaven.

"Listen, listen!" he commanded, wanting Esau to join his rapture.

"It's the wrong religion," Esau sensibly answered.

But Jacob knew he must have this music and more like it in his life.

As soon as he found his courage, Jacob told his father, "I would like to be the man who sounds the shofar at Rosh Hashanah and Yom Kippur." As preparation for his lungs, Jacob proposed he take up the trumpet. Soon he realized his mistake: the trumpet was too brazen; the mellow French horn was just right. And he liked stuffing his fist into the bell to modify the pitch or to act as a mute. It was as though he himself had entered into the life of the music, as if he had joined with the instrument, from his lips on the mouthpiece to his hand inside the metal bell. He had become an instrument of the instrument and of its Glory.

Both boys, then, had their spiritual side. Esau said he wanted to become a settler and help reclaim the land for God's chosen people. Jacob said that God's kingdom was not of this world, and he had no interest in claiming a patch of dirt. He thought of orchestras and French horns playing Handel's *Water Music* and of von Karajan's Beethoven when he thought of where he wanted to be.

When the boys were thirteen, on the first day of school, they entered the public bus with special excitement. At Jacob's insistence, they had hatched an exciting plan: a new variation on an old theme. Jacob had insisted that they sign up to study different languages: Greek and Hindi. But actually they would both study both languages, by swapping places every day. They whispered and giggled like girls, and then the bus blew up.

Jacob was spared, but Esau was decapitated and his body almost entirely destroyed. What Jacob saw when he opened his eyes in the wreckage was their two school satchels leaning together as though in conspiracy. The blue and yellow bags were covered with dust, but he knew their contents—their lunches, their wallets, their books and new blank notebooks—were safe inside. His brother was gone. Jacob reached out for one of the bags, opened it, and saw the Greek grammar that belonged to Esau. With all his heart, he grabbed the satchel to his body and let no one take it from him.

Beside his hospital bed, the orderly opened the satchel, saw the wallet and the identification card, and gently spoke to the boy, calling him Esau. Jacob felt his own eyes narrow, and in that moment he became Esau.

When his parents came to his bed, his mother put her fingers in his hair, but she had no point of comparison; the amount of dust in his hair was distracting, and the dust made his hair feel thicker, too. No, Jacob would not let his brother die. To become Esau he resolved to give up music and to study the scriptures, seated patiently for long hours beside his father. When other boys in yeshiva made careless errors, Jacob-now-Esau flew into a rage.

One day one of his teachers said, "And do you still want to take on the hazards of being a settler, now that your dear brother is gone? Would you break your parents' hearts twice?"

"No," he answered thoughtfully, "yet my faith is strong that God promised this land to Israel, in perpetuity. I will find other ways to do the work of the Almighty."

"And how shall you love God?"

"Thou shalt love the Lord thy God with all thine heart, with all thine soul, and with all thine might."

Esau, born as Jacob, became Rabbi ben Ezra, a rabbi of narrow and exacting precision. Often he studied with cotton in his ears, lest some accidental strain of heavenly music tempt him. He grew to dislike commentaries on scripture that were imaginative, and asked always what was the letter of the word. His disdain for anyone unfortunate enough not to be among the chosen people hardened into hatred, though he collected paintings of the archangel Michael wearing medieval armor regardless of the religion or ethnicity of the artist, and also paintings of the fiery cherubim sent to guard the gates of Eden.

When a wealthy diamond merchant, an oil sheik, and an American real estate broker paid him to organize an interfaith group to guard the glory of God the Creator, Rabbi ben Ezra proposed the name Perpetuity.

It was he who selected an Arab to wrest the unholy secrets of astrophysics from the scientist Thom Bergmann, and he who reviewed the files of Christian fundamentalists to select a Texas businessman for the Genesis mission. It was God who packaged both threats in the possession of and on the person of an American widow.

# GETHSEMANE

LIKE A CRUEL and prodding finger, a shaft of Middle Eastern sunlight abused the raw flesh between my shoulder blades where I had been burned. With absolute determination, I focused my gaze on my feet and slid them through the shallow margin of the sea toward the shore. When I left the water, my soles made contact with firm dampness, then dry sand. I was dazed with pain and the terrible brightness of the beach.

Desperately, I remembered the nude man lying on his side on the riverbank. His image became a talisman, an amulet against the torture of my burns. He had seemed too perfect, his torso and limbs too smoothly sculpted, to have been dead. Surely his body had curved in mere repose, a graceful arabesque.

Of course there should have been no sea near the position where I went down. From the beginning, I realized I had fallen into a place that was no place. Like a person in a Rousseau painting, I inhabited a landscape and a situation that combined realities with imaginative vision. Nevertheless, I would find where the river met the ocean, then follow the river backward to the place where the nude man lay. As I walked along the beach, I felt stronger, more clearheaded. Almost, I could imagine myself healed.

Suddenly I vomited. Even my sense of my own condition was entirely unreliable. All I could do was hope to find the river and to follow it. If there was a river, if there was a man with ivory skin—or was he carved of Carrara marble? Upstream, I would rinse my mouth and throat and drink fresh water. That simple idea seemed hard-won and profound. Sometimes I walked with my eyes closed to save them from the terrible brightness, but nothing sealed away the agony of my burns. I envisioned myself walking across a floor inside an enormous oven.

The shade of the trees set back from the shore beckoned. I might stumble. Their thick roots lying on top of the ground might be full of snakes. The shady, inviting trees might be a snare and a delusion. "Straight is the way, and narrow is the path," my grandmother used to say sadly. From the beach I saw giant ferns springing up like so many green fountains among the roots webbing that shady forest floor. Below a chartreuse branch, the hairy tail of an animal hung down and curled up like a fiddlehead fern.

For a moment, I envisioned papyrus scrolls. Had I been carrying scrolls home to Grandmama in a brown grocery bag, with their ends stuck out like the long noses of French bread? But Pierre had not told me what shape the codex took.

Just ahead, the river emptied itself into the sea. I felt heartened.

*Turn left.*

It seemed to be Thom's voice telling me what to do. He used to joke that way: "If you're undecided about going left or right, always go left." It was a socialist's joke.

Actually, there was no choice: to survive, to follow the river inland, I must turn left.

The geography of all the far-flung earth was gathered together here. At times it seemed I was trudging blindly across an extension of an endless Sahara; other times, trees crowded down close to the edge of the river, and I was refreshed by the moist shade of Tennessee. I saw the snowy peak of the Matterhorn and an Antarctic shelf freighted with penguins. I imagined the burn on my back was smaller than it felt—about the size of my hand. I touched the wet black cord around my neck and followed it with my fingertips to the memory stick hanging between my breasts. Had Thom been murdered?

I would bend my mind to any question to escape awareness of the pain.

Had I almost been murdered? Pierre Saad's plane had fallen apart around me. System after system had failed. Those who had murdered Thom should also want to murder me. Surely we were alike in our innocence, Thom and I, though our minds were furnished in wildly different ways. Who could account for people's hatred—or their love? But the ancient manuscript—clearly Pierre Saad had loved the codex. Scrolls? Pages? Perhaps the heavy French horn case had been filled with cans of soup.

I came to a place where the bare bank was wide and flat and sloped very gradually toward the river. My unshod feet enjoyed the damp, sandy clay of the bank. It had the grainy texture of sugar cookie dough, though more firm. There, close to the water's edge, was a scuffed place where a man might have lain. I fancied I could see the vague imprint of a manlike image. He must have been able to rise and walk.

*Go on. Keep walking.* I wanted to sink to my knees and die.

The river was wider here, and the water was shallow and slow-moving. On the other side, I envisioned a man's large footprints in the sandy clay as surely as Robinson Crusoe had seen the print of Man Friday's unshod foot. I would track and find him.

When I stepped into the river, the flowing water gently cooled my ankles, and it was a delicious cooling. As I progressed, the water covered my feet and came as high as the calves of my legs. Knee-deep, I stood still for a moment. Like freshening stockings pulled up as high as my knees, the water enveloped my legs. A flat fish, its sides striped orange and white, swam by just beneath the surface. Under my bare soles, I felt a large, smooth rock tilting upward. A midget octopus—a clot of roots—withdrew its suctioned tentacles under the rock's edge. Glancing back as I walked toward the far shore, I saw a sticklike gar, long as my arm, moving down the middle of the river. Near the shore, where I stepped off the rock paving, mud oozed between my toes. Then came the firm bank. Ahead of my muddy feet hopped a brown toad with a bumpy back. For a moment, the pain between my shoulder blades flashed in conflagration.

I lifted my face to implore the heavens for release.

Far overhead, it appeared that two silvery jets would collide, but they crossed unscathed because one flew at a lower altitude than the other. From my vantage point below, their contrails formed a sign, a large X in the sky.

I thought a hurt dog was walking beside me; then I heard myself whining. Where the man's footsteps left no mark, I merely walked ahead past the thick trunks, through shady groves, across small, sunny meadows. Why not suppose he had walked this way? I not only hoped but also trusted I was following him. Why not trust I would find help, salvation from my suffering?

When I passed the bright zinnias and marigolds, the mythos turned ordinary and comfortable. Memory spoke, and I thought, Grandmother's Garden. And here were *rows* of roses—red, yellow, and pink—planted within an earthy rectangle prepared just for roses. Weren't those rows of roses? Or mere streaks of color shooting like pain through my brain? The Stimsons had had a rectangular rose garden back then, with a silver reflecting globe at its center. Only adults—not Janet nor Margarita nor I—had been allowed to cut bouquets for the table.

Somewhere, I had seen such a garden ball—shattered. Some malicious child or adolescent had been tempted and had succumbed to his power to break the beautiful. How amazingly thin the shards of glass had been. The insides of the shattered curves of silver had been an astonishing royal purple. *Igtiyal!* Thom's mind had been like a silver reflecting globe lined with royal purple.

The salt in my wounds bit like a billion diamonds.

I glided past two pear trees in full bloom, just like the Stimsons' pear trees. Their shaggy flowers spoke of when childhood was paradise and pain was fleeting. Here was a drift of iris—purple, white, and lavender—and there a clump of blue pansies. Like a curled gray cloud the size of two fists, my disembodied brain seemed to float just above my head—a repulsive object, my brain, convoluted, too nasty to inhabit the open air.

Long ago, decades or centuries ago, in a ruined orchard, Thom and I had chanced to see under an apple tree a sleeping stag who must have gorged himself with fallen apples. I remembered the beautiful branching of his antlers.

Like little apple trees they grew from the stag's head, but now: even now, a man was sleeping, on the ground, his shoulders propped against the base of an apple tree.

A human, a man, nude like myself, but he was not so young as he had appeared from the sky. Thirty, perhaps, maturely muscled, well formed, powerful, innocently turning, as I watched, to lie on his side. He pillowed his cheek on his large, folded hands just before they branched into fingers.

In the middle of his forehead, he had a single black curl—like a question mark. He was beautiful. So as to cast no shadow over his face, I dropped to all fours and crawled toward him over the twiggy orchard floor. From under my knees, I heard the soft, betraying pops of breaking twigs.

I would join rather than disturb his repose. In sleep, I, too, would take on flesh whole and perfect, smooth as myth.

Lying down beside him, I turned myself so as to nestle against his side, but I kept the burned part of my back away from making contact with his chest. For a moment I feared my singed hair with its repugnant odor might disturb his sleep, but he sucked in air all the stronger, as though he were not afraid to breathe hellfire and brimstone. My buttocks found a place to fit roundly against his warm loins.

# PART TWO

# MESOPOTAMIA

ADAM OPENED HIS eyes from an afternoon nap and saw that from his own body, here in the sunshine of Mesopotamia, God had created his helpmeet. The place where she had been joined to his chest was a raw wound between her shoulder blades. He himself was as intact as ever. Her buttocks were warm, sweaty, against his loins, and he drew back from her. His member was as beautifully relaxed as that of Adam on the ceiling of the Sistine Chapel.

As her own life awoke in her, she began to stir. Adam looked around quickly to see if he might have a daylight glimpse of God himself retreating from his handiwork, perhaps stepping into the deep shadows of a grove of trees. Always, always before now, God had come to Eden in the cool of the evening, in the hushed mystery of dying light, when dusk veiled vision. But the God of his childhood, for whom Adam still longed, had been a forthright god of sunshine, or rain, and diurnal weather. That God of childhood had wanted the brightness of noonday about him—that pinnacle in time when equality spread out on all sides, and objects tucked their shadows under themselves as securely as hens sat on their nests.

But here she was, even if God was gone. She was not young. She was not thin. Her skin lacked the luster of freshness; gray, sometimes a thread of bright silver, was to be found among the dark brown hair of her head. Her face? Because she lay on her side with her (mostly) dark hair splashing across her cheek, he could only study her profile. Ordinary: a straight nose, a smallish chin but a rather nice jawline. Could she have been the age of his mother? Probably so, if his mother had mated young. And this woman was marred, or at least hurt. Not only was there the raw patch between her shoulder blades, big as the palm of his hand, but also, he saw now, on the back of her head, another ugly, raw patch, the size of his thumb and forefinger brought together in a circle. Her hair was burned off to the scalp, charred black like the remains of a campfire. Around the bad spot her hair was frizzled, broken, and burned. She was damaged; God had left damaged goods on his doorstep.

But then, too, so was he.

And had he ever known a single person whom life had left undamaged?

Didn't we all deserve each other and nothing better? Suddenly he wanted to draw her, the char circle like a crown slipped down the back of her head.

How had Michelangelo rendered Eve on the ceiling of the Sistine Chapel? God had brought Eve, looking frightened, behind him, enfolded in a flare of his blue robe. Had God's fiery hand touched *this* Eve's reluctant back, shoved her toward Adam?

A garter of sand encircled both her legs just above the calves. Sparkles in the yellow grit glinted in the light, ornamental and pretty. Perhaps she had risen from an older mythology—Venus rising from the sea, marked with rings of sand around her legs.

Adam licked one finger, reached down, and pressed the finger against her sandy skin. Numerous grains stuck to his wet finger, and he brought them to his lips, his finger like an offered Popsicle. He licked once, felt the discrete graininess of it, and glanced into her now open eyes.

"Eve?" he asked. To say her name, his voice turned into liquid velvet and poured from his mouth.

First her eyes answered, with a twinkle, claiming consciousness. Then she asked, "Are you Adam?" and good humor twinkled also in her voice.

"Yes," he answered. His breath clotted, suspended in his mouth.

"My name is Lucy," she replied.

"No," he said. He shook his head slightly in the negative. Not Eve? He closed his eyes for a moment and felt something like shame cross his face.

"I'm hurt," she said gently, with just an edge of urgency.

He opened his eyes, noted that hers were midnight blue, and said, "I saw. You've been burned. Purified. As by a Refiner's fire."

"My plane crashed. On the beach."

"An airplane."

"Yes. An antique Piper Cub. Why are you here?"

"God put me here."

Some idea passed over her face. She sat up, turned her body, and faced him now as they continued to sit under the apple tree. Soft globules of light spotted the grass.

He could not have deduced her countenance from her profile. Her face had a wideness to it, an openness across the eyes. She was not afraid. Her gaze softened as though she had seen someone familiar, someone she recognized and accepted.

"Why did God put you here?" she asked.

"To try again."

She nodded and was silent for a while. Finally she said, "We have no clothing."

"No," he answered. It was a pleasure to look at her. "That's how it was, in the beginning." Her open face, especially her eyes looking right into his eyes, was—yes—a *pleasure* to see. Perhaps if she wore clothing, she would not look at him so tenderly. He wanted to touch the curve of her cheek, to fit his hand just there, to cradle her face. He wanted to care for her.

"There are flowers here, in this paradise." Her voice was full of hesitation. "And fruit. Flowers I knew as a child. Almost exactly like them."

He found himself saying, "I know," though he didn't know. He felt confused. When had she been a child? He, too, could remember, both far back and recent harsh realities. His captivity and rape in a truck. To reel forward more quickly, he closed his eyes: the kindly monkey-boy. His head began to throb. With the hand that would have caressed her soft cheek, he covered his face.

"The back of my head got hurt," he said like a child. Was not Eve the mother of us all?

"Mine, too." She reached out and stroked the nape of his neck. "Feel better," she said quietly. When he stretched his hand toward her, she quickly added, "Please don't touch me." She withdrew her own hand.

He stopped and bowed his head, reprimanded, quietly sad. He glanced at her body as she sat in the sunshine: breasts neither large nor small, a pleasant pearish shape, a little rounded sag of belly fat around her middle. Her private hair was concealed by the fullness of her thigh and the way her arm crossed her body.

"I'm thirsty and weak," she said. "Very weak. My burns hurt."

"I know an aloe plant," he said, looking into the distance. "At the ranch, my mother put aloe juice on burns." When the burned woman did not reply, he continued, "You should be in the shade. It was shady here when I fell asleep, but you know the shade moves." He stood up and felt he was rising successfully from a pool of sadness. "I'll get the aloe and bring you some fruit. What do you like best?"

"Oranges and pears, if they're ripe," she said without hesitation.

"And cherries?"

Unperturbed, she was looking at his nakedness, his height.

He knew how he looked—sculptural and strong—but it meant nothing.

"Thank you," she said simply.

# LUCY AS EVE

I HAD FALLEN into Eden, despite its floral references and their convincing recapitulations of my local childhood themes. There seemed to be an inaudible music in the air, wafting just under the threshold of my hearing. When Thom had sung art songs to me, my favorite had been Handel's "Where E'er You Walk." I heard it now—a song in which the beloved was so adored by both man and nature that even trees would crowd into a shade to protect her from the sun. Whether the music emanated from memory or from the beauty around me, or from the mind of a madman—and surely this naked Adonis, this Adam with an American accent, was mad—I was loath to decide.

I shamelessly watched his naked back as he walked away to gather fruit and balm for my burn: I watched the slight groove acknowledging the presence of a mortal spine hidden under his flesh, the rounds of his moving buttocks, the shapeliness of his strong legs. His head was held high. His bare feet moved him swiftly away as though he had no thought of feet or their necessary work in traversing the short, dry grass. In his physical perfection, he seemed a human worthy of the sky, the complement of its gentle bright blues and satisfying heaps of clouds.

I recognized who he was, or rather I knew where I might legitimately have expected to meet him, instead of in this demi-Eden. He could have been one of my patients, of the gentle variety. A mental case, someone in whose mind reality shifted its shape more rapidly than metaphors of shifting clouds. Someone who was surely terrified, at times, by uncertainties, and yet someone who loved his own imaginings and where they could take him. Was I myself just a figment of his imagination? Had he been powerful enough to draw me into his reality?

"Eve," he had called me, as though he were the proprietor of this territory and might name me as he pleased. Was I so weakened that I would let him define me and the reality of my world? No. I had told this Adam, straight and directly, My name is Lucy. Had I let Thom, when I fell into the world of the university, only eighteen, define my reality? Yes. And it had been good. But I could still tell the difference between a genius and a madman.

When Adam returned, I rose to meet him. Though the effort made me feel faint, I wanted him to see me full—no concealment, secrets, or pretense. I stepped forward, out of the shade, into the sunlight so it could reveal and brighten my body. I wanted to establish our nakedness as ordinary, natural as sunlight, not erotic.

He walked toward me with fruit in his hands—three small oranges in one hand, two pears with speckled skins in the other, and cherries hung over his ears. Two steps short of where I stood, he stopped and said, "You are just like me."

"Yes." Two human beings. Certainly we were alike.

"But you need to stay in the shade so you won't get sunburned. You're already burned."

He handed me the pears, and then with his hand he removed spears of aloe, having transported them clamped between his ribs and the inside of his upper arm, though I'd not noticed them at first. He had come to me like a painting from the Renaissance—a man whose body was composed of vegetables.

Obediently—because it was reasonable—I stepped back into the edge of the shade, sat down, and leaned forward so he could minister to my back and scalp. I imagined the raw ugliness my back displayed—worse than a painting of a sore, it *was* a sore. As he knelt behind me and dripped the soothing sap into my wounds, I bit into one of the pears. He had not washed them, and the skin tasted of dust.

"Do you like the pear?" His voice was as uncomplicated as that of a schoolboy. Drip, drip, drip, without contamination, the aloe fluid dropped patiently into my flesh.

"The pear? Refreshing as water, but more enticing," I reported. "Mealy, a little, but slippery, too." He had asked me; so why not find the words for the whole truth? What else was there to do? I would not hold back but find the real, precise language for every moment of being alive. I ate some more and offered a new report. "But I feel surprised instead of satisfied when it's gone. That's the way it is with eating pears. In your mouth they just disappear."

When he said nothing, I asked, "Do you want the other one?"

"No. It's for you. Does the aloe sting your back?"

"Not at all."

"Lean over more."

I did, glancing at myself, my hanging breasts and nipples as they pointed toward the ground. I regretted that some of the juice from the pear dripped into the grass. How unremittingly the juice fell straight down. The airplane and I had fallen otherwise—a gentle, slanting glide. We had stepped downward as through dreamy levels of consciousness. When I had released the French horn case outside the open door of the plane, the case plummeted. Straightaway, Pierre Saad's codex was gone. Lost. Rushing down the straight facade of the seventeenth-century Dutch house, the grand piano had fallen plumb onto Thom. I had always imagined his face upturned, literally facing it, maybe even calculating its velocity with lightning rapidity.

Drip, drip, drip, like fairy pearls, the aloe dripped into my burn and dissolved.

Adam said, "To be honest, I ate the first pear from the tree. I wanted to be sure they were ripe."

Had I seen any vegetables growing in this garden? Not yet, only fruit and flowers. Perhaps some nut trees. (Already my back and the back of my head were soothing themselves under the influence of the aloe juice.)

The image of my plane smoldering on the beach came to me. Perhaps small flames still smoldered in the wreckage. Should I ask him to fetch fire?

No. I thought not. The natural temperature was so warm I did not want for clothes or any other source of heat. I had had enough of fire, but still I asked, "Do you have fire here?"

"Fire?" he asked as though he didn't understand the word. Certainly he had earth, air, water in abundance. But fire? It seemed a troubling element.

"Do you need fire?" I prompted. "How long have you been here?"

"I came here . . ." He hesitated. "I've been here some time."

"More than a week?" I asked. He seemed in such perfect health.

He extended his hands, one of them clasping a stalk of the dripping aloe, over my shoulders for me to see. He seemed to be presenting the backs of his hands for inspection.

"My hands. My hands are no longer blue, you see."

I said nothing. *Blue?* A small cloud of depression passed through my mind. He had seemed all right enough to be treated as though he *were* all right. Something balked in me about considering him among my patients. I didn't want to work at redeeming him. Not here. I wanted to enjoy. I was alive—Wasn't that enough to be? Alive?

At the lower edge of the canopy of the apple tree, Adam inserted banana leaves; the next layer of leaves was woven through those branches slightly higher, and when a third layer was in place, I was provided a roof. The three stages of big leaves were like overlapping shingles. Providing shade or shelter from possible rain, the banana leaves converted the tree into a garden pavilion. Nested on fern fronds, I lay comfortably on my stomach. For three days, and then three more, I slept and ate and dreamed.

Adam brought me grapes and fuzzy kiwi to eat, and water in a large curved leaf. He cracked pecans between two rocks and picked out the meat for me, making sure to avoid the bitter pith. Once he placed an enormous coconut on the lower rock and, raising another stone high above his head, smashed the coconut shell as hard as he could over and over. The blows made me wince, but he was too intent on his work to notice. Eventually the shell cracked. Though the thin coconut milk was mostly lost, Adam fed me delicious meaty curves of coconut, each a crescent of amazing whiteness.

"Pure as snow," he said wonderingly, his forehead and cheeks streaming with sweat.

After we had eaten the coconut, the empty shell suggested itself to Adam as a dipper for carrying me water. He made a second coconut vessel, one created more carefully, which was almost the equivalent of a small pot in size, so that I would have a reservoir of water with me always. To hold the rounded container upright, he arranged a supporting ring of stones. Before I drank the water, I usually liked to smell it. Seeing me do this, Adam often squeezed a lemon or a lime into the water to give it a slight flavor.

I considered volunteering to make a basket for carrying fruit, whatever, by weaving together the long grass, if there was suitable grass here, and if not I could use the strong, bladelike leaves of the iris I had seen. But I decided not to make the offer. Let it be this way for a while—that he would bring to me only what I needed in his bare hands, or clamped against his body, or dangling from his ears. I recalled again Renaissance paintings of people composed of robust vegetables.

One day he brought home a section of waxy honeycomb that he had stolen from the bees. He pronounced it to have special healing power. After I had sucked the honey from the comb, I bit off a hunk and smacked away on the wax in a noisy way, like a preteen girl chewing gum—uninhibited oral pleasure.

Another day he arrived with an even larger flat rock balanced on top of his head and steadied with both hands. Protected by a layer of large fig leaves, the upper side of the rock itself was upholstered with a deep pad of green moss. Up till now, I could choose to either stand or lie, or sit awkwardly on the grass. He said the mossy rock was to become my soft seat. To elevate it a foot or so, he brought other rocks to form its legs. He constructed the bench in a particularly shady spot, near the trunk of the tree. Because the pad of moss would dry quickly in the warm air, he explained, he would water it twice a day, to keep the moss happy.

During this time of healing, we talked lightly and sparsely.

My thoughts came and went as uncertainly as clouds. I was never bored. I felt myself to be in the process of absorbing it all—the weather, this strange place, the strange man who presided over it.

And what was my responsibility to this man who called himself Adam?

None, I decided. Not now. I would rest. I would heal. Here in this verdant Eden, surely located somewhere between the Tigris and Euphrates rivers as they flowed toward the Persian Gulf, if it were located anywhere outside the realm of imagination, I would loaf and invite my soul, as Whitman had written in *Leaves of Grass*.

Perhaps I myself had potentials of soul, mind, body, I had neither explored nor recognized. Perhaps it was the same for Adam, and we were both fortunate beyond our wildest hopes.

Adam was, I hoped and then decided again, a gentle soul.

But did I myself even have a soul to invite to this picnic on the grass? Did I have one left? Or had it been allowed to evaporate and disperse into the air? No doubt, someplace in Japan, my missionary parents were praying for me. Surely my absence from the round world had been noted and reported. I wished them Whitman's encouraging words, "look for me under your boot-soles. . . . Missing me one place search another, I stop somewhere waiting for you." But I doubted I was waiting for reconciliation with the parents who had abandoned me for their idea of God and duty.

Sometimes in the heat of the day, Adam fanned me with a leaf from the elephant ear plant until I fell into a dazed afternoon nap. Always, three times a day, he treated my burns with the drippings from a spear of aloe. Every other day, he brought tangerines for me to eat, and when he did, he made something of a ritual of it. "I should like to feed you the tangerine sections, one by one," he said, "and if you don't mind, I'd like you to feed me, as well."

"All right," I answered, a bit uncomfortably. "But why?"

"God sent Noah a rainbow as a promise. To me, God gave a tangerine. He caused me to notice it and to take it for myself. It was juicy and delicious. Its goodness restored me to life."

"Where did I come from?" I asked gently. I had disabused Adam of the idea that God had created me from one of his own ribs.

"The sky."

"And where did you come from?" I asked for the first time.

"The earth. My name, Adam, means that I came from the clay of the earth."

For a terrible moment I remembered the last morning with Thom, how he had spoken of the Hebrew meaning of the word *adamah.*

"I've troubled you," Adam observed.

"No," I said reassuringly. "I was remembering—" I wanted to say, "I was remembering my husband," but somehow I could not bring myself to say it. The fact of my former, complicated, and civilized life contradicted this fantasy too flatly. It would be no kind, caring act to crack open this world with the stone of memory.

I was at rest here in this demi-Eden. Not at work. No need to tinker with versions of reality.

"If a storm comes," he said, all serenity, "I'll take you to a place I know. There's a shelter in the rock, and we'll be safe under it."

"A cave?" After flourishing in a world of open sunshine, I didn't like the idea of going into any sort of cold, dank cave. Here everything was sunshine and shadow, gentle breeze and waving grass, a garden of delights.

"Not really a cave," he said. "It's an overhang, open on three sides. But it's a big overhang, and if we're sitting in the center of it, we're as safe as though the air around us were a wall. There's a wall of stone but only at the back."

Neither of us spoke of the past or the future. I had taken a leave of absence from my work at the hospital in New York. During that long cocooning of marriage, I had made no close women friends. The only people who might worry about me were Gabriel Plum, and Pierre and Arielle Saad. If I could have, I would have relieved their anxiety, but I was not much worried about what worry they might experience. Like an inconsiderate child at camp who has no compulsion to e-mail home, because I knew I was more than all right, I assumed somehow they'd know it, too.

At night, the spectacle of stars enthralled me and made me think of Thom, who had studied them with such ardor. I wished that he could see this contrast of absolute blackness with the sparkling lights. In Mesopotamia, we were about at the latitude of Kentucky, I believed. In Iowa the star view would have been a little more to the north. When Thom and his parents visited Israel, he would have seen this sky from a slightly more southern exposure. Who would want to murder anyone whose life was the study of stars? *Igtiyal?* During those moments flying the Piper Cub, the question had burned my brain like a brand. Now I gulped the darkness and felt the sparkle of stars tickle my throat as I swallowed.

At night, Adam slept on his own bed of ferns, softer than feathers, at a short distance from me. His pallet was under another small tree, where he had also constructed a kind of roof to match mine. Under our separate shelters, we were a little settlement of two, surrounded by wilderness and bits of garden. *Igtiyal?* The question was more remote than starlight.

Because of the discomfort of my burns—less discomfort all along once I had suffered a peak of pain on the third day—I woke often, though Adam seemed always to sleep till dawn. Throughout the nights, I heard Adam talking in his sleep. The distance between us was great enough that I could rarely catch just what he said; I doubted if it were coherent anyway. His nighttime monologue reminded me of the experience of sleeping to the sound of someone's low radio in the next dormitory room.

Sometimes he cried out sharply, as though he were terrified or terribly hurt. My heartbeat quickened when I heard him in distress, but always the moment passed and he seemed to drop back into an untroubled dream. If the cries had continued, I would have risen up, made my way to his side, and gently shaken his bare shoulder. Often he slept on his side, facing me, and sometimes I noticed the moonlight illumining one shoulder rounded up higher than the rest of his long body.

My own dreams consisted of colors and textures rather than scenes: Thom's unshaven chin; the sweet rumple of his curls; a certain thick yellow from the painting of a patient who had lost both parents in the Holocaust. Completely lacking in story or even situation, the entirety of my dream space filled with these magnified details that had been a small part of a more significant whole in my waking life. This close focus dominated the infinite visual field of my dreaming mind from side to side and top to bottom.

I knew the prickly chin and the rumpled curls to be Thom's, but he was not there. These frame-filling details displaced any larger context or meaning. I dreamed of the *sensation* of softness—my grandmother's lap—and of the smooth, worn nap of her flowered aprons. The strings of the viola against the fingertips of my left hand—merely the sensation of touching the metal-wrapped A-D-G or heavy C string—filled hours of dreams, or the sensation in my right hand of the drag of my horsehair bow rubbing through the well-worn groove in my rosin cake.

Colors borrowed again and again from the canvases of my art therapy students filled the shapeless, unending space on the backs of my eyelids, but the vivid hues of paint were only themselves; they suggested nothing of the ornate pitcher or kitchen sink or jewel or car fender they had been employed to depict. Once I spent the night dreaming of a beveled camel hair paintbrush; its fine-grained softness made me want to squeal with wonder.

All these dreams were pleasant ones. The most pleasant ones were of the pink blossoms of mimosa trees—the whole blossom, not just its pinkness—how they swayed in Memphis beside the Mississippi like the skirts of ballet dancers.

The color cherry red repeatedly filled my mind. Only occasionally did it take the shape and shininess of actual cherries hanging over Adam's ears.

"Six days have passed," Adam said one morning. "On the seventh day, today, it would be good if you began to walk about. You need to regain your strength."

I agreed.

He held out his hand to me; I stood up and wobbled out into the open sun. The effort made me dizzy; I would have fallen if he had not held my hand. I realized the seriousness of my weakness; I had tarried too long in my sickbed convalescence. I knew better than to indulge in the horizontal. I knew from my grandmother's illnesses that patients should be up and on their feet as soon as possible. I knew from the treatment charts of even those with mental ailments how crucial exercise was to the achievement of any kind of health. And yet I had banished such knowledge from my mind. I had not wanted things to change. I had made a demigod of Adam, in whose care I wished to be perpetually cradled.

—

Our first quarrel occurred when I asked him to bring fresh ferns for my bed. I had never asked him to do anything particular for me before; he had always just anticipated my needs.

He looked startled, but he replied, "Of course," and left immediately.

I felt annoyed. I hadn't meant he should do it right that minute. I had thought we would sit down and chat. If we were not to sit together and chat in the shade of the tree, I thought petulantly, then I would sit by myself and think.

What was I to do about my situation? Our situation. Unbidden, the image of his genitalia presented itself to my mind, the pleasant curve of the end of his penis. Immediately I was furious with myself. He was mentally ill. He was practically my patient. Hands off! I was the sane one; I needed to take charge. Nationally, 50 percent of the patients in mental hospitals suffered from religious delusions. Many of them believed themselves to be Jesus—thoroughly divine, not human. Well, it was the same here in the Garden: 50 percent of the population suffered from religious delusions.

Immediately I thought of his gentleness, his sense of my needs, how he had courteously constructed his own bed under a different tree. I thought of the sincerity and simplicity with which he spoke, when he spoke of God. There was nothing proselytizing about it, nothing that pressured me to believe, no coercion. I felt nothing of fear and little of curiosity. Cared for and content, I found it difficult to think of *next.*

He made me feel helpless. The situation made me angry.

Then I looked out into the sunshine, the simple way it lay on the grass. It was as though the grass had been mown; it was like a large, civilized park, left to go partly natural. Idly, I thought of Kew Gardens—"It isn't far from London," Alfred Noyes had written. "Come down to Kew in lilac time, in lilac time, in lilac time. . . ." In the distance, I saw Adam moving toward me. His arms were heaped so high with fern fronds that it looked as though a pile of greenery, with legs, was making its way across the plain.

I got up from my rock-chair and cleared the shriveled fern from my bed place under the makeshift roof. I didn't want Adam to have to build a new roof of banana leaves, though a few splits had developed, turning the edges of the leaves into a coarse brown fringe. Probably the roof would need to be refreshed soon enough, but perhaps piece by piece.

As soon as Adam finished spreading out the ferns, fashioning a thicker mound at one end to suggest a pillowed place, I startled myself by asking him in a rather presumptuous manner, "Do lilacs grow here?"

Adam straightened up and put his hands on his hips. He looked at me in a level and direct way. "Yes," he said. "I'll get you some." And he turned and walked away.

I was glad to have him go. I hadn't finished thinking about our situation, what we should do.

If he was insane, he was only mildly so. He could cooperate. He could follow instructions. He could *anticipate* instructions. His affect seemed appropriate. He seemed relaxed. Not at all anxious. He seemed as though he wanted nothing, as though he was perfectly content.

These conclusions about my companion awakened a certain sense of frustration. Where was ambition?

Thom had been a person who worked very hard. So had I. We had loved our work, had always kept each other on a loose leash concerning the freedom to work. And Thom knew how to take his pleasures; he made room for attending the concerts we both had loved since our first meeting. After he spent the day at the physics department, Thom enjoyed a good meal and good conversation, even if he came home quite late. Here there was no work, and we might as well be grunting at each other, so monosyllabic were our exchanges. Sometimes I *did* grunt. Thom had focus and insight about everything—art, politics, literature, above all his work in spectroscopy, his knowledge of the starry sky in all its aspects, visible and invisible. He could *listen* to the heartbeat of space, through the radio telescopes.

For the first time since I had fallen into Eden, I touched my talisman, the titanium case that held and protected Thom's last thoughts. While my fingertips caressed the smooth case, I savored our last morning in the hotel when he had projected his valentine on the ceiling: *To all the Lucys in the Universe.*

Could there be more than one? The thought jolted me. Talk among the astrophysicists about parallel universes never seemed very serious. But was it possible that I had not been Thom's one and only object of affection? What bizarre language! I was not an *object* of anything! Suddenly I realized my mind had become irritable. It was like a wound that itches as it heals. The patch on the back of my head itched. So did my back. It was irritating.

And yes, we ourselves had known more than one Lucy. One of them was a cousin of Thom, a woman about the age of Adam. Thom had sent her to work with our friend Gabriel Plum in England. She had come to Thom's funeral and bawled her eyes out. I remembered how Gabriel had taken her into his arms, comfortingly, and even then, at Thom's funeral, the idea had flickered through my mind that Gabriel and she might be an Item. Maybe I had glimpsed a sliver of their intimacy.

Then I'd forgotten the impression. Apparently if there had been any warmth between Gabriel and young Lucy it had not lasted, *because Gabriel proposed to me*. That moment in the big jet, flying over the spine of northern Italy, the gray Dolomite peaks arranged below like dragon vertebrae, belonged more to a dream than to reality. That scene of Gabriel and me inside the airplane seemed to float like an untethered balloon in insubstantial space.

My train of thought had branched and branched, and now I couldn't remember what it was I had set myself to consider during Adam's absence.

Moving across the hot meadow was a lilac bush in full bloom. Its aroma preceded it. I closed my eyes and rapturously drew in a long breath. When I opened them, I began to laugh, for of course the lilac tree had two long and manly legs. It was the ridiculous abundance of the bouquet that had made me laugh. It was like something a lover might offer in a Chagall painting. The bouquet would crowd the lovers to the frame and become the bloated centerpiece itself.

When Adam arrived, I joked, "I'm afraid I don't have an appropriate vase."

An anxious expression crossed over his face, then he suddenly knelt and began to place the lilacs around my bed, branch by branch, in a border.

"That's all right," he said. "I'll just arrange them here."

Their color was perfect, purple and deep as Concord grapes, but with edges of lavender that helped to define their texture. There was a robust springiness about the panicles, a lollipop-like delectableness. Only a few of them had begun to droop from the heat. He held one of the floppy ones up to my nose.

"These have the heaviest fragrance," he said.

The panicle lacked the turgor to raise its head, but it drooped gracefully over his hand. If I were to paint it, if Chagall had painted it, it might have been titled *The Offering,* with no mention of its wilted nature. I wondered if Adam had an artist's eye.

"What say you?" Adam asked. "Should the wilted, like the wicked, be cast into outer darkness?"

"Where is outer darkness?" I asked, surprised at the softness in my voice.

"In Greek mythology," he mused, "sometimes the honorably defeated were placed in the night sky to become constellations."

"Are you defeated?" I asked gently.

At first he averted his face, but after a moment his gaze returned to meet my own.

"Yes," he said. "And so are you."

"And why am I?" I had told him nothing of my losses—of Thom's existence, let alone his death, of how I had become unmoored, of the loss of meaning in work and the loss of joy in being alive.

I heard myself catch a breath, as though my body were fueling itself to tell the truth, but before I spoke, he began his reply to my question.

"Because you fell from the sky."

"My plane crashed," I said, insisting on a literal explanation.

"Yes."

"You know, it may be the plane is still smoldering on the beach. I'm hungry. I'd like to eat some fish. If we had a fire, we could cook some fish."

"It's been many days."

"And before I crashed, I threw a hard case—a French horn case—out the plane door. Maybe we could find it."

"You would like to leave here, wouldn't you?"

"Could you check the wreckage? Maybe something there is still smoldering."

While he was gone, I peeled back the skin of a banana and ate it. I knew that bananas, like oranges, contained potassium, which I needed for strength.

Without deciding, I knew I had decided: Yes, I wanted to heal and to leave this place that was no more meaningful or serious than a giant playground. I wanted to talk to people who had their own energy and purpose, who could be roughly categorized as sane, who were not defeated. And what had defeated this unbelievably beautiful man, age—I was guessing—thirty? Who was looking for him? Who missed him?

And who missed me?

Pierre Saad and his daughter would worry, I knew. For him, the loss of the ancient manuscript would be an irreparable disaster. But he knew he had taken a risk in giving it to me. He must have felt a great deal of urgency to have initiated such a risk. I had a cool and rational ability to assess risk, but why hadn't I questioned his degree of risk taking and understood it as an index to his degree of desperation? No doubt he hoped that at least the manuscript had not been destroyed. Perhaps he would hypothesize that I had stolen it to sell on the black market.

No. Pierre Saad had assessed me. He knew I was not a thief, that I would try my best to deliver the codex, as I had set out to do.

And Gabriel Plum? He would have been frantic when I had not returned to Cairo from the Nile cruise. But had I left enough trail for anyone to follow? The tour guide would have reported I had left the group; I had not told him I intended to visit the museum at Nag Hammadi. Gabriel would not have imagined that I had met with a man Gabriel actually knew, the host of the Cairo symposium.

Squinting my eyes against the piercing brightness of the sun, I imagined this triangle of accomplished men, all of whom knew of one another, had had at least conversation—Thom, Gabriel, and Pierre—as a constellation in the night sky. And then there was Adam, relaxed in his mythic nakedness, whom none of them could have possibly imagined, not in their most extravagant dreams.

I imagined Adam crossing their constellation; he was a planet, a wanderer through the night sky, not a fixed star. A loose cannon. Someone who wrestled with his demons at night and cried out when they pinched him or scorched him with their breath. Someone whose day-self carried all the sweetness of the honeycomb. Who called me Eve.

For him, I had no history before my fall. He awoke and found me curled against his side, hurt by the fiery passage into Eden, more like Lucifer than Eve. Once he told me he had begged God for me, and I had appeared.

A bit the worse for wear, I thought ruefully.

Why not leave well enough alone? That question seemed the true answer to the uncertainty that hovered over me. I got up to test the strength of my legs, to take a few steps, literally, on the path that would lead to my restoration. Again I found that I was truly very weak. As I upbraided myself for lounging so long, I imagined my childhood friends—Janet and Margarita—walking on each side of me, encouraging me. "You can do it, Lucy," they said. "We know you can. Keep going."

It was what they had said when I tried to learn to walk on tall stilts. And I had become a wonderful stilt walker, their intrepid leader into the challenges of climbing steps on stilts and walking long distances over gravel or through tall grass. When I had suggested we joust like knights of old—riding stilts instead of steeds—we charged each other to see who could knock the other off balance. We had had such a fine time, enacting anything we could imagine. Only when I had talked about walking on clouds had Janet reined me in, pointing out the scientific fact that despite their solid appearance, clouds are insubstantial, consisting of nothing but water vapor catching the light in certain ways that have the power to attract and amaze.

When I saw Adam coming toward me, I decided I would try to walk to meet him. I knew I had been peremptory, practically ordering him to do this or fetch that for me. And Adam had taken umbrage. As he approached, there was a new rigidity, a lack of grace in his body. He seemed hulking, more like a comic-book caveman. His face, too, was concentrated, his brow contracted.

"Do you want to leave here?" he had asked. I had neither answered his question nor offered reassurances. While he was away, scavenging for me, he had perhaps brooded on the matter. Would he try to prevent my leaving?

"Adam, Adam!" I hailed him. "I'm coming to meet you."

Usually I avoided calling him by his name. I had not wanted to participate too fully in his fantasy of Genesis.

His face filled with happiness. Though his fists were strangely clenched, he hurried toward me and held his arms out. Fearing that I had signaled acceptance of him and his world, I felt my knees wobble with trepidation as much as fatigue. Before I collapsed, he caught me in those pronglike arms, carefully avoiding my still-healing tender back.

I felt the top of my head fit under his chin, my sun-warmed flesh pressing against his, the utter safety of his support. Our nakedness, and the naturalness of it. I had liked to stand under Thom's chin like this.

"You made it," he said, the delight in his voice as warm as his body. He folded an arm across the top of my shoulders and the other across the small of my back, and I gave myself to the bliss of it. "You came to me of your own free will. God said you would. If I was patient."

Feeling tears gush from my eyes, I took a step back.

"No, I haven't. I wanted to please you—that's all. You've been so kind and so good to me."

He was smiling at me. A tear like a clear jewel stood at the corner of his eye.

"It doesn't mean anything," I insisted. "Everything is the same as it was."

"I see," he said. "It's all right. Don't be afraid."

With the back of his still-clenched fist, he wiped away the clear bead of tear. Blood defined the lines between his curved fingers. His hand was bleeding. Quickly I reached for his other closed hand and saw that it, too, was oozing blood from the knot of his fist. For an instant I thought, I've crucified him, but then he opened his hands. Amid the blood, his palms sparkled.

"There was no fire left at the plane," he explained. "But I found this—a broken mirror. We can make a clay base and push the pieces into the wet clay. It can be a mirror again, just a bit cracked. Perhaps we can use it to make a flame."

As he walked home, he had squeezed the shards into the flesh of his palms.

"There was a mirror on the cockpit door," I said. "Like a rearview mirror on a car, so the pilot could glance back without turning her head."

"When we have a fire I'll catch a fish in the river, and you can cook it."

Staring at the mess of his hands, I said, "But you're bleeding."

Now he looked away from me. "I squeezed too hard. I was angry. At you. You said you wanted to leave. I thought you wanted the fire to make a signal."

"Not for a long time," I answered softly. "I need to find the case I threw out of the airplane. It looked like a case for a particular musical instrument, French horn." Trouble passed over his face. I took a deep breath and said, "This is a beautiful place. It's beautiful to be here with you, as your friend."

"Yes," he answered, and smiled shyly, embarrassed and pleased. But I saw his lower lip tremble a little, though he tried to conceal his anxiety. He seemed newly hatched; he seemed ten years old, not thirty, despite his large and powerful body. He seemed ten years old not mentally but emotionally—fresh and vulnerable, lacking in sophistication and social pretense, wanting to please.

"Let's go fishing," I said. "Sometime soon."

"When you're stronger, we'll fish together. Now I'll fish by myself."

I began to feel overheated in the sunlight. My mind went dizzy, and I felt my body sway when the slightest breeze touched me.

"Are you strong enough to make it back?" he asked.

"I—I—don't know," I stammered.

All at once he dropped down on all fours, his hands still closed over the sharp shards of the broken mirror.

"Climb up on my back," he said.

"You can't crawl all the way back on all fours," I said, though I could easily picture him doing just that, with me astride.

"No. I'll stand up," he explained. "Just hold around my neck and shoulders when I start to stand up."

The arrangement worked. He slowly stood, and with me riding piggyback, we began to progress slowly back toward the shade of the apple trees. I realized the fruit trees had been spaced regularly; we lived in the remains of an old orchard. As soon as we grew comfortable and confident, Adam adjusted his stride to a certain jauntiness. He began to whistle "Oh! Susanna!" through his teeth.

I could not help but laugh happily. I would not spend the energy to sing, but I thought the words, *Oh! Susanna, oh dontcha cry for me.*

Still, I was weak and dizzy, and soon I rested the side of my cheek against the stalk of his broad neck. His tune modulated into a slow lullaby, *Hush little baby, don't say a word; Mama's gonna buy you a mockingbird.* When he reached the ferny pallet, he got down on all fours again so I could dismount with ease. As I slid onto my soft mattress and lay on my stomach, the fronds seemed to sigh and yawn.

"Wait," he said. "Don't go to sleep yet. Drink a little water before you sleep." When I moved to lie on my side, propping my head with my bent arm and hand, he lifted the coconut shell to my lips. "We don't want you to get dehydrated," he added. "That's good. Thatta girl," he crooned.

When he poured the scented water between my lips, my teeth clamped about, looking for wispy shreds of coconut, but only faint flavor was there. I could almost see and taste our fish—flaky, white, and tender. The protein and oils from the fish would make a superb addition to our diet, though we had already gotten protein from the nuts he cracked. Iron, I needed that, too, to strengthen my blood. "We have date trees, don't we?" I asked.

"Yes," he answered. "I've always loved dates and raisins."

Straightening my arm, I pillowed my head on it, and my mind drifted downward to sleep.

A small sun had come from the dark sky to sit burning in the grass. Alarmed, I sat up in bed. Suppose it started a prairie fire?

No, it was not a visiting sun.

What I saw was a campfire, and the silhouette of Adam sitting beside it. He held a stick in one hand, roasting something over the fire. Now I smelled it, and I could even see its shape.

He was cooking me a fish.

As quietly as possible, I approached him stealthily. With care and patience, I placed each bare foot in the grass. As I grew closer, I could see that he had packed the fish in clay so that it would roast more evenly. The stick, too, was protected by an insulating sleeve of clay that ballooned and became the casing for the fish. I smiled to think that he might have been a Boy Scout, or perhaps a member of 4-H, if he had had a rural background. I slipped up behind him and was just about to put my hand on his shoulder, rosy with fire glow, when, without turning his head, he spoke.

"Is that you, Eve?"

I stopped my hand in midair and withdrew it. "Lucy," I said. "My name is Lucy Bergmann."

"Friend," he answered, keeping his eyes on the roasting fish. "I know you as my friend today. But God willing, someday I will know you as my wife—"

I said nothing. When he had called me "friend," my heart had wilted in disappointment—I had to admit it. But the word *wife* made me feel as though a cup of scalding water had been tossed onto my flesh.

"—and without sin, we shall dwell in the House of the Lord forever and ever."

After a long pause, I asked him, in a new key, if he thought the fish was almost done and how he had caught it, and how he had kindled the fire, but I did not listen to his replies. I was monitoring my naughty hand, lest it stray to his shoulder.

When Gabriel Plum had asked me to marry him, I had laughed. Now I felt I was attending a wake. I wanted to cry, to mourn the passing of Adam's hope. But still, Adam and I were alive, sitting in the dark in a grassland, beside a campfire, an isolated twosome. Reflected flames played orange and rosy on our flesh. He knelt before the fire; I sat on my buttocks, my knees drawn up, my arms hugging my knees. Who knew what might happen next? How much time had really passed? I could feel the thin new layer of flesh stretching between my shoulder blades. Perhaps healing was sped up in Eden. The patch on the back of my head was healing faster than my back.

"How does my back look these days?"

"Better."

"How are you feeling, Adam?"

"Happy."

I hesitated and then asked, "How happy?"

"More content than joyful," he answered promptly. "When God created the animals, he made them in pairs—male and female. When Noah took them into the ark, they marched two by two."

"What do you think of couples of the same sex?" I asked boldly. I wanted to knock him off his biblical pins; I wanted to make him acknowledge the contemporary world. In the pause before his reply, I listened to locusts and tree frogs. They could have been in Memphis, Tennessee.

"That's all right with me," he answered. "I can understand that."

He spoke in a steady—no, studied—voice, and I wondered about his past, the past of his hauntingly beautiful body. Surely both men and women would have been drawn to him, would have wanted him, or wanted to be him.

"Adam, I can picture the animals going into a wooden boat, but I need to tell you, I don't believe that story. Not in any literal way."

He said nothing.

A streak appeared in the dark sky, and I exclaimed, "Look! A shooting star."

"No," he said. "That's a fighter jet going down."

I felt foolish, felt the blush of embarrassment at my sentimental error, but knew that even though he glanced at me sharply, the fire glow would mask my blush. If he was the child capable of naive belief, I was the child who had to be right.

To console myself, I imagined the two halves of his brain like two gray elephants side by side—one a creature of ancient mythology, the other a practical, sure-footed beast wise in the ways of the world he inhabited.

"I've set the table," he added. "Did you notice?"

I looked at one large, flat stone, almost covered by a single strongly ribbed leaf and two small stones draped with plate-sized leaves.

"This one is the cook table," he said. "I'll crack off the clay, then you can pass me your leaf, and I'll serve you."

He proceeded to carry out the acts he had previewed.

"Tomorrow I'll look for some wild vegetables," he said cheerfully.

"When I was walking in, I didn't see any vegetables."

"'Seek and ye shall find,'" he quoted.

"If I were you, I'd look in that area where there's a cultivated rose garden. Probably some farmer, before he deserted this place, planted a vegetable garden. In straight rows, with stakes for the tomatoes."

"This is a strange place," Adam said.

"It's a place on earth like any other place," I asserted. I picked up a shred of the white meat of the fish. Never had I tasted anything so fine. Better than ambrosia, I thought.

"Like any other," he repeated. "Is it?" When I did not reply—I was as busy as a monkey using both hands to pick up morsels of food, sliding delicate meat from needlelike bones—he added, "It's good to be able to take care of somebody."

"I'm not that sort of woman," I said. "I don't want a man to take care of me. I take care of myself."

In the weeks that followed, delusion and daze haunted my mind. I seemed always to be awakening, and always to be wondering if what I remembered was a dream or reality. Wonder seemed the best state of mind. It was less irritating than certainty, less taxing than the process of deciding—anything.

I knew I was growing stronger.

The morning after the first fish, I awoke to see a broken basket filled with squash—long striped green zucchini squash and yellow bulbous goose-necked squash. Vegetables. They were decorated with a gorgeous star-shaped golden yellow squash blossom of bodacious size and two not-quite-open red roses, big as fists.

"You were right," he said. "Near the rose garden, there was a rectangle of vegetable garden. And an abandoned basket."

He was sitting beside the basket but a short distance away, in the attitude I had assumed the night before—on his buttocks, his knees cocked and his hands clasped around his knees. I could not remember when I had left that posture. I had sat sideways, with my legs crossed to eat, but then—I must have slumped over. He must have carried me to my bed.

"We need something like a skillet," I said. "So we can sauté things." The squash bodies looked clean and healthy.

"I could take a piece of metal from the plane," he said.

I thought of the painted fabric wings, the struts over which the cloth was stretched.

"The fuselage was metal," I said as much to myself as to him.

"Yes. I could wrench out a flat piece, batter up its edges for a skillet."

"'Batter my heart, three-person'd God,'" I quoted.

"John Donne," he answered, and murmured in an echo, "'Batter my heart.' That poem used to puzzle me when I was a freshman in college. Now I understand. John Donne meant he was willing to learn from God, even if he had to suffer to learn."

He stood up—a gesture that usually meant conversation was over, and he was off on some errand.

"I never understood the concept of the Trinity," I said petulantly. "'Three-person'd God'? What sense does that make? If there's a guy on the cross and another one up in the sky, and the first one's talking to the second one, that's two gods. And then the bird—that's a third."

Adam just stared at me.

"Christians don't really believe in one God," I went on. "The Muslims do, but the Christians don't. The Muslims say 'There is no God but God,' and they say Muhammad is his prophet—only his prophet." I stopped, then added, "Not his only prophet."

"The Holy Trinity is like an egg," Adam answered, but I saw he was shocked and amused at my tirade. "An egg has three parts—the yolk, the white, and the shell—but it's just one egg."

"God is not a chicken egg," I snorted with laughter.

"But He resembles a chicken egg," Adam calmly suggested.

I felt I was watching him make what he considered to be a daring move on the chessboard of the conversation. "Not literally," he added.

"Not literally!" I exploded. "I can't believe you're saying 'not literally.' Who do you think you are? Adam!—that's who you think you are! Adam! And you think I'm Eve."

"I'm going," he said. "I've got to go now."

"You don't want to face the truth," I said.

"The truth?" Now he was amused. "*Your* truth."

"Then why do you have to go right now, at a crucial point in our discussion?" I suddenly hated myself for sounding as bossy and rude as a preteen girl. He was corrupting me. He was robbing me of my maturity. Over and over, he was making me feel like a kid. A spoiled-rotten kid.

"I want to take some of the fire to the overhang now and keep it there," he explained. "Like putting money in the bank."

"If it rains? If the wind blows it out?" I asked. "Why not just start another fire?"

"I . . . I . . . I . . ." Now he was stammering for real. Suddenly confessional. "I destroyed the mirror. I drowned it in the ocean last night." He bent, picked up a stick of fire, and began to walk away.

"Where did you go to college?" I yelled.

"Boise State," he answered.

"For how long?" Something just told me to ask that question, to get the dates, the facts.

"I dropped out after my freshman year." He was walking so fast, his gait seemed more like a running walk, and then he broke into a slow run—leaving me—and then a sprint.

"It figures," I muttered to myself. He was too erratic for rational inquiry. *Eccentric*—that was the word I wanted to describe him. *Off-center.*

*Peevish*—that was the word I next applied, to myself.

"What wood burns best?" I asked him when he returned.

I was glad to see him returning—no doubt about that, I admitted to myself. The way he walked, the way he moved across the grass, made me think of some animal, perhaps an antelope, but something more sturdy—an eland perhaps, with an amazing confidence of straight long horns, swept backward like antennae.

"Pine," he answered, "to get a fire started. In Idaho it would be ponderosa pine. Because it's full of sap. Then hardwood—oak, or maybe maple or elm."

"Are they all here?"

"Everything's here," he answered. "That ever was or ever is to be. 'God in three persons'"—he suddenly sang the dying-fall chant of the doxology in a deep and resonant voice as though he could fill a cathedral. "'God in three persons, Blessed Trinity.'"

I was speechless. Yes, I told myself and swallowed, he's obsessive. But I looked at him then with the most friendly and normal of expressions.

"Everything's here and *more*," he went on in a quiet voice, matter-of-fact, explanatory.

"But, Adam," I said, "how can you say everything *and more*? Everything is *everything*. You can't have *more* than everything. You don't use language right."

"Words disappear in the air," he explained. "Words are volatile. That's their essence. Who can say how they bubble up, how they break free and disappear?"

I started to counter, *Not if you write them down. Not if you put them on a disk and project them on the ceiling. Not if they're full of love. And meaning.* But my words seemed less true than his.

"Scientists say," I said carefully, "that nothing escapes from a black hole. Not even information. Not light. But I never understood how they could speak of *information* in that context."

When he said nothing but continued to present his friendly, handsome face, I asked him if he thought God could be a black hole.

He answered with his body. He suddenly lay down, his back on the grass, his legs spread, his arms spread wide open and then lifted openly toward the sky. "'Maker of Heaven and Earth,'" he quoted again from Christian creed. His penis lolled to one side. He had forgotten his penis, his nakedness, again.

Just a little, I envied him. I looked away. I lifted my eyes to the clouds. *They* were ethereal enough for me. For a while Einstein had believed in the ether, and then he had recanted and called the "cosmological constant" the biggest blunder of his life, Thom had explained to me, but then hadn't Einstein recanted again? To Thom's great interest, a woman in Kentucky had theorized that the WIMP—weakly interactive massive particle—constituted dark matter.

Adam's lifted arms were rounded, curved like the sides of an egg. He wanted to embrace the elliptical planetary orbits, no, the universe beyond the clouds. The open space between his hands—that opening was to let it all in. He wanted to cradle the universe.

He was crazy, but he was happy. That was not true of most of the mental patients I had known. Their delusions were like demons. They were tortured. They lived in an agony of paranoia and pain, guilt and disappointment, the elusiveness of identity, the impossibility of certitude, fear of whatever was next. I supposed Adam might be termed "a wise fool for God." Somewhere I'd heard such a phrase. But Adam did not seem wise in his innocence or foolish in his practicality.

"Why are you so happy?" I asked him.

He turned his face to look at me, pressed his cheek into the grass to feel the flank of earth. "Because you're here."

I felt my own head droop with sadness.

Finally I answered, lifting my head. "I don't know what to say to you."

"There's no need," he answered gently.

His truthfulness seemed to bathe me. His words were a trinity of raindrops catching sunlight: *Because you're here.* Had anyone ever wanted to hear more? Or less.

*Here.* You're here. *You're* here. I'm happy to be here *because you're here.*

"But there's something I need to say to you," he went on. "I want you to feel safe." He sat up in the grass, his body as patient as a lion's. "You never have any need to fear me." He looked down at his clasped hands, their idle nakedness, and then back to me as though suddenly through a veil. "I'm a little off. You know that. I know that, too. But I have never been violent. I will never force myself upon you in any way."

Part of me protested: *Don't say that. That should never even have to be said between a man and a woman. You offend me by saying that. You live in a bad myth, the bad old myth between men and women—that I am weak and you are strong.* But I said nothing. Instead I tried to make myself forgive him for his presumption, for cloaking his eyes behind a veil of confusion.

"We live in a world where women can arm themselves," I answered, in spite of myself. But to myself I acknowledged, *I am weak, I can barely walk. And he is strange. An Adonis. And he could rape me.*

"Not here," he said. "No guns in Eden."

He sat up straighter, cross-legged, his genitals resting in the grass, the rounded end of his penis touching the bent blades of grass. He reached out one arm to me. "I will never force you. But I will want to marry you till the day I die."

The words rang through my body. It was a promise that I knew I would never forget. For a moment not only his words but the entire scene evanesced.

Only a blank of future hung in front of me. I curled my bare toes downward and made them dive rootlike toward the soil. I would ground myself in the solid reality under my feet, not in some clutching after him.

In my stubbornness, I whispered, "What is my name?"

He didn't hesitate. Undaunted in his confidence, sitting under his blue-black hair, on the grass, sunshine like a cape on his shoulders, he smiled and simply said, "*You*. I mean you."

# PIERRE SAAD

WHILE PIERRE SAAD waited, days, weeks, months, he often imagined that he would look out through the window of his library and see her—Lucy—crossing the stony yard on foot, carrying the black French horn case. As she walked toward him, her body would be bowed sideways, but her arm straight as a plumb line with the awkward case as the weight. Perhaps one or two local people would be with her, escorting her. According to the flight plan, she would have parked the plane at the little runway not too far away, and the locals would have offered to show her the way.

Other times he imagined that Lucy Bergmann would fly over his house while he sat at his library table, at his reading table. At the sound of an unmistakable engine, his ears would prick up. His plane had found its way home; she was bringing the codex. *Bonne chance*, the course passed over his house as she piloted her way to the little airport. He would run to the large glass window, throw up the sash, and lean his whole body out just in time to see her dip the wings, an aeronautical hand wave.

She wouldn't know whether he saw the greeting or not, but she would make the gesture anyway.

Once when he was a desolate child, he had waved at the moon. He had thought that even if her face was blank, he would wave. By day, he used to watch the passengers on cruise boats steaming in opposite directions on the Nile. When two boats passed, the tourists on each boat waved at the waving people behind a railing much like the one behind which they themselves stood. They would have no time, going in opposite directions, to fasten their attention on individual faces. Their flurry of hands was an acknowledgment in general. *We're here; you're there.* There was a certain touching human recognition in their mutual gestures. *No time to stop. No, of course not. Not even expected. We'll never see each other again. Good-bye.* But still that passing moment—Hello!—hands agitating the air, was worthwhile. He had thought so, when he stood as a boy, dressed in white, on the bank of the Nile, and watched the boats passing one another, going in opposite directions.

Yes, he imagined Lucy would dip her wings as she flew over. She wouldn't even be sure where he lived, but maybe some intuition would prompt her to wave, to acknowledge his possible presence.

Many days passed while he read at his worn table and listened for the sound of the Piper Cub's engine, more recognizable than his own thumbprint. Weeks passed, and Lucy had not walked across the yard with the precious French horn case. What *had* appeared, quite unexpectedly, while he sat opening his mail at his reading station, was a letter from the president of France.

Before he opened the important seal, for just a moment, Pierre abstracted the envelope into only its whiteness and then morphed it into a feather dropped from the tail of the Holy Spirit, who, Christians claimed, had appeared in the form of a dove.

So, what message had arrived from on high?

The president broached the idea that there should be a new unified ministry of prehistoric cave art and wondered if he, Pierre Saad, might consent to be its director, were such a ministry to be established. The president wrote that new technology, a device created to look under the surface of distant planets to see if inhabitants had fled underground, had been trained on the Dordogne Valley, the entire Aquitaine in fact, and the device meant to explore the nature of outer space had revealed many as yet undiscovered caves in the interior of the French earth. The caves gave evidence of having been visited by humans. The bones of animals, even of the extinct gigantic elk, megalasaurus, and huge cave bears, had been detected, and these bones had been cracked open and the marrow extracted as prehistoric humans had done.

For a moment Pierre paused in his reading of the president's letter to try to imagine the kind of device that could detect bones deep in the passages under the earth, identify their species, and note their condition. He thought of Madame Curie and her colleagues, and their surprise that the new X-rays could see through skin and flesh to find the human skeleton.

No doubt many of the caves, showing evidence of having been visited in just the same ways that Font-de-Gaume, Pech Merle, Lascaux, Chauvet, and dozens of others had been visited, once hosted Neolithic humans. People had cooked meat to sustain them while they engraved the images of animals, or outlined their shapes on the rock, or suggestively painted their three-dimensionality in polychrome pigments onto ceilings and walls. Perhaps those caves that had been detected under the skin of France from outer space even predated Chauvet, with its polychrome animals more than thirty-five thousand years old.

Pierre Saad knew that the speculations of the president's advisers were correct. His own house sat on top of such a cave. Intending only to establish a wine cellar like a good Frenchman, Pierre had accidentally broken into a deeper chamber. It was not that unusual. Rouffignac had also been discovered through a resident's excavation of his own basement. That man had wanted to lower the floor so the basement could be better used for storage. Pierre's eyes moved from the crisp, official paper—where did they buy such paper, unique in its importance?—to the expensive rug on his library floor.

Pierre wondered if the space eye had looked through his house as easily as it looked beyond the earth's surface and if it had already mapped and numbered the corridors and rooms below him at that moment. Apparently the space eye could register geological aberrations and objects but not drawings; it could not detect the spectacular array of paintings he knew he harbored, though the eye would know of the scant animal bones scattered here and there. What the president wanted to know was *whether* there was art, galleries and galleries of it, in the numerous passages seen from outer space.

Pierre winced when he encountered the word *galleries*. Cave art had not been transported to galleries for sterile display. It had been created underground. The contours of the rocks sometimes dictated the type of animal or the posture of the animal who emerged from it.

"Knowing of your interest in these sacred texts . . ." the president had written.

Pierre Saad's eyes lingered on the phrase "sacred texts." Yes, that was what they were—all of the cave paintings. Even the hordes of tourists who had crowded into Lascaux II, the mere replica, to the extent that they had had to create Lascaux III and then Lascaux IV, replicas of replicas, knew that somehow they must get in vague touch with their origins as humans. In the beginning, what *were* people? When people had evolved to the point of knowing themselves as people, how did they think and feel? How did they treat one another? What knowledge did they seek when they turned to making art? What yearning sought satisfaction when they mixed their colors? How had the president known the exact phrase—the recognition that cave paintings were a sacred text—that might seduce Pierre Saad away from scholarship and into administration? The cave paintings were as sacred a text as the Dead Sea Scrolls, or the Nag Hammadi gospels, the Genesis codex of 2020, or the Bible.

In the next paragraph the language betrayed the crassness of what had actually been of official importance. The president wrote that the south of France could become a greater draw for tourists than the pyramids of Egypt. The cave paintings were older. Much older. With global warming, Egypt was fast becoming an oven blasted with sandstorms; underground, under the ground of France, the caves were at a constant temperature cold enough to require a jacket. It had always been that way; it would always be that way. Oh yes, the art in each cave was unique and compelling. If the new caves detected from space also held significant art, the length of time spent by the average tourist in the Dordogne Valley would increase from one or two days to a week. Hotels, restaurants, interpretive centers, transportation . . .

While the state would bear no expense for the natural air-conditioning characteristic of caves worldwide, of course it would be necessary to control humidity, bacteria, molds. . . .

Perhaps the tourists would need to rent something like space suits, which would increase their sense of adventure. Their defiling exhalations would be piped back into their high-tech outfits and used to inflate and insulate their suits. Earth tones—umber, red, the black of magnesium dioxide found in the palettes of the cave painters. Perhaps the cave clothes would display replicas of the face of a lion, or the profile of a mammoth, the palmate antlers of the megalasaurus. In some instances, people could wear outfits that glittered like cut crystal if there were more caves like Cognac, naturally filled with crystalline stalagmites and stalactites.

Pierre Saad shook his head in disgust. Was it just that easy to betray the quiet spirituality with hoopla? A mere hop, skip, and jump of the greedy imagination.

Yes, Pierre Saad might consent to becoming the national director of parietal art. He would protect cave art from his own imagination and the imaginations of those even more corruptible than himself. Imagination—Einstein had thought it the most valuable of mental powers for the scientist. Imagination and curiosity. But the purity of scientists was becoming as obsolete as honor in the age of chivalry.

Pierre spent hours drafting his reply with the conditions attendant on his acceptance. At the fringes of his thought, disaster rippled: no codex. He assumed Lucy Bergmann was all right. She had grown up flying such a plane. How had she gone astray? Had she betrayed him?

No. Pierre was never wrong about the people he trusted. He had survived as an orphan boy in Cairo because he could tell intuitively whom to trust; he could also tell when his own best interests required of himself a certain chameleon quality. He knew he could not trust the president—Pierre's own invitation to the appointment as national director was in part a political ploy. The president wanted to signal the Muslim population that some of them could partake in the government, some of them were respected for their learning and integrity, some, such as the Franco-Egyptian Pierre Saad, had entirely assimilated and could be trusted with the irreplaceable past of the French.

In his own past, Pierre had not been able to receive permission to visit the Chauvet cave. He had resented his exclusion from Chauvet, as though he, as an Arab, had secret folds about his person that would allow him to smuggle in the most virulent of microbes, devourers of magnesium dioxide. A visit from him and—who knew?—the black outline drawings of animals might disappear. He wrote the president that before making a firm commitment, of course he (accompanied by colleagues of his choice and his daughter, the artist Arielle Saad) needed a tour of all the caves already known to house prehistoric art, including Chauvet.

He reassured himself that Lucy Bergmann and the Genesis codex would appear in due time. Was he using the American widow as an unpaid and unwitting courier to transport materials for which she might be waylaid and robbed? Of course he was. But no one else had been available. He congratulated himself on being honest with himself. Self-knowledge was another tool in his survivor's kit.

He reflected briefly on his conversation with Mrs. Bergmann while they sat at the table in Nag Hammadi. He had propped an old-fashioned armpit crutch near at hand. Not knowing the moment of her coming, he still wore a support boot, to continue his ruse.

"Must you trick her?" Arielle had asked her father. Pierre had replied that if he appeared to be vulnerable, impaired in fact, she would be more likely to help him. "I am an Arab," he had said. "She fears and mistrusts me automatically. She is middle-aged, a widow, and to some extent she fears all men. There is a certain freedom in widowhood, which she fears to lose."

"She's drenched with grief," his daughter pronounced.

"Yes, that too." He shrugged. "I *do* have sympathy for her," he had insisted.

As he sat in his library, drafting a letter to the president of France, those words he had insisted on as truth hovered in the air around him. He remembered Lucy's pale face, hanging like the disk of the full moon above the podium. Her face had seemed to fracture into a network of fine lines as she looked at the scientists, minus her esteemed husband. While he had been touched by her grief, he also calculated it to be an index to her capacity for devotion.

When she virtually ran from the symposium, he *had* followed her, out of sympathy. After he had seen her disappear behind the closing doors of the elevator, he *had* hurried down the stairwell, intending to speak to her again. But he had not slipped on the steps. He had not broken his leg. Instead, he had changed his mind about comforting her.

As he had watched her go out the door of the building into the light, the way she pushed open the door—her power and determination to leave the scene behind, her anger—caused him to hesitate. She was not crushed by grief, he had decided. She needed no sympathy from him. The event at the symposium was going to be a turning point for her. She was about to resume her life. She would not drown in a lake of tears; she had reached the bottom and was now swimming for the surface.

Only later, in a conversation with Gabriel Plum, had he learned that she had indeed gone off with a tour group. And still later, that Plum had been notified she had left the group—her old friend had laughed about it, bragged about her independence, though no one knew where she might have gone. Pierre had been appalled; Plum had no idea of the possible dangers. When Pierre had mentioned that a lone woman, an unveiled Westerner, had no business visiting desert towns alone, Gabriel had said Lucy lived in New York City, where there were certainly more murders and rapes per capita than in Upper Egypt.

Then Pierre remembered that she had mentioned the name of a place: Nag Hammadi. But he did not enunciate that phrase for Gabriel.

Instead Pierre had asked in a soft voice if Mrs. Bergmann were religious.

"A blank, frank, militant atheist," Gabriel had replied with a rather pleased grin.

"Really?" Pierre had asked. He would have labeled her as one of those secular Americans who dwelt in some sort of perpetual quest for spirituality.

"Her parents are Christian missionaries. She's still in some sort of eighteen-year-old rebellion."

"And you?" Pierre had presumed to ask in his least intrusive tone.

"Church of England. I'm a Brit, you know."

"Wonder where her parents do their work? Africa?"

"Japan. They went off and left her with her old grandmother when she was a child. She's never forgiven them."

"I don't think she's safe traveling alone in Egypt," Pierre said.

"I'll go fetch her when the symposium is over."

Foolish man, Pierre thought.

At that moment, Lucy's usefulness had occurred to Pierre. Even before the symposium officially ended, Pierre had left for Nag Hammadi and contacted his daughter to meet him there.

As his conversation with the British scientist evaporated from his thoughts, Pierre's hand strayed to a blank page on his desk. While he had only seen photographs of the parietal art at Chauvet, he had memorized every curving line drawn on the cave wall. The angle from which the photographs were taken made the curves balloon or shrink; it was difficult to tell which shape had been most intended by the artist. From his memory of a photograph, Pierre began to draw the heads of two rhinoceroses. Their keratinous horns almost interlocked, and they were often interpreted as engaging in a confrontation. But were they? he wondered. Interpretations of any depiction of two animals constituting a single painting often varied diametrically. Some saw the animals as fighting or preparing for conflict; others saw them simply as meeting, perhaps trying to make connection.

The cave drawings often came to him as emblems of his own inner states. They were like dream images, suggestive of inaccessible feelings and ideas. Did he have two conflicting attitudes toward Lucy Bergmann—was his sympathy in conflict with his predatory impulses? Or was he simply acknowledging his own willingness to use her? He had thought in terms of animal imagery since he was a very young child—not of course the cave drawings. Parietal art had come into his life as a college student in France. As a child in Egypt he had found strange kinship in the images of gods that combined human bodies with the heads of animals. *Amun* with his ram's head; *Bastet* the cat, *Horus* the beaked falcon, *Hathor* the cow . . .

In Nag Hammadi, while he masqueraded as a man with a broken leg, Lucy had brought out the politeness in him. For a few moments, in her presence, he had become the person she thought him to be. He remembered himself as having truly felt what she seemed to assume he felt.

In Cairo, standing behind the podium, when she lifted her bowed head and showed her full round face to the group, she had impressed him as moonstruck. He had imagined her former life, how she might have been sitting safely at her breakfast table in New York, with many buildings far below. A few misty skyscrapers rose toward her like stalagmites thrusting up from the floor of a cave. She was reading the *Times*, with bowed head. When her husband came into the kitchen and she lifted her face, how had he regarded that full quiet face? Back then there would have been nothing melancholy in her mien. The scene he imagined must have happened in Iowa City, before Thom Bergmann's death. In New York, when Lucy resided among the mist and clouds, no one would have interrupted her reading of the newspaper.

What had been her life before her loss? Pierre had liked the sound of Thom Bergmann's voice the few times they had talked on the telephone. His voice, the way he moved from word to word, had a certain thick-edged carefulness to it. Pierre had pictured him to be large in general, quite tall, and when he studied a photo on the memorial cover of Thom Bergmann standing next to Gabriel Plum, whose height he knew, Pierre saw he had guessed correctly. Bergmann had a large head, with a fleshy nose and lips, lots of salt-and-pepper curly gray hair. He was not a person who would have left his wife in a scruffy desert town while he hobnobbed with his colleagues. Pierre had always liked that English phrase—salt-and-pepper—when applied to hair. *Hobnobbed,* another idiom to embellish his English. *Hoopla:* he had liked that expression, too.

What had surprised Pierre was how much older Thom was than his wife.

At his desk beside the rhinoceroses of Chauvet, Pierre sketched a shaggy mammoth from Rouffignac; everyone, including himself, particularly liked the depictions of animals now extinct. The mammoths had died out ten thousand years ago. As he doodled, he wondered if Lucy had been grief-stricken for the entire three years since her husband was crushed by the falling piano. He thought most people could not sustain a sense of loss for such a long period. She moved like a somnambulist; she was a woman in love with a ghost.

Pierre felt his lips curl toward a self-aware, ironic smile. For how long had he sustained his own sense of loss? Of losses too bitter to swallow.

—

Pierre Saad's most vivid early memory was of the graffiti on the outer wall of a Coptic church near Cairo. Even his childish eyes could see that the slashes of Magic Marker covered other images. In later years, he would acquire the term *palimpsest*. Beneath the electric blue lines he saw other, older drawings and traces of color. He could detect the flat image of the Virgin Mary. Flakes of her mild blue robe still clung to the wall, but where the gentle blue was worn away—was that the image of a falcon's head? As he huddled against the wall waiting for his mother to come for him, it had frightened him (he was only six years old) that one image could be placed right on top of another. He knew the Coptic Christians had taken over and defaced many of the abandoned temples of the old gods.

For a moment his six-year-old hand had explored the hard, shaping cartilage just below the surface of his skin and wondered if his own head and neck were a hood for some sharp-beaked falcon. The falcon's profile incised on the Cairo wall had been painted over by a heart. Anxious and weary of waiting for his mother, he had lifted his gaze, hoping to see some real bird perched at the top of the wall, a bird who could fly and be a bird out there where birds were supposed to be, not imprisoned and immobilized in the flat of a wall.

What he saw again higher on the wall were more pictures, carvings that resembled the falcon masked by Mary's breast. In one place the entire stone wall had been chipped away. Whatever face or head had been there originally had not been painted over but entirely removed. Nothing was left but a patch of rough stone. He thought of it as a small battle zone. Beyond that height nothing had been mutilated or painted over. High up were the messengers from the pure past. Those sharply incised pictures, he was sure, had been chiseled there in the time of the pharaohs.

Up there was a cow with the moon in her horns—Hathor, the goddess of beauty, worshipped in the days of the pharaohs, before Jesus, before Moses, before Abraham. He had seen her illumined at first dawn, having waited hours in the darkness for his mother's return.

It had been near midnight when she had left him at the wall. As they hurried through the crooked streets, she had leaned down and explained into his ear that home was no longer safe for them, that she had been forewarned.

Her voice and her breath, explaining and warm so near his cheek, had been a comfort to him. He was an obedient child: often she asked him to do this or that, then later explained why. Always there was an explanation that was reasonable. It had trained him to trust her. When she awakened him, before their hurried passage through the streets, he heard the Christian church bell tolling midnight. Though it was a sound that signaled the outside world was now dark and cold, she had not stopped to pick up his jacket draped on a three-legged stool. Her urgency surprised him—even he knew what midnight meant about outside temperatures.

Positioning him in a dark shadow against the wall, she had taken off her scarf and tied it over his head and under his chin. "Remember," she had whispered, "do you remember that most of the heat of the body escapes through the top of the head? Keep your head warm."

Also whispering, he had answered that he remembered.

She had taught him many things about the body that other boys seemed not to know, and about the world as well.

He was six years old, but she had spoken to him of governments, and that his father was French, and that the French were not all bad, despite their domination of Egypt once upon a time. "No worse than the British," she had instructed. "No worse than our dictator now." Once his father had loved her well, though his love had not lasted. "There have been benevolent kings and queens," she had taught. "What counts is not so much the form of government but the generosity and care with which it is administered."

Before she left him against the wall—if there had been some heat in it at first, that warmth had entirely dissipated well before dawn—she had kissed him on both cheeks in what he recognized as the manner of the French. As she held his face between her hands, his mother's instruction had taken a new turn: "Think of the kindest person you know. Think about him or her while I'm gone. Then think of the most powerful person you know who is also kind. Call that image to your mind. You may think of the richest person you know, but remember richness and power do not always lie in money but in knowledge of one's own self, in one's determination and resilience. Remember: kindness, power, riches." And she was gone.

He listened and memorized, not so much her words as the gritty sound the soles of her sandals made, moving away so quickly over the sandy street.

Because the night chill was in the air, he had drawn his knees to his chest as he sat huddled against the wall and hugged his knees with his arms to keep in his warmth. After many dark hours, he watched the rays of the rising sun brighten the smooth sandstone surface of the top of the wall. Sunlight illumined the horns of Hathor the cow and the disk of the moon she held between her horns. Next, sunlight washed over her wide-spaced eyes, receptive and open. *Beauty*—his mother had not charged him to remember beauty, but he had thought of his mother and her beauty, how slender she was and how gracefully she moved.

Then he thought of cows as simple animals, their funny four-leggedness, of the fascination of their out-jutting hip bones. Of course, he had seen many cows led by ropes as they ambled through the streets of his village. He had always loved the luminous eyes of cows, their gentleness.

Who would not want to draw them, and the other animals as well? Who would not want to put on something of the power of the animals? Who would not want to unite the limited human body with their various mysterious powers? In memory, he saw again the upright body of the goddess at the top of the wall, still as a mummy in the morning sunlight. A real cow had passed him, raising her tail as she went to deposit her waste onto the street. The bell at her neck made a soft clanking. The man who led her with a worn rope walked with a staff in his other hand.

Pierre knew him or someone like him. He was a Sufi mystic with distinctive bowed legs, deformed but able. His mother had explained the mystic had not had enough vitamin D as a child. Thinking again of his mother, Pierre had raised his eyes yet again to the ancient image of Hathor, the cow goddess of beauty.

I have worshipped her, he thought. As a grown man sitting in his own library, a man of enough reputation that he received an invitation from the president, a man contemplating his own corruptibility and his harsh past, he knew that he had worshipped beauty embodied throughout the centuries in art. *I have worshipped beauty.*

In memory, at that moment, his mother dashed into the street. The force of a shot caught her and sent her reeling against the wall, which she hit with her shoulder—her lips opened in a silent O—and then she slid down, her eyes closing, onto the road. Not a second passed till Pierre felt the iron grip of the Sufi cowherd around his wrist, pulling him upward and making him walk slowly along, in step with the cow, beside his own bare, bowed legs. Pierre saw that the tip of the man's wooden staff poked itself into the sand, swung forward, entered the sand again as though nothing had happened. Before they turned the corner, Pierre-the-boy had managed to twist his body and look back just once. He saw his mother's unmoving body lying near the wall. Her blood was spattered and smeared red over the bright blue graffiti.

# RECOVERY

I SLEPT WELL. I ate well. I exercised.

I dreamed, but I trained myself to wake up when words from Adam's dreams traveled the discreet distance from the deep shadows under his bed-tree to mine. When I heard the muttered words, I stored them in the granary of memory and promptly went back to sleep. I wanted to help him exorcise his demons. Each morning when daylight worked its way through the woven mat of my makeshift roof, I lay still so that some minute shifting of blood in the vessels threading my brain would not wash away what I had deposited there of his midnight words. Nonetheless, I recovered nothing. When I opened the door to the cupboard of memory, its shelves were bare, with one exception.

I was able to understand and retain the word *sin* as one of his nocturnal utterances.

To know his past, I would have to ask him. However, as I studied Adam striding over the grasslands as though he were the lord of creation, or even when I only considered his handsome, forward-looking face, I knew it would be a sin to drag him back into his past. With every gesture and every cheerful matter-of-fact expression, he was determined to step into the future. He wanted us to inhabit the future.

When Adam called out from his nightmares, terrified, I began to make it my practice to call back, "It's just a dream. It's just a dream." Once—only once—half asleep myself, I had called out, "I'm here!"

He had sat up, half awake. "Are you? Are you here? Eve?"

I had not replied. I breathed as quietly as I could to minimize my presence. After a while, he lay back down.

One morning as we ate nuts and apples together, I asked Adam if he knew that sometimes in the night he called out the word *sin.*

"Do I?" he asked. "Other words, too?"

"Such as?" I smiled encouragingly.

"Names?"

I told him that if he did, I could not decipher them.

"Rosalie?" he asked.

I only shook my head.

"She was my first girlfriend in Idaho. In high school. We fucked."

I was shocked to hear him use the vulgar term.

"I wasn't faithful to her. She wanted to marry." Adam spoke more and more slowly. "I wanted . . . to know many girls."

Though I waited for him to continue, he said nothing. So I asked softly, "And did you?" I watched the vague orbs of light projected through the pinholes among the leaves onto the ground. There was a swarm of the gentle, light disks, visitors from the sun at last arriving onto the earth.

"I had . . . had a lot of girlfriends. I was thought handsome, you know. Unusual."

He pulled gently at a few tufts of grass.

Finally I said, "Many young men do, don't they? Young women, too."

"So many. I remember some of their names. Probably I might say them in my sleep, sometimes."

The silence lasted a long time till I looked at him and smiled a little. "And you still feel guilty."

He flushed.

"One girl's father complained to my father, and he took me to the barn and beat me. For punishment. He used to punish me, too, if he found my drawings. Crotches, breasts, sometimes myself, erect."

After he felt the touch of my hand on his, he looked up at me.

"Adam," I said, "most artists, painters, and poets are inspired by the erotic."

"He beat my hands."

I lifted his hand to my lips and quietly kissed his knuckles.

My favorite food became the fish he caught and cooked for me. *Wild-caught,* I told myself smugly, thinking that these fish of various varieties possessed the best of fatty omega oils, good for the mind and good for the body. Now that we had the skillet he had wrenched and shaped from the steel of the Cub's fuselage, the fish could be sautéed with the tomatoes, and I again congratulated myself on the healthfulness of our diet, knowing that cooking the tomatoes released the nutrients not nearly so available in the raw vegetables.

While the skillet was our most prized possession, I also appreciated the metal skewers Adam fashioned from the cross struts of the wings. To keep the end of the rod from burning his hands as he roasted the fish, he had jammed one end into a short, rotten limb for a handle. Though I had been tempted to taunt him with the idea of rottenness in Eden, I restrained myself.

Instead, I explained that we should let the peppers growing near the straight rows of staked tomatoes ripen to redness because then they would become more nutritious, replete with vitamins. I enjoyed the yellow and green squash as well, but somehow the squash vegetable itself never lived up to the robust promise of the squash blossom. In my mouth, squash melted away, seedy but mostly water. I supposed seeds were worth something and chewed them vigorously.

In the rectangular garden plot, there were only those three vegetables—tomatoes, peppers, and squash—but when I took long walks alone I kept an eye out for wild lettuce, dandelion greens, and watercress. Once I found a stand of morel mushrooms and remembered how Thom and I had hunted them in the woods south of Iowa City, on a farm gone back to woods called the old Bourjailly place.

Back then, Thom and I had conditioned our eyes to recognize the sponge-like texture of the morels by staring first for long minutes at corncobs, which had a similar reticulated surface. Fried in butter, the morels had been heaven to eat, we had agreed. Thom had looked up through his thick glasses, smacked his lips, and simply said, "Heaven." When I slowly savored the butter-drenched spongy texture of the morel, I had pronounced, "Paradise."

In our garden, when Adam and I cooked the morels in tomato juice in our battered and blackened skillet, I wished for butter. Without it the morels' flavor lacked the sinful richness I had relished so much. *Sinful richness*—when I once characterized our sex life that way, Thom had laughed and fed me from a collection of Godiva dark chocolates kept at our bedside. To Adam's delight, I sautéed our morels in a reduction of coconut milk, and that did add some richness to the flavor.

One day, when Adam and I had just sat down in the grass, a silver jet roared over the plain, not much higher above our heads than the top of a tall skyscraper would have been. The plane slightly rotated its torso as it ripped across the sky, and Adam began to count, "One thousand and one, one thousand and two," and on up. The grazing wildebeests off to our left jerked their heads up and ran a short distance.

My mouth fell open and stayed open till a fly buzzed close by. Of course I knew the jets were up there, but far above, very far away, thirty or more vertical miles into the stratosphere. It was the large, close-up view, the terrifying speed and sound, that had seemed unreal. When Adam reached one thousand and ten, we heard a soft and mushy thud.

"Impact," he said. "There are low hills that mark the boundary. About ten miles away."

"How do you know?"

"Sound travels about a mile a second."

I felt shaken, as though the reverberation that entered my ear had set off a quake within. "What boundary?"

He lowered his eyes and smiled a slight secret smile. "Eden's." He did not look at me.

"And did you meet the cherubim with the twisting fiery sword when you came in?"

"Yes." He bit his lower lip and looked ashamed.

One day a Jersey cow, lowing pitifully, wandered out of a group of zebra and walked purposefully toward us as we were eating. Butter, I thought.

"The milk wagon," Adam said. "Look at her udder."

Though I was not at all a farm girl, even I had noticed the fullness of the cow's udder hanging so low that it barely cleared the ground. When the cow stopped close to us, I saw her teats were leaking milk.

"She's in pain," Adam explained. "Lie down close to her and I'll squirt milk into your mouth."

"Really?" I asked. "Can you really do that? What if she steps on me?"

"I won't let her," he said. "I'm a farm boy—didn't you guess? Besides, you won't be that close, not underfoot."

Lowing more insistently, the cow fixed her eye on Adam. He petted her neck and then stroked her flank. When his fingertips smoothed her udder, the cow shivered all over.

"Now lie down," Adam said quietly to me, pointing to a place some five feet away from the cow's four hooves. "And turn your face this way. Not too much, or the milk will just run out. Open up."

I obeyed. When a zing of milk tickled the roof of my mouth, I laughed out loud and choked.

"Don't scare her," Adam cautioned. "We'll have to practice till you get the knack. Didn't you ever see anybody shoot milk into a barn cat's mouth?"

But I couldn't answer. I was choking and drooling and smacking the warm milk. Trying to be ready, I watched the milk rhythmically spurt across the short distance toward my face. I marveled at how thin and laserlike came the squirt of milk. Somehow I had expected it to pour obediently in a thick rivulet as from the spout of a pitcher or from the opening in a carton. I had expected to lie underneath to catch a thick stream twisting slightly, as though it were falling into a wide-mouthed glass. But no. To trap even a little of the milk in my mouth, I smacked my lips and tried to use my tongue to lap the liquid backward into my throat.

"You could practice snapping flies," he teased.

Occasionally, Adam squirted me in the eye, and I suspected that he did it on purpose.

Soon my face was bathed in milk, and my neck was sticky with it. I tried cupping my hand beside my mouth to catch the drippings, but the method didn't work well.

"I hate to waste it," I sputtered. "Can't you slow down?"

Adam laughed. "You don't have any idea how many gallons of milk she has. Now watch this."

He changed his hand position and suddenly the milk squirted upward into his own mouth. He drank and drank and didn't spill a drop. Finally he paused, then expertly squirted the milk just once more toward his face—up one nostril.

I shrieked, and he laughed, too.

"I guess I've had enough," he said, grinning, and he again took aim at me. The cow was the model of patience through all his antics.

My ineptitude embarrassed me, but I had not gotten enough milk down my gullet to want to quit. I suggested a solution. Adam could just milk into the skillet, and I could drink from that.

"Sure."

He was perfectly good-natured about it all, and I rolled over playfully, sat up, and fetched the skillet. The burn on my back was so well healed that I hadn't thought twice about rolling over. When the shallow pan was full, and he passed it with a steady hand to me, the cow looked around reproachfully that her relief had ceased. Adam stroked the veined udder and quietly reassured. "Whoa, Bossy, whoa, girl. It's not over."

We made no attempt to tie her up, and after a few days she wandered away. To create a tether, we would have needed to gather grasses and braid a rope. When Adam offered to hollow out a log and make me a churn for butter, I said just the milk was sufficient.

The next week, when a domesticated she-goat wandered by, we enjoyed her milk and let her go, too. So much did we trust our habitat to provide whatever we needed that we made little effort to store up resources for the future.

For exercise, I walked and walked. When I gently reiterated that I preferred to walk alone, Adam willingly complied, respectful of my wish. We woke up together in the morning; we met and ate together in mid-afternoon; before bedtime, we enjoyed a snack of sweet fruit. While we chatted cheerfully over our meals, I decided it might be wise not to spend entire days together. On all my walks I hoped to discover the French horn case with the codex that I had jettisoned, and I earnestly asked Adam to look for the case, too.

I liked to walk at a respectful distance around the various grazing animals as they pastured on the plain. Once I saw our fawn-colored cow at a distance. Once I spotted a lone donkey trotting along right through a herd of Thompson's gazelles as though he were going home.

Sometimes I saw a pride of lionesses sitting chin-deep in the tall grasses, watching the wildebeest. I never saw them take an animal. Perhaps they can't, I fantasized, not in the Peaceable Kingdom. Perhaps they've been forbidden. Maybe they had been hypnotized, or perhaps in this strange place they'd not yet come fully into their own nature as predators. I didn't mention the lionesses to Adam.

During this time, I had little sense of time passing. I did not know if it were stretched or compressed. This was Eden. My grandmother had suggested that perhaps a day during God's creating of heaven and earth equaled millions of our years. My days of strolling and recovering seemed timeless.

While I walked, I often admired the flowers, whom I regarded as friends. Colorful as a circus, a crop of jolly zinnias gazed back at me. As I looked at them, I fancied each straightened up taller to shout its colors at me: *Pick me.* Once Adam had garlanded my bed with lilacs; I felt there was no harm in returning the kindness with the almost articulate zinnias.

While I walked, not only my legs grew stronger but my whole body. Sometimes I carried stones in my hands and exercised my arms as well, doing curls, or exercising my triceps by raising my elbows and kicking back my forearms from the elbows. Sometimes I thrust smooth, heavy stones up over my head, first one arm, then the other, sometimes both arms. That routine remained challenging for days and days.

While I walked I visited memories—only happy ones, first with Thom, then with my grandmother. The sequences and images from the past seemed almost palpable, as though I could handle them. I felt as though I were folding clean laundry, fresh and warm from the dryer. Sorting my memories had something of the same soothing, almost mindless rhythm. I was tidying up the past, making it as nice as possible, getting ready, perhaps, to put it away.

Often I thought of the good times visiting the Stimson sisters, especially when I strolled in the garden that was reminiscent of the lilacs and roses, the iris, the two pear trees that had bloomed near their house, though the flowers and trees in Mesopotamia bloomed all at once, not in the sequence of seasons I had known in Tennessee.

I rarely pictured my parents, but I sometimes thought of good moments playing the viola, or of orchestral friends, music teachers, and conductors who had gathered our disparate contributions into marvelous bouquets of sound. I considered it healthy and healing to luxuriate in happy memories.

When I accidentally touched the back of my head, I found a soft, short patch of new hair. When I winged my arm back so I could finger the place between my shoulder blades, I discovered the skin was smooth and slick. It was not like normal skin, but who would ever see that scar unless I were wearing a bathing suit? Unless I were swimming in a public pool. For a moment I could almost smell the chlorine from a pool full of people sporting bathing suits more colorful than the petals of zinnias.

I would return to civilization, to my old self. Of course I would. Someday. Did I dwell in a real place? Or had I projected some potent combination of memory and imagination onto airy nothingness? Whatever the status of this Eden in reality, it was the healing place. I was healing, and I was ready to prepare to leave.

What I hoped most to see while I walked was the rigid reality of the French horn case, a crafted, dark emissary from another existence. I supposed the case might have burst open upon impact, but perhaps not. Probably Pierre Saad had made sure that those were no ordinary clasps for the average instrumental case but ones that would hold even if the case were dropped from an airplane. When I looked up, I imagined the black case was caught in the branches of a yellow acacia tree, but the dark object hunched there was only a baboon.

I supposed the scrolls or the loose notes within the case to be rather small; I pictured a square stack of pages nested in the center of the irregularly shaped case. A dark plum-colored slippery silk lined their nest and flowed over the padding all the way to the edges. If the ancient text had taken the form of long, rolled scrolls, surely the Egyptian would have chosen a trombone case to house them.

Watching as I walked for any scraps of inscribed parchment or papyrus lying loosely around—had the case broken open and spilled its contents—I supposed Pierre Saad must be worried, but I could not worry about his worrying, I repeatedly told myself. As I walked, I literally plodded out this plan: I would heal and grow strong; I would recover the lost texts; I would find a way to return to civilization. My stark plan lacked any emotional content.

And what would become of Adam? I would be happy to take him with me, to rescue him from the fog of mythology, to help him adjust to civilization, to help him secure proper medication. I could not keep myself from admiring him, but he was too young and too troubled for me to envision any real attachment between us. He seemed as exotic and inaccessible as the strange, powerfully muscled antelope-like animal he had identified one bright day as a bongo. Its beautiful russet coat had strange narrow lines of white running through it, and its wide, flat horns rose up in a loose twist, like candy. The loosely twirled spun-candy decorations on Thom's and my wedding cake, I realized, resembled the horns of the bongo.

At times, as I wandered through the endless grasslands, the groves of trees, and the cultivated garden-transported-straight-from-childhood, I wondered if I had lost my mind. Or if I had died in the crash and this was the afterlife, a place more African than Middle Eastern. No. I had been hurt in the crash, but I had been lucky. Lucky Lucy: I had found help; I was healing. I had fostered a plan with one, two, three steps in it. What else defined my existence? I never asked how I might absorb my experience and re-form myself.

The weather was always fair and hot enough to walk about comfortably in the absence of clothing. Here night followed day, and at night there were the same stars I had seen in Tennessee, or in Iowa with Thom. Of course when I had moved to New York after Thom's death, I saw few stars. What else impressed itself on my senses or filled my thoughts? I had wanted to know if Thom had been murdered. Yes, I had wanted to find an answer to that riddle. *Igtiyal.* What root tethered that notion to reality?

The vividness of the world around me, the weakness of my recovering body, the confusion of my own mind—that was the business that must occupy me. Thom was dead. Of that I was sure. How could I ever know the *why* of his death?

Was this natural place any more unlikely than the unnaturalness of New York City? I thought of Gershwin's music incorporating the sounds of taxi horns. Pausing before crossing the river, I imagined the sounds of traffic as though I had stopped before crossing the avenue. Gershwin's music hovering over the brownish water. I was neither dead nor insane. I was here. Naked as Eve.

One afternoon, Adam pointed to the horizon to show me a rising pile of dark clouds.

"We'll have a thunderstorm and rain by afternoon," he said.

"I didn't think it ever rained here in paradise."

He went on speaking, explaining that at certain periods it must rain very hard and very long to balance the long dry season we had been living in. "The roots must hold a great deal of water, not so far down." If it should rain as hard as he thought it would, our trees and woven roofs would provide inadequate shelter.

"And so?" I asked.

"We'll take what fruit we can carry with us—maybe make satchels of the elephant ear leaves—and go to the overhang. Where I keep the reserve fire. I already stored firewood at the rock shelter," he said. "We have a lot."

Having considered the particulars of the immediate future more carefully than I, he must have gathered fallen branches while I was taking my meditative walks. The clouds looked like bruises billowing at the collided boundary of meadow and sky. Far away. A turmoil of purple, dark gray, and yellow.

"In Idaho we sometimes watched thunderclouds build, like those."

The rain began while we hurried up the stony path to the shelter. With damp hair and skin, I felt chilly, but Adam set about borrowing flame from his established hearth to build a second fire on the rock floor. A whole truckload of wood, it seemed, was piled safely back in the driest part of the shelter. Rivulets of rain cascaded over the high rim of the overhang to form a flowing curtain between our cavelike room and the rest of the world. Sometimes the wind puffed the curtain back into the room and sprayed us with a cold mist.

Near the edge of the floor, the blowing spray quickly coated a large pile of rocks, each about the size of a fist. Those nearest the drop-off glistened with wet. When I reached to touch one, Adam quietly said, "I'd rather you not disturb the rocks."

It was an odd request. He'd never before told me that he'd rather I not do *anything.* I didn't like it—this new possessiveness—but I complied. Maybe he thought of this space as his own, a kind of den especially for his use. His castle rock. Because the second fire was built near the back wall, it smoked, and I saw the soot had left its mark on the sandstone wall.

Although I thought the rain would certainly stop before sunset, the sky beyond the streaming rain grew increasingly gray and then black. On the inside of the rain curtain, the light of the flames from the two fires reflected the glamour of silver and gold. I was glad for the fires, but being in a more defined space hinted of primitive domesticity.

While it was warmer farther back under the rock shelf, it was also more smoky. Adam warmed himself beside the fire. Occasionally he held out one of his sturdy arms at shoulder level over the flames, as though he were roasting himself. The dark pocket of hair in his armpit somewhat embarrassed me, although I was used to the black cloud around his pubis. In the middle of the rock shelter two pallets of moss had been arranged for our sleeping, parallel but separate. Probably a whole clan could have been sheltered in the overhangs among the bluff.

"One bed looks fresher than the other," I remarked, somewhat nervously.

"I just finished it yesterday," he said. "It's for you."

"Why did you start making one for me yesterday?"

"It was yesterday when I first saw the storm beginning to build. Just a little. I wasn't sure then."

So he had suspected a change in the weather even earlier but not told me. The moss on the one pallet was beginning to turn brown in places. I judged his bed to be about five days old.

"Sometimes I nap here in the afternoons. I change my bed about once a week," he said.

He, too, seemed nervous.

Whether my question rose from fear or hope, I don't know, but suddenly I blurted, "Adam, could there be other people here?"

"I don't know," he said.

I was amazed. "You don't know?" I questioned. "Wouldn't you have seen someone, or some sign?"

"They're . . . sort of monkeys. At least one. A sort of boy monkey."

I was incredulous. "Does he come here?"

"No. I don't want him up here."

Full of curiosity, I asked if he minded that I was here, in his special place. He replied no, that he wanted me here with him. When I asked about the monkey, he told me that he was rough, hairy in places, his head was shaggy, but he was bare of hair in other places. He had not seen him since he first came to Eden. When Adam said the hominoid had human hands and eyes, I grew alarmed and tried to change the subject. Adam wouldn't let me, not till he'd conveyed one more fact.

"When I first came here, I was hurt. Beaten . . . to say the least. I couldn't close my fingers. My hands were blue with bruises. He fed me. Fruit and meat. Raw meat."

But Adam had not encountered him again. He did not know if the monkey had left the Garden, he said.

A gust of wind slapped the rain into one of the fires, and it died, hissing.

"We can share," Adam said. "I shouldn't have built that one so far out."

When I moved back near the smoky fire, I suggested we place apples near the embers. "It'll take a while, but wouldn't roasted apples be good?" I asked him. "Something warm to eat."

"My mother used to roast Rome apples in the oven, Idaho potatoes sometimes, in the stone fireplace, for us."

"Your mother?" I was surprised. He was admitting to a human past. "Adam, you've never mentioned your mother."

He said nothing, but he brought two apples and placed them on the pitted rock close to the fire, then pushed them closer with a stick.

"And brothers and sisters?" I asked.

"I had five little brothers." He rose and stood at the fluid curtain. "I was supposed to set a good example for them, my father said." He turned his back to me, and I realized he must be pissing into the rain. I turned away from him and surveyed the back of our cave.

At our camp, Adam kept a series of holes ready for waste, each with a neat pyramid of dirt beside it. When he had scraped out the holes with the edge of a coconut shell, he had not needed to explain what they were for. I wondered if my menses would commence, when my burns were healed, and how I would handle that natural phenomenon. They had become, at age forty-two, somewhat irregular.

Except for our nakedness, ours was a rather sanitized Eden. I liked it that way. Do no harm. Listening to the force of the rain, I knew I did not want to venture out into it. When I surveyed the cave floor, I saw that in a back corner—one would have to squat to fit under the low overhang there—a shallow dip had been lined with a large leaf. Our toilet. The waste to be enfolded in the leaf and dropped over the edge, not on the gently sloping path where we had ascended but over the other edge, a genuine cliff. A stack of banana leaves lay on a flat rock, near the basin.

Before he turned to face me, I watched his elbow give a sharp double jiggle. Familiar. What woman would not recognize that characteristically male gesture? With perfect matter-of-factness he walked toward the stockpile of branches and twigs, gathered some in his hand, then squatted and began to feed the fire.

"Yes," he said, "like everyone, Eve, I had a mother and a father."

"Adam," I said as gently as I could. "My name is not Eve."

He winced. "Don't say that," he replied. "Please don't say that now."

If I could not speak the truth, I decided, I would say nothing at all for a while. I would enact the mildest kind of negative reinforcement for his insistence on delusion—silence. Though I walked to the curtain of rain, I knew it would be ludicrous for me to try to piss into it. No posture would serve. The scene would be more comical than my trying to catch milk in my mouth, though I had performed better with the goat than with the cow.

I stretched my fingertips into the cascade and let the spatter bounce into my face. It felt good—a relief to my skin after the dry heat of the campfires. I stayed at the rain curtain a long time without even looking at him. When I got tired of playing with the rain with my hands, I stuck my toes into it. When I looked again at his pyramid of stones, it occurred to me they might be a kind of munitions storage. Would not someone who prepared a latrine also want an arsenal? They were just the right size for throwing, not for me, but for a strong man who wanted to do as much quick damage to anyone below the cliff or approaching on the path as he could.

Finally I asked, "When did you gather the stones?"

"As soon as I got here," he remarked, somewhat sullenly.

"Did you know they would get wet, where you've stacked them?"

"No. I didn't know it would rain this hard. I'll move them, another time."

"Adam," I said, finally turning to look at him again. He had quit feeding the fire, but he still stood looking into it, with his arms crossed high over his bare chest. The firelight played over his rosy skin, and in the middle of his forehead hung the black scythelike curl. "Adam, don't be mad at me," I said. "I said the wrong thing."

Now he glanced at me and held my gaze.

"I'm sorry," I added, as blandly as I could.

Immediately, he smiled and came to me. Very carefully he placed both hands over my shoulders and turned me. "Come back to the fire, Eve," he said. "Won't you?"

I came to the fire and neatly sat down sideways on a stone, on my hip with my legs bent to the side. Under my hip, the stone close to the fire felt hard but warm.

"It'll take a while," I said, "for the apples to roast."

"I know."

"Do you want to talk?"

He hesitated, glanced at me, and then back to the flames. "No," he said quietly. "Let's not. Let's just wait." In a few moments, he coached, "Listen to the rain."

That was what my grandmother used to say when bedtime in Memphis came during a rainstorm. "Listen to the rain," as though that were a sound to be let in through your ears and into your mind, like a friend.

"Adam," I said, "what do you want to do with your life?"

"I used to want to draw. And paint."

"That would be easier to do, if you went back with me."

After the apple skins began to wrinkle and glisten, we mutually pronounced them done enough. With a stick, Adam rolled them over the stones close to where we sat. To avoid burning our fingers, we waited again, and Adam mentioned he had brought some cherries and also some walnuts and pecans to crack.

"Plenty of rocks for cracking," I remarked, in return.

Finally he said for me to cup the apple in both hands and just take a bite.

A patch of peel slid right off with a touch of my teeth, and the hot juice and warm fruit delighted me. When I finished, I even lapped up the little brown seeds from the palm of my hand and chomped on the stem. Only after licking my sticky fingers like ten lollipops did I go to the water curtain to wash them. The water was shockingly cold to the touch, and it stripped my skin of the mellow warmth and lingering aroma of the apple. The sharp rain fell like little spears against my spread hands, punitive as sleet, and my whole body felt vulnerable. I wished for clothing.

When I turned from the blackness, I saw that Adam was already lying down on his pallet, his back turned toward me with his knees drawn up. The whiteness of his flesh looked miserable and chilled. My gaze followed the rift of his backbone to his buttocks, rough with goose bumps. The cave looked dismally primitive and dirty, unbearably confining. *Lucky Lucy,* I reminded myself. Lucky I had not been killed when the plane went down. Lucky there was somebody willing and able to take care of me. I remembered how he had looked from the plane, lying on the bank of the river—glorious, like ivory, in the sunlight. Like a piece of art, not a miserable human being. Even in the extremity of my situation, he had seemed a marvel.

After I lay down, I found it difficult to get comfortable on the moss. The stone floor was much harder than the grassy earth that usually padded my fern pallet. I focused on the pile of throwing stones—yes, that was what they must be, a primitive arsenal. To distract myself from discomfort, I began counting the stones in his arsenal and noticing their shapes and textures, speckled, like granite eggs. Especially against my head, the hardness of the floor came right through the moss.

I felt excluded by his delusions, but I had made myself behave as neutrally as I could. That was how I had trained myself; if I had no warmth to give my patients, at least I could find a blankness to offer, not my own uncertainty or pain.

I decided I should give myself some definite time limit for finding the texts Pierre Saad had entrusted to me. After such a period had elapsed, then it would be reasonable to leave, empty-handed. I was strong enough now. I tried resting on one side of my face, then the other. Why had I jettisoned the case? I had thought that even if I died, perhaps it could be salvaged. I had wanted to do that for a person who had trusted me. I still had Thom's flash drive. At least I could return that to the scientists.

Most uncomfortable was the obdurate pain where the convex of the back of my skull encountered the flat of stone.

"Lucy," Adam said—how strange to hear a voice; I had felt utterly alone. There was his kind, strong voice. "If you like, you can pillow your head on my stomach."

"I'd like that," I answered.

"Stand up," he went on, a certain neutrality in his voice. "I'll move your bed over here, at a right angle to mine."

He had already nimbly risen.

"I'll fix everything," he said. He sounded like a willing child, an eager Scout.

When I stood up, he quickly began to move my pallet. The fire was very low now, and he interrupted his work to put on a large limb. "Our night log," he said. Then he lay down on his pallet and patted his stomach. It did not look soft but ridged with muscles—a six-pack, the bodybuilders called it. Still, I lay down and placed my head there. Yes, this was much better. His body was my cushion. It relieved my shoulders of the weight of my head and neck to lie this way, perpendicular to his side. Very slightly, my head rose and fell with his shallow breathing.

"I won't touch you," he said. "Not in any way."

Even his voice seemed disembodied; it hovered in the air, pretended to be words formed by the tongue of flame in the cavern, rather than in a human mouth.

Only as I drifted into sleep did I realize he had called me by my name. I hadn't even noticed. "Lucy," he had said. "Lucy, you can pillow your head . . ."

I opened my eyes in surprise, then closed them and listened to the licking of the small flames and the falling of the rain. It made no difference what we called each other, I told myself. We were who we were, I thought, regardless of label.

Yet when he called me by my name, the core of me had responded.

From that night when I pillowed my head on his body and he first called me Lucy, the name he used for me became an index to his state of mind.

# PARACHUTE

NO NIGHTMARES VISITED Adam's sleep that night, and when I awoke, I found my head had moved to his shoulder, and I had thrown my arm across his chest. That was how I had loved to sleep with Thom, with my head on his shoulder. Adam lay on his back, as though he had not stirred at all in his sleep. Very carefully, I sat up; then I studied his body in repose. Not entirely in repose; there was a clenched quality about his muscles. The features of his face seemed more chiseled, set, and beautiful than ever. I glanced at his penis. It lay to one side, not hard but rounded and somewhat tumescent. Rosy, his egglike testicles, ruddy and tender, lolled against his paler skin.

I stood up carefully and walked to the lip of the rock shelter. The curtain of rain had vanished, the sun bathed the nearby trees, and the world was a peaceable kingdom. I could see and see yet farther and yet beyond, over the meadows of the great plains divided into zones by stands of acacias. The flowers and colors of our garden were too small to carry to this distance, but I recognized the clear geometric shape of their plot. On one side was the river; tall grasses tucked here and there against its curves, and in the far distance the glittering ocean. Was it the Persian Gulf? A mirage? On the other side, a band of lavender clouds gathered again on the horizon with their hint of *could*. Could it rain again tonight?

Without warning I heard a rumble and then the sound of tearing sky. Not in the distance but nearby and coming nearer, something was ripping the great blue sheet of cloudless sky, booming and coming closer. I felt the warmth of Adam's body standing just at my side when two jets sped into view, turning and twisting their contrails together like DNA. They flew much higher than the lone jet that had passed over our luncheon on the grassy plain, but still the double power and speed of the twining two was terrifying—the sound of their unbridled engines, the shriek of their silver massiveness.

Suddenly something orange, packagelike, shot out from one of them, lengthened, and began unfurling, while the two planes narrowed with astonishing rapidity the blue division of sky between them. As we gasped, the planes collided and exploded in a single fireball that continued the momentum of their motion, then plummeted, exploding again in a shatter of fire.

"Wait here," Adam said, and began to run down the path.

Before the question could leave my throat to ask, What is it? he answered over his shoulder. "Parachute!"

Mesmerized, I stared at the almost vacant sky while he hurried down the path. Yes, an orange parachute hung in the blue, and a blob of human almost too tiny to see dangled below the carapace. Halfway across the sky where the planes had converged, only a cloud of smoke smudged the air. I looked closely at the terrain where the parachute was descending, and I recognized a familiar landmark. When my own Piper Cub had lost power, while it was still gliding, I had noticed a grove of redwood trees. They had risen above the greenery of all the other trees to an amazing height, like many spires of a super cathedral, like Gaudí's Sagrada Familia. And there they were again, with the billow of orange fabric hovering above their tall green points.

I wondered if Adam had noted the redwoods as a marker.

Of course he had. This was his hideaway, his stronghold, his private place. He was keenly observant. He would have seen the redwoods. He would have admired them as I had.

Had he instructed me to wait? Of course I would not wait. He would need help. Perhaps *they* would need help. But I would not run. I knew I was not yet strong enough for running. Quickly I looked for the store of fruit and nuts we had transported to the shelter. I draped my ears with bunches of the long-stemmed cherries the way Adam had done when he first brought me fruit to eat. In each hand, I held an apple. Then, following Adam, I started as rapidly as I could down the rocky path.

# ARIELLE

"I'M HERE, PAPA," she said.

Pierre Saad shivered and then sprang from his chair to embrace his daughter. He shivered because, ever since her puberty, his daughter's voice had assumed exactly the same timbre as his wife's.

More than a decade had passed since that day when the similarity had taken him utterly by surprise. Arielle had been thirteen. She had come back to Jean-de-Luc from boarding school in Paris. Electrified by surprise and joy—"I'm here," her voice had rung out—he had thought his wife, Violette, had returned from the dead. His body believed. His ears rang with the miracle. When his eyes fell upon his little girl—taller, her hair caught up in a more sophisticated way—he had had to press his breastbone. The pain of false recognition exploded in his heart, as though he had been shot.

Thoroughly alarmed at his expression of pain, the sudden movement of his hand to his breast, she had run to him.

"I'm all right," he had stammered in French. "It's all right. You've grown. In just these months you've changed so much."

"I have a secret," she said, the dimple in one cheek showing. Now she looked like a little girl again.

"You've become very beautiful," he said. "Is that your secret? You scared me."

"Poor Papa," she said. "It's just me. I'm not Princess Charming."

He kissed her on both cheeks and, still feeling weak, invited her to sit down with him in the library.

"Next time," he said, "you must say, 'I'm here, *Papa*.' Then I'll know it's you."

"All right," she replied happily. "I'm here, Papa, and I want to tell you my secret."

"What is it?"

"My periods have started. I look the same, but really I'm a woman."

He wanted to say, *You do not look the same, you do not sound the same; it seemed my wife was alive again and returned,* but instead he had assured, "You are growing up, *sans doute,* but always you are my beloved daughter."

From within the circle of his fatherly embrace, his independent, now truly grown-up daughter, a successful artist, teased, "I knew you'd be in here. Always working in the library."

"My favorite room," he answered, still unsteady with joy. Daughter or wife, it was almost the same joy.

"Our favorite room," she said. She glanced around, taking it all in (he did not need to look; he saw it in his imagination through her beloved eyes): the oak bookshelves and the matching oak library table, the walls painted a rich red, the vase of white midsummer daisies he kept there on the golden oak table whenever daisies were in bloom. He knew she was making sure nothing had been changed, except the flowers. Naturally, they were allowed to change according to the season, even within the eternal compass of home.

"But Lucy Bergmann has not arrived, I take it," Arielle said to him. Her face was very serious.

"How do you know?" he asked, teasing.

"Because she would have left her mark. Here in the library, there would have been . . . a slight mutation."

"Why do you think that, dear daughter?"

"Because she will change our lives. I had a dream about it."

Pierre frowned. "Dreams do not always come true."

"I remember my mother's charm. Put six pomegranate seeds under your pillow, and whatever you dream will come true. In six hours, six days, six weeks—maybe six years."

"Because Persephone ate six pomegranate seeds, she was confined to the underworld for six months of the year."

"I know that story," Arielle replied. She smiled at her father, lowered her face, and made her eyes turn six shades darker. "The Greek story has nothing to do with our Arabic charm."

"I think your mother made it up. I never heard of such augury. You didn't like pomegranate juice. You would never drink it."

She continued to shift her gaze from the floor to his eyes, like a little seductress. "Still, Lucy Bergmann will change our lives."

*Change nothing* had become their unspoken credo. It had been their bulwark against cataclysm and horror. Arielle had been only six when they had fled Egypt for France. Only six—as he had been when his own mother died against the wall near Cairo—when Arielle's mother, his beloved wife, Violette, had been blown up by a car bomb. The bomb had been meant for him, the author of *Muhammad, the Man.* Even now he wagged his head back and forth a bit, as though to shake out the memory, the impossible, endless recapitulation of loss.

Although every instinct had shouted at him to take his little girl and flee to France, he had refused to be exiled entirely by terror. He had gone back to Egypt every year, at least for a week or two. He knew he was probably watched by some wing of the dictator's government, but he didn't care. Until the discovery of the Genesis codex, he had nothing to hide and no inclination to be politically active. He visited his Sufi stepfather and Violette's family. For serenity, he needed to see the images of ancient Egypt. When Arielle reached the age of twenty-one, she, too, had insisted on returning to Egypt periodically, and she had embraced her mother's Muslim faith.

Though his professional focus had become the cave art of southern France, northern Spain, and Italy, Pierre Saad had also continued to study the stone carvings of ancient Egypt, with a special emphasis on how depictions of Hathor and Isis had evolved. The goddesses and gods of the Nile had rewarded him for returning more faithfully to the land than the floods, now that they were contained by the high dam at Aswan. The gods had saved a special discovery for him alone to make.

In the hills around Nag Hammadi, in the year 2019, he had stubbed his toe on what he first took to be a smooth stone. Later he would tell his daughter that it was simply because he knew the story of the peasant boy's discovery of the so-called Gnostic Gospels, in 1945, that he had looked down. The curve of the stone raising itself slightly above the sandy soil was too perfect, too smooth, to be natural. Glancing around and seeing no one, he unearthed an alabaster jar, not a human-size one like the 1945 discovery, but one much smaller.

This one was only the size of a human stomach. Weighing perhaps seven pounds, it was squat and almost oval in shape, with a lid that fit so closely one could hardly see that it was a lid. The thick lid had no handle, but a slot chiseled down into the top; at the bottom of the slot a recess on one side accommodated the tucking under of fingertips. Yes, a person inserted straight fingers into the lid, then curled their tips into the recess. The slot was just the size for three of his fingertips, but probably when hands were smaller it had served as a grip for four ancient fingers. He tried to pull up the lid, there on the spot, though all his professionalism said *No*, not to do that. The alabaster casket was wiser than he. It would not open.

Nervously he glanced around, saw only three donkeys, and put the oval box in his knapsack. He took time to walk slowly, to eat leisurely at a tavern before going to his room. There he tried again with all his might to lift the lid. To no avail. A housekeeper came in with a broom and swept the floor; he saw her eye the alabaster oval.

To steady his nerves he took a single long and deep breath; involuntarily, he smiled at the recalcitrant vessel, as snug as an ostrich egg. Its vague, tannish mottling mingled with its creamy tones. Even when the maid left, he continued to sit. He would regard it as an object of fascination, not vexation. Then it occurred to him to see if the top would *slide* off the base. Yes, a lateral motion, not the preemptive arrogance of entry from above. He must *set aside* the lid. Perhaps it would slide in only one direction, from right to left. When he pushed the lid with his thumbs, he heard a slight grating, as though minute particles of sand had worked their way into the fine space where the lid fit the base. Of course there was a reluctance of stone to slide over stone. Perhaps originally—how many thousands of years ago, in different hands, in a different world—there had been oil to facilitate the motion.

Very carefully, he held the stone casket on the horizontal.

As the lid grated to one side, he saw a hollow space containing small, flat sheets of papyrus. The brown lettering was unlike Hebrew, more primitive in shape. The letter forms had the laborious rigidity of ancient Phoenician letters, like little clubs or angular ladles. Meaning, a phrase, emerged.

. . . *not a story of one creator.* . . . Pierre's hands began to shake. These little pages, so fragile, perhaps a dozen of them, like a stack of thin, dry crackers. His eyes raced along the marks, searched for another phrase.

. . . *In the beginning* . . . Very carefully he looked at new pages. When his effort yielded no understanding, he went back to the first page. Was that the word for "friend"? Did the phrase mean "my friend who writes"? Single words suggested *rivers, sun, moon, sheep, donkeys, birds.* But what did these names mean? The animals seemed to rise from the page into the air. His eyes flew back to the phrase *In the beginning God* . . . , and a great chill swept Pierre's body. It was the idea of Genesis: *In the beginning God created* . . . But what was the reference to "friend who writes"? And had he not seen the phrase or something like it farther on in the text? Yes. Another version: *In the beginning, there was something and there was nothing.* . . .

Now heat flooded Pierre's body and brain. The words appeared to contradict, at least to amend or to approach from another angle, the Genesis story, the grand opening verses. Again, Pierre made his shaking hands move carefully while his eyes searched and found *dust* and then *clay.* The yolk inside the alabaster egg was a vision of creation. And perhaps it provided a context of a writer or writers attempting to articulate the vision.

His hands trembling, Pierre replaced the loose pages back into the cavity that had held them, then slid the covering stone back into place. He leaned forward and kissed the alabaster as he had seen Orthodox priests kiss the Holy Bible. He picked up the protective casket and cradled it against his bosom.

He must find a way to disguise it and take it to a safe place. He closed his eyes and began to memorize what he had deciphered. *In the beginning, there was something and there was nothing. . . . Birds, donkeys, clay, friend, dust . . .*

"Genesis," he whispered.

Had he been watched? Surely the author of *Muhammad, the Man* was regarded with some suspicion. Was he being watched now as he stared at his treasure egg of mottled alabaster?

As casually as possible he glanced at the corners of the room. It was not an expensive room, but it was one he had returned to for six years. For the last five years Arielle had often rented the room next to it, and there was a connecting door so that one need not pass into the hall before entering the other room. It had been cozy having his daughter close at hand while preserving his own privacy. Again, he glanced around, trying to detect if some tiny camera eye were watching him. Perhaps so. Perhaps not. Or an ear tuned to his whisper?

He sat back down and deliberately picked up the alabaster egg, glanced at it, set it down again, and pushed it away with a casual gesture as though he counted it of no special importance. Having been careless, now he must try to cover up his rapture. Was he a fool to think this writing referenced creation? He picked up a common catalog from the Coptic Museum and leafed through it as though the egg held no more interest for him. Perhaps only now was he under surveillance. Perhaps they had not seen him place his lips on the stone. Pushing back his chair, he put his feet up on the hotel desk in the rude manner of a Western male, letting the sole of his sandal almost touch the alabaster box. He chewed absentmindedly on the fingernail of his index finger as though he were so bored that he welcomed any distraction.

Finally he got up restlessly and rapped with his knuckles on Arielle's door.

"Want to go out?" he had called to the closed door. "I'm bored out of my mind. I want to shop."

Arielle opened the door. "Shop, Papa?"

"Let's buy some alabaster—vases and boxes—to take back to our friends. The French love that sort of stuff. Maybe some goblets?"

"The goblets are usually onyx," she answered. She was looking at him carefully.

"Get a large bag," he said. "I'll take my knapsack."

Her gaze went over his shoulder to the box on the table.

"I have a piece I want to return," he added.

"Cracked?" she asked.

"Yes. We can find some better stuff."

At the Cairo airport that distant day in 2019, when they were beginning their journey back to France, every package was unwrapped from its newspapers, unsealed from its cellophane taping, opened, held up to the light, and examined by uniformed guards, finally by two sweating men in coats and ties. The father and daughter were respectful and patient; they chatted of this thing and that person whom they would soon see at home. Only someone who knew the pair very well would have noticed their eyelids were slightly lowered. Behind their gaiety, there was conspiracy. Days before they entered the Cairo airport with their packages, they had managed to visit Arielle's aunt, Violette's sister, to leave the treasure with her.

Recently Pierre had been visited separately by two grave men. Though he tried to shrug off their visits, he was glad that Arielle was still working at her studio in Paris.

The first visitor had been an Orthodox Jew, Rabbi Esau ben Ezra, from West Jerusalem. He appeared at Pierre's office in the Dordogne with a proper letter of introduction from a mutual acquaintance. The rabbi started the conversation casually by noting Pierre had recently been in Egypt. He asked questions about artifacts dating to the period of Moses and early textual versions of the Ten Commandments; then he pretended to let his mind wander as he spoke of texts dealing with Jacob and Esau, with Isaac and Ishmael, finally of Seth, the third offspring of Adam, brother to Cain and Abel.

"Of course it is not merely what the stories may have meant to those to whom they were originally told," he said, "but what they have come to signify today. To us."

Pierre replied, "I ask exactly those questions about cave paintings. Would you agree that they, too, are a sort of sacred text?"

His visitor spluttered a bit, then said decisively, "Not in the same way, of course. Cave art has only recently been discovered or at least recognized for its true antiquity in the last hundred fifty years or so. No culture has surrounded the animal paintings because they were unknown for many thousands of years. The sacred is a quality relevant to cultural context. The paintings have had no influence—"

"Perhaps an influence on artists?" Pierre asked. "Genetically, vaguely, if not directly?"

"The biblical stories are the thumbprint of our Creator," the scholar answered. "They reveal His identity to us. Their veracity has sustained my people. Some of us, in Israel, take the responsibility of being guardians—"

"Of course," Pierre said.

As he stood, his visitor adjusted the folds of his long black gown; he positioned his rope belt so that it became a level equator dividing the top half of his body from the bottom half.

"We have resources," he said, "as well as a sacred right—"

"A right to—"

"To what God has always intended us to have. Even now, I could—"

"I think our interests are not really the same," Pierre said. "Of course they overlap, but . . . but primarily I am considering now only the cave paintings, the underworld."

"The underworld. Italy? Mafia? The Vatican—"

"Oh, no," Pierre said. "The world we stand on. What is beneath our feet. Literally, I would go so far as to say. The prehistoric *human* thumbprint . . ."

They continued to shuffle the words between them till both grew weary of the game. Just before the visitor left, Pierre remarked, "It seems your true interest is in biblical stories of brothers. Do you have a brother?"

"I am my brother's keeper," the rabbi answered, then rose, bowed, and left.

The second visitor had been an American businessman, sincere and direct. "Thank you for seeing me," the American began.

"Please," Pierre said encouragingly.

"Thank you for speaking with me," the man repeated. He settled himself in a chair across the table from the anthropologist. Pierre noted that the man's face was worn and lined, as though he had once lived hard and fast. He wore snakeskin boots. "I won't take too much of your time. I have an opportunity to offer you. I take it you're a Muslim?"

Pierre made no reply. The two men let silence lie between them. Then the businessman began again.

"The Bible begins, 'In the beginning God created Heaven and Earth.' You ever run into any old papers might've had those kinds of words on 'em? I got somebody willing to pay a cool million."

"Who?"

"Ever hear tell of the Creation Museum?"

Pierre laughed. Then he asked, "Where is it?" but he was thinking of the alabaster egg. Somehow others knew of the words he had only tentatively deciphered. Perhaps there were other documents that referred to the existence of his codex.

"Northern Kentucky. You can fly right into the Cincinnati, Ohio, airport." The man's voice began to relax into a drawl. "But the museum is in Kentucky. From lots of places in Europe, you can fly right into Cincy. Be at the museum in less than an hour after touchdown, you got anything to sell. I don't represent the museum. I'm a broker. An idea broker. We could go straight to Cincy, bypass New York City entirely."

"I'm sorry," Pierre had answered. "I don't know what you're talking about."

"You sure 'bout that, buddy?"

Pierre said nothing.

The visitor stood up. With one hand he patted the discreet silver buckle of his belt. With the other hand, he pinched the top of the crease in his pant leg to straighten it.

As a screen for his activities, Pierre thought of the idea of hosting a symposium of scientists to honor the memory of Thom Bergmann, the astrophysicist. Before the scientists convened, Pierre knew the alabaster egg must be replaced as the container for the codex. He had a new receptacle prepared by a man who fashioned special cases for delicate electronic devices and expensive musical instruments. *Not really for a French horn,* Arielle had explained to the clerk, *but for a small stack of papers of these dimensions.* Before the symposium commenced, she had presented the order.

But here was Pierre's daughter standing in the library, predicting Lucy would change their lives. Yet he had no news of the American widow to give his daughter.

"Mrs. Bergmann should have been here long ago," Arielle told her father.

"Of course. I tried her telephone, called the hospital where she worked in New York, sent her e-mails."

"Who else knows her?" Arielle asked. "How can we inquire?"

"I'll call her old friend, her husband's friend. The British physicist. Gabriel Plum."

There had been an air about Gabriel Plum, his cocksureness, that made Pierre wonder if he had slept with Lucy Bergmann. But perhaps not. In her eyes, there was something newly virginal. Pierre would have to confide to Gabriel that Lucy had agreed to smuggle an ancient manuscript out of Egypt, but Pierre doubted the ethics of that would matter to Professor Plum.

"Do you trust him?" Arielle asked.

Pierre saw a shadow pass over his daughter's lovely, expressive face.

"No choice."

# RESCUE

WHEN THE SKY screamed with twining airplanes and the air exploded, Adam watched a parachute unfurl in rich orange, the signal of danger and caution. Yet the parachute swelled open with a color joyful as a zinnia, quite the opposite of that oddly shaped black egg the bird plane had erroneously laid upon the air.

Appended from the chute was surely a man, a brother, a soldier. On his own cheeks Adam felt the cold air rushing like two adzes made of ice past the soldier's cheekbones. How had Adam himself come to this world? The descent of Adam, having been thrown from the scalding back of a truck, was shorter.

Who was coming? He stared and waited.

If the chute dropped plumb, it would land to the left of the tall trees, and if it descended in a drifting course, as surely it would, then it would settle like an orange drape among the high spires of the redwoods. And there the paratrooper would hang.

His body broken? His blood shed?

Adam glanced down at his naked feet, their clean, bare whiteness, and knew that they would take him where he needed to go. *How beautiful are the feet of them who preach the gospel of Peace.* If not a well-winged angel, then let him be mountain goat and more, sure-footed and practical.

Adam thought of his own five younger brothers, and he remembered the five not-brothers, Arab soldiers, God's avenging angels, the Eumenides of Greek mythology, the five young men in the truck who had savaged his body and left him, dumped out, like a dung pie in the road left to bake in the sun.

But the monkey-god came, the hominoid or little homunculus had come to Adam. At first he had thought the creature was stuffing a gag into his mouth, but no, it was a juicy wad, a handful of fruit, wedges of tangerine, pomegranate seeds slimy as the jeweled sperm from a frog, oval grapes, and then the tapered end of a soft banana. The Samaritan monkey had fed him, had pulled and boosted him upright, had placed a skinny arm of surprising strength around his back and made him walk into the shade.

Having reached the bottom of the path from the rock shelter, Adam paused to enter the room of his mind that was not memory but the dwelling place of *now*, the place-time for planning and thinking. Here a forest of scrubby pines, there he would run through the aspens, green and flickering in sunlight, and he would come to the grasses, short and thick, dear cushions for his feet. Quickly, quickly he would run past the staked tomatoes and the rose garden with its tempting silvery gazing ball, past the twin pear trees eternally afluff with blossoms and attendant bees, because this was Eden—half-created, half-perceived, as Wordsworth said of all of nature.

Running, not just thinking of running, Adam passed through oaks—he loved those boldly, irregularly lobed leaves—and past the dogwoods, here as yet uncursed or dwarfed because their wood would form the tree whereon Christ died. Not the sacrificial future, now, this, he panted as he ran, was the beginning, the Genesis.

Here, in the beginning, God placed humans, a man and a woman whose nature it was to help each other because they were made mortal. Magnolias. The air was redolent from the perfume of their wide-open white blossoms, big as cereal bowls.

Suddenly Adam tripped in a tangle of ivy vines. He should have gone around. He didn't fall, but the tough vine cut the flesh on top of his foot. Snared, he looked up and saw the redwoods, their height stretching sunward. Near the pinnacle of the tallest tree wavered the orange parachute, its lines terminating some twenty feet lower in the hanging man. He was suspended not over empty space, but above a branch that stretched flat as a floor only a yard or so below his feet. A soldier, yes. High above, dangling in the treetops. Dressed in desert camouflage, an American. Adam thanked God, who had yanked up double handfuls of redwoods and transplanted them to Eden.

The soldier's eyes were closed, his head drooped, his jaw hung askew as though it were badly broken. He was missing one boot, and the ankle was turned in awkwardly. A boot was still laced onto the other foot. His arms swayed loosely from his shoulders, and for a terrible moment, Adam thought perhaps the soldier's neck as well as his jaw had been broken. Then the booted foot moved. Purposefully, the hanging man toed the air to search for a firm place to stand. He could not quite reach the flat evergreen limb below. As his eyes opened, his face ignited with terror.

Adam waved both arms and shouted, "I'm an American."

The words seemed very small shouted upward in the vast, sunlit air. He watched the soldier locate the origin of the voice, the amazement cover his face. Very slowly the soldier lifted one hand and carefully made one fan-shaped pass displaying his open palm. A wave of recognition. Then faint, desperate, urgent gurglings issued from his throat.

"I hear you, man," Adam shouted. "Don't try to talk!"

Adam would ascend. But how? When he entered the trees and stood among the shadows, the girth of their trunks asserted imperial stability and their soaring height signaled majesty. Would not any wanderer who entered here want to worship? Adam resisted the impulse to fall to his knees. The gigantic presences grew in loose family circles, as though each group embraced a room-size space where perhaps an ancient parent tree had stood. As quietly as he could, Adam passed from one grove to another, a brown church of many chambers. Finally he stood still and listened. The silence seemed imbued with their odor—not quite cedar, not quite pine, but aromatic and subduing. He stood in the center of the irregular circle rising around him. The towering trunks offered a conduit almost to the infinite. Skyscrapers, the trunks merged in a ceiling of greenery.

No tree trunk offered the slightest foothold, but only a sheer, unbranched and unknobbed verticality for a height of three stories and sometimes much more. Which tree to climb? And how? He passed from grove to grove looking up. Finally the canopy allowed a glimpse of orange parachute.

He called upward. "Man?" and again, "Hey, man?" but there was no reply. Perhaps the soldier had lapsed into unconsciousness from pain. First Adam must gain the canopy, then cross from tree to tree.

The light came slanting between the strong, vertical trunks, and then Adam realized that one of the trunks also slanted. A tree had fallen, a broad-trunked grandfather, but it had been caught and lodged among the trunks of the others. It provided an avenue of access, *a highway for the Lord.* Adam could walk or crawl along the incline up to the height where interlacing branches of upright trees would become his ladder.

Without hesitation, he began to walk up the fibrous bark. *I know that my Redeemer liveth.* Without formulating any additional plan, Adam trusted his strong, self-preserving body to find a way.

Near the top of the ramp, Adam felt the temptation of flight, simply to launch himself into the deliciousness of sky, but then he glanced down at his feet, at the small red cut across the top of his foot, and he remembered the reality of his body. *Feet and hands; no wings,* he told himself, and laughed at the solid simplicity of the idea. Truth had never seemed so simple or so real.

And suddenly there was the gentle fluttering sound and the swaying orange of the parachute, more vibrant in color than the petal of an enormous tiger lily.

And there high above the earth hung the man in his harness, his eyes closed, his lower jaw partly turned athwart the bottom of his face. "F. Riley" was stenciled across his shirt pocket.

"Friend," Adam said softly, "I've come to get you."

The man opened his eyes.

"Riley," Adam said, "I'm going to take you down on my back, fireman's carry, but first I have to cut you loose and tie you to me."

Riley merely stared, dazed beyond thought. Adam climbed the limbs till he moved nearer to the soldier. It was amazing how close together they were in the tops of the redwoods, high above the ground but speaking as they might had they met below—two men high as angels, one harnessed, suspended in a mottled uniform of desert camouflage, the other naked, standing at ease on the limb just below, speaking conversationally.

"Or I can make a sling out of the parachute, lower you that way. That sound better to you?" Adam moved so near to Riley, he could have reached out and touched him.

Ever so slightly, Riley nodded yes, or Adam thought he did.

Adam said these things because they were pictures of possibility in his mind. He had no idea how he would implement either idea. Looking at the cords of the chute, he pictured himself gnawing fruitlessly, gnawing on and on, and unable to sever the cords, when without even thinking he heard himself saying, "You have a knife, don't you?" and his hand reached toward the scabbard at Riley's belt.

Before Adam could touch its hilt, he felt Riley's hand close slowly and warmly over the back of his own hand. He stopped. Riley squeezed, warm and warmer, tender, thankful. And once again the squeeze like a pulse, thanking, thanking.

"That's all right," Adam murmured. "Glad to be of help."

To cut off a section of the collapsed orange fabric, Adam climbed higher. With the cloth bunched in his hand, he came lower again and spread the fabric out as though on a bed below Riley's feet, one bare and already swelling, one booted. While he prepared to cut Riley free, Adam held the soldier around the waist with one arm, but he needed both hands for cutting. He would have to let Riley partly slide, partly fall onto the fabric. Then he would use the cloth like a sling and make a web of the cords so he could lower the man to the place where the fallen tree slanted among the stalwarts.

Riley was sometimes conscious, but mostly he was not. Adam had to climb up and down, back and forth, his body working like a shuttle of logic, so that he could sequence himself to do the work of three or four. Most of the chute he left caught high in the tree.

Once Adam slipped and slid down till his foot found an intersection of branch and trunk. Once, he glanced down, and the world spun below him on the axis of the trunk to which he clung. Trembling all over, he closed his eyes and held on tightly till the tremor subsided. *Learn,* he whispered to himself, *be more careful.* There would be no more looking down. Before he trussed Riley up in the sling, Adam replaced Riley's knife in its scabbard. By degrees, tying, untying, retying the cords, Adam lowered the soldier to the inclined tree.

While he balanced carefully, his bare feet moving cautiously down the long ramp of the trunk, he carried Riley like a baby swaddled in bright puffs of drooping parachute. He envisioned Jesus in a nimbus of light walking down from heaven to earth, to help mankind. *Da, da, da:* that was the lesson of Eliot's *Waste Land*. *Give, control, sympathize.* Adam could give help, if not alms, here in the wilderness. He could control his lust. He could sympathize with the inner life of others—their fear and pride. His consciousness swooned at the glory of fulfillment, with the honor of becoming himself.

When Adam could no longer think, his farm-boy body knew how to continue—to work when work was impossible. His eyes focused on his long white toes bracing against the bark. He ignored his trembling thighs. If he fell, then he would try to fly. His body would do that for him. Then he saw a woman, surely Eve, far below looking up at him. Her face was the pale, full moon. She had come down from the sheltering rocks to the forest to help him. His helpmeet.

# INTIMACY

"WE'LL TAKE CARE of him here," I said. "No need to move him again." My eyes went to the large, useful knife in the soldier's scabbard. "Can you build a shelter here?" I read his name on his shirt: "F. Riley."

"First a splint for his foot," Adam said.

We both took inventory of what we had acquired: yards and yards of orange fabric, cords, a knife, and a badly injured soldier. I leaned forward and very gently touched the askew jaw. "Dislocated," I said. "Likely broken, too."

"First we pop it back in place," Adam answered. "Then we try to squeeze closed any fractures and bind his jaw shut." Adam sat on the ground and took Riley's head between his spread legs in order to begin the work.

Placing his thumbs behind the corners of the lower jaw, Adam pushed down and forward. "Sorry," he said as he then pushed laterally. Riley's eyes flew open in the horror of pain, then rolled back into his head as he passed into unconsciousness. I remembered my own pain when I had arrived in this place.

"Cut strips, several inches wide," Adam instructed, "long as your arm and half again."

With the tips of his fingers, Adam felt the jawbone for fractures and shoved the fragments toward what seemed to promise a smooth contour. I could sense Adam's immense fatigue like an aroma, but his hands were deft and sure. His sweat fell like beads and then splattered onto Riley's blanched face. Riley's eyes were closed. Adam and I passed orange strips under the jaw and tied their ends over the top of Riley's head.

"He has red hair," I said. I passed my hand over the ends of the red stubble.

Adam glanced at me curiously, then looked more closely at the face of the unconscious man.

The pilot breathed evenly.

"Now his foot," Adam said quietly, and I rose to find long sticks for splints. Then we cut and tore more strips from the chute to pad the splints before binding them to Riley's foot. Throughout our work, F. Riley remained unconscious. We said very little, and we avoided each other's eyes until the last binding knot was tied.

"The primal work has come to us," I remarked.

"Primal?" Now he looked into my eyes as though to clear his own confusion.

"The work of taking care of one another."

For a moment Adam looked at me as though he were well. "Didn't I take care of you, Lucy?"

I thought of our night under the rock shelter. I had wanted him. In that new location, enclosed in rock behind a curtain of rain, in his castle, I could not deny to myself that I had wanted him. I extended my hand to Adam, and he took it. There was nothing particular about the gesture, but it was the beginning of our intimacy, only now, because Riley was with us, we had lost both simplicity and privacy.

"Yes," I said. "Yes, you took splendid care of me when I needed it most. But . . . but—" I hesitated.

"But what?" He watched me, how I searched for words that might be true, clear, and significant.

"What I said was, 'The primal work has come *to us*.' To us, together, Adam. For us to do. For us to take care of somebody besides ourselves."

—

When we finished binding up the injuries of the pilot, Adam turned his attention to our need for shelter. As he went away to cut saplings, I admired his straight, strong back. Because of the rain, the grass beyond the redwood groves had turned a deeper, brighter green. The sunshine blessed the conjunction of flesh and verdure.

Over the framework of sticks for our lean-to, we layered elephant-ear leaves and the broad leaves of banana trees to ward off hard-pelting rain when it would come. The shelter would need sides, too. From the distance, we heard growling, lions but not lions—thunder. Perhaps the interlacing redwood branches high above would sieve the raindrops and diffuse them into mere mist.

In his sleep, F. Riley moved his hand to grasp his dog tags. I closed my own hand around Thom's memory stick. My knuckles bumped against one of my breasts. I had almost forgotten the nakedness of my breasts and the titanium-clad pendant that hung between them.

"You'll be all right," I crooned to Riley, but nothing in his face changed.

Still and hot, the perfumed air among the tall trees made breathing difficult. Sometimes I stirred the air above F. Riley's nose by waving my hand like a fan. While Adam came and went, bringing the materials for the lean-to, I whispered encouragement to Riley.

# GABRIEL PLUM

IN HIS LONDON apartment on Baker Street, Gabriel was waiting for a visit. He knew the arrival of his guest was imminent. Just now, looking through one of his curved windows down into the street, he saw the black-clad emissary of Perpetuity.

Almost no one in London wore black anymore. The color was as passé as New York City. When the dollar came in at four-to-one for the pound, everyone in London dressed in white. Clothes in Paris reverted to a pleasing medley of colors—a vivid Postimpressionist palette. But here was a blackbird—conspicuous, dignified, self-righteous.

A well of darkness, Gabriel thought, ready to absorb all light that comes to him. For a moment he thought of the dark hole to the interior of a box designed to illustrate black box radiation to beginning physics students.

Against the background of the upright black garb moving over the walkway below, Gabriel immediately spotted a white slip of paper. The bearer held it in one hand, and the paper fluttered like a small flag. With his other hand the rabbi adjusted his pince-nez to better view what was written on his flag—without doubt an address! This address, Gabriel thought. He sighed.

The rabbi's footfall on the staircase was as light as a dancer's. He moved as though he enjoyed climbing stairs—who knew what was at the top? Gabriel wondered if the man's thoughts moved from one to another with as much nimbleness as his feet. Anticipating a knock at the door, Gabriel moved as quickly as he could across the worn carpet. The jute threads were visible in some areas. He took care to make no noise at all and swung open the door.

"Professor Plum, I believe. I am Rabbi Esau ben Ezra. I have read your latest articles with great interest."

"Then you must be a physicist as well as a man of the cloth. No other sane person would have done so. Please come in." Did the man have news of Lucy? Gabriel decided to prolong the pretense that his visitor was a colleague in physics. "Your specialty?"

"Many body calculations employing domain decomposition."

Though the knowledgeable answer startled Gabriel, he pushed the game a step further. "To business, then. Come in. Please sit." Gabriel closed the door to the hallway. "I suppose you come to inform me the matrices must be positive-definite and self-adjoint. I have already thought as much."

"Domain decomposition—yes." The rabbi slowly removed his pince-nez and made it disappear within some placket of his robe. He rubbed his eyes, retained his hat. "Yes. But we are not speaking of quite the same domain. Mine is not material."

"Exactly the problem with all mathematics, is it not? My reason for being a physicist, instead of a pure mathematician. I prefer my math, no matter how subtle, to refer to physical realities, don't you?"

"No."

"Explain yourself." Gabriel felt as though he were going mad. He was greatly tempted to begin to sing "Jerusalem, the Golden." Free association was running out of control. Hamlet had pretended madness as a prelude to real madness. Gabriel took a deep breath to steady himself and then merely said, "What about domain decomposition?"

"I was not referring to Professor Bernard Belecki's mathematical exploration, which he names 'domain decomposition.' No. I refer to the domain of the spiritual, which I fear may be about to undergo a certain amount of decomposition. I speak of dogma—Jewish dogma fundamental to the faith, to be exact."

"Your exactness lacks precision, my friend."

"Very well—the dogma of Jew, Christian, and Muslim, fundamentally speaking. I'm afraid I have rather bad news and need to enlist your services. Your concern is the key to the future, the flash drive. My chief interest is in the past. Perpetuity has an interest in both."

Fear for Lucy swept over Gabriel. From Pierre Saad's phone call, Gabriel knew that she not only wore Thom's flash drive but also carried a manuscript that might well undercut Genesis as being literally true. He had been expecting a visitor from Perpetuity, and yet he had hoped not to be so firmly linked to the group.

"But do you really know physics," Gabriel asked the rabbi, "or has some scientist read my article and written you a script?"

"Science was an interest, and so of course I have some skills, still, in math."

"What's gone wrong? Still no flash drive?"

"The Arab who was commissioned to retrieve the flash drive has committed suicide."

"Where?"

"In Amsterdam, as it happens."

"How?"

"He plunged from a high window on Prince Street. Familiar location?"

"To be sure."

For a moment the conversation rested. Gabriel stared at the rabbi, who took an inventory of the furnishings of Gabriel's room. Finally the rabbi said, "Isn't it all rather Sherlockian, these digs? A Persian slipper on the mantel? Surely you don't smoke shag. The Arab had some stomach for violence, but not enough."

With as much regret as irony, Gabriel asked, "Then he dropped the piano on Thom, didn't he?"

"Well, he assisted. But he refused to go after Mrs. Bergmann. First he dallied—we waited patiently for the war to quiet, or at least for a lull. But the battery embedded in the case—"

"The case?" Gabriel asked. "The titanium case for the flash drive?"

"No. The French horn case. You don't seem to understand."

Gabriel pushed the tips of his fingers together and said, "I believe I do see. Perpetuity is two-pronged."

"God has condensed our mission. In one person, our two objectives are united."

"Mrs. Bergmann disappeared."

"You, Professor Plum, failed to relieve her of the flash drive, though you were her companion in Egypt."

"You were speaking of a battery in a case."

"The Genesis codex—"

"I know of the existence of the codex—"

"When Pierre Saad had a French horn case prepared for transporting the codex, we had a global positioning device placed in the case. Its battery has begun to weaken. The Arab should have secured both the codex and the flash drive; he failed. One story is, he committed suicide; another is that he was murdered. In any case, he's out of the picture. Now you must try again to retrieve the flash drive, which interests you, and the codex, which should interest you but apparently does not. I believe you fly rather well. Airplanes."

"Why, for God's sake, did you ever let her carry the case out of Egypt?" Gabriel asked. "And why haven't you gone after her before now, if you knew where she was?"

"We did not expect it would be entrusted to her. Monsieur Pierre Saad was barely acquainted with Mrs. Lucy Bergmann." The rabbi cleared his throat. "And to your second question—the area where her plane went down is a doughnut hole. A little oasis of peace, but totally surrounded by the most vicious warfare the world has ever seen. A little Armageddon, a Christian might say."

Gabriel realized that should he fail to cooperate, two stories about him might be circulated: committed suicide or murdered. He maintained his seat and tried to take comfort in the ordinary nature of his surroundings. "And you want to send me there?"

"Things have quieted down. You and I and an American businessman will visit Eden. I'm having an airport constructed in the wilderness not far from Baghdad."

Gabriel wondered what value had been placed on the life of Lucy Bergmann.

As though he knew Gabriel's thoughts, the rabbi said, "It is not the person of Mrs. Bergmann that interests us, but the things she carries. However, at some point you may need to consider, Professor Plum, whose life you value more—hers or your own."

Gabriel stood up. "How do you know what you know?"

"Eyes. Eyes and ears. Sometimes they ride on donkeys let loose in Egypt; sometimes in the broom handle of a maid; sometimes in the black spot on the back of a tiger's ear in India. There is no place where we of Perpetuity do not watch and listen. We have watched you, friend and rival of Thom Bergmann, many years and anticipated your sympathy to our cause. You did well to inform our office that Mrs. Bergmann had gone missing with a flash drive full of information on perfected spectroscopic methods and extraterrestrial life."

"Why do you call me Thom's rival?" Gabriel knew it was unlikely that he'd ever be permitted to ask such questions again.

"You never wanted his search for extraterrestrial life to succeed. You rejoiced over each sterile planet. You wanted science to affirm that we are special, unique in the universe."

"Are we?"

"In a word? No."

# THE AMERICAN PATIENT

AT THE MOMENT when F. Riley opened his eyes, I was looking at his face. I was not contemplating his closed lids but the set of his jaw, bound shut with strips of orange fabric from the parachute. He had a jutting chin, a fortuitous happenstance because its size had made the binding easier to secure. I worried, though, that the back edge of the binding might be pressing too closely against the patient's larynx. Just as I was about to test the tightness of the bandage with the tip of my finger, I noticed the slow, theatrical rising of his eyelids.

Trying to draw him to consciousness, I shifted my eyes to look steadily into his unfocused gaze. When I smiled a little, he made a quick, surprised sound, like a yelp.

"You'll be all right," I soothed, repeating my litany of reassurance. I reached for one of his hands and held it in both of mine. It was a large and knobby hand. "You'll be all right." Dulled by the fragrance of redwoods, was I hypnotically crooning to myself or to the patient? I took his hand to my lips and kissed the back of it, noticing the red-gold hairs curling sparsely from its paleness. While holding his gaze, I registered the color of his eyes for the first time—a striking reddish brown. Yes, I had occasionally seen such eyes of people with dark red hair.

The soldier gave his little yelp again, but this time it resembled the question Why? and so I quietly explained that my friend Adam and I had seen his plane go down, and his parachute open. Adam had climbed up through the trees and brought him down.

"Your jaw was dislocated and broken, too, so we've immobilized it." I watched him watching my lips forming the words. Without thinking, I brushed my own lips with my fingertips, and then I reached out and touched his lips. His eyes now seemed focused, comprehending. "Your ankle was broken, too."

Tightening his muscles, he lifted his neck and his foot to inspect the splint. Without doubt, he understood my words and their import. Carefully, he lowered his head and closed his eyes for a moment as though the effort had caused him pain.

I said gently, "You're bruised, of course. Probably better just to lie still."

He made a sound in his throat that sounded affirmative. As he drew in rapid breaths, I watched the stenciled name on his shirt pocket—"F. Riley"—rise and fall. Gradually he resumed breathing in a more normal fashion. Slowly he opened his eyes again, and I saw the question in them.

"This *is* real," I said. "You're not dreaming." An unspoken explanation was gathering in my own mind: *This place is where we come for peace and healing. Pieces of the past are here—gardens and trees. We call it Eden.* Instead, sensible words passed from me to him. "You're going to be all right, but you're hurt."

His gaze shifted to my naked breasts.

Instead of replying, I withdrew my hand from his and crossed both arms modestly over my nakedness. "We'll take care of you—my friend and I. I promise."

When Adam brought back saplings and a bouquet of huge leaves for our hut among the redwoods, he also carried a stalk of sugarcane and two oranges clamped between his upper arms and his ribs. Before he began to construct the shelter, he cut off a joint of the sugarcane stalk and, with the tip of his knife, hollowed out the pith to make a narrow cup. I remembered my grandfather, how he had carved away the hard casing and cut off rounds of sugarcane with his jackknife for Grandmother and me. At one end of the segment of cane, Adam left the pith undisturbed to form a plug.

He used the pilot's sharp knife again to cut the oranges into sections and with one hand squeezed their juice into the cup while I held it upright. Pulling F. Riley's lower lip out to make a small pouch, I poured less than a teaspoon of orange juice into the lip-well. "Close your lips tightly and see if you can swallow. Don't try to open your jaw."

When he succeeded, his lips made a small smile. With surprising energy, he gave the thumbs-up signal with both hands. I poured more sips of orange juice into his lip pouch, then waited as he swallowed the juice around his clamped teeth. It was a slow process.

After Adam had constructed a lean-to wide enough to accommodate the three of us lying close together, rain began to fill the air. I folded the parachute and laid it over the pilot. Adam suggested he and I lie down under the shelter on our sides with our backs to Riley. "Human heaters," he said softly. When we were in place, I lay still, staring into the hastily constructed weave of poles and large leaves that made up the side of the lean-to.

In my mind's eye, I also saw us from a detached viewpoint: the soaring tree trunks surrounding a dwarfish hut huddled close to the ground. I pictured the air filled with mist formed by the shattering of raindrops as they fell through the high redwood foliage. Yes, that was the explanation for the moist veil we breathed: the high branches of the redwoods had sieved the rain into the fine mist that blurred vision and made us want to lie still. The mist gentled the scene.

Dampness and new chill impinged on my unprotected skin every time I moved. At that moment, the pilot used his hands to open and spread the parachute on both sides so that Adam and I in our nakedness were covered also by the silky orange fabric.

"Thank you," Adam whispered.

Adam's voice is beautiful, I thought. I heard myself saying back to Adam—to this man who had taken care of me, as well as the pilot—"Thank *you*. He would thank you, too, if he could." I recalled some of the mental patients at the hospital, capable of real kindness and understanding despite their impairment. When I spoke, I had tried to give my own tone the same gentle timbre modeled by Adam. With both hands the pilot reached out to give each of us two quick, comradely pats.

As I grew drowsy, I thought of F. Riley's broken ankle and realized that it would be weeks before we could consider walking out of Eden. Adam would be pleased. Was I? A blip of new thought occurred: perhaps the air force knew F. Riley had ejected; perhaps they would send troops to find him.

As fatigue and sleepiness set in, I mused on how the low roof and sides of the hut kept us somewhat dry, but the open end was letting in enough diffused rain to dampen our feet. In the morning, it would be necessary to unsplint Riley's ankle, dry the bindings or make new ones and tie it up again. We needed to make a mat, I mused sleepily, like a door we could close, once we three were inside for the night.

High overhead, even through the sound of rain, I fancied I could hear the whine of a jet plane.

In the morning, Adam and I were awakened by the startling sound of the man's clenched voice.

"I can talk—just moving—my lips," F. Riley said, "if that's all right?"

I gasped. Already I had assigned him the role of silence.

"What does the 'F' in your name stand for, buddy?" Adam asked, sitting up.

"Freddie. My name is—Freddie Riley." He propped himself up on his elbows.

"Adam Black, from Idaho." Adam reached across his body to shake hands. "And this is Lucy." Without hesitation, my true name came clicking out of Adam's mouth.

"Lucy Bergmann," I added, not moving but opening my eyes to stare again at the weave of branches and wide tropical leaves less than a foot in front of my eyes. Through the cracks in the side of the hut, I could see sunlight slanting from a great height through the redwoods into the grove.

"Lucy, I don't believe I knew your last name," Adam said softly.

Normal, I thought. Adam wants to pass for normal. Now that we are three, he wants to be a part, not alone with God and his delusions. At this point, sometimes patients resisted the gathering strength of the outer world; they insisted on their visions, their unique individuality. Good for Adam, I thought.

"Are you Jewish?" Adam asked.

"My husband was," I answered.

"Was?" Adam asked.

"He's dead."

Through set teeth, Freddie Riley asked, "How long—y'all—been here?"

I heard the Virginia Tidewater in his speech.

"Several months," Adam answered. "I think it's been several months. She came from the sky, too—"

Quickly I cut him off. "How do you feel today, Freddie?" I sat up and glanced at his face—swollen and discolored purple.

"Hungry."

"Breakfast! You stay still," I said to our patient. "Freddie, try to say only what's absolutely necessary for a few days."

"Gotta, latrine."

Adam extended his hand to Riley (who spent a few words to tell us he preferred to be called by his last name) to help him rise. With his arm around Adam's shoulder for support, Riley hobbled from the grove.

To my delight, the milk goat presented herself in the redwoods. When Riley and Adam returned, Riley indicated he wanted to sit with his back propped against the largest tree trunk in the grove. While I carefully held the cane-tube cup in place under one of the goat's teats, Adam quickly and accurately milked her.

"Calcium for your broken bones," I said cheerfully, and knelt down to help my patient drink small sips of the milk. Riley reached out and took the cup from me, eyes a-twinkle. With his other hand, he pulled out his lower lip. Already, I saw, he wanted to be self-sufficient.

After Adam and I mashed fruit on a flat rock, Riley used his finger to place the juicy pulp behind his lower lip. Sometimes he used his finger to push the mash back along his teeth on the unbroken side. Once he got choked, but despite his bound jaw he coughed successfully and continued eating.

Adam explained he would fetch fire from the cliff shelter; then he intended to fish, then cook. To my surprise, he added, "If you two can stand it, save the talk till I get back. I don't want to miss anything."

"Sure." To Riley I said, "It'll be better for your jaw to have as little movement in the area as possible."

His eyes glowing, Riley inched his thumb and index finger together and made the motion of writing; he raised his eyebrows in questioning. His index finger was wet with bits of apple.

"We don't have anything to write with. In fact we don't have anything much at all."

Riley applauded, his eyes making a quick glance up and down my body.

Looking back over his shoulder, Adam said cheerfully, "I'll be back soon."

When Adam returned, he was speeding over the grasslands in full sunshine carrying a blazing pine knot. Close to our sleeping shed, he placed a circle of protective stones, then built a tall, open-sided peaked roof to shelter the flame. Throughout the morning Adam came and went, always hurrying to beat the storm clouds building from the western horizon. When Riley made running motions with two fingers, I explained the need for hurry—rain would likely come again in the late afternoon and on through the night.

Riley let his other hand make a second pair of hurrying legs, and then he flicked the back of his hand to shoo me away so I could help fetch and carry. Surveying my patient, I saw he was pale and in discomfort, but he had no need for constant monitoring. His face was full of life and bounce. I rose and ran after Adam, calling to him to wait. I explained we had a considerate patient, one who had sent me to help.

As we hurried over the grasses, Adam told me about the food he wanted to gather. There was a warmth in his communication, a series of sudden smiles when he looked down at me, more directness in his affect. Not far away I could smell a herd of gazelles grazing.

"You're feeling better, aren't you?" I said to Adam. Even the way he put down his bare feet seemed to suggest he felt himself substantial, defined.

"You think so, don't you?" he remarked.

When I nodded, he simply added, "I do, too."

Why should we discuss Riley or speculate on what his presence implied? Why should I ever mention to Riley that Adam was sometimes visited by delusions? Adam had become competent now—kind, practical, decisive.

At noon, as we walked through the orchard, I stopped at a fig tree. I tore off two of the large, lobed leaves. Remembering Riley's deliberate survey of my body, his eyes looking slowly up and down my torso and legs, I held a fig leaf over each breast and asked Adam if he knew a way to make them stick to my skin.

"Sure." What refreshing enthusiasm he packed into that single syllable. He went on, "Fresh rosin will do it. I'll just nick one of the little pines over there." He went about the task immediately, selecting a place where sap had already oozed out a sticky white crust. I thought of my days with the viola, when I used a dried, hardened cake of this same substance to rosin my bow. Applying the stickiness with one finger, Adam stroked gooey patches on my chest just above each breast. As he finger-painted, he asked in a matter-of-fact way if I'd like a skirt, too. "I could make one, sort of Hawaiian style, out of long grass."

"Would you? Later, when we have time."

"You'll want to be careful around the fire."

He plopped a dollop of goo on my belly below my navel just above my pubic hair and stuck the largest fig leaf there. We both laughed out loud. I was a parody of every modest medieval or Renaissance painting of Eve. Adam maintained his unself-conscious dignity, naked. He smiled down at me, some combination of good humor—which he'd learned already from Riley's manner—and handsome, shy lout, like the comic-book Superman. I liked his combination of sweetness and power; I felt about fourteen instead of forty-odd.

When Riley saw me approaching in my new covering, he made binoculars of his hands and placed them around his eyes. As we walked into the shady redwood grove, he said loudly through his bound-closed jaw, "Shit!" but he shrugged, too, as though to say, "Whatever." We all laughed.

As we cooked fish on the makeshift skillet, we heard thunder revving up in the distance. The goat came by to offer milk again, and I made a cherry sauce for the fish, along with a fricassee of squash. While Adam and I prepared our meal, Riley held out his hand for an apple, and twice again; then he began to juggle the apples higher and higher for our entertainment as we cooked. He made one apple land so that it bounced off the top of Adam's head. Remembering how Adam squirted milk at me, I chuckled to see him get some of his own.

"What did you do, back home?" Adam asked.

"Farm," he answered, and when I asked if that was in Virginia, Riley nodded yes.

"Cows?" Adam asked, and Riley nodded yes.

"Do you have a family in Virginia?" I asked, and again he nodded yes.

"Children?" I inquired.

"Sisters," he said distinctly with only the movements of his lips and little kisses at the beginning and end of the word.

"How many?" I asked.

Riley held up his hand with all five fingers spread.

No wonder, I thought, full of ease and fun, the darling goof-off brother. Till the draft probably prompted him to join the air force. I imagined his sisters, some of them with dark red hair and eyes to match. I was too old to be even the oldest of the Riley siblings.

Riley made a V with his fingers, then drew a line straight down from its point, then lifted his arm on the same side of his body as his broken foot; he placed the V'ed fingers under his armpit.

"Crutch," I said. "You'd like us to make you a crutch."

Riley bent from the waist and touched the orange bindings around the sticks we had prepared for his splint. He made a wrapping-round motion.

"A *padded* crutch," I amended, and he nodded.

As I leaned forward to pass the vegetables to Adam, the fig leaf detached from my right breast and fluttered down onto the rounds of squash.

"Lucy," Riley said to get my attention.

Embarrassed, I glanced at him, but he was not embarrassed. He quickly pointed to the cloth around his jaw, then gestured with both hands across his own shirt as though to form a bandeau.

"Of course," I replied. I took the knife and went to the folded parachute cloth to cut off a proper strip.

Riley made another gesture around his waist and said, "Sarong."

Each night the three of us lay down together, side by side, in the lean-to. The redwood branches and lacy sprays of needles continued to break up the torrential rains that came in the late afternoon and lasted well into the dark of night. Most of the rain was sieved into mist by the time it reached our level on the ground. An occasional plop of water crashed its way down more or less intact as it struck the broad leaves that roofed our lean-to.

The smaller shelter Adam had built over the fire kept it from going out, but occasionally we heard the fire hiss in the darkness when a spear of rain penetrated its covering. Despite the campfire, we were chilled by the moist air, but the layers of parachute fabric spread over the three of us helped to hold in the warmth of our bodies. When daylight came, we were all grateful for our sunny mornings and for the heat of the day that would collect itself by noon.

Over the next few days Riley became adept on his crutch. He could keep up with Adam on excursions, and he went exploring on his own across the grasslands with the grazing herds and through the orchard into the flower and vegetable gardens. Riley discovered the remnants of the mat roofs in the apple tree where Adam and I had our beds before the hard rains came. Because of the rains, our world grew more and more green. Both Adam and I found our world enriched by Riley's enthusiasm.

After a few weeks, Riley was strong enough to hobble with the crutch all the way from the redwoods to the cliff dwelling. He swung himself along up the rocky path with aplomb, though I noted that Adam had apparently come before and cleared the way of loose stones.

When Riley suggested we move from the redwoods to the rocky overhang where we'd be warmer and drier, I found myself hesitating. It was a special place: Adam's retreat, his castle. Vaguely I felt Adam and I had unfinished business at the shelter in the rocks, though we'd only spent one night there together before Riley fell into our lives. Riley quickly registered our hesitation and added in the jerky way his bound jaw dictated, "I mean—if it's—okay. I don't—want—to intrude."

Together both Adam and I said, "It's fine." We would be warmer and drier housed under the great rocky overhang.

"Clan," Riley said, and drew a circle in the air that included all of us.

"We ought to be wearing fur instead of orange nylon," I said.

Adam said anxiously, "We don't kill animals except for fish."

"No," I answered soberly. Would things change if we did? Would things change in any case? Then I added, "You need to wear something orange, Adam. To match Riley and me."

To my own amazement, I untied my bandeau. After all, they'd both seen my breasts before. "Think Tahiti," I said. "Gauguin." I handed the cloth to Adam. "Tear off a strip," I instructed. "It's got too much fabric in it anyhow. I'll make you a headband."

Adam ripped the cloth with a sound like a jet parting the sky, and I neatly folded the fabric so no raw edges showed. When he bent his head down for me to tie the orange strip around it, I commanded, "Kneel." He obediently dropped to one knee. I liked the effect of the slick orange against his dark hair. After I tied the knot at the back of his head, I arranged a few of his black curls to fall over the headband. "The Matriarch of the Clan," I pronounced, "hereby officially names you—"

"Adam," he said, bowing his head again. "My name really is Adam."

When he lifted his head, both the men exchanged a rather sober glance. I wondered if they disapproved of my little ceremony or the title I playfully had given myself. I didn't care. Maybe they thought I was losing my grip on reality.

That night the rain did not come till we were already beneath the shelter and cooking over the fire a large salmon Riley had caught. I luxuriated in the reflection of the undulating flames on the rocks. The stone reflecting the heat made our room in the cliff face almost too warm, but when the rain began, we would be glad for the stored warmth in the massive rocks.

Looking at the neat pile of throwing stones, Riley observed to Adam that he practically had a fort. "Here's your arsenal," Riley said. "The nuclear stockpile."

The term *nuclear* was like a stone striking my forehead. I think Adam felt the same way. We'd asked for no news of the world, but here were the words of war.

"I guess nobody's gone atomic yet," Adam said slowly. "Out there." He lifted his eyes to the horizon.

"At least not by the time I bailed out," Riley answered cheerfully. He picked up a rock from the pile and hurled it forcefully out into the distance. The air shifted with the aftershock of distant thunder.

"What year is it?" Adam asked.

"Twenty-twenty."

"It was 2020 when I took off from Cairo," I said. It amazed me to think that I had known Adam perhaps for only a few months. My hair had grown out now, and I never thought of the scarred skin between my shoulder blades. We had entered a peaceful and timeless dreamworld. Even the rumbles of thunder sounded benign, and the torrents of rain, another of which would soon erupt, were obviously a needed part of sustaining life for the flora and fauna of Eden.

"Did we create this," I asked them, "or did it create us?"

Riley announced, "I want—to take off—my jaw bindings."

"Feels ready?" Adam asked.

Riley nodded and began to untie his jaw.

"Don't open wide," I cautioned. "Be really careful."

With urgent fingers, Riley untied the knots on top of his head and let the streamers fall to the ground. "Free—at—last," he said slowly and obediently as though his jaw were still bound. Suddenly emotional, Riley swallowed and turned away from us to regain his composure. It was his endearing style to take things in stride, to be jovial and upbeat.

A gust of wind blew in a sprinkling of rain, and then the sky split with a torrential rainfall. Adam got up to put dry logs on the fire.

"I wished for salmon," Riley said. "It was in a dream, but now it's happened."

Though Riley seemed a bit spooked by the satisfaction of his wish, Adam and I had come to take the fulfillment of our wishes for granted. What we wanted here, we could have. Or maybe it was that here we only wanted what we could very likely have. Now I knew I wanted Adam, and it seemed very likely that I could have him.

I wished that I had some milk to follow the salmon and squash. My eyes fell on the globe of a red tomato, and I considered biting into it for its juice. Having milk would be almost as good as ice cream, I thought. Vanilla, anyway.

Suddenly Adam was standing in front of me with a clay jug in his hands. "Look," he said, "I made it out of river clay and fired it hard. Days ago." The jug was a round globe with a very wide neck. "You can get your hand down in it to swab it out." His vessel was practical as well as beautiful. The clay had been fired a purplish black, and its color and shape suggested an artful version of an eggplant. I remembered Adam had spoken of wanting to draw.

"You even made a lid," I said. I thought the piece was really quite lovely. The lid had a knob on it for easy grasping. "You could make a whole set," I said, "if you wanted to." Then I asked, "What's in it?"

"Milk. I thought we might all enjoy some goat milk."

I smiled. So it was my destiny to have what I wanted. At least in Eden.

By the time we finished eating and drinking, a curtain of rain hung all across the opening, and we watched the reflected firelight flash gold and silver and bronze across it. The water curtain fell straight and hard for over an hour, then in rivulets and trickles from the runoffs down the rocky slope above us. It was good to have all the warm, dry space around us instead of the close quarters of the damp lean-to. As the night storm passed, Adam occasionally added more wood to the fire, and our talk, too, flared up and then died down in fits and starts.

When I had spent nights with Janet and Margarita Stimson, or with my friend Nancy, it had been like this. Anyone could speak, but gradually, in the most natural way, the restful silences began. A few last water droplets clung to the rock lintel and dropped singly, elongating as they fell. The only curtain across the large open side of the overhang was the soft darkness.

I could easily imagine the landscape now obscured by the night, how in the morning the sunshine would flood the valley. In the far distance, we would see the green spires of the redwood grove we had formerly inhabited. How strange that step by step we had been able to come from there to here, leaving something of ourselves behind.

But there was Riley now, in front of me. His hair had grown out—dark red, as I'd expected, made mahogany by the fire glow. His face was almost free of bruises and swelling.

"I forgot to tell you, Lucy," he said. "I crutched myself down to the beach."

"It must have been hard," I answered, "with the crutch sinking in the sand."

"Not too hard," he replied. "I wanted to see what was left of your plane."

"Not much," I said.

"That plane had sort of a little glove compartment," he went on. "I pried it open with one of the broken struts."

"And?"

"A piece of needlepoint. My sisters used to do needlepoint and crewel, cross-stitch—that sort of thing. There were needles, yarn, and thread."

"Really?" I pictured the somewhat frail circle of an embroidery hoop, its ends connected with a metal screw. I thought of holding a loose, floppy skein of six-ply embroidery thread, how one could pull the plies apart into two sections of three threads each. My grandmother had done that, stitching and telling Bible stories all at once. I recalled Arielle Saad—perhaps crewel or cross-stitch had been a hobby for her.

"What was the picture?" I asked Riley, brother of many sisters. "The image on the canvas?"

"It was a big jar. Kind of a fountain."

At once I vividly recalled how I had admired the fountain at Nag Hammadi. The dazzling sunlight and the heat. In a distant life, I had stood in front of a museum dedicated to texts found in a jar on the slopes of Nag Hammadi in 1945.

"When the plane came down," I said slowly, gathering the attention of both Adam and Riley before I went on, "I was transporting some ancient texts. For friends." I envisioned myself following Arielle, wearing sunglasses, through the streets of the little town, and my hurrying to catch up whenever she disappeared around a corner. I envisioned Arielle's father, in the white room beyond the pit of baby crocodiles, the man sitting at the rough table, a crutch leaning nearby, the Bible open before him on the table. His tawny lion eyes gaze at me.

"The texts I carried—I was smuggling them, really—were housed in a reinforced case, like a French horn case. Before I crashed, I opened the plane door and threw out the case. If you see something like that—it might have broken open when it hit—let me know. It might have caught in a tree, or even landed in the water." I thought of the river, though I had never considered that possibility before. There had been so much land beneath me, an endless green carpet, trees, grassland. And then the sparkling ocean, or something like an ocean. "It's precious. What's inside. Probably irreplaceable." My sentences had become staccato, like Riley's when his jaw was bound and he could say only a fraction of what was in his mind.

"Why are you wearing a flash drive?" Riley asked.

"A memory stick. It belonged to my husband." It represents his mind, I thought but did not say.

I sighed and looked up and around at the sheltering overhang and the rock walls on three sides that held the three of us. *Us* used to be Thom and me. Now he had been replaced with the two of them. Only I was the same. Now *us* was Adam and Riley and me. No one asked me questions about my husband. Not even his name.

I wanted to say, "My husband was the first person on Earth to discover the location of extraterrestrial life." For a moment, I burned with the desire to emblazon Thom's name on history. But this was Eden, and we were all caught in its web of non-time. History was not just insignificant but irrelevant. What mattered was *here* and *now.*

I had spent the day bringing armloads of ferns to the cave so that each of us would have a fresh, soft bed, piled nearly a foot high. There would be no need for a large fire tonight. I placed my bed in the middle, as far back in the crescent-shaped room as possible, and each of theirs as far away on both sides, as near the tips of the crescent's bow, as I could make them. I had some idea of providing private space after our cramped quarters in the lean-to. Having had our fill of slow chatting and unasked questions, we retired to our pallets.

I heard the tapped placing of the tip of Riley's crutch—wood on stone—as he moved to the perimeter. When Adam put his bare knee in the midst of his ferns, they made a slight creaking. I heard him settle his body and knew he was lying on his back, as he always did, though later he would be rolling around first to one side, then to another. In the lean-to, he had rotated in place, on the other side of Riley.

Hesitating, I stood at the side of my pallet, looking outward. Such a sense of space in our cavity—the ceiling high above us, the front of the shelter entirely open to the night and to the landscape below. I wished for stars, but there were no pinpricks of light. From the embers of the small fire, my peripheral vision caught the motion of Riley laying his crutch down beside his bed, bending over to catch his weight on the palms of both hands, then gracefully pivoting on one arm so that he sat, somewhat heavily. His knee was bent, and he put no weight on his splinted ankle.

I had the impulse to kneel beside my bed and pray, but instead I stared at the fire. I thought of a prayer I had sung when I was a child, much to the approval of my parents: *A little star creeps over the hill / When woods are dark and birds are still. / The children fold their hands in prayer / And the love of God is everywhere.* Only there was no little star. The night was utterly dark. Of course I could build up the fire, if I liked, but I thought it was time to let it die.

Adam said enigmatically, "When I have time, I'll make a flute."

Both Riley and I had sunk too far into our own thoughts to respond with a question.

I lay down and let my body suffer the softness to envelop me. "Suffer the little children to come unto me"—that was what Jesus had said, and for the first time I loved the word *suffer,* meaning "to allow," and I thought how natural it was to allow my body to enjoy the softness of the ferns I had gathered. My weight released the faint odor of cinnamon from the fern fronds. But I did not close my eyes. First I turned my head to stare again out at the unchanging blackness. I liked the way the campfire coals continued to glow between me and the curtain of dark, whether we were all sitting around it or not. Then I turned my head to look at the back wall of rock. It was built in strata, some reddish, some more golden, some dark gray. My life, too, was laid down in strata. Perhaps each layer was a decade, though the divisions were not quite so neat as intervals of ten years might suggest.

"I shouldn't have made the beds so far apart," I said into their silence. My voice sounded plaintive.

Neither of them answered. If the beds had been closer together, we might have chatted longer against the darkness. The regret I had voiced was a spontaneous utterance against the desolation I suddenly felt.

There was childhood with my parents in their apartment, and then their leaving for Japan as missionaries and my moving in with my grandmother and grandfather in the bungalow in Memphis when I was nine, and then the years of powerful childhood growing up with the Stimson sisters, how I practiced the viola, and my grandfather's death, then the binge of studying psychology and graduation from high school. There was the move to Iowa City, my quick engagement as an undergraduate to Thom Bergmann, our happiness as I finished my degrees; our travel and our meaningful work, his international connections. A decade with Thom; the loss of my grandmother; another decade with Thom. The loss of Thom. Again I saw the flap of the black wing of the falling piano, felt the hardness of the pavement under my thin shoe soles as I ran down Prince Street toward the Blue Tulip Café. *Igtiyal.* What did it matter? Thom was dead. What did the manner of his dying have to say about the nature of his life?

*Everything.*

What did my own survival tell me since I had come to dwell in this most accommodating of places?

*That I knew nothing of who I was.* And even less of Thom. *Good-bye, Thom.*

Of Adam and Riley?

These two men, one impaired of mind, one of body? But those conditions would pass, for each of them—I was sure of it. I was slipping into sleep. For each of us, it was his or her own dream story that would matter. Each was like Earth's consciousness before Copernicus; each was the center of his or her universe, and there seemed no way for the center to move beyond the infinite arms of its radii. Sleep embraced me. Let all else circle round me. The unconscious breezes of memory and imagination toyed with the kite of my already dreaming mind. Thom lifted his arm and scattered the stars in the firmament. He breathed the deep breaths of passion.

Riley's breath said sleep had claimed him. Then I floated in my dream to Adam and said, "Love me." And we did. After we had made love, he disappeared, and I drifted home to my pallet and its scent of cinnamon. I rose again and wafted to Riley. Crossing the stone floor of the cave, my bare feet, though ghostly and immaterial, felt the slight variations in the rock, the places that were cracked, and those that seemed smooth and without blemish. Passing the dying fire, I felt warmth underfoot lingering in the rock. I moved more quietly than the spirit of darkness. When I reached Riley, I slumped to my knees and whispered into his ear, "Love me." But I awoke too soon, shocked at how thoroughly I had been inhabited by desire.

In the morning, we all three woke up at the same time and sat up on our wilted fern beds.

Both Adam and Riley breathed deeply, and so did I. In unison, they looked at me and said, "What did you dream?"

I glanced at them and kept my secret. Then a piece of another dream visited me. "Toward morning, I dreamed of the sound of an airplane engine," I told them. "And of flying on and on, from Nag Hammadi to Cairo. It was a memory dream. There was a Muslim girl, Arielle, with me, a young woman, really pretty, at the controls, Egyptian, with shoulder-length black hair. She probably left the needlepoint work in the Cub. The engine was loud and grinding, like teeth spitting and grinding in sleep."

"Anything else?" Riley asked. "I sometimes used to grind my teeth."

I hesitated. There had been something else. "I dreamed . . . several dreams . . . a monkey crouched beside my bed. A large monkey, with a hairy head and a naked body, like a boy. Like an incubus."

"Not very likely," Riley said. "I mean not with Adam and me posted like two sentries at either end of this cave or shelter or whatever you call it."

"I've called it 'The Cave of Artemis,'" Adam said.

"Why?" I asked.

"It's bow-shaped. And the first night I was here, there was a crescent moon smiling at me. Like the first night . . . on the beach."

"When you first came here?" I asked gently.

He just nodded. His face became blank and still. He turned away.

Finally I said, "Let's gather breakfast."

Looking back, I'm unsure of what happened that night. Perhaps we all dreamed the same dream. It didn't matter. We were the same people as before. Perhaps closer.

Each of us sniffed the air once, as though we had detected the odor of sex.

# THE INCUBUS

EVERY DAY THE rains came later and lasted for a shorter period of time. One morning we saw no rain clouds at all gathering on the western horizon. The sun shone with special brilliance. Through the day only a few small, puffy clouds floated by as though they were lost sailing ships abandoned by the fleet. In the garden, in response to the extra warmth and light, roses of every color bloomed.

Adam proposed that we sleep in the orchard again, under the apple trees, that we weave new mats to sleep on and others for grassy roofs just over the beds. I proposed to gather roses—there was such an abundance of them—to wreath our beds. I think we all longed to situate ourselves in the center of the great openness that spread out around our orchard.

The change in the weather changed Riley's mood, too; feeling optimistic, he announced he would unbind his ankle. "I'll still use the crutch," he said. "At least at first."

"Don't waste the bindings," I instructed, but added whimsically, "You can tie them on the branches of your apple tree for decoration."

"You all know we *could* build ourselves something more substantial, dontcha?" Riley said, but neither Adam nor I answered.

Finally I said, "When your ankle is strong enough, we should leave."

"Why?" Adam asked. His head swiveled quickly to give me a piercing glance.

"I want to find the French horn case. People are waiting for me to deliver it. Help me find it, will you? Both of you." And I wanted the world to know of Thom's discovery.

"Do you know what's in it?" Riley asked of the French horn case.

"Yes. I think so."

"What?" Adam asked sharply.

"Something about the book of Genesis—an alternate version."

That night, after we cooked fish and roasted apples out in the open and let the small campfire burn on, not rain but warm breezes blew over us. In our new camp in the orchard, close to the gardens and the plains, I smelled the aroma of distant desert, dry and slightly dusty, but with the scent of roses. Having harvested their blooms, I had inscribed our three pallets with borders of red, white, and yellow.

I dreamed again that I was in an airplane, but this time it was a big one. It was night, and we—a huge planeful of people—were drifting down for a landing. When I glanced back at the rows of seats, I saw the Stimson sisters drinking tomato juice, pouring it from the spout of a small silver teapot, their wedding present when Thom and I had married. On both sides of the plane, out the windows, was New York; a vast number of lights twinkled and glimmered at the bottom of a dark transparent ocean. I knew I would see Thom when I landed, and there *was* Thom waiting for me behind the security gate. "*Igtiyal*," he said, and goosed me in the ribs.

I woke up to the sound of struggle, fighting, with Riley cursing and yelling, "You devil."

Adam sprang from his pallet and ran toward the struggle, calling to me to bring a light. Without hesitation, I pushed the end of a dry pine stick into the embers, waited a moment for it to flare up, and then hurried toward them.

Holding the light above my head, I saw in its glow a silhouette, a dark blob with three parts moving together and then away to become individuals. Riley rolled away, and Adam held a third something, person? He forced the animal or person—someone small—against the trunk of an apple tree. Reaching up, Adam jerked down one of the streamers from the tree above Riley's bed. Quickly Riley secured whatever man or beast it was to the trunk. Still the person or baboon kicked his feet, but Adam stood out of reach of his thrashing, and Riley knelt at one side.

When I got closer, my taper illumined dark splotches on Riley's shirt and dark smears around his mouth. His eyes were wide, terrified and outraged.

"He tried to make me eat something!" Riley exclaimed. "It's still in his hand."

Adam continued to kneel beside the boy—for the beast was a boy with a long and shaggy head of hair—who kicked to no avail all the harder. As I approached, and my firebrand brightened the scene, I could see color. Riley's face was smeared with blood.

Quickly Adam took the light and held it close to the boy's face. His bowed head was a shock of straight black hair that curtained his features.

"Sit on his legs, Riley," Adam said, and Riley moved over—careful of his incompletely healed ankle, I noticed. His weight was enough to quiet the struggling legs of the boy, who was small. I thought him about twelve or thirteen. His chest was bare and hairless, but hair straggled from his armpits. Like Adam, he wore no clothing. The boy's pubis was shockingly dark with hairy growth.

Holding the lighted stick well back, with his other hand, Adam gently gathered the hair from around the boy's face. Suddenly Adam sprang back.

"I know him."

I was stunned.

Adam handed the torch to me, and I moved closer as he knelt down beside the boy.

"Hello," Adam said, carefully and quietly.

The boy glared at him.

"I remember you," Adam said gently. "You took care of me. When they threw me out of the truck, you fed me." He stopped and touched Riley's shoulder. "My friend was trying to take care of you. He was trying to feed you."

"Not goddamn likely," Riley said, as I stared at the blood smeared on his face.

"He doesn't understand us, of course," Adam said. He held out both his hands in front of the boy. Slowly he opened one of his hands and brought it to his own mouth to mimic eating, then pointed at the boy and then at himself. "You fed me," he said, pointing again at the boy and then himself, and then making the gesture of eating. "You fed me," he said again. "Thank you."

Adam stood up. "Lucy, do we have anything left we could offer him to eat?"

"No," I answered.

"We have to untie him," Adam said, "and let him go."

"What in God's name was he trying to stuff down my gullet?" Riley asked. He rolled off the boy's legs.

Slowly the boy flexed his knobby knees. Like a frightened animal, he began to pant. Adam went behind him and untied his hands. The boy jumped up, his chest heaving. With his fists still clenched, he parted his own unruly hair with a finger from each hand and looked first at Riley, defiantly, and then at Adam, sullenly. He only stood as high as their shoulders, about my height. To him, the two men must have looked like giants. One of the boy's clenched fists was oozing blood.

Adam opened his own hand and pointed to the boy's hand.

Slowly the boy opened his hand.

"What the devil is that?" Riley said.

At first, I thought the boy held a mouse, skinned, bloody, and raw. When I looked at Adam, I thought he might be about to vomit. He averted his eyes, gagged, then made himself look again.

"It's the heart of a lamb," Adam said softly.

The boy started to move away, but he looked back at Adam and moved his head in a gesture that surely meant we, at least Adam, were to follow him. The boy was slight, but his body looked wiry and agile. Though he moved quickly, like a purposeful animal, the boy was not running away. Adam followed closely behind him. I followed slowly, realizing Riley had picked up his crutch and was trying to join us.

The wild boy led us into the garden, past the vegetables and the iris, to the roses, the garden in the heart of the garden. On the ground, a woolly lamb lay on its back. The white woolly arms and legs were stretched out and pegged to the ground with sticks. Its bloody chest, slit open, was an empty cavity.

Adam sank down before the lamb, covered his face with his large hand, and wept.

The boy slid back into the darkness, as though it had been opened for him, and disappeared into its black pocket.

I knelt beside Adam and put my arm across his broad shoulders. He seemed felled by grief.

"It's all right, Adam," I said. "We're all right."

On the other side, Riley knocked against Adam's arm with the side of his crutch. "Hey, man," Riley said, "what kind of damn craziness is this, huh?"

I could feel Adam gathering himself together. Still kneeling, he reached over for a moment and rested his hand on my thigh. I placed my hand on top of his and pressed his hand firmly against my leg.

"How'd you know that—that damn heart come from a lamb?" Riley asked.

"I recognized it." Adam rose from his knees. "We raised sheep in Idaho." He put his hand on my shoulder to steady himself. All the way back, he kept his hand on my shoulder, as though I were a trusted crutch, though the weight on me was only that of his hand.

When we returned to the orchard, Adam said that he and Riley would move their mats to sleep next to me.

"You don't think he's dangerous, do you?" Riley asked.

"I don't know," Adam said. "He saved my life."

"I guess he was trying to help me, too? Like a bat out of hell, he just swoops down on me trying to stuff a goddamn heart in my mouth." Riley clutched his throat and spat. "Makes me want to puke."

Adam said nothing.

—

In the morning, I heard Riley asking Adam if he thought the boy had any kind of weapon.

"I wouldn't think so," Adam answered.

"Then how'd he get the heart out of the lamb?"

"He crushed the breastbone with a large rock. Then he used another rock to drive a broken stick into the chest. Then he pulled the heart out with his fingers." Adam shifted his gaze from Riley to me. "It was a little lamb. Not even half grown."

Adam took a strip of orange fabric nearly two feet wide and wrapped it around his waist and hips to make a short sarong. With another strip, he made a belt for himself and tied the handle of Riley's military knife in a knot of the belt.

We buried the lamb among the yellow rosebushes. Lacking a shovel, we found digging hard work, a matter of finding flat stones to scrape aside the soil.

Because of that grotesque night, we stood within sight of one another on the banks of the river while we fished, and we moved together as a group to gather wood to replenish the fire. "I want a lot of wood," Adam said. "Enough for a bonfire."

All the following day we stayed close together and kept an eye out for what I thought of as the feral boy, but no one saw anything of him. It was a sad day, though the powerful sun brightened every gesture and move we made. With not a single cloud to shield us, the unremitting sun almost made me nauseous. All day I hoped to see the French horn case. Yet when I mistook a black, humped rock beside the river for the bell curve of the case, it seemed a malignant thing. I wondered where the boy had taken shelter during the torrential rains. Had he found a cave? Or visited ours? I remembered my dream of someone like him hovering over me.

That night, after we lay down under the still-full moon, a sound came from the distance that made the air shake and creak. The return of thunder, I surmised, or the shudder of a volcano, but soon I realized it was only lions roaring from the grassland. Because the moon was so bright, perhaps the male lions were urging the females to hunt by its light. I had never seen them hunt by any light, or even found a carcass from a kill. Then I heard a new sound from the plain, a persistent, drumming thunder.

"The zebras are running," Adam said, "hunted by the lions." As the frenzied drumming grew nearer, he rose and built up the fire, till the flames were almost as tall as he. "Come stand behind the fire," Adam told us.

"Did you know they would panic?" I asked. "Is that why you wanted lots of firewood?"

"I didn't know. Something just told me to stock up. To provide."

"Like your rock pile, huh?" Riley commented.

Before Riley came, Adam would have said God had told him what to do. Now he was less extravagant. There is a grammar of vividness, I thought, a persuasive rhetoric. What we can see or imagine, we can convince ourselves to believe.

With increasing volume, the running of the hooves came closer. The herd was veering toward us. The zebras were crossing the grassland, now through the garden, and now toward the apple orchard. Our wall of darkness was shattered by white stripes on their emerging faces, then the black-and-white necks and running shoulders of the zebras. They wouldn't plunge through the bonfire, I felt sure, but Adam reached out both arms and drew Riley and me close against him so that we were all squarely behind the protective flames.

The striped flanks of zebras rushed past us on both sides. In their springing and leaping, the black and white moved in a zigzagging design, disorienting and frightening. The undulating pattern confused our eyes, while the thunder of their running baffled our ears. I wondered if the lions, too, would run past. I thought I saw tawny sides of lionesses streaking fast and low past the straight rows of palm trees. Finally only the stragglers of the zebra herd, their sides heaving, were passing the bonfire. I turned around to watch their striped hindquarters disappearing into the darkness, and finally the tassels on the ends of their ropy tails.

"Before tomorrow night we'll move back to the cave," Adam said.

Gradually the din of hoofbeats diminished, and Adam laid no more wood on the flames. Gradually, I let go of the tension in my body. When any of the three of us glanced at another, there was a faint smiling in the fire glow. We were survivors. Then, from far away, there was a sound like growling, a faint recapitulation, and I thought of Beethoven's Symphony no. 6, how after the intensity of the storm has passed, the composer lets a few diminuendo growls from the kettledrums precede the return of harmony. When I sat beside Thom in the concert hall, I had imaged a gathering of villagers coming out to make merry when safety replaced the receding storm. Maybe we would hear the sound of piping, even in Mesopotamia, with a village congregating for a country dance. Had Adam said he would fashion a flute? Such a small village were we—only three. Four if I counted the feral boy.

As soon as dawn came, the air filled with birds and insects on the move. First the green parrots burst out of the tops of the palm trees as though the leaves themselves had taken sudden flight. Clusters of monarch butterflies and then their imitators, the viceroys, rose up out of milkweed and joe-pye weed at the edge of the garden, and then the majestic tiger swallowtails lifted themselves from the garden phlox and the modest little gray hairstreaks from the low red clover. Locusts began to whir around, and a flock of crows swooped down to feed on them.

When the three of us visited the garden, we saw that the beds were pockmarked by the curved hooves of the zebras and the cloven hooves of ungulates. The rosebushes were battered to the ground. The flower garden was devastated, and the stems of the tomato and squash plants were also broken and mangled. Occasionally a pomegranate, like a broken jewel box, had been smashed and lay on the ground with its glistening seeds exposed. Cardinals came to peck at them.

I thought of how medieval gardens were often enclosed by wooden fences to protect them from the surrounding animals. Now, since the zebra stampede, I saw the necessity of dividing garden from wilderness, something that previously had seemed unnecessarily exclusive to me. I thought that someday I would like to make a medieval garden, if I moved from New York to some more peaceful place, the South perhaps, or back to Iowa and the Midwest.

The men regarded the ruined garden with less distress than I. There was Adam, newly clothed for the new day, with his short sarong around his waist and thighs, but I knew his body so well, it was as though he still stood open and nude before me. I noted his knife belt and his headband. The orange referenced by way of contrast his black wavy hair. There was Riley, with his lengthening red hair, who had never taken off his camouflage uniform of sage and sand, already moving with his crutch toward the rock shelter.

Would the garden recover? Not during our tenure, I thought.

When we were resettled at the shelter in the cliff, I felt disinclined to go down at all. I left it to Adam and Riley to fish and to gather fallen vegetables, fruit, and nuts, firewood and ferns for our beds. They used squares of parachute fabric to carry home the harvest, like sheets tied for bundling laundry.

After a few days in the cave, still not wanting to go down, I decided to entertain myself by sewing. Because Riley's foot gave him some trouble, even walking with the crutch, I asked Adam to visit the beach and to bring back the yarn and needles Riley had found in the dash compartment of the Cub.

Sitting on a benchlike slab of rock near the wide mouth of the overhang, I set about stitching up clothes I had envisioned—a full skirt with its drawstring waistband, and a more proper blouse, it, too, with a drawstring neck and full sleeves gathered just above the elbow into soft puffs. The days grew warmer as I sewed, and really the bandeau was a more suitable top, but I wanted to be making something congruent with our changing circumstances.

I think I knew even then that we must prepare to leave our Eden. With the sacrifice of the little lamb and the presence of the feral boy, violence had entered our haven. It was time to go, with or without the sacred codex. At least I had Thom's flash drive. The boundary between our peaceful paradise and the violent world had turned out to be imaginary. I knew these things, and yet the thought occurred to me that I might teach the boy to talk, to communicate, to express himself, and in that ability—if we only understood each other better—a measure of safety for all might be redeemed.

Often as I glanced out from the overhang at the surrounding forest, I imagined where Adam might be—under what tree, stooping to gather pecans or walnuts, fishing with a line. In my mind I made pictures of paradise to take with me when we left. Sometimes I merely stared at the beautiful world, unenhanced by any artifice save the vague boundaries implied by the periphery of my vision; I memorized the vast, wild landscape all the way to the straight-line horizon of ocean stretching across the gap between hills. I rarely imagined that the two men were together, but sometimes because of the heat I imagined the three of us, naked, refreshing ourselves by splashing in the stream. At odd, startling moments, sharp as a sudden thorn, involuntary memory presented the splayed lamb and its bloody, vacant chest. I thought of Rembrandt's painting of a splayed ox, and I thought of Adam's desire to draw and paint. I hoped he would find other subjects for art.

One night around the dinner campfire, Adam told us he had met the feral boy in the woods. "He watches us," Adam said. "He noticed Riley's knife and how I use it to peel sugarcane. He came to me and put his hand on the knife. He wanted me to give it to him."

"I hope you didn't," Riley remarked as he glanced to see if the knife still hung from Adam's sash.

"No. But I showed him how to chip away at a likely piece of stone. How to flake the chert with another rock."

"He'll make a stone knife," Riley said.

"I expect so."

Before they left the overhang the next day, Adam tried to give the knife back to Riley, but he refused. "It's better off in your hands," Riley said as though Adam were his revered older brother. With a quick grin, Riley added, "I'm going to rob a beehive today. I'll take one of your pottery jars, if you don't mind, to collect honey."

Neither of the men urged me to come down with them.

I was surprised when sunset had pinked the sky, and neither Riley nor Adam had returned. I didn't mind because I had only the hemming of the skirt left to finish to complete my outfit. I had decided on a balloon hem for the skirt, to echo the puffs of the sleeves. A regular hem with its definite edge would be too stark. It made me smile to think I would somewhat resemble a pumpkin—probably the vegetable look was not haute couture this year in Paris. Nor the color orange. It seems strange now, looking back, that an interest in the aesthetics of clothing began in the wilderness for me, a woman who had always been rather indifferent to fashion.

It had been a sweltering day, even in the shade of the overhang. I could almost taste the sweetness of the honey Riley intended to bring home, and I lined up halves of pecans and walnuts on a stone for later honey-dipping. Little pieces of candy, they'd be. I set the stone closer to the fire to warm and returned to my sewing, enjoying the slick feel of the needle in my fingers. If only we had chocolate to add to nutmeats and honey—

Suddenly I realized I couldn't see well. I brought the fabric up closer to my eyes and then glanced into the distance. Only the last blush of sunset hung in the sky. A wave of worry washed over me, and I set aside my sewing. I built up the fire to be a welcoming beacon and moved the heavy stone with its array of nutmeats closer to the fire. On one of the shallow clay bowls Adam had fashioned, I arranged a pyramid of various fruits.

Finally, after I put on my new outfit, there was nothing else to do. I sat still and studied the darkening landscape before me—how the loss of light shaded the vastness and melded the varieties of trees and spaces. Eventually I began to eat the warmed nuts and selected a yellow-green pear to bite into; I let myself idly wish for a good Stilton cheese as a complement. I thought of Thom, how on the airplane flying to Amsterdam we had been surprised when the flight attendant served Stilton and pears in a basket and a small carafe of sauvignon blanc. I saw Thom's face again, his springy graying curls, his thick glasses. His restless leg syndrome had set in, and he had been shifting uncomfortably in his seat until the little picnic basket of cheese, fruit, and wine was presented. Such a large man, and, I realized, he had just been beginning to put on weight.

How difficult would it be to make cheese?

Probably Adam had some idea about how to do it. Odd, how he never suggested projects for other people, though he had an endless supply of ideas for himself. I enjoyed thinking of the perfection of Adam's body and of Riley's freckled grin. The more he stayed in the sun, the more freckled Riley became. And boyish, too. This so-called Eden was a place where we could revert to something we hadn't finished being.

In high school, with Janet Stimson, I had sewn a lot, though Janet was the better seamstress. I remembered a plaid jumper I'd made with six gores—in rich fall browns and golds, a touch of red stripe—with suspenders. I had sewn the whole thing together on my grandmother's ancient treadle sewing machine before I showed it to Janet, who then pointed out, or rather asked, why I hadn't matched the plaids. My homemade jumper was all higgledy-piggledy. Still the colors were nice, and I sometimes wore it. Autumn leaves, I had thought; fall is a jumble of color, not lined up in neat stacks and rows.

There was Adam.

In one hand, he carried a pair of neatly folded men's trousers, and he was wearing a shirt, unbuttoned like a jacket with the tail hanging loosely over his short orange sarong. It was Riley's shirt, and when Adam came nearer, I read the label above the pocket: "F. Riley." As Adam came to me he held out his arms, his face a mask of misery. Automatically, I rose and walked into his arms. With one hand he held my cheek against his bare chest. The pad of folded trousers pressed like a flat cushion against my back, against the burn scar.

"Lucy," he said. I heard him swallow. "Lucy, I had to bury Riley today."

"My God," I said. I swayed and would have fallen but Adam supported me, led me to sit down. "What do you mean?" I was engulfed with horror. It couldn't be true. This moment wasn't real. I had never imagined this.

"The boy killed him," Adam said.

"Why! Why would he?"

Adam shrugged and shook his head. "The boy must have dropped down, out of an acacia tree. He must have waited till Riley hobbled along under the tree, and then dropped down like a panther onto his shoulders."

"But Riley was strong. The boy was just a boy."

"His weight would have taken Riley down—his weak ankle—and . . . And I think he cut Riley's throat before they hit the ground."

"I want to see Riley."

"I buried him. That wasn't all the boy did. He . . . he defaced him." Adam began to weep. "And . . . and he cut out—"

"Stop," I cried out. "Stop."

My God! I thought of the Aztec sacrifices.

Adam took his arm away from me, covered his eyes with both hands, and sobbed into the folded trousers. As he gasped and wept, he said he shouldn't have let Riley go alone. He said he shouldn't have shown the boy how to make a knife. He asked what did it mean to save Riley, if he hadn't been able to save him, finally. Incoherently, he said these things many times, that Riley was like his younger brother Fred. That Fred had saved him once . . . that Riley was innocent. That the war, the war, the war, the war—and here he began to slide into incoherence. Finally he stood up and said that we must leave.

"The cliff?"

"The whole garden. Everything here. We have to leave."

"Yes," I agreed. "We'll go in the morning." I thought about the French horn case, but I said nothing.

Nothing—certainly no message hidden in a bottle—was worth staying here. The peace was broken. It was violence, murder—*igtiyal*—not knowledge, that blighted Eden. The Bible story was rotten at the core, truly wrong on that score. Knowledge, creativity, were two keys to salvation; killing was the hermaphroditic mother and father of all sins. I pictured the slender savage boy dropping down, a chipped stone blade in his teeth, onto freckle-faced Riley's shoulders and back—Cain slaying his brother Abel.

"I'll give it to you now," Adam said, but I couldn't think what he might mean. Riley's heart?

Adam turned to the pile of stones. He picked up one and hurled it as hard as he could into the trees below. We heard it strike among the leaves and fall. Because Riley is murdered, I thought, he wants to stone the world. It was dark, and he was exhausted, but one after another, Adam hard-hurled rocks. They thunked and bounced and crashed with distinctive impacts into leaves and grass, against boulders and tree trunks. With a degree of awe, I watched Adam's fluid power in the cocking and release of his body as he hurled stones from his arsenal till the pile was diminished, and I saw what they had concealed. He heaved a sigh and turned toward me. There was the hard black case of what might have housed a French horn.

Panting, he sighed again.

"You hid it," I said slowly. I made my voice explanatory, not accusing. "Because you didn't want me to leave."

With averted eyes, Adam slightly nodded.

"I understand."

When he raised his eyes, I saw shame, sorrow, repentance, trust—and hope. That sweet sincere mingling of trust and hope—where had I seen it before? In the tawny eyes of Pierre Saad, when, seated in the whitewashed room, he had lifted his eyes from the Bible, read the opening verses of Genesis, looked at me, and asked for my help.

And so, now, because Adam repented of his theft, I was to have another chance to deliver the sacred texts. I was to have another chance to salvage failure. I would be able to bring back something valuable to Pierre Saad, should Adam and I find a path back to the world.

"Come sit by the fire," I said, in a voice that seemed unreal. "You've had nothing to eat. I ate up all the nuts, but we have fruit, many kinds of fruit you can eat."

Like a child, he did as he was told. I handed him the earthy clay bowl he had made filled with the medley of fruit—apples, pears, bananas, oranges, quince, pomegranate. We were both very tired.

"Why is there no blood on Riley's shirt?" I suddenly asked. "What about the trousers?"

"Riley had taken off his clothes before the attack. The trousers were folded, just as they are now." Adam's sentences moved by fits and starts. "He had hung the shirt on a thornbush. He was wearing only his underwear."

For a long time the words hung in the rock room.

"Why?" I finally asked.

"Maybe he wanted to wash his clothes."

Was I thinking or speaking? Lull, lull, lullaby. It was a place for lulling that I wanted to create. For myself. For Adam. How to relieve his anguish? Could peace be fashioned like a bowl from river mud?

*Put your head in my lap, Adam. Cry. Sob. Curse. Try to rest. You'll be all right. We'll be all right. Riley's gone. We'll leave here. We'll leave here in the morning.*

Before he slept, Adam asked me if I did not want to open the French horn case. I explained it was not only locked but sealed, the better to protect its contents. I thought of the ancient words cradled within. Words describing how it all began, Pierre Saad had said, how people came into being on Earth.

That night I dreamed I was walking among the redwoods when the wild boy dropped down on my shoulder. His hair was flaming, and he blazed like a cherubim, his mouth full of dagger teeth. I woke up and stifled my scream with my own hand.

Before our flight from Eden the next day, we put on clothing. I dressed in my new skirt and blouse, and Adam wore Riley's shirt and pants. All day we walked: past the ruined garden, beyond the magnolias and redwoods, and over the grassy plains into the rough wilderness. Riley's pants were a little short on Adam and left his white ankles exposed.

Before we passed the boundaries, we encountered the feral boy once more. He leaped from above, as he had done to Riley, as in my prophetic dream. All his weight and force hit my chest, and I fell backward and down. His member was erect, he gripped a chipped stone blade in his hand, and he was wild with passion. He straddled me and tried to enter me in the single desperate moment he had before Adam pulled him away. He succeeded only in tearing open the seam where the sleeve joined the bodice of my new orange blouse.

Adam took the stone knife from the boy and tossed it aside; he placed the boy on his feet and shoved him roughly away from us. Adam did not try to hurt the boy; he just shoved him, each time farther and farther away. I sat on the ground, legs spread, tears streaking my cheeks, my face set in appalled and furious defiance. I bared my teeth, ready to bite.

The boy would not be shoved away. He snapped his jaws and pointed at me and at himself. With contorted face, he strained to speak but only made strangled noises, none of which were necessary to express what was evident: that he believed I should belong to him.

Because the boy fought to come back after each rough shove, Adam began to strike his shoulders and arms with his fists. Each time Adam hit the boy a more forceful blow—sometimes a slap across the face, sometimes a kick on the backside, finally a hard blow to the side of his belly.

The boy retreated a little, but he found his stone knife and returned. The gray knife resembled a dirty icicle. With complete coolness, Adam easily leaped away from the boy's frantic assaults and made no attempt to wield his own steel knife. Tears of frustration dashed from the boy's eyes, and when he could not land any slash or stab, he began to spit at Adam. To stop him, Adam caught the boy's wrist, wrenched the knife from his hand, and threw the knife on the ground behind himself. Then Adam slapped first one cheek, then the other, very hard. The boy cried out, and tears gushed from his eyes. Suddenly, he turned and ran.

Still sitting on the ground, I watched the boy cross a field of large rocks, picking his way around the big ones and leaping over the smaller ones when he could. Without speaking, Adam picked up the primitive knife from the ground, stowed it behind Riley's khaki belt, and then held out his hand to me. His face was chiseled and set hard as stone.

For a long time, we walked quickly and silently toward the boundary. The terrain became rocky and barren, the soil a packed and baked red clay. Occasionally a single large red rock stood up like a jagged tooth or flame. Though tinged everywhere with red, the place seemed a moonscape, a wasteland of broken rock, gravel, and soil dry as powder—sometimes gray, sometimes a grainy red. Finally I saw in the distance two smooth gray boulders, rising over the jumble of red sandstone like granite shoulders. "The Gates," Adam said. Beyond them a few clusters of pampas grass waved in a slight breeze, and beyond that we saw scrubby specimens of Russian olive and just the shaggy tops of tall royal palms. Perhaps there was a ravine or a river out there. Just before we passed between the boulders, we looked back.

Behind us, the boy was standing on a red-streaked rock, his naked, hairy body erect and yelling, trying to speak.

"I don't know what he's trying to say," Adam said sadly.

The boy's face contorted; the shaking of his skinny chest, his clenched hands, bespoke his snarling fury.

I knew what he was saying. He was saying that he would make another knife.

# LIFE OF A SUFI

THE ARAB HERDSMAN first saw his son in a dream, although he had neither sired a son nor even taken a wife to his bed nor even any animal, though he had loved all the animals of the herd and did not consider them unworthy of human carnal love, since it was clear that their spirits were in harmony with his own—most of the time, which was as much as you could say about any living creature. Of course the Holy Book forbade congress with animals, and as a good Sunni he did not want to violate its tenets when there was no necessity to do so, but still his imagination had considered the idea.

What is our connection to the animals? he pondered. Is not our flesh and blood very much like theirs? At times, even our joys and sorrows resemble theirs.

Before he was grown, he thought of his own imagination as being goatlike, familiar and friendly, playful, companionable. After he had spent his young manhood out in the desert, after he had been alone enough to feel his brain curing among the stars like meat cures from the proximity of myriad sugar grains, he came to believe imagination resembled not an animal but the brightest of stars—Capella. How many Arab men, when they became mature and proper herdsmen, had seen the bright star Capella and let it inspire a mirror brightness in their own hearts, in the depths of their hearts? (Capella was called the Goat Star, anyway, and it was essence of goat, lively and twinkling.)

As an aging man, after he journeyed to Cairo and became full of natural wisdom and of Sufi learning, he would know they were the same—the depth of his heart and the height of the stars. It was those unattainable and distant points of light that made the flatness of the earth meaningful to him. What was life if it had only length and breadth like a rectangle drawn on a flat of sand? No, it was the third dimension, that of height or depth (they were infinitely the same), that he had sought and found.

Even when he was still young, he first found meaningfulness as height in the heavens above when he stood watch at night alone on the dunes with the animals. He had thought of the shepherds in the story of the birth of the prophet Jesus and how with his birth a brightness had come to their minds and their inner voices had been allowed to speak and sing, "Behold, I bring you good tidings of great joy, which shall be to all people."

Second, he had found transcendence in the depth of his heart. Sometimes he told himself his own story (when he had no child near enough to listen):

> *One night when I had felt loneliness like the jaws of a nutcracker and myself the nut, when the starry sky was a jaw of teeth, the stark earth the lower jaw and I between— One night when I had felt unbearable loneliness, sky and earth came together and squeezed my brain till I knew I must take my herd to town and sell them and live in the city. (My own town was originally Nag Hammadi, and it had been my grandfather's village when he himself was a boy who had stubbed his toe on the buried jar that held buried wisdom for the Christians, though most of them have learned little from it.) And I thought, out of my solitary pain, though I am a man and not a schoolchild, I must learn to read and write and all that the teachers can say to me in the city, and that will be the path to salvation so that I will not go mad because I think I am alone in the universe, as all mortals are alone and wretched, not just ignorant but stupid and blighted, because they do not know reality but only these empty visible forms, these shapes we use as guideposts.*

*For weeks and months, perhaps years, I herded my goats toward the city on the Nile, and as we progressed, their bells tinkled in what Westerners would call a symphony of sound. It was the sweetest music I ever heard, that of my herd, and whenever we passed camels who had the talent for dancing, they recognized that this was music and began to dance, and the sounds of their harnesses and jangling gear added their own notes. This earthly music is too sweet to take to town, I sometimes thought. I hesitated and thought, Allah is telling me, Go back, do not surrender the unbearable peace (and loneliness) of your pure life in the desert for the city. There were many voices in the music, but finally I took this confusion to be a snare and a delusion, and I decided to obey the bright, clear idea that had first come to me. I continued to follow the flow of the river northward almost to the place where its waters bifurcate and fan into the Mediterranean.*

*But my hesitation, my ambivalence, had been real, and I had wasted time going first one direction and then backtracking, then going off at an angle, and reversing that path till my footsteps printed their own star in the dust as I tried out many directions. But finally again, I remembered the necessity of pursuing the road beside the north-flowing river, and I came to the city. I was to find my son, you see.*

*That was Allah's will for me: to have the son I never had.*

*It was the crack of dawn when we came, the herd and I, not back to Nag Hammadi because we had not just traveled in a circle, but because my journeying in the wilderness for a long time had led to the very outskirts of the city of Cairo, which looked like a village to me, though I heard a kind of murmur that might have informed me had I paid attention and might have caused me to realize that a whole vast city lay beyond the villagelike outskirts. But this seeming village was only the fringe of the city, the frayed edge of the garment of the city.*

*BANG! Such a noise, and again BANG!*

*I recognized what startled me was the firing of a powerful gun such as no one should carry into the city where the most fierce animal is only man whose skin is so very tender and can be so easily pierced by even the weakest bullet, or even a knife. One can also kill another man with a wire for a garrote. And there is poison. Or one can drop down a simple rock from a high place. One can plant an evil seed such as a coiled snake or several scorpions under the blanket where his enemy sleeps. What is the need of a powerful gun?*

*I left my dog with the herd and took only one goat with me as a sort of escort because it was early morning, and I was a stranger in this place, and I did not want some ranger or policeman asking, "What is this man doing walking in our streets?" No. Instead they would see me with the fine goat and think, He is here to sell his goat, and they would let me pass.*

*My goat—his name was . . . His name is a blank. My goat's name and even his meaning to me have become like two blank eyes staring over time at me. His name and his features have been erased from my memory, but still I remember he was. In any case, I turned the corner, and there we saw a young woman sliding down the wall of a building, leaving a smear of her own blood behind her on the whitewash of the wall. She sagged down onto the street. In amazement and horror, I turned for an explanation to my goat, but now he had grown large and turned into a cow—yes, a cow. (Usually to turn a goat into a cow, there must be a trade between two men each of whom owns one of each, but in this case that step was simply stepped over, and I looked into the sweet, gentle eyes of a cow.)*

*And then I saw my boy where once there had been nothing but a blank wall. He was wrapped in a woman's shawl, but I knew him to be my boy, all huddled at the place where the wall met the flat street, that juncture where two dimensions meet—like an incomplete corner. I simply reached down and took his hand. We hurried. Hurry was essential. It was from my desperate fear for his safety that the idea of real hurry was born.*

*And then I knew the depth of my heart. It matched the height of Capella the Goat Star. I knew my own essence, which was to love this boy with all my spirit, and all my mind, and all my heart, and in knowing this love I would know God beyond myself but within me as sure as the stars sprinkled the sky above me because what is inner is also outer.*

*Amen.*

*That is my story. This is the end of the story that swooped me up in its wings.*

---

But it is not the end of what happened. When we left the bloody wall, he seemed both to know and not to know that his mother was gone. The boy was very young, but he knew his name. He told me his father was French, and from that he had been named Pierre, but he used his mother's last name because his father had left them (though his mother said he was a good man), so his name in its entirety was Pierre Saad.

I told him that I had come to the city to learn the mystic ways of the Sufi. He asked me how I had found him, and I told him how I'd followed a star and found him.

He asked me which star, because dawn was just breaking and we could still see a few bright points in the gray sky above the edge of the city.

And I answered it was the star named for my goat, who had just turned into a cow.

When he laughed and squeezed my hand exactly the way a boy should who is sharing a secret with his father, I knew that he was a boy who would find joy in his life.

You may ask me, Did your boy who must be a man now find joy?

And I will say the path is not always straight. On its own—not just through our hesitations—it twists and turns. I would tell you he found joy and lost it. He keeps his own joy in his child, now a grown woman but not married and who may or may not marry because she is married to her work. My son has also found joy in his work. Like me, he loves images.

He understands images to be the mediators between what is mortal and what is divine, what has form and what is real beyond any shape or form. The image is not the betrayer, as some Muslims think; it is the gate. My son is not a Sufi; he is a scientist. But he is a good scientist; he knows he does not study reality; he knows that he and his colleagues only work to construct a picture of reality. He has told me this many times so that I do not worry about him.

But I do worry about him. Violence has visited his life twice to take from him those who are dearest to him. His mother and then his wife were taken from him by those who would lock religion in a box bound with metal. Patterns sometimes run in threes, and it may happen again. I only hope he does not lose his daughter, because she is the future that rightly belonged to both his mother and his wife. Finally I hope only that my son remains safe and alive till I am not. I hope that in the afterlife I do not ache with anxiety about his safety or his happiness. I wish him protection. Beyond that I wish that joy may visit my son named Pierre Saad again.

Voices braid together to tell a story. Sometimes one section disappears behind another. How many strands are there, and where do they come from and how does one story disappear or emerge unexpectedly?

Pierre Saad trusted his father and took his hand because his father was accompanied by Hathor the Cow, the goddess of beauty, and the little orphaned boy believed in the truth of beauty that depends on imagination. The Sufi father taught the boy as he grew that the text is always open to new interpretations because story conjures images, and pictures partaking of the infinite transcend both space and time. Pierre Saad wanted to read the earth—pictures left in caves when humans were original, close to their beginnings as humans. He wanted to read the artful images painted on, etched in, shaped from, stone, carried in the hand, or abandoned on a cave wall, or buried with the dead, or simply dropped and lost by those earliest humans.

For almost forty thousand years, images begat images through the hands of mankind, and most men went away and forgot the cave art and did not understand even what it was. Incised or painted on an envelope of rock, the mail was left undelivered. Only a few people knew the rock images were addressed to them and to their children's children.

Pierre the anthropologist was curious, too, about reading the starry sky—such as his friend Thom Bergmann (really only a voice on the telephone at first, then the voice arising from printed letters on a sheet of paper or on a screen, finally the man bleeding under a broken piano) had wanted to share with him. "What will it mean," Thom had asked through his letters, "if we can picture a universe with others Out There? What will it mean about humanness?"

Sitting in his oaken library in the Dordogne Valley of south-central

France, smelling through his open window the fragrance of wheat ripening in the sun, Pierre Saad held a sheet of fine stationery between his fingers and read a blackly inked text suggesting he might become national director of parietal art for the country of his father, who had deserted his mother. Though his adopted father had taught him that only God has power and glory (and yet He is nothing), Pierre Saad began to want them both for himself.

# THE ROAD TO BAGHDAD

ADAM LOOKED BACK over his shoulder at the two rounded, upthrusting granite boulders and thought them like the open sides of a giant vise. The figure framed between the jaws, standing on his own high red rock in the distance, was the boy—"the feral boy," she had called him—full of fury. Adam touched his own mouth, then looked at his fingers. No sign of blood. It was not he, but the feral boy, who had eaten Riley's heart. What connected Adam to the wild boy? Only that the boy had fed him when he himself lay bruised and bleeding, beaten and raped, on the hard-packed sand road? This road? The road he and she would walk to Damascus. No, Baghdad. But he knew Baghdad had been destroyed.

Politicians and troops had used the language of their fathers, of Vietnam—"We had to destroy the city to save it." Yes, before he was captured, Adam had heard another soldier explain it just that way, and then his head was blown off, and from the stem of his neck, blood leaped up high into the air like a fountain.

Adam began to hum and to match the words to the rhythm of his walking, but he did not sing the words aloud: *There is a fountain filled with blood / Drawn from Emmanuel's veins. / And sinners plunged beneath that flood / Lose all their guilty stains.*

"What is a sinner?" he had asked the chaplain at the mental hospital in Idaho.

The man had explained it. *We are all born sinners. Because of Adam and Eve. When we are born into this world as human beings, we are born stained with sin. But there is redemption. Ask forgiveness. Believe that Jesus, fully human and fully divine, is in fact the Son of God.*

"Was there ever a child who never committed a sin, aside from being born?"

"That was Jesus. And only Jesus."

"The Son of God, or the Child of God?" Adam had interrupted to ask.

"Certainly the child of God. But Jesus was a man. The Son of God. We can all be children of God. Believe in Jesus as the Son of God, and ye shall be saved."

"Ye?"

"You. It means you."

*What have I done?* Had Adam actually asked the question of the chaplain, or only thought it? He knew what he had done. He had disobeyed his father. Adam had hated his father for his rock-hard tyranny. He had lusted after his mother. He had fornicated with innocent girls. He had drawn lewd pictures of female bodies. He had masturbated. He had shirked his work and resented the unending labor the farm required of him. He had felt deprived of money and of the culture of the city. And yet he despised the city and its wickedness, and the intellectual pride of the university and the smug professors who had recognized him as Piers Plowman and mocked his rustic ways behind closed doors.

What had he done? He had lost his mind. He had contended with God.

How had he failed? He had failed Riley, his friend, and many others.

Adam looked down at the front of the shirt. There was the name, upside down, since seen from above: "F. Riley." But he was not F. Riley. And her? What was her name? It changed: it had been Eve; it had been Lucy. She was particular about getting names right. When he had murmured, "the road to Damascus," she had corrected him. *Baghdad.* She had not heard the news about Baghdad. Saul was on the road to Damascus when he was converted and his name changed to Paul. Saint Paul, the Catholics called him. Before he saw a great light on the road to Damascus, Saul had persecuted the Christians.

And then he became one. But before and after—was he the same person, or different?

Was he, Adam, the same person he was as a little boy full of brightness?

And this woman beside him dressed in orange, her brow beaded with sweat. Who was she? He thought her nature was a good one. But damaged. Burned.

Purified? In the Refiner's fire?

The music of Handel's *Messiah* began to dance in his brain: *For unto us a child is born, unto us . . .*

"Adam, Adam," she said. "Is there any water along this road?"

"I don't know. I was blindfolded when we passed this way. I heard something sloshing in the truck. They might have had a five-gallon jug of water, or gasoline."

"'No blood for oil,'" she mused. "That was the slogan on the signs we carried when we marched on Washington, Thom and I, before we went to Iraq."

"Thom was a soldier, too?"

"No. I meant 'we, the United States.' Before the United States went to war. Thom was a scientist."

"What did he want to know? From his research?"

"If there was life—some sort of real life, not little green men from Mars—in the far-flung reaches of space."

"You said he was dead, Lucy." He was amazed: sometimes her name came to him without thinking. Other times he was confused and afraid of offending her. "I remember that right, don't I? He's dead. What happened?" He glanced down at her. He took her hand. She was short, barely came to his shoulder, and he had noticed there was something childlike about her, something stunted.

"He was crushed to death, in Amsterdam, by a grand piano that fell on him."

Adam began to laugh. He couldn't help himself. He took his hand away from her and put first that hand and then the other one over his mouth, like a bandage or gag to try to stifle the laughter, but he couldn't. The laughter flew out of him, spit, too, and he staggered drunkenly as he laughed and choked on laughter.

She hung her head and said nothing.

Finally he got control over his laughter. He knew it was inappropriate. Sometimes he had laughed at his father that way. Adam's exuberant, spurting humor made the old rancher bite his own lips and clamp them together in disgust. To Lucy, Adam managed to say soberly, "God works in mysterious ways, his wonders to conceal." Then he spurted again with painful mirth.

*Wonders*—was that the word? Or was it *horrors*?

"Where are we going?" he continued. "I mean, Lucy, where did you say we were going?"

"To Baghdad. To civilization. To see some friends in France. To give them this." She lifted up the black case.

He had forgotten about it. He wished it were a keg of water. "Here," he said politely, "let me carry that for you."

She stopped and transferred the French horn case to his hand. Her face and neck red with heat, she looked dangerously hot, he thought. He looked away, scouring the landscape with his eyes for relief.

"Look," he said, "there's a palm-leaf hut. Maybe people are there. Maybe they have water. We'll sit in the shade. I'll fan you."

She nodded.

The hard-packed sand road smelled of scorching. He remembered that odor from his mother's iron. In a debased kind of way, he had rather liked the odor of scorching, as a boy. Once he had gotten into the brewer's yeast she had used to make bread, and he had eaten it by the spoonfuls. He had felt debased then, too. He had done something else in his mother's world that he shouldn't have done. Once he had taken Rosie into his parents' bed. He had imagined she was his mother that time, just for the forbidden fun of it. He had been afraid that Rosie and he had left their fluids on the sheets, but he saw they were already stained. His father had been there before him, recently, and Evie, Evelyn, had not changed the bedclothes (as she called them) before they went to town.

"I'm so sorry about Riley," she said.

Yes, Adam could see the sorrow and trouble in her face. More than grief, the footprint of trauma was in her eyes. "He was a good boy," Adam said. *All you could have said, all anyone can say,* the chaplain had consoled him, *is something simple and true.* "It's sad," Adam added.

"Sort of an all-American boy," she answered. "Even had the freckles."

Adam could tell her tears were flowing. He wanted to say to her, Don't waste the water, or catch your tears with your tongue, even if they're salty. Made of poles and large leaves, a hut sat green and wilting on the sand.

He could hear bees buzzing all around the palm hut, and Adam remembered Riley had wanted to rob a hive. Perhaps these desert people had done just that. On the horizon, he saw an emerald line of forest. There were trees ahead—palms and acacia and maybe Russian olive—and that meant the likeliness of water. Still— No, the buzzing insects were not bees, but flies.

"Wait," he said. He led her to the back of the hut where it cast a short shade and told her to sit down and to rest in the shadow.

After he left her there with the black case, he went around to the frail front door, the only door. It, too, was made of palm leaves, each one hanging down from a wooden slat at the top and another slat across the waist of the frame. He started to open it, but then he saw the long palm leaves sway, and instead he just took a finger and gently pushed one aside so he could see in. Like the pendulum of a clock, the long leaf was something you could move to one side with the tip of your finger.

There lay the family on the floor. He stared to understand. They were dead, and the sandy dirt floor was soaked with their blood. Their hands and feet had been staked to the floor. Then they had been severed at the wrists and ankles, each with a single blow, he thought. Now their hands and feet, even the baby's, were still staked to the floor, but they were no longer attached to the bodies. These people had known a secret. Or soldiers had thought they knew a secret. Probably they had started with the baby, just one foot, and moved up the line, ending with the father, and then started again.

Adam could hear the voice of the father roaring like a lion. His mouth—still open in the hollow shape of a curse.

At their feet, before the threshold like a doormat, Adam saw the sign of a cross.

But he felt sure that Christians had not done this. Someone, he felt sure, had made the cross to cast blame, to create a scapegoat. There were other marks inside on the dirt floor: the crescent moon. And that tangle of lines and points—the Star of David.

Yes, Adam thought. The idea seemed to split his brain: They all did it. He staggered and took a step backward. He worked his jaws and gathered what saliva he could, and then he parted the leaves with both hands and spat through the opening, randomly, toward their political signs. To be sure of the reality, he looked once more between the palm leaves. There, there, the crack in the wall behind them? Down low. Wasn't that her eye, just an eye, unblinking, peering in?

When he walked around to Lucy, he simply said that they were all gone. And there was no water. "But ahead—"

She interrupted him. "How many were there?" Her brow was corrugated with puzzling—as though their number was the only question to ask.

"Five," Adam answered. "And the parents." He knew he had not really counted. "Five or six," he amended truthfully.

"I saw," she said.

Now, now, he looked into her eyes, filmed and dazed. He drank from them as though his own eyes were flies come to gather at those unprotected pools.

She was holding out her hand to him, for help. Yes, he could do that. He could help her rise. He caught her wrist instead of her hand and pulled hard. She seemed to rise miraculously. She was very light, or was it that he was very strong? *We are weak, but He is strong*—they'd sung that in Sunday school the year he came as Superman, five or six years old. He was not weak. He'd been a strong boy. Superboy. Leaping, almost flying. He was a strong man now. When anyone saw his manly jaw, they recognized him as Superman and gave him tight-fitting blue and red to wear.

Like a marine's colors. But he had been a foot soldier, in camouflage imitating the hues of olive green, dry rock, desert sand.

"Let's walk," he said. "It isn't far."

"'Come down to Kew in lilac time / In lilac time, in lilac time. / Come down to Kew in lilac time— / It isn't far from London,'" she quoted.

"Shakespeare?" he asked.

"No. Alfred Noyes. Also wrote 'The Highwayman.'"

"'The road was a ribbon of moonlight . . . ,'" he quoted.

"No, it isn't," she said. "The road is a white-hot poker."

She stumbled, and he caught her quickly under her elbow and took the black case from her again.

After walking, trudging, stumbling, in silence in the broiling heat, Adam thought he could see oil oozing out of his skin, or melted fat, not just sweat. When he looked up from his skin, there was the bubbling green of the tops of trees, probably acacia trees, surely visible at the meeting line of sky and earth.

"Broccoli," she said suddenly. "I always think of that when I see the tops of trees from an airplane."

Like a brand on the buckskin flank of sand, a black circle off in the desert distracted him. He pointed to it. A black doughnut. Large. "Looks like a campfire once," he said.

The stones were arranged very nicely so that the inner edges of the flat stones created what appeared to be a perfect circle. The ash in the center of the circle was gray, and sometimes it wafted in a ghostly way up from the circle in a twisting column. He wished the breeze would come over to the road.

"They've been cooking, like good Boy Scouts," she observed.

Yes, he could see two Y-shaped sticks, and a horizontal rod resting at the bottoms of the V's of the Y's, passing from one upright to another.

"They've left some meat, I think," he said.

"It looks charred," she responded. "Inedible. A waste of energy to go there."

Hadn't he warned her about waste?

"I want to see," he said. "You're probably right. The stones are probably black with soot. The rocks around here are white, or gray."

"The sticks must be some kind of rebar, construction iron."

He told her to keep walking; he would catch up. Did he hear her murmur, "And I—I had just wanted to cry?" Maybe there would still be some moisture in the meat. He was hungry, anyway. Then he saw the place where an army jeep, or some other vehicle with heavy treads, had left the road to drive over to the campfire. He hurried along, but he looked back to check on the woman, his companion. She was shuffling like an old woman, but he had remembered her as someone pretty, desirable, though he'd acted the part of a gentleman.

The terrain was beginning to slant upward; the circle of stones had been constructed just before the crest of a sand hill. He couldn't see what was on the other side. For a moment he worried that men might be lying out of sight, hidden, with their rifles stretched out in front of their bodies, with the sights of the guns waiting for him. But the imprint of the tire treads looked old to him. He had a mounting curiosity about the site; he had been in 4-H, not Scouts, but he had made just such campfires. The other boys loved to set their marshmallows on fire. They claimed to like the black char and almost-liquid goo inside, but he always carefully browned his marshmallows. They were golden-sided, deliciously browned, never burned.

He stopped. Not hands. Not feet. But human parts had been skewered. He would not name those parts, but he knew their shapes. Parts such as he had drawn. Parts such as he had touched on his own body. He retched once, twice, but no bile was left in him.

He would not look there again. He turned and went back, not following the tracks but cutting across diagonally toward her new position on the road. He took note of the speed of her progress and calculated how to angle his path so that he would intercept her at the right moment. He had played football. He had been a quarterback. Not his mind but his body knew how to calculate the intersection of two trajectories moving at different speeds. Only this was slow motion.

The principle was the same. At the movies, he had always loved the mysterious moment of sudden slow motion. It sanctified things, sometimes.

When he caught up with her, they would be close enough to see the brown trunks and limbs of the bubbling broccoli trees. Maybe a clean blue creek would flow near their bases.

When he reached the road, and Lucy on it, shuffling, she tilted her bowed head, looked him square in the eyes, and greeted him.

"Hi, gal," he said. He would not remember what he had just seen. Erased.

A blank. Even the crossbar spit was gone, and he saw only two upright Y's. "It was nothing," he said. "I should have listened to you."

"Let's camp in the trees," she said. "Maybe it's an oasis. Maybe there will be fruit trees. Or dates or olives."

Not until close range could they see that most of the trees were thorny acacias; some were yellow acacias, and the tips of the branches drooped with sprays of lovely yellow leaves. Beyond the trunks was a ribbon of blue water. Eve broke into a trot. "Come on," she called, like a teenager—eager, full of her own energy.

Then she stopped and began to sob. Walking rapidly to her, he saw blanched bones; human and animal rib cages arched up in the sunlight, beautifully white with the blue water flowing through. Threaded with scraps of cloth, purple and red, many human skeletons lay in or near the water, where the sandy bank was almost white.

"Never mind," he said. "Never mind, Lucy." He made himself call her by her right name. "We'll just walk upstream a bit. Out of sight of all this. Upstream, where the water is clean."

"But, Adam," she said, "suppose it's poison. Suppose they died because they drank poisoned water."

He took her hand. "Come on," he said. He made himself smile. It was a flirt's smile. He remembered how to smile that way. He'd never known a high school or college girl who could resist that careful, no-teeth, fragile smile. It melted resistance. "Let's go see."

They trudged through the loose, fine sand, their feet sinking almost up to their ankles. "We'll just take our time," he said. "Don't try to hurry now."

Despite his encouragement, she finally sank to her knees.

"This is just the place I thought we should stop," he said. "Here, let me carry you to the water." He put down the French horn case and scooped her up in his arms. Black spots appeared before his eyes, in a rectangular grid. Deprivation spots, he thought, but he was not afraid. They were too close now. Whether the water was poison or not, now they would drink. Eve would understand. They would do it together, at the same time.

The sun was setting rapidly behind them, and their own shadows stretched out long across the sand toward the trees and water. The short, shaggy trees looked humped, four-legged, like a distorted camel. How light she was in his arms, her arms around his neck. He still carried the French horn case. Among the trees, he saw shaggy movements with humps. Two creatures. One golden as a sand pile, the other dark, almost black. Two camels. Two wild camels. He named them Day and Night.

He sat Eve on her feet.

"Look, darling," he said. "Wild camels, among the trees." But he savored the word *darling*, delicious as a fig or a date on his tongue.

"Are they dangerous?" she asked, and answered herself, "They're beautiful." To steady herself, she clasped his arm.

"See what they're doing?" he said. "They're drinking. The water is safe. Let's just wait. Then they'll move. They might not be wild. They might have escaped from a caravan."

"Like us," she said softly.

As the camels lifted and curved their long necks, water streamed silver from their muzzles.

Slowly, their big bodies began to glide on. Adam listened to the gritty sound of their large splayed feet sinking a little, compacting the sand.

What the humans wanted most was to drink. Then they wanted to submerge their bodies in the cool, flowing water.

Automatically they pulled off their orange and camouflage clothing: the hand-sewn blouse and skirt, the borrowed shirt and army trousers. Orange parachute and tan camouflage fluttered to the ground. Over her head, Lucy lifted the black cord and the titanium-cased memory stick and placed them on top of the soft mound of orange. They looked down at their bare, worn feet and laughed. Their feet would be the first part to relish the water. Yes, happy tadpoles for toes, wiggling and laughing. Then there was a plopping down, female and male, bottoms first into the water, which was beautiful and cool, clear, only—say—ten inches deep. But it covered and refreshed their private parts, male and female. And then there was nothing else to do but to lie down fully in it. Sometimes on their backs with their necks tilted up so they could breathe. Sometimes on one side or the other, with a bent elbow to prop up their heads. In that posture they talked and laughed and every utterance was joyful, in praise of water, which they gulped by the handfuls. Then they flopped onto their stomachs, and he let the scant hairs in the center of his chest over his heart have their fun, and she let her breasts float and bobble.

When they propped again on their elbows, facing the stream and catching the flow of it on their chests, they might as well have been kissing. They cupped their hands into scoops and splashed their faces. Finally they sat up and wetted their hair, bowing the crowns of their heads into the stream or bringing water to their scalps with their hands. For each other, they made bowls of their hands, filled them, and then opened the seamed bottom of their bowls to let water drop down on each other's heads.

"God is good; God is great," they chanted. "And we thank him for this food."

"What food?" they both exclaimed, and laughed.

They tilted their heads and exposed their throats to the air and looked up in the sky for manna.

Skyward, sustenance did sway among the branches of fruit trees. Fruit ripe and ready.

What they envisioned were men hanging head-down from trapezes without lines, their bent knees hooked over the lineless bars; trapeze artists free as angels were swooping down and bearing in their hands white china platters filled with fruit—oranges, lemons, pears, apples. Or maybe the woman and man had climbed the trees and picked the fruits. In any case, mercifully, magically, sustenance appeared. Lucy and Adam sat down on the sand beneath the trees, reached into the branches, took, and ate. *This* is Eden, they insisted.

*Any oasis is Eden*, they amended, their mouths full of the mush of fruit.

*Shall we put on our clothes now?* they asked.

*We're dry now*, they agreed.

*And the air is chilly.*

*It's night.* And they covered their bodies again, he with Riley's clothes, and she with the orange ones she had sewn herself for the journey back. She replaced the memory stick around her neck.

*But look at the stars.*

*A starry, moonless night is the most blessed of all nights.*

*Diamonds.*

*Worlds unseen.*

*Stars galore.*

*The word* galore*—it comes from some place deeper than the throat.*

*From the belly of God. When he's generous.*

"Lucy," he said. "Make love with me."

She smiled at him. A smile she had never given anyone before. She felt its newness on her face.

"Tonight, for this moment," he said, "I know you for who you are, Lucy. I know your name. Let's make love while I know who you are."

"I'm new," she said. She laughed a little. "Clean and fresh, refreshed," she said, denying the warning implied by his invitation. "Adam—"

He held his finger, upright, sealing his lips. *Shhh*—he signaled, shy of his own name.

She reached to his chest, to the smooth button beside the label *F. Riley*. "Adam," she whispered again despite his signal for silence.

He nodded. She unbuttoned the first button. Gesture was the only language. Down the row of buttons, each slid more easily from its fastening than the one before; each felt more silky to her fingertips than the others and more precious than pearls. He pulled the tail of her orange blouse from the waistband of her skirt and lifted loose handfuls of blouse over her head. She drew the black silk cord over her head and laid the old talisman among the orange puffs. There were her breasts for him to kiss. To cherish by starlight.

Before he leaned toward her, with a single downward glance he memorized the shapes of her breasts as he had not done before. In a future, given soft pencil and creamy paper, he would draw them.

But now was bliss, as she folded her arms across his shoulders and pulled him closer. Then there was kissing. Sweeter than the berry, she thought, an echo of a half-forgotten song.

Finally she said softly, “Stand up now,” and she reached to unfasten the army trousers. “Country people in the South say, ‘Shuck out of them pants.’ That’s country talk.”

“Like shucking corn?”

“Like shucking an ear of corn of its wrappings.”

“In Idaho, we grew wheat.”

“But you’re stalwart as Iowa corn. And golden. Sweet.”

*Smell the air.*

*Perfume. Lemons.*

“Anoint my head, my hair with lemon juice,” he asked.

She reached for a half of lemon they had squeezed and sucked for its sour piquancy. He knelt on one knee, and she squeezed the juice into his dark hair and rubbed it in with her fingertips.

“The stars should smell like lemons,” she said.

*Lie down again.*

*Hold me.*

*Hold me.*

*Your body.*

*Your body.*

*You.*

*You.*

## THE ODOR OF LEMONS

IN THE MORNING, he called me Eve. While we still lay flesh to flesh, he looked at me, his eyes coated with the sort of blear I had sometimes seen in patients, and said, "My Eve."

I burst into tears. Had I not held him as dear as I had ever held any person—in my heart, with my body, as dear to me as my husband and only lover had been? Had we not *known* each other—Adam and I—in every biblical sense? The fragrance of lemons was still on my hands. From the sunlit grass came the mingled perfume, close to rotting, of the rinds of all the fruits we'd ravaged. The grass itself, dappled with leaf shadow and sunlight, had the odor of wheat. Adam was unresponsive to my weeping.

He got up and walked away a short distance. In full sun, turning his back to me—the sun stroking his back with its warm dry light—he knelt in a sandy depression edged with grass. On his knees, he thanked God for granting his prayer for his rightful wife.

In the dark that had been ours together, all of his masculine attention had shaped itself to me and to our desire. He had seemed to be the only man and the first man. I had gloried in his strength and passion. Had this kneeling child-man been that tender lover?

When I rose and walked to him, my body, too, gave thanks for the pleasure of the night and for the warmth of the morning sun. As he continued to kneel, I stood beside him and looked down at his dark eyelashes resting on his cheeks. At his beauty. While he prayed, I bent over him and smelled the odor of lemons in his black hair. When he stood up, I studied the two round bowls his knees had left in the fine, dry sand. He was gone from me. What we had shared had been real, and now it was over. He had become the confused soldier, ravaged by the acts of war. I was rested and restored, determined, but I could not stop sighing.

Adam asked where we were going.

"We're going to walk along the road. To Baghdad. Carry the case for me, please."

By tucking my blouse back into the waistband of my skirt and tying its drawstring securely, I devised a carrying pouch into which I dropped several oranges and apples, two pears, and a banana through the neck opening of my blouse. The fruit clustered around my waist and swayed against my bare skin when I moved. Pregnant with bounty, I felt mythologized, an earth mother—Ceres. Instead of a daughter, I had a large and innocent son whom I must try to protect. Perhaps he would come to me again, a stalwart man, all of a piece, strong and loving.

Beside the stream, we knelt to drink as much water as we could hold before we left the oasis. How foolish for us to have abandoned home empty-handed—no clay jugs, no sling satchels for carrying. Had I bought into the Genesis myth? Surely the biblical Adam and Eve had left Eden empty-handed.

At least as real people returning to the unmythologized world, we had clothes to protect our flesh from the sun and from the eyes of strangers. Under the bloused fabric, I could feel the round jostling of apples and oranges and the long curve of a banana, all held securely just above the tight drawstring of my skirt. I thought of Riley caught in the spire of a redwood tree and dangling from his parachute. The vision melted. The trees behind us turned to ash and sank down without a trace. I thought of the Twin Towers blazing and sinking in New York, though at that time, nearly twenty years ago, I had been a young wife in Iowa City.

—

Each time we crossed a river, the vegetation on the other side became more lush. With no way to test the potability of the flowing waters, we simply knelt, hoped for purity, cupped our hands, and drank before we waded across, but Adam was skittish and afraid. As we walked, he talked to God and prayed. I said nothing. Although I had become his guardian, the memory of his ardor and the shape of his body was fresh inside me.

As we walked down the road, Adam prayed for God to make him blind, and then he closed his eyes so that he would see nothing more of horror. Holding out his hand, he asked me to lead him, and I accommodated his fancy. Occasionally, I asked him to switch the French horn case to the other hand and changed also the hand I held.

For a while, we passed through what could surely be called a jungle or at least a subtropical forest with a canopy so dense the sky was obscured. Here the terrain grew flat again. Overhead I could hear an occasional airplane. Some were small planes and flew rather low. We were grateful for the coolness of the shade. Occasionally Adam stumbled in his blindness, but he easily regained his poise and followed happily, never releasing my hand. He hummed "Amazing Grace."

Abruptly the forest ended. Full of wonder, I stopped and saw we stood at the edge of a cleared runway. In the distance, in the sky, a small plane, a Cessna, lined itself up with the strip.

"Look," I commanded.

Adam opened his eyes but said nothing.

The grinding buzz of the Cessna's engine meant the plane was coming closer and lower, would surely land. "Someone in the plane might help us. The army might have sent someone to look for . . . for Riley, or you." The idea seemed unlikely—surely they would have sent rescue to Eden, where Riley had ejected, but I wanted to jolt Adam with hope.

"Are we afraid?" he asked.

"We should see who it is before they see us. I'll go. You stay here. Keep the black case safe. Will you do that for me? And stay here. Hidden?"

His eyes tried to read my face. He asked, "You won't leave me behind?"

I leaned forward and kissed him fully on the lips. Why not? Why not? The man had entered my body. "I'll come back. Stay here. Don't follow me."

As I hurried away from him, I looked back to smile and thought he looked pleased. Bemused, but pleased, as though my kiss might have awakened a memory. A sense of how we had been together might have wafted through his mind. He dropped to his knees, bowed his head, and pressed the palms of his hands together. I blew him a kiss, but he had already closed his eyes in prayer. Then I heard him softly singing a Western tune he must have learned in Idaho:

*Come and stay by my side if you love me. Do not hasten to bid me adieu. . . .*

The airstrip, I realized, had been only lately cleared. Uprooted bushes and trees pushed along the sides of the runway still had green leaves on them. The tarmac was freshly laid. In fact I saw no sign that it had ever been used. No tire marks. An unwritten page, a pristine surface. Who would go to such expense to prepare a landing strip in the jungle? Surely it was not far to fly on to what was still called Baghdad?

And how had bulldozers and trucks gained access to the heart of this wilderness? There was no sign of an access road. I felt the frightened thumping of my heart. Why be afraid now? Construction was a sign of civilization. The bulldozers, the asphalt, the structural steel—all of it must have been transported here by helicopter. Perhaps by a fleet of helicopters.

The plane touched down too fast and made a dangerous, even reckless landing. As it bumped past my hiding spot beside the runway, I saw that people were seated inside the Cessna, one an elderly bearded man wearing a black hat. The plane taxied on toward the end of the runway but then turned and came back. Watching the propellers turning more and more slowly, I calculated they would stop almost exactly where I stood. Perhaps my orange clothing had given me away, though I stood behind the trunk of a palm and thick vegetation rose almost to my chin.

The airplane stopped, the engines were cut, and gradually the two propellers lost their momentum. A door cracked open, hinged down, and a flight of steps unfolded.

The first man to clatter down the steps wore a gray cowboy hat and blue jeans, though he was approaching middle age. His face was worn, and his eyes darted about warily.

He was followed by the white-bearded man with the black hat I had seen through the porthole window of the Cessna. He was dressed in a black cassock cinched by a rope belt. Priest or rabbi, I thought, calm and curious.

The two men waited while the pilot took off his headphones. As he turned, I saw only the sleeve and shoulder of a distinctly European gray tweed jacket with black suede patches at the elbows. Through the narrow window of the cockpit, the pilot appeared to be straightening the knot of his tie. I had forgotten men did that. His gesture spoke of manners and civilization. As he appeared in the open door of the airplane, I was thinking no one but an Englishman would straighten his tie before greeting the jungle, and then I shrieked in recognition. "Gabriel!" I charged out of the clearing onto the asphalt.

His body jerked to attention, his face opened in joyful disbelief as he descended the stairs and ran toward me, a laptop computer case in one hand. The other arm flung open wide as a door. The asphalt surprised the soles of my bare feet, but I ran hard across the surface. The other two men drew back and turned their shoulders as though bracing against an assault. From my old friend of the proper British tweed, I had never received such a welcoming and joyful smile.

Could it be? Could it be? My arms were around his neck; he was saying, "Lucy, Lucy, Lucy," and I inhaled the wool of his jacket. I could not restrain myself from sobbing. Here he was. He had come after me. A sane and capable man. An old friend, the essence of civilization. I was saved. How soothing the words he spoke, but I could not understand their meaning. His presence, his solid, well-clothed body. These were reality.

To the other men, Gabriel said casually, "You can get back into the plane." I understood that much from his utterances. To me, he looked down and smiled. "Let's get out of the sun." With his fingers lightly on my shoulder, he steered me across the tarmac toward the edge of the jungle, into the shade.

"Now let me look at you," he said, placing both hands on my shoulders. "You've made yourself something quite different to wear," he teased. "And what's this familiar cord?" He fingered the narrow black silk around my neck as he continued speaking. "Thom's old flash drive worn like a millstone. I should have known. Didn't you miss me a bit, Lucy, here in the wilderness?"

I laughed, tried to steady myself, and replied in a mirroring, somewhat British manner, "Gabriel, I simply can't say how glad I am to see you. And very surprised. And thoroughly, completely, overwhelmingly grateful."

His blue eyes sparkled with pleasure. He looked younger. There was nothing cynical in his face.

"Thank you," I added. "Thank you very, very much."

"I say, don't I rate a kiss?"

I kissed him immediately and fully on the lips, and he kissed me back. A thoroughly satisfactory kiss for a daytime greeting. Appropriate. Reassuring. Nothing like Adam's tender, lingering nighttime passion.

"I suppose I should do this more often," he said, grinning. "But I *am* surprised—the way you just popped out of the greenery, orange as a pumpkin, onto the runway. To tell you the truth, I thought we'd have to hack through a bit of brush to get to you."

"I saw the plane come in for a landing. A runway! In the middle of the jungle."

"A bumpy one, to be sure. Don't you have any luggage, my lady?"

"Luggage? How did you find me?" In my mind's eye, I saw the French horn case, but how would Gabriel know of that? "You've come with a strange pair of fellow travelers," I said with sudden caution. "Who in the world?"

"They are an odd duo, aren't they? You can get acquainted as we fly back. A cowboy, American, of course. Actually he's a broker. An ultra-Orthodox Jew of some sort."

I felt sobriety rising up in my body like dark water in a quick-filling well. "They're not scientists?"

"Nor is this Kansas," he quipped. "Perpetuity. It's a kind of club they work for." He shifted the computer valise to his other hand.

"What do they have in common with you? A chartered plane? A runway materializing out of the jungle?"

"How did you get here?" he asked. His voice was full of sprightly affection.

"I think you must know," I said soberly, with more wariness in my voice than I had intended to exhibit.

"You know, Lucy, I'll tell you all about it on the plane. Where's your bag?"

"The Cessna's a five-seater, isn't it?" I asked.

"Yes." He eyed me curiously.

"I have a friend," I said.

"Really?" Gabriel looked mildly shocked. "I hadn't thought of that possibility. I don't suppose you want to leave him behind, since you've mentioned him."

All of my giddy joy seemed to solidify. I felt heavy as stone. Suddenly I remembered the baby crocodiles standing up in the corners of their pit, and a warning phrase came back to me. *Fundamentalists of every stripe*—hadn't Pierre cautioned me about that? The cowboy would be the Christian stripe. I found I could not look at Gabriel as I slowly said, "He—my friend—has . . . the luggage."

Not my friend, my lover, I thought.

"I've found you, Lucy," Gabriel said. "That's the important thing." He reached toward my neck again and tenderly picked up Thom's memory stick with his fingertips. "Whatever you've done here, whoever you've known—leave it all behind, Lucy. Come with me."

"You're not here for . . . the luggage?" I asked uncertainly.

"I want you, Lucy. Always have, always will. You're right, my entourage, they've paid me—very well—to help recover certain texts that rightly belong in Egypt, but I came to find you." He gave a slight tug on the flash drive. "Let me take this," he urged. "Give up the past. Really and truly, my friend, you should let Thom go."

"Tell me honestly," I said, looking Gabriel squarely in his eyes. "Why do you want Thom's memory stick?"

"It's a kind of pun, isn't it?" he said. "It's symbolic for you. Your steely link to him."

"Why should I let go of Thom's memory?"

"To live."

I said nothing. I *had* returned to life. I had been broken, but I had healed. I wanted to salvage what was available in the world for me.

Gabriel sighed. Then he added, "Thom didn't deserve you."

As I stepped back in surprise, Gabriel let the titanium case slide out of his fingers and lie against my flesh.

He returned my steady gaze. "If you don't want to give this abomination to me"—he nodded at Thom's flash drive—"leave it here, under a rock, like the snake it is."

Abomination? Stunned, I looked around as though to find a suitable rock, but I said falteringly, "I haven't seen the file. Not once again. Not since that last morning with Thom." My thinking collapsed into incoherence—*abomination*? "Not since we were together in our hotel room in Amsterdam." My knees felt wobbly. I needed to sit down. What did the word *abomination* mean? The word detonated like a bomb in my psyche. The pendant had been a talisman, a touchstone, not an abomination.

"Do you want to see the file, Lucy? Once more before you let it go?"

"I . . . I don't know. Thom's valentine. It was in the context of—"

"Aren't all texts embedded in context?"

"The file had a valentine on it, just for me. We lay in bed and watched the universe—galaxies, stars, intergalactic dust—together, on the ceiling. . . ."

"I brought my laptop. Just in case you needed to see it—"

"Needed?"

"Needed to be convinced to let go of Thom."

I turned, walked quickly past a gigantic philodendron into the thicket, and sat down on a large, flat rock. The leaves of the philodendron, the deep incursions dividing the leaves into lobes, filled my mind. I felt spiked, lobotomized.

It was not the ancient texts but the flash-drive file that Gabriel wanted. Carrying his computer, he quickly followed me, sat beside me on the rock, and began to unzip the laptop case. I thought of Matisse, how Gabriel had promised to fly me to the Hermitage in St. Petersburg to see his paintings. I thought of the painter Rousseau; I wanted to lie down on a bed of sand, to wait for a lion to come and lick my dreaming forehead. But here there was only rampant fecundity, split-leaf philodendron, a plant large as a room.

"I gave you his notes already," I stammered.

"Thom thought on the computer," Gabriel answered. "There may be something on the file not in the hand notes."

Suddenly I did want to see the universe represented again as it was on Thom's file. I wanted to lie on a bed in Amsterdam, weary with transatlantic flight, with Thom. I wanted to feel small and humble, to be in awe of vastness, to quote Emily Dickinson and claim, "The brain is wider than the sky"—I had believed that of Thom. I wanted to see his red letters, Thom's valentine, emerge from the profundity of space bearing my name—and yet I did not want to see or prove anything.

When I closed my eyes, an image appeared to me of Adam on his knees, eyes closed, summoning from some distant corner of his mind a plaintive cowboy song: *From this valley they say you are going*. . . . And what of the Texan businessman, and the other man, stepping onto the tarmac as though they owned the world? Was that the image of sanity?

Gabriel took my hand and said tenderly, "Lucy, Lucy, you don't have to do anything you don't want to do. I love you, Lucy. I don't want to hurt you."

"I want my heart to hurt," I blurted. "That way I'll know I'm still alive."

Gabriel nodded. He released the lid, touched the power key, waited for the machine's tonic triad to blare, and slipped the end of the flash drive into its port. I felt as though he had entered me. But when had he lifted the cord with its memories over my head? When had he unsheathed the working end from its metal case so silky to the touch? I saw the list of file names on the screen, Thom's files, his work, dim in the mottled, penetrating light of the jungle. Gabriel made the cursor speed down to "Universal Valentine"; he adjusted the screen to daylight viewing, and there it was, on a screen only seventeen inches wide, the known universe.

There were the brilliant pinpoints of starlight; there were the clouds indicating probability—pink, red, magenta, royal purple for the most likely areas, according to spectroscopic interpretation of light-emitting molecules—the probabilities of finding life out there. As though they sensed my excitement, the mammoth leaves of the jungle stirred around me.

"It's a view looking past the center of the Milky Way, past the black hole at our center," Gabriel murmured.

A view? Just a view? Had he said that? So it was not the whole universe, of course not, just a certain perspective.

Sensible-sounding, I asked, "I wonder if he made pictures encompassing different sectors?" I thought of an antique cyclorama I had seen in Atlanta, a battle scene from the Civil War with its devastation encircling the viewer in every direction. That was the kind of view that lived in Adam's brain. A different war. The same horror.

Gabriel said nothing. He had become totally absorbed in the residue of Thom's genius.

I heard myself panting. Thom could be beside me again, the two of us seeing it together, dazzled and thrilled and happy. Thom: large, curly-haired, kind, brilliant, graying. Even when Thom studied the computer screen, he never forgot my presence; he kept a corner of his mind for me, if I was present. Here was Mesopotamia; here was a jungle of greenery; out there was an airplane with two strange men waiting; behind me was a single deluded man, my lover, praying and singing. Didn't I smell the odor of lemons from his hair?

"The words are starting to emerge now," I said, pointing at the bloodred dot on the screen. "See, 'Valentine'"—I had forgotten the 'a' in Valentine was shaped like a schoolboy's lopsided drawing of a heart. Had it been that way before? Now all the letters were emblazoned across the starry cosmos:

*A Valentine to all the Lucys in the Universe*

Gabriel took my hand. "Shall we go on?"

"That's it," I said. "That's the end. He promised he would stop it during his presentation. He'd stop it before they saw the inscription. That's why it emerges so slowly, so he'd have time to cut off the file."

The night sky faded from the screen, but it was replaced by an image of myself—younger, so much happier I was hardly recognizable. Quickly I glanced over at Gabriel and smiled. I watched myself coming toward the camera, holding out my arms, delighted, then blurred when I came too close to be in focus.

I exclaimed, "I didn't know he—" Then I realized I must have kissed Thom when the image blurred. He had filmed me somehow; he wanted to keep my happiness and anticipation as I came to him. Yes, that had to be the reason he had filmed my joy. I began to cry.

When my image blurred and disappeared, then another woman, Italian perhaps, came walking toward the camera, happy, welcoming, younger—then blurred, and another woman followed, Japanese, equally excited and pleased, open, fresher and younger, and then—

"It's Lucy Hastings," I exclaimed. She, too, approached the lens, her face happy with unmistakable anticipation. "His assistant. Your assistant! The other Lucy." Something detonated with a dull thud in my chest.

Lucy Hastings was quickly replaced by yet another welcoming woman. Gabriel touched a button, and the series sped up. Dozens of ever more beautiful women came rushing toward the lens, their lovely, intelligent faces aglow, arms lifting for embrace. I was speechless. And there I myself appeared again, and Gabriel slowed the speed to that of real time. I was in bed now, wearing a favorite nightgown, lime green, holding out my arms, happy, willing, alive, the camera coming closer. And then the Italian woman wearing black lace lying on gleaming sheets—

"Stop!" I screamed. "Stop! Were they all named Lucy? Were they?" I felt hysteria rising.

"At first," Gabriel said. "Later Thom just *called* them the Lucys."

"My valentine," I sobbed. I jerked the flash drive out of Gabriel's machine and stood up. "You betrayed me," I yelled. I had not been enough for Thom. Then I sobbed out the impossible words "Thom betrayed me," but now I was whimpering and gasping.

"Give the flash drive to me, Lucy." Gabriel closed the computer and slipped it back in its case.

"Why? To smear Thom's name?" I retracted the tip of the memory stick and placed the cord over my head. It pleased me, despite everything, to feel the familiar metal against the skin between my breasts once again. "It's a fraud. Those women couldn't have happened. It's something you already had in your computer. It's an illusion, a computer trick."

As he stood up, Gabriel said calmly, "You recognized Lucy Hastings, I believe."

"She was your girlfriend. You could have made that video."

"Actually, we shared her. Thom had a very small camera built into the corner of his glasses. Did you ever notice how carefully he positioned his glasses on the nightstand—as though they were looking at you?"

I thought of the heavy frames of Thom's glasses, but the lenses were also thick and heavy. He had needed a durable frame.

"I've watched the videos. In the next sequence you and Thom are making love. And then the others and Thom—"

"Stop!" I screamed. "Stop, stop, stop!"

Gabriel did stop. My chest heaving, I stood and stared at Gabriel, watched from my own detached distance the two of us standing in the tangled jungle, confronting each other. He held the computer; I closed my hand around Thom's memory stick.

"Why would he?" I demanded. My mind whimpered, *We were happy!* My body whispered, *I trusted him.*

"Thom lusted after an integrated life; he liked to keep his best equations near his private life." Gabriel watched me with remote curiosity. "Thom was a risk taker, a gambler." Gabriel spoke in a dry, informative way. "It excited him. It spurred his thinking to have astrophysics and earthy sex dangerously cohabiting on his drive. He was so much older, Lucy. It made him feel alive, his collection."

I marveled at Gabriel's coldness. No. He looked slightly amused, disdainful of Thom and of me. "I won't give it to you," I said.

"I'm sure there's something scientifically important there on the file. Something beyond the briefcase notes you gave me. Thom always finished preparing his lecture just before his presentation. Did you realize that, Lucy? You two would have lunch or dinner; then he would take the flash drive from you. I'd be sitting across the room from you—shop-talking with my colleagues. He'd open his laptop, take the flash drive back from you, fiddle around for ten minutes or a quarter of an hour at the table to claim the brilliant conclusions that were always there waiting for him at the edge of his brain. You'd have a chocolate dessert." Gabriel chuckled with a sneer. "Thom never ate dessert. He wanted to keep his youthful figure."

"Just like you," I added, glancing up and down his lean, fit body. He was a serpent.

"Of course you hadn't opened the flash drive before you came back. You'd been shopping, visiting a museum—"

"The Anne Frank House."

"He liked the risk—suppose you'd lost the flash drive or were delayed?"

"No. He trusted me. I was trustworthy about punctuality."

"About everything. He liked the pressure and drama that come with procrastination."

"You killed him?"

"Whatcha got, boss?" the American voice asked: jeans, a Stetson, chewing gum. His body was relaxed, languid but alert.

"Where is the case of the French horn?" the old man in black asked in accented English.

"We'll get it," Gabriel said casually. "No rush. This wilderness is almost Eden, my friends. Let time stand still."

"I want to go home, Gabriel," I said. I forced myself to speak calmly. Nothing had ever been harder. I made myself swallow. I felt my own tears clinging to my eyelashes. Now I must focus, think, be smarter than all of them.

"Cool as a cucumber," Gabriel said. His voice took on a cruel curl. "Do people have that expression in little Memphis?" The tip of his tongue wetted his thin lips and seemed to taste the air.

Although I felt a strong impulse to run, I hesitated. Could I start the plane? If I outran them to the plane—I was younger than any of them—if I could start the Cessna, I could escape. With the flats of my fingers, I pressed the memory stick against my breastbone. Could I come back for Adam? Would I? What constituted treachery?

"I've always wanted you, Lucy."

"Wanted me?"

"All those years you were with Thom, the two of you growing older together. You always the trusting child to Papa Thom. I wanted you to look at me that way and then have the power to betray you. As Thom did."

"Leave," I answered. I tried to filter the hatred from my voice. "Just leave me here. You've got what you really wanted, Gabriel."

"Oh, no," the rabbi remarked. "We also want the texts, the Genesis parchments."

I feared I might faint. I closed my eyes to steady myself and drew in a deep breath. *Lemons!* Distinctly, I smelled the odor of lemons.

Adam had followed me!

He had disobeyed.

At that moment, his voice rang out, "Run!"

As I spun around to run, I saw Adam burst into the clearing, swinging the French horn case at Gabriel's head. Though the Texan lunged toward me, I evaded him and ran. In an instant, I was sprinting toward the Cessna.

At the edge of the jungle, without hesitating, I ran across the tarmac and up the steps into the plane as though they were the stairs to heaven. Freedom and joy canceled every feeling but determination. Panting, I rushed into the cockpit, sat in the pilot's seat, and pushed the ignition square. The twin engines sputtered to life.

Certain of our triumph, I imagined Adam subduing his enemies as he wielded the French horn case, like Samson with the jawbone of an ass. Soon he would join me. Soon we would fly. Quickly, while I waited, I picked up Gabriel's knapsack and looked in it. Yes, a wallet. Money.

I would fly to the cradle of Western civilization, to Greece; we would abandon the plane, buy new clothes, take the train to the south of France. Would they follow? Would they perish in the wilderness? Never mind. Money! New clothes! I laughed hysterically to think of dressing Adam, like Barbie's Ken, in expensive casual clothes. Myself, too.

I was out of my mind with joy and foolishness. *Run, Adam*. He would look like a fashion model, strong and cruelly handsome. I could not stop myself from giggling; nonetheless, I fastened my seat belt in preparation for takeoff. People on the train to France would surely wonder how I had managed to snag someone so young and comely. *Run, run!* But he was mine, yes, he was mine! And I would marry him—I vowed it—and make him well.

Adam hurried across the tarmac toward the plane, but he did not run. The sleeves of Riley's camouflage shirt were rolled up, and I admired Adam's sinewy forearm and the hand that grasped the black snail of the French horn case. We would take the Genesis codex to Pierre Saad. I imagined Adam had knocked the thieves out cold. Now all three were lying crumpled together among the jungle greenery, stars orbiting the interiors of their skulls. Perhaps dead. Their venomous brains registering blackness. I touched the titanium case of Thom's flash drive.

With perfect competence, Adam efficiently mounted the Cessna's stairs, pulled them up after himself, bent to kiss my cheek, assumed the copilot's chair, and buckled his seat belt as I began the taxi for takeoff.

Glancing over at Adam, I thought he had never looked so handsome. The plane and my propeller heart roared into the sky.

# PART THREE

# THE FRENCH QUARTET

ARIELLE WAS KISSING her father's cheek when a shift in the quality of the light made her glance out the large library window. While the sunlight in the south of France was always alluring, this light had an unusual tint of red in it. "Butterscotch," she said out loud. To get closer to that rich light before it transformed, she began crossing the room to the window. "We should go to Tanzania," she said to her father over her shoulder. The exotic quality of the light stimulated a longing for adventure. "See the lions and the big animals sometime."

"If you like," Pierre Saad answered nonchalantly. Sometime soon Arielle's frenzy to create art would be tempered by her desire to find a mate. Their life together would modulate into another key. But he liked the key of father and daughter, and he would prolong it to the degree he could. Since his daughter wanted to go there, Africa—the gigantic bulbous root of Egypt—suddenly seemed appealing. Before the light shifted, she had announced that she would call a cab, go to Lyon, and from there fly back to her studio in Paris.

Pierre took a deep breath and released it. Lucy Bergmann had been missing for nearly nine months.

"Father, don't sigh." Arielle smiled as she glanced back at him.

"The human chest is a rudimentary pipe organ," he said. "No doubt one could breathe very deeply on the African plains." He took in an enormous breath of air.

"Father, there's a taxi approaching. From Lyon, its advertisement says."

"My Sufi father said the rhythmic act of breathing mimicked creation when one breathed in and annihilation when one breathed out."

"A taxi!"

"To know the divine, we must become nothing."

"It's a long drive for a taxi," she answered. "I might bargain with him for my ride to Lyon, since I'm packed."

The taxi stopped. From the backseat, a woman popped out, not waiting for the driver's assistance. Arielle observed she was dressed in beige linen, with caramel-colored high heels and a cocky little hat, with a long pheasant feather jutting out behind—a throwback to the time of Princess Diana. The woman carried a valise, lavishly trimmed on the flap with flat autumnal feathers, but no purse. Her body moved not gracefully but crisply, as though she were stronger and more decisive in every gesture than she needed to be. Before Arielle could decide if this visitor looked familiar, from the far side of the taxi, the head of a man emerged over its roof. He was tall, with blue-black hair.

When he came around the back of the taxi, Arielle noticed that his slacks and jacket were a vanilla color, the complement of the woman's outfit, but they fit the form of his body with amazing exactness. No one should be so good-looking, Arielle thought.

"Shall I tell the driver to wait for you?" Pierre asked, rising from his desk.

"No," she answered. "I won't be going quite so soon, after all."

That being the case, Pierre took his time in joining her at the window. So Arielle had changed her mind. Restless. Why not savor their moment together in the south of France instead of rushing here and there?

He enjoyed the plushness of the Persian carpet under his feet as he moved. A rug dealer had once told him that in Persia the adage was that you could judge a man's wealth by the *thinness* of his carpet, but the idea of symbolizing munificence with thinness made no sense to Pierre. For his library, he had bought a carpet that felt like a sponge through the thin leather soles of his fine French shoes.

His daughter stood at the window as though arrested, with one hand raised—but not as though to wave. Of course she looked like her mother in that moment. The explosion that had killed his wife had been so powerful that the largest piece of her found intact had been her little finger. Pierre joined his daughter at the window and placed his hand protectively on her shoulder.

But Arielle stepped forward eagerly.

Pierre looked out and saw the black French horn case, and a young man with matching black hair in a vanilla suit, and the woman.

"It's Lucy Bergmann!" he said. "She made it."

Yes, that must be the French horn case and the codex! His joy was only slightly diluted by incredulity. "And it appears they took time to go shopping in Paris." He wanted to sound offhand, shrewd, and knowing, but his heart was sputtering like a skyrocket.

"Not Parisian fashion—Rome," his daughter answered. "Or Milan. His hair is Italian dark, but he's so fair." Was that anxiety in his daughter's voice reflecting the reality of her own olive skin? "Who in the world . . . ?" she speculated.

"I don't know him from Adam's house cat," Pierre answered over his shoulder as he turned to hurry toward his front door. Why not begin to use a few American expressions? A Southern one. He liked that one—a house and a house cat in Adam's garden. The idiom caused the mythic world to jangle in pleasant discord against the bourgeois one.

Right behind her father, Arielle rushed to greet the new arrivals, but when she stepped into the sunshine, she let Pierre hurry on ahead of her. Arielle wished to appear composed—friendly but in nothing of a frenzy. She had liked Lucy Bergmann. She had thought her terribly lost and exceptionally naive for a middle-aged woman, but capable of basic honesty and caring. To what extent did Lucy care about her handsome traveling companion? Arielle wondered.

When he said his name was Adam Black, Arielle could not restrain herself from laughing. "Not Adam's house cat, but the man himself?"

To her surprise, the young man blushed, looked concerned, and became silent. Hers was just a tossed-off, spontaneous laugh, but she saw he had some strange sensitivity about him. He wasn't so very young—maybe thirty.

Despite his clothes, he was lacking in sophistication. His mind lacked nimbleness, boldness.

"And where is my father's plane?" Arielle asked, turning to Lucy.

Both of the visitors answered at once, but Lucy's reply rang out more clearly. "I wrecked it." Could it be possible that Adam had mumbled, "In Eden"?

Wary, Arielle could not stop herself from glancing at him askance.

Suddenly her father was shouldering her aside. He held out his hand to Adam, and then enclosed Adam's hand in both of his. "We are delighted to welcome you. *Enchanté,*" her father said with just his particular mixture of warmth and polish.

In Adam's face there was open gratitude. She watched their eyes meet—her father and Adam beginning to know each other. Perhaps even trust. He's all right, then, she thought.

The taxi driver handed out another suitcase, large, to Adam.

"Is there another bag?" Pierre asked Lucy.

"No," she answered. "We're sharing."

Together the quartet—Arielle thought of them that way—walked the stone path toward the house, her father ahead with Lucy, and she beside Adam, who carried the French horn case in one hand and in the other the suitcase that matched Lucy's valise, though it had no decorative feathers. In the style of her father, Arielle just said, "We're very glad you've come," and let the rest of the short walk continue in silence. When she glanced back to watch the taxi disappear down the hill, she was glad she was not in it.

Her father walked with one arm loosely across Lucy's back, his hand resting on the curve of her shoulder. Had he been wearing his Arabic robes, he would never have assumed such a familiar arrangement.

Later that night, after dinner, she would say privately to her father, "To my knowledge, you only met her at Nag Hammadi." He would reply, "Not so. Remember I had spoken with her in Cairo, when she nearly broke down trying to address the symposium. And that is not all. When the piano fell in

Amsterdam, I happened to be next to her. I put my hand under her elbow to keep her from falling." Arielle would smile slightly even while giving her father the eye of suspicion. He would redirect her attention to herself: "And what are your intentions concerning the handsome Adam?" Instead of answering, Arielle would ask her father what he made of him, and her father would reply, "He has the perfume of a rare flower. He would require extraordinary care, more devotion than most people are capable of giving."

But that afternoon, in the hallway to the bedrooms, Pierre asked Lucy in a direct fashion, "Shall you share a room?"

"I think not," she said, "but would a connecting door be possible?"

"But of course," Pierre said. "Exactly the arrangement my daughter and I have when we travel abroad together."

"I don't think he's quite young enough to be my son," Lucy murmured.

"Some people have young souls," her father replied as he led them down the hall. "Some of us dally along the road to wisdom, or even to age." Without even looking over his shoulder he tossed back the idea, "Perhaps you yourself have a soul that has rested as much as it has journeyed." He stopped. "Forgive me." He turned around to offer an explanation for his impertinence. "My stepfather is a Sufi, and sometimes my own thoughts take a rather mystical direction, that is, when I feel I am with those who might as well be family."

Lucy said nothing.

Arielle wished her father would zip his lips. She didn't want them to think either he or she was weird.

"We don't eat meat," Adam suddenly said, out of the blue.

After Pierre had telephoned his friend at the restaurant in Bordeilles to bring up his most exquisite fish offering for their dinner, and after the guests had bathed and rested, they all seated themselves at the candlelit library table, Pierre beside Lucy but facing his daughter; Adam beside Arielle and facing Lucy. Pierre explained that he always used the large library table for the rare dinner party, as it saved the expense of building a dining room.

"The table is elegant," Lucy said. "I can't think of a better place to feast, literally or figuratively, than in a lovely library."

"We are a quartet, are we not?" Pierre replied.

Arielle was both surprised and pleased to hear her father echo just what she had thought but not said.

"What instrument would you choose to play in a string quartet?" Pierre asked the table at large.

No one responded. They picked up their white damask napkins and smoothed the cloth over their laps.

"What a relief to be out of high heels," Lucy remarked candidly.

Arielle was delighted with this down-to-earth, nonsequential response to her father's whimsy. It was as though Lucy had steadied the boat that held them all. Like old friends, they could just blurt away.

While Lucy had changed from her skirt into linen slacks without changing her blouse or jacket, Arielle had shed her jeans to wear the most richly exotic of her gauzy, flowing gowns. Quite on purpose, she had decided to look as strange and alluring as possible, lest Adam take her for an ordinary person. Like Lucy, he had dressed down by replacing his smart-cut jacket with a casual white cotton knit sweater; a narrow band of pumpkin color encircled his chest and back. Already Arielle wanted to ask if she might sculpt his head, but the impossibility of representing the inky blackness of his hair parried that impulse. She regretted that she knew nothing of the art of love.

How is it possible for merely his appearance to promise so much? she asked herself. And yet it did. His form spoke of his essence, surely.

"Without your heels you are just my height," her father commented to Lucy. Too much candor, Arielle thought. Too much, too soon. She felt herself blushing for her father's sake. He really did not understand proper boundaries. Then she censored herself for being censorious. Lucy didn't seem to mind his comment any more than he had minded her segue from chamber music to foot comfort. The smile Lucy gave her father—Arielle could see perfectly well sitting on the diagonal with her—was sheer friendliness. But Lucy was contained, too. Oddly self-contained, Arielle thought. Lucy had changed.

"And so," Lucy said, "we have brought you the ancient texts. At least we assume they're inside the case. Of course, we've not opened it."

Arielle's father helped Lucy to a portion of stuffed sole. Arielle noticed he had chosen the new Nall pattern of Haviland porcelain. It was rather unusual: flowers combined with patches of reticular geometry in strange contemporary colors Nall was said to have invented himself. Pierre hesitated in replying until he completed the transfer of fish so that it covered the lavender pansy painted on Lucy's plate.

"Perhaps you will accept on faith not just the sincerity but the profundity of my gratitude," Pierre finally said. "I am sure this mission has cost you dearly. Do you think you are pursued?"

Lucy said, "We don't know. We left our attackers in the jungle. No doubt they each suffered injuries. They could have died. In any case, it might be a long time before they escape the wilderness. Adam destroyed their computer."

Arielle's father looked squarely at Adam and asked, "Did you kill them?"

"I used the horn case as a defensive weapon," Adam said.

"On whom?" Pierre asked as he prepared to serve Adam's plate. The rose on Adam's plate was such a dark crimson, its crevices were black. Arielle wondered if her father had matched the plates to the guests in a conscious way.

"Gabriel Plum," Lucy answered.

"The scientist!" Pierre exclaimed, though the name meant nothing to Arielle. Pierre asked, "Where did you meet him?"

At that moment, a rush of sweet bells passed under the library window. It was the kind of sound that Papageno, the bird man, made on his xylophone in *The Magic Flute,* but in a less predictable scale, note to note. Pierre's hand froze in midair; the sole dripped its sauce back into the serving dish.

"What is it?" Adam asked.

Pierre placed the silver serving tool back in the dish. "It is my father," he answered solemnly. Pierre picked up a silver bell and jingled it. All of them noted that its tone and timbre matched the sweep of sound passing under the window, though it was but a single bell instead of dozens.

When the server appeared, Pierre said, "Please set a fifth place, next to me, at the head of the table."

"It's possible," Lucy said, "that we have been followed. Be careful. We *expect* to be followed."

"No, no. It is my father. The very Sufi I spoke of earlier."

"In Egypt," Arielle explained, "his camel always jangled a blanket of little bells. Here he would be traveling with—" She hesitated.

"A donkey." Pierre hurried away, calling out in Arabic.

"Never before," Arielle said, "has Grandfather visited us in France. I have no idea how he found us. He's very dear. A creature from another universe."

Arielle noted that Adam glanced rather anxiously at Lucy, and Lucy, in return, extended her hand across the table, palm up, to Adam, who took it and held it tightly.

# LOVE AND ART

SAFE IN FRANCE, in the library of Pierre and Arielle, I loved the feel of Adam's large hand in my own. I knew Arielle was puzzled by Adam's demeanor. From the front of the house, we heard Pierre welcoming his father and his father's reply—an ancient, dry voice—then the sound of the donkey's small hooves entering the house, a quiet clatter on wood, a muted footfall on carpet.

"Grandfather is a bedouin," Arielle explained. "He would expect his animal to be brought inside, like a brother."

She rose from her chair as a tiny old man swaddled in flowing robes led his soft-faced donkey into the library. The bedouin's skin was like leather, and a staff towered above his head. I felt Adam abruptly release my hand. Both Arielle and Adam hurried to the little man. Arielle bent to embrace her grandfather, but Adam fell on his knees as though he knelt before a holy manger.

The old man spoke in Arabic, which Arielle immediately translated: *"Here is one come from the West, a young man, a prince, neither king nor magus, who bends the knee and gives reverence not to a babe but to an aged man as though he were the Prophet himself."* (Yes, I thought, Adam is a prince.) The Sufi laid his hand on Adam's black head and let his fingers play in his hair. *"The true Prophet will not come again. That is not promised to us. We are to go to him, to make a holy pilgrimage to Mecca.*" His gaze shifted to Arielle, and his face crinkled in a smile.

"And now he is asking me," Arielle reported, looking at me, "if I have made my pilgrimage to Mecca." She spoke to her grandfather in Arabic. "And I am telling him that it is my intention to do so, sometime soon." She glanced at Adam. "Actually I'd rather go to Tanzania and Zanzibar, the Serengeti Plain, and the Olduvai Gorge."

Pierre spoke to his father rapidly in Arabic and then explained to us that he was inviting his father to sit at the table. "A quintet," he said. "Do you know Schubert's quintet," he asked me, "the one referred to as 'The Trout'?"

As he spoke the words, playful strains of music filled the air.

"The system is voice-activated," Pierre explained in English.

I smiled, but I felt unnerved. In the music, the trout gleefully cavorted in the water. My ear followed the viola part, as it always did because I had played the viola in my youth. Adam remained kneeling on the carpet before the tiny Sufi. Surely the others were finding Adam peculiar. He folded his hands in prayer, and his tears bathed his knuckles. Did Adam weep in sorrow or with joy?

Waving his hand at the donkey to shoo him away, the grandfather circled around Adam to claim his proffered place at the head of the table. The obedient animal turned and retraced his steps down the carpeted hallway toward the entrance. I heard someone speaking politely to the donkey in French—no doubt leading him away. Adam's eyes were closed, and he moved his lips in silent prayer.

I stood up from my seat, my eyes meeting those of Pierre, Arielle, and the grandfather in turn. "Please believe that in no way do we mean to give offense," I said. "Certainly we wish to do honor to each of you, and especially to Monsieur, who like ourselves has traveled a long way. Nonetheless, for the sake of Adam's health"—I paused—"we must beg you to excuse us. We need to retire."

The grandfather threw back his head and laughed, nodding vigorously to assure he understood intuitively.

"You honor us with your trust," Pierre said, "in sharing your need, as all true friends must ever do with each other. Of course you must eat before you sleep, and your plates will soon be with you." Immediately he began to address his father and his daughter in happy Arabic.

When I held my hand out to Adam, he rose from his knees, and I led him down the hall.

When I closed the door of Adam's room behind us, I kissed Adam on the lips. He held me close against his body. For a moment we stood together, swaying. Then he tugged at the neckline of my sweater and said, "May I?"

I nodded consent and smiled. Carefully, he began to remove my clothing, and we both entered the realm of serene ritual. As he had whenever we entered our hotel rooms, since our flight from the jungle, Adam unbuttoned, unzipped, and took the clothing from my body. I stood perfectly still and smiled at him. When he had finished disrobing me, he took a pad of exquisite drawing paper and a wooden case of pencils from the valise decorated with pheasant feathers. Now he made a slight movement, sliding back the lid of the box to display a palisade of sharpened points.

"Where shall I sit?" I asked. Always he wanted to draw me, to practice his art, before we made love.

"Sit on the bed."

I pulled back the covers and sat on the sheet, my bare feet resting on the floor.

"Hold the valise," he said. "The feathers are like you."

I stood the valise on end so that its edge rested on my thighs. It was tall enough to hide my nipples.

"Like this," he said gently. He laid the valise flat across my thighs. "Like a dinner napkin." Humor tweaked his glance.

I smiled at him, and he began to draw. I watched his eyes move back and forth from my body to the page and listened to the slight erotic rub, almost a scratch, of the graphite against the receptive page. My thoughts wandered to the two flowers on our plates, the open full-faced pansy for me, the black-crimson rose in flowing profile for him, as though it were a smoldering comet about to let its color slip off into space.

When he finished the drawing, Adam laid the pencil back into the wooden box. He turned the pad of drawing paper to face me.

"It's beautiful," I said. "All your drawings are beautiful. I can never decide which one I love the most." A rather narcissistic statement, I knew, since they were all of me.

Obligingly, he turned over the pages so we could review together the drawings he'd made. The early drawings had the loose lines of a sketch. The first one showed me sitting nude in a chair near a window; I was looking out at the Acropolis in the distance. The rectangular shape and pillared sides of the Parthenon were faintly suggested, and its geometry contrasted with my curves. "The Greeks had no more fear of the naked body," I had said, "than we felt in Eden."

In another sketch, I lay flat on a small sailboat, my face turned toward the artist, as though he stood in the water, though he had not. We were alone on the little boat in the Aegean, relaxing. I had spent Gabriel's money freely.

A later drawing showed me in a roomette on a train. As he turned the pages over, the sketches became more detailed and erotic. With the fifth or sixth one, I had asked him if he were making a calendar. "Yes," he had said, "a calendar for all times and places, of one person whose heart I love and whose body my hand loves to draw."

When he actually touched me, each time we made love, he obliterated everything of my memory of Thom. In the drawings he never included the fact that I wore the flash drive on its black cord around my neck.

"Rembrandt loved to paint his Sasha," I said, thinking of her wide waist and aging thighs. I recalled *The Lagoon* of Matisse, in which an apple green form spread over a bluish one, their curves undulating in the rhythms of loving bodies. Not people at all, but abstract forms, yet the concept was thoroughly erotic. Surely art has its deepest root in sensuality. "How many sketches do we have now?"

"This was number eleven."

When I looked again at this newest drawing—*Lucy with Feathered Valise,* I thought—I noticed that my body seemed older, more sagged. "Do you think of them as particular months of the year?"

"No." He pulled the cotton sweater over his head. "Do you want me, Lucy?" he asked.

"Of course." Then I teased him a bit— "Who wouldn't?"

Afterward, I listened to Adam's breathing change and knew he was asleep. I sat up to admire his amazing beauty, memorizing, storing up for the future. Sighing softly, I remembered that we had not eaten. Pierre had said we should eat, and of course he was right. I padded to the door and opened it a crack. Yes, there were two trays, with decorously covered plates. Down the hall, very faintly, a trio of Arabic voices chattered in quick exchanges, and I heard the faint bubbling of a hookah; I inhaled the odor of Turkish tobacco and thought of the richly flowing—concealing, revealing—dress Arielle had worn.

After bringing in both trays, I slipped on a nightgown from our suitcase, for warmth. Then I ate all of my dinner, even the fattening baklava. While I enjoyed the honey sweetness, I continued to admire Adam, lying on his side, facing me, his cheek pillowed on his hands pressed flatly together. He had been lying in this posture, I remembered, a long time ago, when I first saw him under the apple tree. When I finished the food, I used my finger to swipe up the last of the honey and flaky pastry. Then I rose and passed through the door that joined our rooms.

I wanted to sleep long and undisturbed. When Adam got hungry, he would wake up and enjoy his food. He would feel strong and whole. He would have a clarity about him—perhaps for days—till something jolted him backward into a morass of guilt and confusion. If he perceived or imagined danger, his focus would become steely and his body and mind would contract into purposeful action. But he was not naturally a person of action; he was a dreamer.

In my own bed, alone, I wondered yet again, as had become my habit since Gabriel's betrayal in the jungle, whether Thom had been faithful to me. I had relived seeing again and again my own more youthful face coming unself-consciously toward the camera. Was a camera hidden in the corner of Thom's glasses? Was he possibly even a spy? Had he seated the camera close to his natural eye to record classified scientific documents? For whom would he have been a spy? For his own records? His own library? I saw my face and body replaced (preferred?) by a series of other Lucys. But wouldn't that have been a simple matter, with Gabriel's vast computer expertise, for him to engineer? Perhaps Gabriel had filmed them from the corner of his own tortoiseshell glasses.

Again, Thom's valentine emerged from the dark cosmos, declaring itself to be for all the Lucys in the universe. When that message had been engraved on my heart, there had been no sense of any sinister connotations.

I pictured the Lucy whom I had actually known, the young assistant I had assumed was Gabriel's girlfriend. "We shared her," Gabriel had claimed.

A film such as the one Gabriel had tricked me into watching could so easily have been faked. It was pornographic, not artful. Gabriel could have hidden the images on the drive of his computer, coiled in the chip, waiting till he gave it some signal I never noticed so that it would seem to be part of Thom's memory stick. He could have caused the film to embed itself in Thom's flash drive, too.

The answer was either yes or no. Thom was the person I had always believed in, or he was not. I thought of the probability problem referred to in physics as "Schrödinger's cat." Tonight it seemed more likely that I had been mistaken about Thom. Was letting Adam draw me the way he did, and come to me as he did, the acting out of some feeling of degradation or of revenge on my part? Or was it liberation, joy, therapy, friendship, love, transition? I sighed and closed my eyes.

I remembered the abundance of Thom's graying, springy hair. My own hair had its graying threads now. No curls. I thought of how Leonardo had loved to draw curls of hair, in angels, in men, in women. Sometimes he had drawn streams of water that swirled and curled like hair. Drowsy relaxation claimed me, and I thought of Schubert's trout, a fish that smiled. When I slept, I dreamed of Fred Riley standing patiently beside a stream, hoping to catch a trout in a hand terminating in pale claws. Seated at a concert grand, the bedouin fingered ivory keys, interspersed with black ones grouped in twos and threes. Near the piano in a wooden chair, Arielle sat on Adam's knee. Once again I tucked the viola under my chin.

# ADAM'S DREAM

DEEP IN THE night, curled in the cave of sleep, Adam dreamed of himself walking in the garden. Alone, he knelt beside the crisscrossed bark of a palm tree and prayed God to give him Eve. The side of the tree creaked open like a door, and graceful, nameless animals passed before him. A young woman appeared, richly dressed in the desert manner. "I'm here." With a little gasp, she apologized, and her wide eyes looked afraid. "There will be blood on the sheets."

Sleepily, he said, "They're already red, aren't they?"

He held out his arms to her. Many women had walked willingly into his arms, whether he was sane or not. Rosalie? Always he was a tender lover. He hoped so. This time he would live tenderly with her, too. No betrayal.

This he devoutly intended.

In the morning, Adam heard a light rapping at the door. When he opened it, a slender arm thrust through, holding a lightweight but beautiful dressing gown, purple with gold threads and small mirrors.

"There's one for everybody," the voice said—certainly it was Arielle's voice. "Grandfather brought them on the donkey."

Adam expected his robe to be too small, but his arms entered the sleeves as though they were entering air. He liked the thin, crisp fabric.

"Come to the library for coffee, please," she said from behind the closed door to the hall.

Adam crossed into the adjoining bedroom, but Lucy's room was empty.

When he entered the library, the four of them were already tucked into soft chairs. Their bodies bent this way or that—relaxed, chatting, eating, licking their fingers. It appeared to Adam that they had been talking for hours, sitting in their comfortable chairs grouped together on a lovely woolen carpet. Perhaps the carpet would rise and transport them to perfuméd Arabia.

Their robes and the food—glazed and braided breads encrusted with slivered almonds, goblets shaped like funnels filled with small round golden plums, the sprinkling of pink rose petals over the table—everything spoke of luxury. The word *Venice* formed in Adam's mind, though he had never been there, and he felt the glide of a gondola.

"Such uniformity—all of us in robes," Lucy exclaimed, but because the colors of the robes varied from person to person, Adam thought her choice of word to be not quite right. *Unified,* not *uniformity,* he thought. How composed and unified we are, like diverse people in a single painting might be. A Renoir married to a Matisse. He thought of the valise stuffed with art books Lucy had insisted on buying for him as they traveled. "They drew," she had said, "yes, but, remember, they also painted."

Lucy's robe was scarlet shot with gold; Pierre was in verdant green, Arielle in azure, and Adam in royal purple like the prince the grandfather had said he was. Why did the grandfather resemble a turtle? It was the way his head thrust forward almost horizontally from his shoulders. The grandfather's robe was the colors of sand and birds' nests.

Quickly, Arielle said, "Beautiful. The robes our dear grandfather has brought on his donkey make us beautiful, one and all," and Adam loved Arielle for the kindness in her courtesy.

While they ate breakfast together for the first time, their hosts asked how Lucy and he had met and what had happened to delay their arrival in France. Lucy's sentences seemed curved, Adam thought, then straightened like a drawing that wanted to be a portal more than a picture, and he wondered if what she said was true. She told her tale briefly, and then Arielle wanted to know his own story before he met Lucy.

The touch of Arielle's question caused Adam's history to contract and repackage itself within his brain. His story was like an insect, a roly-poly bug that could curl itself into a smooth gray ball concealing its many legs like small hairs along its side and also obscuring its beginning and its end. Rapidly rolling the small ball of narrative, he spoke even more briefly than Lucy had.

"I was captured, and beaten and left half dead. I found myself in a place, a garden, that seemed like Eden. Like the first day of creation. Like the beginning of my life. I have recovered my health." After each of his sentences, he provided a space that Pierre filled with Arabic for his father. Neither Lucy nor Adam mentioned the feral boy or how F. Riley descended from the sky in an orange parachute, or his death. Together, they described how Gabriel Plum had betrayed them. Because Adam felt that what he had said had a mistake in it, when they finished their duet, Adam looked into Arielle's eyes and said, "I should have said, 'I am recovering my health.'"

Immediately, Arielle translated the reshaped sentence, passing it along—like a well-rounded apple on a platter—for her grandfather. She opened her hand and made the palm flat as she spoke.

Suddenly the grandfather began to speak in Arabic. The strange words bubbled and flowed from his lips. Arielle quickly folded in her fingers and brought her hand, balled something like a fist, to rest in the V of her body, where her legs met. Both Arielle and Pierre sat perfectly attentive, as he talked on and on. He never made the slightest pause for translation.

A long time later, he still was speaking. Who would think, Adam mused, the old man would have so many words in him? The old man was like a mountain spring, and the words from his lips flowed unceasingly over jagged rocks and smooth, flat stones, over toads and watercress. Minnows swam in his words, and then a gigantic whale whose passing was interminable. Yards and yards of gray whale blocked Adam's vision like the passing of a freight train at a rural crossing, till finally the way was clear and that moving assemblage no longer blocked the vista. Then Adam felt Lucy glancing at him, no, a steady gaze. In their garden life, her gazing eyes had been a calming hand.

Someplace in another room a clock chimed ten times. Adam realized the grandfather would talk forever. They would die listening to his wet voice, the way it snagged on twigs and ruffled around a sharp rock. It was a room of fathers: Arielle's father, her father's father. His own father, the old rancher, might come to stand beside the grandfather, two eagles like harbingers of eternity. The distant clock chimed eleven times, and still Arielle and Pierre sat still as foothills before the mountain. The gonging of noon, twelve strokes after the clock cleared its throat, and a server stood in the door, listened, and disappeared. Very slowly, Lucy rose. She stood behind Adam and put her light hand on his shoulder.

At the stroke of one, the old man stood. In his body, he himself became the figure of a short, straight number 1; and the words ceased. He bowed his head to each of them, and like a sand dune walking, he moved without moving, across the room and away.

Pierre blurted, "My father has told us the history of everything. We must make a pilgrimage."

Pierre stopped speaking as abruptly as he had begun. He looked vastly uncomfortable, pained, as though his gut cramped him and yet he could not release his bowels. Finally, with a grunt, he said, "You share all but one of my secrets. I must share now my unshared secret with you. My father has said I must take you to a certain place immediately. My secret place. No one but me has been there, not for thousands of years, not for many tens of thousands of years. I am shaken because I had no idea that my father knew this secret. Now we are to go to our rooms. Arielle and I must put on warmer clothes, and we will lend you jackets and caps."

"Where are we going?" Lucy asked.

"To see cave drawings, paintings, etchings, the bas-reliefs that use the shapes and colors of the rock as inspiration for particular animals. And one small statue."

"How long will our trip take?"

"A few hours."

"Why—"

Pierre stopped her speaking by putting his finger across his lips. "In this story," he said playfully but nervously, "you are allowed only two questions."

When Adam turned, he saw a flush of anger pass over Lucy's face. Her face was almost as rich a scarlet as her dressing gown. Had he ever seen her angry? Alarmed, he glanced at Pierre.

Immediately Pierre crossed the three paces that separated them. He took both of Lucy's hands. "I have made a mistake," he said earnestly. "It was wrong of me, not clever, to set limits on your need to know. I'm very nervous, too eager to follow my father's instructions and to begin my task." Astounded, Adam marveled at how quickly Pierre had understood and analyzed the causes behind his inappropriate speech. Now he was saying he hoped Lucy would forgive him. "Not even for my father's sake, Lucy," Pierre said, "would I have enmity come between you and me."

"You don't know what cave paintings have meant to me," Lucy said. She was roused by the imperative to explain. "To me, they're the emblem of the human spirit. When people first knew themselves to be people, not just survivors, they felt the urge to create. Probably they danced and told stories, too, but what have endured for us are the paintings. When I encourage my patients to paint and draw, I'm encouraging them to know the root of their humanness and that they're not alone. Their work bridges the space between them and any other human." Though she seemed to empty herself with her speaking, she added yet one more question: "Why did your father say we must go on this pilgrimage?"

"For Adam's sake. To heal his wounds."

Lucy leaned forward and slowly kissed Pierre on each cheek. The anger drained from her face. Pierre reached out both hands to her, and their misunderstanding was over.

Adam's whole body felt a surge of relief. The cosmos wanted to heal his wounds? Then Lucy would know and forgive what was inevitable and necessary.

Adam held out his hand to Arielle. She received his large hand with her little one, squeezed, and released it more deftly than an expert angler could release a lucky trout.

Pierre said, "My father says we must journey together, the four of us. Perhaps there is danger."

Well capped and coated for their journey underground, the quartet reconvened. The old man was not with them, but Adam saw the Sufi outside explaining things into the long funnel ear of his donkey. When Adam looked into Arielle's luminous brown eyes, he fell into their depths and fell and fell, though he knew his feet were still standing on the polished oak floor. Pierre placed flashlights into their hands—blue, yellow, green, and red, their stalwart barrels full of batteries.

"The door to the cellar stairs is in this room," Pierre explained.

Lucy was surprised. The room was lined with bookcases. Adam quickly looked around but saw no other door. Arielle began to smile.

Pierre took a red leather book from a shelf. Its gold-stamped title read "Revolve."

"In the original house, the cellar stairs began here, where I built my library room. On an impulse, I made one of the bookcases revolve, like a door." He opened the book; in the center, pages had been cut away to house a switch. He touched the button, and a bookcase turned on its axis, revealing the stairs.

"My whimsical papa," Arielle said. "Grandfather will love it."

"It's a remote device," Pierre explained. "It can be activated from anyplace in the house."

As Pierre began to descend to the cellar, Arielle and then Lucy quickly followed, but Adam paused.

Looking at the elongated flight of stairs, Adam felt his strong legs quiver with uncertainty. The angled tree trunk among the redwoods had seemed less threatening than these down-diving, dusky stairs. Where the original wooden steps ended, earthen steps had been carved as the floor was excavated. At the top of the tall wall of the basement were ordinary half-windows, but the light entering the basement fell so far, it became weak before reaching the earthen floor. Adam hesitated. Below was the land of nightmare. Everywhere, just under the surface, pulsed the possibility of war or violence.

Embedded in the far wall lay two great flat stones almost together but with an opening between their heavy lips, like stomata on the surfaces of leaves. Botany, the peaceful science. It was a calming thought. Who could have guessed, without a microscope, that a host of lips dotted the surfaces of leaves? Adam had loved to draw in the botany class in college; it legitimized his desire to look and draw. *Lips, lips, labia.* Adam closed the revolving door. *Cellar door.* Hadn't he read somewhere that scientists had determined that phrase to be the most euphonious in the English language? Adam hurried down the stairs to catch up with the others.

To pass from the basement into the underworld, they each folded themselves in half and entered the mouth of the earth through the stone lips. When he bent himself to enter, Adam impulsively turned and backed through. "Breech," he said softly. "Ass-backward I am reborn into the realm of darkness." He would ask Lucy if Shakespeare had written that. *Macbeth?*

"Are there witches here?" Lucy joked.

Pierre answered that he thought not, but shamans perhaps.

A weak splash of light followed them through their entrance. Pierre suggested they click on their torches, which Adam knew to mean flashlights. Silently he denied Pierre's term: a torch must burn. *Flame* was the essence of *torch.* This battery light had no warmth. The light Adam held seemed dim and feeble against the absolute blackness of the earth. He wished he'd come with handfuls of lightning bugs.

"Adam, Adam," Lucy said with some urgency. "Is it all right for you—being here?"

"Are you claustrophobic?" Pierre asked, but in the pause where Adam might have put words of some sort, Pierre went right on speaking. "My father said, 'In the old world, he will find connection and kin.'"

Pierre's flashlight spotlighted a small army of upright rolls of bubble plastic, each tied with a red sash. A platoon of rolled bubble wrap. "I should unroll the plastic to protect the floor," Pierre remarked. "But my father advised against it. Walk gently."

"We will, Papa," Arielle said in the voice of a flute.

# WITHIN THE EARTH

IN A NIMBUS of light, they moved through a corridor rendered smooth-sided by coursing water eons before humans walked there. Carbuncles of flint protruded unexpectedly from time to time. Occasionally Adam's hand reached out to touch a rough patch glittering with mica. Far ahead in the dark, he heard the sound of rushing water, and he was afraid of needing to cross it, but the path broadened and ran parallel to the malevolent stream. Adam was grateful the river, terrible in its power and indifference, did not ask him to put even his foot into it. As the water became wider, its violence diminished and finally the flow spread into a broad, still lake. A small red canoe was lodged on the near shore of the pool, but it had room for only one, and Pierre made no indication that they should try to crowd aboard. Overhead, the ceiling arched high.

In this hollow space below the high stone ceiling, their footsteps echoed and mingled as they moved through the emptiness. Against his face, Adam felt a damp chill contradicting the cocoon of warm-seeming glow that surrounded them. While his nostrils constricted to stem the flow of fetid air, his jaw opened, and the air entered the little cave of his mouth and wiped itself on the plushy carpet of his tongue.

Pierre stopped to point down with his flashlight. The beam illumined a bottomless crevasse, a fissure more than a yard wide running in both directions as far as they could see. A great crack. There was nothing to do but step over it. There was no need to jump, but the step would require them all to stretch.

"Lucy," Pierre said, "you will have to give a little leap. It's not far, but your body will not want to do it."

She simply nodded, stepped up to the abyss, looked straight ahead, and, without hesitating, pushed off and over. Modestly, she stood aside, out of the way, and Arielle immediately followed with no to-do at all about the effort. It was almost as though they had blinked collectively and then Arielle had already accomplished the step she needed to take. Pierre nodded at Adam, but Adam was afraid.

"Like a bull," Pierre said.

Adam stepped back five paces and ran. He would not look down, he would not lower his head, he would look straight ahead like Lucy, unflinching. With every step he was afraid and the soles of his feet tried to recoil as though scorched, but he ran and leaped, landing far beyond on the other side, his entire body shrieking in protest. When his feet hit the stone, he stumbled. His body insisted, *Yes, there was danger.* Like a bad shepherd, Pierre had ordered Adam into danger.

"But you made yourself obedient," Adam said out loud. They all stared at him as though he had referred to them, so he mumbled truthfully in explanation, "My body, like a herd of disobedient sheep, did not want to take its members across the divide."

Where was Shakespeare when he needed him? Shakespeare to give him the words for what was never spoken but only thought before?

Pierre picked up a small rock, knelt carefully beside the great crack, and dropped the rock. They listened to it clatter as it fell, colliding with the walls of the split earth. Their flashlights wavered in their hands while they listened. There was no end to the falling, only a diminuendo like the hoofbeats of a galloping horse dying away in a distance.

"I have to *make* myself do it," Pierre said to no one in particular. "Each time I have to make myself step over." Pierre was not ashamed. "The body rebels, instinctively."

And why had they come to this land of fissures and darkness? To see cave art, but so far there were no pictures. The place itself was a picture, a landscape Adam had never inhabited before. One of the passages opened into a great hall with a huge boulder in its center. So might the earth have fallen from the underside of heaven. Round as a globe, the boulder had dropped from a height beyond the power of their flashlights to illumine, though they all held their torches as high as their arms would reach, and Adam stretched tallest of all. The mass of the boulder was there simply to intimidate, but all they need do was to walk around it. It was inert, helpless.

"'Potential,' I call it," Pierre said.

God's Weight, Adam thought but did not say.

They placed their hands on the boulder as though to hold it in abeyance or to influence its disposition. Adam liked the gritty feel, even the chill of the rock flank, against his palm and fingers. Some of his smaller, weaker fingers were afraid, but his hand as a whole was confident. The flickering light cast their moving shadows on the stone.

The room narrowed to a corridor, and this time its walls were smoothly coated with white calcite. Again Pierre stopped. When he held his lamp close to the wall, its light was reflected in a white glow.

"Look beyond the surface," Pierre instructed, and Adam thought his words were impossible nonsense. "Don't look into the light. Pay attention to what the side of your vision can see."

And then beneath the translucent calcite, Adam began to see the lines of a drawing. Something lived and had its being under the skin of calcite. His eyes traveled those charcoal lines, waiting for them to speak their form.

"I call it 'The Kindness of Animals,'" Pierre said.

And then Adam saw a pair of giant C's, the rearing up and reaching and return of curving antlers, of a male reindeer. The animal's lowered head, even his tongue, was drawn there, and with him was another deer, resting or kneeling, receiving the kindness of that ancient tongue. "It's like a painting at Font-de-Gaume," Pierre said, "but larger. And look behind the female." Then Adam saw curled and sleeping the small form of a fawn. Colors of reddish brown draped the backs of the animals; the pigment shaded in places to suggest the varying thicknesses and contours of their bodies. The color had its own richness, though it was cloaked by the milkiness of the calcite. Their hooves and the moment defining the reindeer eyes were black.

"He honors her achievement in giving birth," Lucy said.

"At Font-de-Gaume, there is no little one," Pierre said. "The tenderness between the two adults is simply there—who knows for what reason."

In Pierre's voice, Adam heard a tremor, a fissure, an abysm.

Pierre added, "Perhaps, at Font-de-Gaume, the female was tired, or dying."

Death? Adam felt the shape of tears traveling his cheeks. He could have swiped the sliding tears away with the back of his hand, but instead he thought of their rounded form bulging on one side, their flatness on the other, of the flexibility of the flat side as it adjusted to the shape of his cheek. He would treasure each tear's short life as a formed thing before it fell and splattered on the cave floor. He wept for himself, for the dark backward of time, and for this stony man Pierre, who would not allow himself to weep, though his voice might quake. Adam counted six tears like large apple seeds on each side of his cheeks as they traveled down, fell, and lost themselves on the stone floor.

What did this painting want to mean, and to whom? To Adam it said, *You can have this. When you recognize tenderness, it comes to dwell in you. The painting of a tongue is a tongue speaking to you. The painting is a gentle, silent licking of your soul.*

When they walked on, Adam felt the broadness of his own back. On that flat place, an image of tenderness could have been painted. The corridor opened again into a stone room. "Look up," Pierre said.

In the wavering light, a multitude of animals ran across the ceiling. Adam gasped. While the reindeer had seemed beautifully arrested, here the giant creatures moved in unison. Pierre had them turn off their flashlights, but he quickly struck a match to light a thick candle from his pocket. Because of the flickering of the candle, a great ripple of shoulders and backs and bodies poured across the sky, the arch of rock overhead. Adam felt his body sway. Shaggy bison and aurochs tossed their heads and stirred up dust with their trampling. Rounded horses shifted their haunches. Lions sped forward with faces like wedges among the herds, and elephantine mammoths moved with curtains of hair swaying from their sides.

The contours of the cave, its bulges and declivities, helped to form their bodies, and the shifting shadows of those irregularities in the undulating light made the animals surge and retreat. Billows of calcite mimicked clouds, though sometimes the hooves seemed to spring from earth-rooted, jagged terrain. There was a single, magnificent elklike creature. Adam could have sworn those lordly nostrils flared with breath. The elk's antlers branched and branched till it seemed he carried an impossible tree on his head, and he himself bifurcated into a kind of outreaching god hand.

Filling the not-sky that was arching rock, the rush and power of the animals overwhelmed Adam, and his heart galloped with their ecstasy.

"Like constellations," Lucy said. "In the night sky, animals and giants populating the sky."

A dark hole ascended upward from the ceiling, and Adam thought it might be a chimney through which all of these soaring creatures could funnel outward and into the night and on to the outermost reaches of darkness. Constellations, yes, they could become even that in distant space.

"See the great black cow," Pierre said, pointing where the ceiling of the cave bent down to become wall. "She's falling upside down from the sky. You can see her at Lascaux, too. No one knows her story."

"Black as a piano," Lucy said sadly. Her pale, fringy hand gestured at the panoply of rushing animals. "But what did it mean to them?"

"These paintings are a text," Pierre said. "They are as much a text as the pages you saved, the ones inside the French horn case now, waiting. For me."

Dizziness swept Adam's mind. Animated by the flickering candle, five lionesses cleaved their way toward the others. Perhaps Lucy or Arielle—her name was fresh and frightening on the tongue of Adam's mind—must become like a lioness, a power, a sister to those with whom she hunted. He closed his eyes for a moment.

"In their time," Pierre went on, "these pictures were read, and they were copied many times, over thousands of years. Some painted twelve thousand years ago replicated those made twenty-four thousand years ago, and those were half inspired by, half copied from, paintings thirty-six thousand years back in time, and these—"

"Is each copy an interpretation?" Lucy asked.

"Who's to say?"

"There." Adam pointed. "A horse is running through feathery grass. Or is he in a shower of arrows?"

No one answered.

"Here are rhinoceroses, like ones in Chauvet and elsewhere," Pierre explained. "Over thousands of years, the artists—shamans, whoever they were—continued to draw in the same style, to copy the drawings created thousands of years before their time. It's the same with stories. Stories begat stories and were passed through the air from lips into ears until they became the written sacred texts our cultures hold so dear, our holy books, our bibles."

Pierre's words rattled and fell, like stones exploring a crevasse. Adam watched Pierre's eager eyes move from figure to figure.

Because the dome of the ceiling was high, the artists would have needed to build scaffolding to create the soaring effect they wanted. They might have lashed poles and crossbars together. Like Michelangelo, Adam thought, painting the ceiling of the Sistine Chapel, but the power of these animals seemed terrifyingly close, less remote than Michelangelo's biblical figures. Except for his rendition of Adam, recumbent and limp, waiting for God to touch him, nothing of Michelangelo's spoke like these beasts conjured with line and color from mute rock.

"Did they already know everything—these artists?" Arielle asked. "Did they know it all then?"

"Picasso said so," Pierre answered. "He'd seen copies Henri Breuil painted of the bulls in Altamira."

Adam had never liked Picasso; he thought his forms were cruel to soft bodies. Who was Picasso to pronounce on this? An opportunist. He hoped that Arielle did not worship Picasso. But Picasso had not seen this cave—only Pierre, and them. When a drop of water fell on Adam's nose, he moved his position slightly and opened his mouth. He waited till a drop fell onto his tongue, and he swallowed. *Shed for thee.*

"How old?" Adam asked.

"Breuil's copies were made in 1902. Picasso saw them when he was twenty-five."

"How old are these paintings?"

"Older than Chauvet, which is older than Lascaux."

"And Lascaux is—" Lucy asked.

"Eighteen thousand, six hundred years. And Chauvet is twice as old. And the style in both is much the same. So little evolution of style in all those millennia. Here—" Pierre stopped and gathered his breath. "Here I know we go back even further than Chauvet. I've carbon-dated. Back nearly all the way to when we, *Homo sapiens,* evolved. Back forty-seven thousand years."

Lucy said, "Lascaux is closer to *us,* in time, than it is to these paintings."

Adam wanted to weep again to think how long humans had labored to bring life from stone.

"There is a reason to paint on walls and ceilings," Adam said. "It subverts their purpose to enclose. The walls become windows, portals to other realities." Arielle moved beside him and encircled his waist with her arm, but it was Lucy's voice that filled his head.

"I believe this," Lucy said. She spoke loudly, making her voice reverberate in the room. "I believe this," she repeated, her phrase like a fanfare of trumpets or the prescient roll of tympani; now Lucy's voice was like elephants braying through their lifted trunks, like zebra hooves drumming the plain: "I believe this: As soon as we were human, it was part of our nature and our necessity to create art. It is as essential—art is as essential to our humanness as food or shelter."

Adam had never before heard her trumpet her belief in anything. He was pleased. Her credo was of creation, if not of the creator.

*Father!* Adam summoned. *Listen to her, Father.* Adam thought of his father's hands, hard and callused, yellowed like horn, with the work of the ranch. His face carved by wind, hardened by the sun. His icy blue eyes. His intolerance for the soft strokes of graphite on soft paper. His disgust.

Finally Arielle asked her father if the prehistoric artists had represented the human form. "They drew all these animals. Did they draw themselves?"

"I'll show you," her father answered. A deepness thickened his voice. Like the tolling of a bell, Adam thought, and he shivered. "In two ways, they represented themselves, male and female," Pierre said darkly.

Pierre led them from under the clatter of hooves and heads past the great black cow falling from her sky. From the domain of the animals, Pierre took them deeper into the raw earth, into one of three openings that branched away from this rotunda like arteries from a heart. The corridor was smooth again because gushing water had once polished its walls. Then the conduit branched, and nodules of flint began to protrude again from the uniform smoothness. Where a side of the wall was ruptured, they stepped across another crevasse into a parallel hall filled with crystalline stalactites and stalagmites. It seemed like a different universe because of their glitter. Adam felt he was walking among stars.

"They were here, too," Pierre said, and he pointed to the heads and necks of three mountain goats lined up in profile like choristers, and then a tiny little goat, complete and set apart, more detailed and appealing than anything they had seen, but abandoned, created and left near the bottom of a wall, as though to emphasize his small, incidental nature, all by himself. If a child had crawled here, and the spot had been illumined by an adult carrying a stone lamp, the child might have reached out and patted the drawn goat with the palm of his hand.

"I have a friend," Arielle said, "who draws just like that." She pointed at the darling goat, drawn so low on the wall.

A red tide of jealousy engulfed Adam. Outside, up there, far away in Paris, in the sunlight, what café, what striped awning, what blue sky did she live under, with artists for friends? The rapid footfalls of fashionably dressed Parisians drummed in his ears. Of course Arielle must be an artist, who lived among other artists.

Their path bent downward, steeply, and Adam felt bewitched by the change in perspective, how if he were sketching this, Pierre's shoulders and back would be drawn lower on the page to suggest descent.

Stopping beside a cave within the cave—a grotto—Pierre lifted his light to the prone figures of crudely drawn men, falling, pierced with spears or sticks. "Here are the wounded. Not unique. Similar figures—but only single figures—have been found several times in different caves."

"War," Adam said.

"'The Killed Man,' some have said of the single figures they've found. Possibly a sacrificial figure. At Cognac, he also looks just like these men, naked, falling forward, the cleavage of his buttocks rendered but the form left unfinished. No head. The lines for shoulders simply stop."

Adam thought but did not say: Like the artist, we see him from the back, like those who have thrown the spears. The artist, knowing that we, too, are men, has made us complicit. Adam closed one eye the better to aim. Unaware of arms or legs, Adam's target was the man's back.

"And so," Arielle said, "humans have always killed each other."

Adam met Lucy's gaze, and together they thought of F. Riley and of the tortured lamb.

Lucy said, "We must not repeat Cain and Abel billions of times. Sin was the joint failure of Adam and Eve to teach their sons the sacredness of life."

Adam put his hand on Lucy's shoulder, remembered the willingness of her flesh, and swallowed tears. He followed the movement of dank cave air through his nostrils and down into his lungs, and smelled the unhealthy rottenness of time. Violence against the body, so pitifully vulnerable, was surely the original human sin. And yet he felt strength and readiness in every fiber of his muscles. Readiness to fight or to love.

"Another image," Pierre said.

They continued downward in a single file. Straight ahead the corridor came to a dead end. A smooth V-shaped rock hung down like a sharp tooth. With bold black lines an icon of womanhood appeared. Without doubt, the black thatch of lines represented the pubic hair of a woman, and at its center the outline of the open vulva.

"And so," Lucy said in a sad voice, "from the beginning we women were reduced to this."

"And we men to killers," Pierre said. "But this is harder than 'The Killed Man' to show you, certainly to show my daughter." Pierre did not turn his gaze away from the large, hairy, open pubes, but Adam watched him reach out and touch Lucy's shoulder. Yes, she needed comfort, as much as anyone could give. But she flinched at Pierre's touch. Adam dared not look at Arielle. Did it come to this? The marks of charcoal gripped in some prehistoric man's hand were rapid, ugly, ruthless.

Arielle's voice asked calmly, "Are there other drawings of women, in other caves?"

Her father answered that there were. But they were all like this: five thousand years later, twenty-five thousand years later. What had been drawn to represent women in the days of parietal art was mainly focused on the reproductive female parts.

"I am more than this, Papa," Arielle said in her pure tones. "We have evolved in our thinking. Some of us, at least." Her voice, suddenly like her grandfather's, reminded Adam of a clear stream on a mountainside. "I do not accept this as the image of woman."

Adam felt depression settle over him. Was his father right to whip the hand that drew a woman reduced to her shaggy crotch? And his own eleven drawings of Lucy? Did he betray the spirit by wanting the body? What was betrayal? After their time in Eden, on the road to Baghdad, in Greece, on the trains, was he betraying Lucy then and now? He thought of Rosalie, the first of his loves, and her apple cheeks. How stirred he had been by the prospect of knowing other girls! And killed men? He winced, remembering the hurt bodies of men he had seen—while he survived.

"This is the wincing place," Adam said. "The mirror of us—violent and lustful. But the animals they painted were beautiful. To my eye the animals were transcendentally beautiful." He thought of the majestic elk, a continent of an animal, with its branching rack of antlers.

Pierre picked up a small carved stone, a bulge of hips and breasts, and placed it in his daughter's hand. "Here she's a bit more whole, a fuller body and head. Some think they're fertility symbols perhaps. Not young and lithe, Arielle—but with pendulous breasts and plenty of thickness to her body. A woman after many birthings."

He put the hard little figure of fecundity back on the cold stone.

"I've seen photos of such small statuettes," he said, "from all over Europe.

They've been given the names of various kinds of Venuses. The Venus of Willendorf, the Venus of Lespugue. Some figures are fashioned from rose quartz. They're composed almost entirely of a lovely abstracting of curves."

"If those who named her wanted to claim in a respectful way that she represented fertility, they should have named her Demeter, not Venus," Lucy replied. "She's a mother, not a calendar girl. Not a representation of idealized, virginal, inaccessible beauty."

"Young females," Pierre said, "are depicted almost like straight sticks—no breasts, but curved behind for the buttocks, sometimes a V scratched on the front." Adam thought of young girls in jeans walking in the schoolyard. "I'll show you two more sites," Pierre said. He sounded tired.

Adam heard the cave make a sound as though it were clearing its throat. Or was it the sound of a single footfall? Perhaps God had walked here in the cave with the artists and breathed over their shoulders as they painted the animals. But Pluto, the rapist, had also guided their hands. Adam himself was tired.

Arielle said that in Germany, in a tar pit, an ancestor of humans much older than the fossil Lucy had been found. A lemurlike creature they had named Ida. And others. Then she asked her father if they would go back the way they came. He answered no, that there was another way out, and it led past other paintings, lovely, inspiring ones. And so they began a long, more gradual ascent.

"Is it a mistake to judge them by our values?" Lucy asked.

"Many men," Pierre replied, "in our time are ready to kill. Many men see women so crudely. Are we so different from people who lived eons ago?"

No one answered. Adam wiped his forehead, as though he were sweating in the cold cave.

"Two great dangers," Pierre said. "Violence and the way men view women."

All the way, as they climbed steadily upward, Adam thought of the first animals they had seen under a veil of calcite: the male deer licking the head of the female, their tender connection. He imagined the free movement of the artist's whole arm circling to create the sweeping C of antlers, how that movement engendered form and volume on the stone. How the artist's moving hand had graciously drawn the flick of an animal tongue. But had a woman represented only by her genitals sat nearby posing for the artist, or had he drawn from memory and desire? Adam wished a cave artist had offered a redemptive vision of humanness, an Adam and Eve, rendered fully, with the tenderness of those deer, not the reductive, dark allure of sexuality.

The cave's corridor fit his shoulders like a cape too heavy to bear. He would walk upward toward openness, remembering the grassy plains spreading around the Garden of Eden, and how the sunshine drenched everything. How he and Lucy had come together in tenderness and respect under the starry sky on the road to Baghdad. He wished they had made love in the sunshine of the open plains of Eden. He thought of the many times he had seen a male wildebeest or graceful gazelle casually mount a female in the daylight. Then walk away. *Dumb animals,* did he hear his father say?

He thought of Pierre's library, the essence of civilization, and their own cozy group around its table, of a crimson-black rose that someone whom he did not know had designed for his plate.

He walked a maze of branching memory, but there was a wholeness, a continuity, to the narrative. One foot followed another.

Lucy walked ahead beside Pierre as they moved through the uptilted corridor. Adam found his hand reaching for Arielle's hand—or had she woven her strong, cold fingers between his? Her hand was abnormally strong and confident. What work had she done with this hand?

He considered the vulnerability of Pierre, ahead of him, safely bundled in a warm jacket and wearing a cap, but how easy it would be to pick up any path-side rock (lying just beyond a stooping down and a reaching out of fingertips), and how easy it would be to hurl that rock into the back of Pierre's head. Adam pictured himself standing on the ledge of the rock shelter in Mesopotamia and looking out on the world, his own neat pile of stones stacked in a pyramid, like antique cannonballs. He had felt himself lord of all he surveyed, and while Lucy slept and healed, he had gathered an arsenal to defend his domain. That he had hidden the French horn case in the rocks embarrassed him, but every day they had spent together had been essential to their healing happiness.

Pierre flashed his beam on a site where the outlines of animals were drawn, one across another, a great jumble with no attention paid to the relative sizes of the animal; a mammoth was drawn partly inside a bison but also spilling beyond to nudge a lion. Adam saw the outlined shapes of bulls, aurochs, rhinoceroses, and lions piled together like a tangle of wire coat hangers. There was plenty of blank wall space. Why had the artists chosen to pile the outlines together?

There by itself someone had drawn the sloping neck and pointed nose of a bear, and close by, the skull of a real bear sat, as though purposely placed, on a hump of dirt. Pierre pointed to claw marks, great gouges torn into the sides of the corridor, and then he pointed to huge shallow basins, dozens of them, and explained that here giant bears had wallowed and slept through prehistoric winters.

Adam longed for snow, for the pristine whiteness, for both the bright terror and the new beauty of Idaho in winter, but he could not imagine Arielle in the snow. He imagined Pierre's father, the Sufi, handing him a pad of creamy drawing paper; he wanted to take the Sufi's hand, to kiss his hornlike fingernails.

Suddenly the two couples turned a corner, and there on the stone wall were beautifully painted horses decorated with spots. Yes, a whimsy of spots, like no real horses ever wore. Pretty spots for all the pretty horses. Surrounding them, blessing them, was a halo of human handprints. Adam heard Lucy's sharp gasp of pleasure at the handprints from the past, friendly and familiar.

A slight smile curled the two corners of Adam's mouth, and he knew he was smiling at them, the invisible ancient ones. He smiled at the black-spotted horses and the swarm of vermilion handprints. Adam closed his eyes. When he opened them, the flickering light played again on the stone wall, the horses, and the myriad human handprints wreathed around. Here was joy and fulfillment and connection.

"The charcoal I found here," Pierre said, "carbon-dated back to forty thousand years ago. Painters blew red pigment through a hollow bone onto and around their hands to leave the prints. Look at the fingers. Their fingers and handprints look exactly like ours."

When he first awoke in Eden, Adam had crawled to the beach, left his own handprint on the shore in the damp sand. Without touching the prehistoric print, Adam placed his hand so that it hovered just above one left by an artist so many thousands of years before. Their work had lasted.

*I am justified.*

Adam felt no need to put his hand into the wounds of Christ. For a moment Adam's hand and spread fingers hovered and trembled, then he closed his fingers and rested his hand beside his thigh.

Finally Pierre said, "Look up." Above them was painted a small figure of a man, not crudely but with the grace of the animals because he was part animal. The man's head and shoulders were those of a stag.

"At Les Trois-Frères," Pierre softly explained, "some people call a similar figure 'The Sorcerer.'" Pierre sounded exhausted, but he continued. "This image, too, combines features of a man, with the antlers of a stag, and that's the tail of a horse. His legs look human, and so do his arms. His fingers seem stylized, split like goat hooves, to me."

Although no one mentioned it, the testicles and penis of the figure hung between his legs but seemed turned backward. The penis was a bold, black, curved line, about to lift itself to straightness.

"His body leans forward," Pierre said, "like 'The Killed Man,' but he has a face, and it is turned toward us. Part man, part animal."

"The Christ was part man, part god," Adam said.

"Some church dogma says 'fully man and fully God,'" Lucy corrected quietly.

"In any case," Pierre went forward with his thought, "the Sorcerer is part man, part animal. Like the Egyptian gods, but so much older. Being partly animal may give him power and help him transcend human limitations."

"He's wearing a mask," Lucy said, "with eyes on the side like a frog."

"I think he's hopping, or jumping," Arielle said. "The other men were crude stick figures, falling. But see how the calf muscles in his legs are defined. They bulge like ours. He may be dancing. *Ekphrastic,* art about art. The artist may be depicting the art of dance."

"He's looking at us," Adam added, peering back.

## A PATH, A STAIR

When we emerged from the cave, we stepped out not between the two flat stone lips into Pierre's basement, but through a hole shrouded by holly in the side of a steep green hill overlooking the river valley. As we reentered the sun-bright world, we shielded our eyes with our hands. After a moment, Pierre pointed west toward two bare juts of gray rock in the distance, where the sides of the valley came closer together but did not adjoin. "The arch broke and fell," Pierre explained, "millennia ago."

Turning to the east as the hillside curved, we saw the Saads' A-shaped house with a blue roof, like a toy, perhaps a mile away, and the thread of road leading to it. Because the road ended in the cleared space before their home, our taxi from Lyon had turned around to retrace its route.

East and west, in all directions, the sunny openness of the landscape of the south of France made the dark caves seem a product of imagination as much as of memory. Here was the bright reality I loved: topside. I had had the privilege of seeing sacred art; for my own eyes it had emerged from profound darkness—yet I wanted to worship the sun, the days of light and breath it gave me.

Pierre gestured toward a footpath progressing from where we stood across the slope and toward the house. As Pierre began to lead us back, Adam fell in beside him, with Arielle and me following close behind. For a while she and I shamelessly listened to their conversation.

Pierre said, "My father insisted I show you the underworld." He added lightly, "I still obey my father."

"Do you?" Adam seemed amazed. "Throughout my youth, my difficult youth, the chief imperative was to escape the domination of my father."

"Perhaps," Pierre asked quietly with the voice of a friend, "it's time for you to accept him?"

"He's dead."

Pierre turned his head and smiled at Adam. "I'm not sure that's relevant."

"Suppose I told you—" Adam hesitated, found his wording, and said, "—that I have walked and talked with God."

Arielle's head twisted abruptly toward me, but I ignored her surprise.

"Who knows?" her father answered, not at all surprised. "Suppose I told you that I *am* God, and that in walking and talking with me, as we are doing on this hillside, you are talking with God?"

Because the path cut across a slope, Pierre's and Adam's eyes were level with one another, though Adam was much the taller man. And younger, and stronger. But there was self-assurance in Pierre's unmocking brown face. And confidence.

Adam said, "That's not what I mean."

"But you could mean it," Pierre went on comfortably. "Each of us has only his own meanings to offer. But in some sense, I'm sure you can see truth in what I say."

Silence fell between them, and the four of us simply continued our walking, two by two on the sunny path curving like a low necklace across the bosom of the mountain. With Arielle, I felt warmly companionable. Nearby two birds fluttered into the needles of a pine tree.

"The air smells like ponderosa in Idaho," Adam remarked. "Why did your father suggest you show us the cave paintings?"

"'Show your discoveries first to those you love, then share them with the world.' That was his advice. In France, such treasures belong to everyone by law, that is, to the state."

"And do you love us?" Adam asked Pierre.

"Certainly, my daughter," he answered. "But I have hesitated to take my daughter to such a place, to such a deep grave." I felt that Pierre was purposely ignoring the fact of our presence behind him. He placed that much importance on being direct with Adam.

"You accept that I love my daughter," Pierre went on. His head was bent, and he appeared to be studying their feet. "But you doubt my love of you and Lucy."

Adam was silent. I, too, studied our feet moving beside the pathside tufts of grass, beside a fallen pine, past a knuckle of rock emerging from the soil, beside a small gnarled bush with dried orange berries on it. Fellow travelers, we four, at least for the nonce.

"It is a little embarrassing for me to say to you that I love you," Pierre continued. "And yet it is true of both you and Lucy, though I have known you such a short time. I love you because you have helped me, because you have brought me my heart's desire, the ancient texts. I know it is a miracle that you have managed to do so." Pierre was trying hard to read his heart for the truth of the moment. "You have brought a priceless treasure to my house. Who does not love those who give them even the ordinary things they need?"

"The ungrateful," Adam said, then he tossed his head like a stallion and seemed surprised that he had said the words aloud.

"It is easy for me to feel gratitude," Pierre said, "and gratitude is the bed-fellow of love."

"Does love have other bedfellows?" Adam asked, but his tone had changed. He sounded like a friend talking to a friend.

"Of course. One of them is desire."

Adam simply let the idea sink like a stone in water.

"And there is longing," Pierre added.

Adam touched the back of his neck, feeling the warmth of the sun there. Perhaps he was thinking it was a French warmth, not the white, high-altitude burning that touched the Idaho mountains, not the sizzling heat of sunlight on our skin in the unfiltered Middle East. He said, "Your name, Pierre, Peter, in English means 'rock.' Jesus told Peter, his disciple, that he would build his church upon a rock, through Peter's faith."

"Your greatest longing," Pierre said, "is for God."

"'In God, we trust,'" Adam answered. He grinned. "In America, it's written on our money."

He used a friend's prerogative to lighten the tone of a serious conversation.

Our curiosity about them satisfied, Arielle and I began our own dialogue, but we let a space open between our voices and their ears. We were glad to walk in the sunshine and to draw the aroma of grass and scattered trees into our nostrils, but we wanted to know each other, too. Walking beside Arielle, I remembered my girlhood friend Janet, and how often we had strolled in some park or boulevard while confiding our thoughts.

"Tell me about Thom, your husband who died," Arielle said. "You loved him?"

Her question struck me as an insult. Beside my elbow, she was a streak of warmth, tall, young, exotic, a presence unlike myself. Because the only bridge to link us seemed to be an arc of language, I began to send words like so many goats across it. Was this how Adam often felt? Cut off from the world with only breath and words, peculiar words, to send to the Other Side? Perhaps what seemed an insult was really an invitation to commune. "I did love my husband—very much—and I do."

What *should* I say to this younger woman, who was doubtlessly filled with real questions about love? Pierre had tried to read his heart to Adam; as the more experienced person, I must try, too. "I don't know if the Thom I loved really existed, or if it was my idea of him." My skepticism blurted out like a protrusion in the path. How blandly abstract my words! Yet I felt I was pulling barbed hooks from the red fish of my heart.

"If he was what I needed—I met him when I was eighteen." My sentence bridge was breaking up into incoherent phrases. I gathered control and said, "I believed in him because I could imagine him to be what I needed." When Thom came into my life, my ties with women friends had weakened. Regret flamed through me.

"And have you loved Adam?"

Did the young woman actually mean to ask me if I had had sex with Adam?

"Yes," I said, but because I feared the falseness of a truth so baldly literal, I added, "And no."

"These answers cancel out each other."

"Exactly," I said, but I felt only silly confusion.

Spontaneously, we both trilled with laughter and liked each other a bit better.

"And are you, Arielle, devoted to sculpting?"

"Yes—and no," she echoed.

"But you don't mean it in the same way I do."

We passed another scrawny bush with puckered orange berries growing close to our path. I thought of the orange blossoming of the parachute in the sky, how Adam and I had stood within the rocky overhang and watched the parachute opening. "You mean," I interpreted, "that you thought you were passionate about your work, and you were, and you *are.* But now—"

"But now, out of nowhere—there's Adam."

"How does he seem to you?"

"Incredibly, fabulously beautiful. . . . And in some way . . . wounded."

"An irresistible combination," I observed, "for those who need to be needed." But my scientist husband, established and admired, hadn't needed me; I chose to be an art therapist partly because I wanted to be needed. When I returned to the States, would I return to my work? I had also chosen the work out of faith in creativity—that which, unfailingly, always, was a positive force. *Ars longa, vita breva.* Even now, for Adam, seeing what the earliest humans created had been wonderfully affirming of his own artistic impulse. Even their depictions of violence and their fundamental absorption with raw sexuality were human realities he needed to embrace. Mostly, I thought, those artists had wanted to celebrate the beauty of the animals, of the Other.

I touched the memory stick hanging around my neck. Thom had said there were Others out there. Would we find them beautiful? Would we find some reason to kill them? Or them us? *Thou shalt not kill*—surely the most important of the commandments.

"About Adam," Arielle continued. "Is it wrong of me—I mean, do you— I feel I shouldn't go on without—"

"Permission granted," I replied, and instantly, how light I felt!

Walking ahead of us on the path across the slope, I watched my lover, my Adonis, walking beside Pierre, saw Adam's straight back and his inky hair burnished blue by the sunshine, but it was as though he had become merely an image. His substance evaporated from my interior landscape and left a vacancy.

Why should I need to love any man now? Why not just feel safe here in the south of France, absorbing this sunlit place with my eyes? After the bleakness of the underworld, the contours of this land comforted my eyes. What other image did I need beyond that of beloved land? The firmness of the very path supported the soles of my feet. Across the valley a number of small stone houses and barns, whitewashed, with red tile roofs, basked in their share of sun. Ripening fields lay in the valley below, and in distant places I could see the blue ribbon of a river. *Love the natural world; love being alive,* I counseled myself.

Arielle mused, "The men Adam overcame in the jungle, they feared any contradiction of the literal Genesis story?"

"Yes."

"And were willing to kill you for the codex? Over a question of religious dogma?"

I left the question hanging in the air. Certainly they had been willing to use force.

"Maybe you'll find someone," Arielle said. "Someone you really love. In a way you have not loved before."

I said nothing. I had loved Adam, but that did not mean I could not let him go.

I listened to the twittering of unseen birds.

We all came home happy, refreshed by the newness of our experiences. A beautiful table was spread and waiting for us in the library. None of us spoke of danger; I don't think any of us believed in it anymore.

Sitting at the head of the dinner table, the old bedouin said, "In the coming days, while my son reads the message of the ancient writing, I shall read the paintings in the cave. If I study them slowly, perhaps the paintings will have a message for me."

"It's unsafe to go alone," Pierre replied, but he meant only that normal care should be taken.

"So it is in life." His father smiled; his eyes made the circuit of the table.

I knew what he had said even before Pierre interpreted the Arabic.

Apropos of nothing, Adam remarked, "A path speaks horizontal, a stair speaks jagged vertical."

# BOUSTROPHEDON

FOR FIVE DAYS, while his daughter entertained Adam and his father descended to the nether regions, Pierre shut himself in the library. He understood that his daughter and Adam had taken up hiking. Sequestered in the kitchen, I began writing long overdue letters, real ones, on stationery, explaining something about my absence.

The third day, through a window over the kitchen sink, I saw Adam and Arielle in bare-legged sport running side by side down the road away from the house. His daughter's bright blue shorts were so skimpy, Pierre later told me he felt embarrassed. They were not tight, but so short she appeared to be wearing a silk handkerchief of electric blue. Adam ran in his pale linen pants, cut short and notched, in makeshift fashion.

But Arielle's father approved. From the beginning, Pierre approved of Adam. Later on, he would explain. *He's made of beaten gold.*

I smiled to see them running together. Adam was clearly about the manly business of courtship, which on that day meant running behind a young woman fleet as Artemis. If Pierre noticed them through the library window, I felt sure he, too, smiled approval. Afterward, he would have lowered his eyes to study a square of parchment covered with signs as incomprehensible to me as Thom's equations.

An hour later, Pierre came into the kitchen, where I was sitting on a stool close to the counter, writing. When he remarked that I couldn't be comfortable, I explained I was writing to my childhood friend. "Janet Stimson. I miss her."

He asked gently, "Has it been long since you've seen your friend?" I was pleased that he had sought me out.

"Years and years. We gradually lost track of one another when I went away to Iowa, to the university. Then I met Thom. Janet and her sister left Memphis, too, for Kentucky, for a wonderful small undergraduate college."

"Invite them to come here," Pierre said. "To France, to visit you."

"Really?" I asked, surprised.

"There's an escritoire—secretary—in the library," he said. He was smiling slightly in his charming French manner. "I'll open the desk for you. You'll be more comfortable."

"Won't it bother you—my being in the same room?"

"Not at all. We will agree not to speak."

He knew there would be plenty of room for me to write at the library table with him, but it seemed more considerate to offer me a private place where I might reconnect with my friends. It was something I wanted to do. Connecting with Janet was something I wanted to do as much as anything.

In the library I watched Pierre settle to his work. Before touching the pages of the codex, he donned thin white gloves to protect the pages from the oils of his fingers. The pages were unbound, a short loose stack looking as casual as a letter. Beside them, he positioned three notepads, two of which held the Arabic and French translations. He worked away now on a preliminary English translation, but after fifteen minutes, he broke the silence. He turned his face toward me and spoke with calm deliberation.

"It makes me happy to have you here. I hope your friends will come." He paused, then added enthusiastically, "I would like to see you even more happy."

"Actually, I don't know their addresses."

Pierre shrugged. "You will discover it. Use the Google."

An hour later, Arielle breezed across the library window. Five minutes after her passage, Adam walked by, panting, his hand clenching his side.

"She runs the marathons," Pierre explained, trying to conceal a smile.

I laughed. "She'll give him a run for his money. I doubt that she could have kept up with him in Mesopotamia. But he's reverted to civilization."

"A *run*? For money?" he asked. "An idiom, no doubt." He pulled off his white gloves and clasped his hands behind his head to signal his willing detachment from his work. "Explain it, please."

At the end of his working day, Pierre placed the loose pages back inside the French horn case, into the velvet-lined pocket created just for them. I had long since finished my invitation to Janet and Margarita, but I had sat still, daydreaming, or meditating on my life with them when I was about eleven. We were wearing the crown of childhood then—strong, curious, self-confident, independent within our friendship. I wanted to loop back to those feelings—not to close a circle, but to complete it and continue on in a new trajectory.

Their home had been located at the edge of the civilized world, to my mind, but really only at the edge of a residential section of Memphis, at the end of an unpaved road.

The Stimsons had a great deal more green yard about their home than the houses lined up close together on the regular neighborhood grid. Their home had been far enough from neighbors so that when their father decided to fatten three calves, he simply enclosed a space beside the house and put the calves in it.

For me, the approach to the Stimsons' property was the approach to paradise. At the top of the dirt road, I would let my bike coast. I would pick up speed and pick up speed, turn from the rough unpaved road onto the top of their long slope of grassy lawn, give the pedals an extra hard push, then swoop and soar down to the land of perfect happiness. Before I flew halfway down the hill, I had spotted the calves and determined to ride them. *Rodeo!* We would be cowboys today. Hooray for Mr. Stimson!

You never knew what Mr. Stimson would think of next. He had made wooden stilts for us. He welded together pogo sticks. He tossed a length of cable high in a tree for our swing. He taught me to fly.

The Metropolitan Opera, brought to you by Texaco, played on the radio while their lovely gray-haired mother tidied the kitchen. As soon as I came through the door that day of the calves, my heart brimming with cowboy excitement, both Janet and Margarita proclaimed in unison, over the music, "Daddy said not to let you ride the calves."

"How did you know?" I asked. It was the biggest surprise of my life. "How did he know?"

Both girls chortled with delight, while their mother smiled. "We just know you, Lucy. We know you," they all said.

Dismay kindled up like tinder, but the experience left a glow that warmed me still—to be so well understood!

That afternoon, sitting in the tree near the railroad tracks on thick, horizontal limbs, each of us in her own place, I said, "My parents off in Japan don't know anything about what I'm like."

"But your grandmother does," Janet said comfortingly.

I said nothing. My grandmother let me make up my own mind, to do this or not to do that, and I had become quite good at making decisions. I thought things over carefully. But Mr. Stimson knew what I would want to do even before I did, and he had said no, in advance.

"You're an open book to us," Margarita said, not without satisfaction.

*Closed* and *open, inside* and *outside;* I liked to think of such oppositions. I thought of the sweep of the Stimsons' yard; their openness to fun and adventure; Janet's readiness to discuss any topic while taking a long walk. She and I never argued; we probed. We listened to each other and responded. It was all as natural as breathing.

What else could compare to that balance and intimacy? There was Thom, and now there was Adam and our time in Eden together. Perhaps there would be Pierre, who understood not just my impulses but my needs.

He broke my reverie by remarking on the French horn case, how it had kept the codex safe through thick and thin. He seemed to enjoy the mild incongruity of pronouncing English idioms with his French-Arabic accent. "Through thick and thin," he repeated. "Why not now?"

At night he slept with the French horn case and the codex beside his bed—easy to grab that way, in case of fire.

At dinner, I looked around the table at Pierre, Adam, and Arielle, their faces bathed in gathering candlelight. They all paused with me to look at one another, at our glowing. Because we always ate by candlelight, we seemed most beautiful, most painted and eternal, at that time of gathering. The bookcase turned on its axis, and Pierre's father entered from his journeying in the caves.

He carried a fresh-cut curly walking stick, and a few pale green shoots crowned its top. Ceremoniously, because the stick was a gift from his son, he leaned the staff into the corner where the bookcase abutted the wall. The green-sprouting crown of the stick rested near the book titled *Revolve*, and the old man stared at the volume a moment and touched its red leather spine with his finger. While he went away to wash his hands and we sat waiting for him, I think we all revisited the images on the cave walls far below the room where we were sitting.

I thought for a moment how Pierre liked *surprises within:* a codex within a French horn case, a remote control device inside a red book, baby crocodiles in a pit in a room. Even the caves were hidden within the earth. His search was inward, downward into the past, while Thom's gaze had been outward turned, striving to enter the future.

"Do I know all the details of your life in Paris?" Pierre asked Arielle in a jocular fashion. "For all I know you have hordes of admirers, bohemians of all sorts, who frequent your apartment day and night."

"Father!" she exclaimed, with a quick glance at Adam.

"So I am wrong," Pierre said, shrugging his shoulders. "Nor do I know what Adam has done in this interminable war in the Middle East, or what has been done to him." At this point Adam dropped his head forward as though he had been struck on the back of his neck, and Arielle reached out to touch his elbow.

The three of us looked at Pierre as though he had lost his mind, or at least his civility. As the bedouin reentered the library, he spoke a quick sentence in Arabic. Arielle translated for Adam and me: "My grandfather asks his son, my father, what has he said to us."

Turning to his father, Pierre replied first in English and then Arabic, "I said that we are all friends who would trust one another with our lives—past, present, or future."

The old man shrugged his small shoulders and remarked something in Arabic.

Arielle quickly interpreted. "He said, 'Life? What is that? A small thing to give away in the name of love.' "

We all picked up our eating implements, in unison, before the meat and vegetables.

"I am no longer a vegetarian," Adam announced.

As he seated himself at the dinner table, the grandfather reported, "With his tongue, he licks to soothe her forehead." For a moment the cave painting of the male deer licking the head of the female hung in all our memories. The bedouin went on to tell that he had taken the red canoe—he had named her *Lipstick*—and rowed across the still pond to the other side. When he said the word *lipstick,* he gave a sly and mischievous look at Arielle and me, though he continued his account. "On the far shore of the underground lake is the sanctuary where dreams originate." He had walked into a cavern full of fantastic shapes that could become whatever the viewer wished, "smooth brown ghosts, some knee-high, some towering high as giants. Very smooth, glazed." In the next chamber, he had been surrounded by the glittering teeth of stalactites and stalagmites encrusted with crystals.

"Because of your words," I exclaimed, "now we journey there, too. We didn't cross the lake but you make us see."

"One should never think of the caves as a *museum*. Some people like to think of Lascaux as a museum, like the Louvre," Pierre remarked. "The art is not hung arbitrarily on this wall or that. The wall is the site of their creation, and it has been chosen in a way that signifies."

"Like an installation," I said.

"Narrative and image, story and picture," Pierre went on. "How are they alike and different?"

He began to carve the rack of lamb that formed the centerpiece of our dinner.

"Whether told or written, a story lives in moving time; the abode of a picture is timeless in space, whether real or imagined," I promptly answered.

"And dance is the art form that dwells in time and place at once," Arielle said. "Remember the shaman was dancing. Some evening I will dance for you, in the Egyptian fashion."

Between the carving knife and fork, Pierre held a slice of the tender, dripping meat toward Adam. "Take and eat," Pierre said.

Embarrassed, perhaps by the bloody meat, perhaps by Arielle's offer to dance, Adam placed his pointing finger next to the crimson rose on his plate. "What was Nall thinking of when he painted this?"

"A Cardinal de Richelieu rose," I said, "because the crimson is almost black in the crevices."

With his mouth full of half-escaping curly greens, the bedouin spoke, and Arielle explained, "He is asking my father which way the writing moves on the pages." She spoke quickly in Arabic to the grandfather. "I've asked him what he means, and he says he wants to know about the direction—left or right—in which you read the writing of the codex."

"Boustrophedon," Pierre answered, and we all waited for him to explain.

"It's a term that derives from Greek, with French trappings. It means 'as the ox plows.' That is, the reader reads a line in one direction and then turns, as an ox would turn when plowing, and reads the next line in the opposite direction."

"Then reading that way is following a path," Adam said. "Perhaps a labyrinth."

"But a very simple labyrinth," Pierre replied, "one in which the visitor cannot be lost. He has only to move his feet to progress."

"Quite unlike the corridors of your cave," I said to Pierre, "where anyone could be easily lost."

"Like good Catholics," Pierre said, "we in this dining room are at communion. Communion, only a little of communication. Old married couples, especially in France, even when there is no speaking anymore, commune."

No one replied.

He tried again. "Our spirits flow round the curves in our life paths, back and forth, smoothly, continuously, as the ox plows."

He rested his curled hand on the tablecloth, and I knew he wished I would cover his hand with my own.

That night Adam lay luxuriantly, I imagined, in his bed as though it were a floating raft. Had he ever been so comfortable? More at peace than Huck Finn enjoying a day on the Mississippi.

He knew he could go through the door to me, and I would give myself to him, as I had so many times, freely, without question or stint. Saint Paul had said it was better to marry than to burn. Or he could go down the hall to Arielle; she, too, would receive him. If he did that, if he did it several times, then for him and for Arielle, both young and still unformed, a new path would flare wide, into a new world.

Tonight he would not choose between us. Instead he would dream. Desire would subside, untouched. Intuitively, he would believe Freud's idea that masturbation was an impediment to bonding.

In his dream, perhaps Adam is back in the ranch house, in Idaho. Confused, he wanders the familial rooms of the house as though he were in a maze. In each room he pauses before at least one shiny mirror, and the mirror bounces light back into his eyes so that he cannot see his own visage.

In front of the rock fireplace in the living room, he stops to remove from the trophy space above the mantel a boss of longhorns, a dusty relic salvaged from the time when Texas longhorn cattle, half wild, roamed the range. He settles the horns on his own head and snorts like a minotaur. Which way lies his parents' bedroom? He will show them his own wild power.

Because of the width of the horns, to enter the long hall he needs to turn his head sideways. He is not entirely a monster, for he has the thumping heart of Theseus. When he dares to straighten his head, the walls of the hall become a hollow stone tube, and the corridor twists like a bowel through the earth. The tips of his horns almost scrape the rock sides as he walks forward.

He needs a guide, a Dante: a wizened old man or a capable Pierre. Or, better, a Beatrice, a fresh Ariadne, young and pliable, to guide him out of the labyrinth, risking all for his sake. Or perhaps a woman embodying the complex certainty of middle life, coming to help him, to coax him toward normality. Young or seasoned, he imagines she comes with a stone lamp in her hand.

The flickering light illumines all the animals who graze the walls around him.

# HOW TO READ A SACRED TEXT

ONE DAY PIERRE invited us to reconvene in the library, not in the evening but in the middle of the afternoon, not to sit round the table but in the comfortable wingback chairs and the deeply cushioned green-gold sofa, before the hearth. We would gather not to eat but to listen.

At last he would read a translation of the codex!

After his reading, we would have a bouillabaisse of memorable fishy flavors with seasonings fresh from Zanzibar. I wondered if the danger Pierre's father had mentioned before our cave expedition was more metaphysical than physical. Would reenvisioning the book of Genesis cause minds to quake? Certainly.

Without hesitation, Adam and Arielle exchanged a single glance and claimed the two seats on the green sofa, facing the fireplace, which hosted a small flame. Left of the sofa were two matching wingback chairs, high and mighty as thrones, upholstered in a feather pattern in French blue, with a small Louis XV table between them. I chose the chair closer to the little fire, while Pierre seated himself at a right angle to the sofa so that his daughter was at his right elbow. He had entered the room carrying the black French horn case, which he now laid across his lap before snapping up the bright clasps.

"Where is your father?" I asked.

The bedouin's low, barrellike chair—replete with cushions whose fabric had been heavily embroidered and set with tiny mirrors—was empty. Pierre shrugged. "Perhaps he chooses to remain below, reading the paintings."

Although Pierre opened the case so we could see the codex, he did not remove it from its safe place. I thought its inscribed signs looked like rivets, as though they were shaped to hold elusive meanings on to the dry, frail sheets. "I place these pages here, for you to see. We will not touch them, though. I read from my draft of the English translation. But I want the codex to be present," he said, "to represent the person whose own hand so long ago hovered above them, writing."

Each of us acknowledged the presence of the codex by inclining our heads in the direction of the case.

"I translated first into modern standard Arabic, the language of Cairo, then into French, the language of the country where I have chosen to live, and finally into English because it is the language we come closest to having in common, among the five of us. Of course my English is not so skillfully deployed or idiomatic as one might wish." He cleared his throat. "I'm sorry my father is not here, but I will read the Arabic translation to him later."

He glanced around at all of us and at the little fire. I thought he wanted to remember the moment accurately—the color and size of the flame, how his daughter was dressed—in a cotton shirt and neat khaki pants, the sort with a zipper concealed in a seam encircling each leg just above the knee so the pants might be shortened if they proved too warm. Her cotton shirt was dyed burnt orange. She had not bothered to change from her comfortable lace-up walking shoes into something more fashionable. Adam and I were both stylishly dressed in the neutral linen clothes we had worn when we arrived. My shoes were fashionable but low-heeled, a tasteful compromise between style and comfort.

"It is a jeweled moment," Adam said. Though he spoke to us all, he turned his head and looked only at Arielle, beside him on the sofa. How lovely it was to hear Adam's voice—calm, warm, assured. It was the voice of a man of cultivation, a man of the world. "Like John Keats, I would ask of this moment 'Do I wake or sleep?' It seems too lovely to be true: to be *here,* with you all, in the south of France." Despite his warm words, Adam rubbed his hands together briskly as though they were cold. He nodded at the sprightly flame dancing in the fireplace, and I thought of the comfort we had drawn from our fire on cold damp nights under the rocky overhang.

"'O for a beaker full of the warm South,'" Adam quoted from Keats's "Ode to a Nightingale."

He hesitated and extended his hand as though he held an imaginary wineglass and were toasting the flames:

*With beaded bubbles winking at the brim,*
*And purple-stainèd mouth;*
*That I might drink, and leave the world unseen,*
*And with thee fade away into the forest dim.*

I knew that he did not quote for me.

Keats's words seemed new-minted when Adam pronounced them. Pierre blushed for the young man, this handsome American, so obviously smitten with his daughter. "Well then, from poetic words to sacred ones." Pierre cleared his throat. "Perhaps they are the same. Let me begin," he said. But feeling the need for explanation, he hesitated again.

"These notes are thoughts written about two and a half thousand years before the time we now live in, before the beginning of the common era. While these words do not compare, in antiquity, to the paintings that exist in the system of caves below our feet—or they to the age of the star-writ dark studied so devotedly by Lucy's husband—this writer's mind, like the minds and needs of artists of parietal paintings and drawings, was like ours. You must not think of him as foreign, or remote. He was like us, a quester."

Pierre shifted his body to look at me, saw with approval my excitement and interest. "We are full of curiosity?" he said, in a friendly tone.

"Of course," I murmured. But I also felt a special calm. The moment, the culmination of all our effort, was too important to be defined only with the froth of excitement. I closed my hand around the titanium case of the flash drive.

"The Neanderthals had bigger brains than ours; those later ones, the cave artists, *Homo sapiens,* and those who lived and wrote in Egypt and Mesopotamia were more like us in brain size and in stature. Dress them as we are dressed, and any of them would pass unnoted on the streets of Paris.

"Even before our codex, a few passages in our own Genesis had been written down by a scribe designated as 'J' because he always referred to God as Yahweh, which is spelled with an initial J in German. About the same time, other passages in Genesis were written down, most biblical scholars believe, by an author they designate as 'E' because he always referred to God as Elohim. Two hundred years after J and E walked the earth, the writings of J and E were brought together by a priest—his work is identified by biblical scholars with a 'P'—who also added his own original cosmic view of creation, the magnificent first two chapters, more or less, of Genesis. The opening of our Genesis was written after the other parts, though it is presented first. We do not know the real names of J or E or even P. The words of J and E were inscribed in the eighth century BCE, or 'before the Common Era,' as scholars say so as not to be so provincially Christ-centered."

"Were they Israelites?" I asked.

"Yes, though their story has deeper, older roots in the creation stories of the Sumerians and the Babylonians, who were not Semitic peoples. J lived in the land of Judah to the south, while E was from the north, the Kingdom of Israel."

"God dictated the first five books of the Bible to Moses," Adam said. "Or so I have always been taught and led to believe."

He spoke as calmly as he had of Keats, but Arielle reached over and rested her hand on his knee. I would have done the same, had I been beside him.

"Perhaps the historical truth is more complex," Pierre said to Adam. "Perhaps to some the idea of Moses represented the spirit of 'the beginning' or 'that early time when Moses lived,' and later people took the era of Moses to mean Moses himself, literally. You are correct—the churches usually do not teach their parishioners that the so-called book of Genesis was composed over a long period of time, and by several authors, none of them Moses but more simple men, not political leaders but poets, inspired but obscure storytellers. Some scholars even think that J was not a single person, but there was a J1, J2, J3. In any case, passages by J and by E were incorporated into the account assembled by P, in the sixth century BCE.

"And now we have been given these words that have traveled in the refurbished case of a French horn, these squarish leaves of papyrus I have translated—at least a first draft of translation—in Arabic, in French, and in English. Our codex, present with us here, in this moment, was also written at the time of P, in the sixth century before the Common Era. P wove the others' verses together, but more important, perhaps, he gave us the beginning of the beginning, the first two chapters of the creation story that trumpet down the centuries louder than a shofar. His words, rendered in Middle English by Wycliffe and later again in English at the time of King James I, who had commissioned the scholars of his court to make a new translation from the Greek and Hebrew, are these: 'In the beginning, God created the Heaven and the Earth.' Of course that is not the only way one could translate the opening passage. Robert Alter in 1996 begins his Genesis translation: 'When God began to create heaven and earth—'"

"Please read what you have translated to us, Pierre," I urged.

*This day is the first birthday of my twins, a daughter and a son, and they are healthy as blushing apples growing on a green tree. My wife and I agree, of life, one can ask no more than this.*

Overcome with emotion, Pierre's voice trembled. He swallowed. "I could have translated 'blushing' as 'red,' but because the children are so young and 'growing' is mentioned, I chose 'blushing' to imply process; they are not yet fully ripe and red. I suppose I could have said 'reddening,' but 'blushing' is more naturally associated with the cheek of a person, and it's more tender." He continued:

*No one knows how people came to this fertile place between the rivers. No one knows why darkness comes at end of day nor why we sleep. Nor why the sun and moon and stars travel the sky, in their turns.*

*Into the mouths of our children and ourselves we give good food and sweet liquids to drink. That is the first requirement of our lives as human animals. Like Tigris and Euphrates, two rivers—of food and drink—enter us, flow through us as through a fertile land, and then these substances leave our bodies as two kinds of foulness. There is no shame, for in this way we live. We ourselves emerge from the nether region of the body.*

*No one knows why sheep and donkeys, birds and cattle and all animals of the water and of the earth and of the air, like ourselves, are created male and female, or by what magic we mate, and from that mating little ones, each of the kind whence it originated, come forth.*

*Only in imagination do creatures come forth who are part this or part that. No men are born with antlers, and no women are born with wings, for that is not the way of procreation. Yet we can imagine demons and angels, though no person, except through wine or fasting or fever or dream, beholds these fantasticals.*

*Surely our creators formed the first of us even as we have come together to form our children. What might have been the food and drink, what might have been the mating, of those first gods? What pleasured them, sustained the god forces, and made them fruitful?*

*My friend, a priest, tells my wife and me a story of one creator who made the heaven and the earth in seven days. His poem begins with the beginning, "In the beginning, God created . . ." I point to our twins. I place one of them upon his knee and the other upon my own knee. Their faces beam like two stars. To my friend, who taught me myself how to write, even these words recorded here, even to him I say, "But life comes from the melding of Two who are the same and yet distinct and different." I suggest another opening for his poem.*

*In the beginning, there was something*
*and there was nothing.*
*When they connected, there was everything.*
*And it was everywhere.*

—

Then, I thought, life is throughout the universe. I closed my eyes and squeezed the memory stick with all my might. We are neither alone nor unique in our aliveness.

"The writer contradicts Genesis," Adam said. "He proposes an alternative."

"Yes," Pierre answered.

"It is only his supposition, his imagination, his audacity," Adam went on, trying to control his rising anger.

"Because we live in our own time, we must each create new myths to represent the truth," Pierre said as nonaggressively as a voice can be voiced. "How, if you were going to tell the story—how would you tell it, Lucy?"

I felt dazed.

Waiting for my reply, he remarked, "I could have translated the phrase 'when they connected' as 'when they collided,' but I wanted to avoid the suggestion of violence. Our author—I call him 'X'—has been thinking of human procreation. Surely *connection* is more in that spirit than *collision*. And, Lucy, how do you think of creation, of the beginning?"

Tranced, I spoke as though I read words chiseled on the air; I knew I spoke of my own need:

> *When the atoms of gray dust began to stir, each searching for the other which it had simply imagined into being (having no eyes with which to search but only yearning), there were forces that caused among the atoms a swirling, bending, curling, both inward and outward. The swirling was like the whorl on the pad on the underside of a pointing finger. And the gathering of the dust was like those distant shining smudges we apprehend scattered in the blackness of space known as galaxies and known to be composed of stars of enormous size and number.*
>
> *When the dust began to congregate, it stirred itself into the idea of fruitfulness, though it lay helpless and dry.*
>
> *Was it the tears of a god, shed in pity of the puny prehuman effort, that added the necessary lubricant?*
>
> *Or was it an accidental splash over the channel of a river that saturated the dust and made sticky clay?*

*Was it a lapping wave from the edge of a salt sea onto a stand of grass that created a fecund marsh?*

*Or was the beginning at a place now known as a dry gorge, a place where rock and clay have crumbled to sand, a place shaken by the distant thunder of the hooves of vast herds of oryx, gazelle, zebra?*

While I recited what had been given to my mind to say, I thought of Thom and of the magnitude of his inquiry, and the question of fidelity evaporated. It was insignificant.

Though words had stopped, I imagined myself and the friends who now sat about me in Africa, at the Olduvai Gorge where the fossil bones of Lucy had been found.

"Your rhapsody, our Lucy, is not so different from that of the unknown scribe," Arielle said. "My father gives him a more casual tone. Your speaking has more of the formal notes of poetry."

Pierre said, "If my father were present, he would say: 'We speculate, we imagine. Because we are human.'"

"I feel bewitched," Adam said, but his face was eagerly turned to Arielle. "I feel I could put my hand through a membrane that we can't see, and there would be the hand of the scribe. I felt that way looking at the human handprints in the cave."

Adam turned to look at me, and I felt frightened by the rush of time and space in my brain.

I saw myself night-walking with Thom, on the outskirts of Iowa City into a low pocket of fireflies, and how he had laughed and flapped his arms and said, "It's like walking in the Milky Way." And then we had walked out beyond the city to a high, dark place and looked up at the real stars, and Thom had murmured, "Behold the sacred text, which each of us must read differently." Surely Thom was good. Surely he had loved me as I loved him, been faithful and loyal. Plum could have transferred the images to my flash drive. I hoped it was so, but I knew that I would never know, and I need not concern myself with the question. My path had turned. *Boustrophedon.*

Pierre went to the library window, looked out, and said, "It's thoroughly dark now."

Preceded by an enticing fragrance, the serving staff quietly appeared bearing to the table a clay tureen of bouillabaisse and an immense cut-glass platter of salad greens. Small glass bowls glittered on the plates.

"Do you see Grandfather?" Arielle asked.

"I see a light coming this way, at his speed, approximately. He's come home across the face of the mountain this time."

"Have you finished the reading?" I asked.

"I've finished the first part; there is a second part, much more abstract, but it grows out of the first."

"Read it, please," Adam said.

Pierre returned to his chair, sighed, and began again to read his transcription of the wedge-shaped marks on the little pages. I breathed in the potpourri fragrance of the hot stew.

*In the beginning, there was something*
*and there was nothing.*
*When they connected, there was everything.*
*And it was everywhere.*

*When my mind meditates on my own nature, and on my origins, I ask, "Am I, then, something, or am I nothing?" Does everything, including myself, partake of both these elements which I call Something and the invisible twin of Something whose name in my story is Nothing? "In the beginning," my friend writes. But the beginning assumes the existence of time. Both time and place are human perceptions. Let us step over those mud puddles. Let us say, "In the Realm of the Ultimate, beginning and end did not and do not and cannot exist. By the Ultimate we may mean the Infinite."*

*I cup my open hand before my mouth, and I puff my breath against my flesh and into the cup of my hand. I do not see the air, but I feel it when it moves. Breath is not Nothing. Perhaps there are other realities not only invisible to sight but also unapprehendable by touch and by all the senses. That Nothing which is no thing to be apprehended by neither eye nor ear, nor tongue nor nostril nor simple skin, might be called the Spirit that resides in its own domain. The Creator Spirit—I imagine it Magnificent and Magnanimous.*

*What is man, then, of whom I can be mindful? Is he naught but dust or clay; so writes my friend, who is a good priest, kind to the poor as well as attentive to his writing and also attentive to the collecting and retelling of old tales so that they might not perish from the earth. He writes, "Man was dust, formed by the fingers of God so that he had limbs and body and a face, an image of God was man, but inert and without meaning till God breathed life into him—Adam." So writes my friend, whom I do not believe, though I am his friend and admirer.*

*What if God is Nothing, without shape or form? And we, too, are, in part, nothing?*

*Then that is good news indeed, for it means we cradle divinity within ourselves.*

We were speechless. Stunned by what the ancient scribe had termed "good news," we looked at one another's faces and felt stricken. I pictured the poet Wordsworth walking with his staff, like the bedouin, and would have said I preferred the ideas of pantheism, but at that moment, the library door banged open and three men came into the room, the first with a drawn pistol.

For an instant the intruders appeared only as impressions or shapes—one, a long dark rabbinical shape with a beard; two, a business suit with a face like an eagle; three, a tweedy British form.

I sprang up from my chair and exclaimed, "Gabriel Plum!" Beyond these three, through the library door, in the hall was a coterie of dark forms.

In a quick, low tone, Pierre Saad said, "Stay where you are, Lucy." Then he stepped near the edge of the carpet, though not beyond the territory it defined, held out his hand in friendly gesture, and spoke. "Pierre Saad here, old chap. We met in Cairo. I'm pleased to see you, Dr. Plum."

Gabriel Plum took a few steps forward, followed by his two cohorts, but he did not advance enough to shake the proffered hand. Instead he waggled the steel barrel of his pistol.

"The demons of literalism," I murmured so that Arielle would have some notion of what was at stake.

"I suppose you've come for the manuscript?" Pierre said.

"And for your pendant, Lucy," Gabriel said, moving the barrel of his handgun to point at me. Did Gabriel fear Thom's starry secrets, or did he covet them?

"How did you find me?" I asked.

"It is less a matter of you, madam, than of the blasphemous codex," the bearded one remarked in curiously accented English.

Pierre frowned. "Then let me give it to you, by all means, my friend. Put away your pistol." Pierre snapped shut the locks of the French horn case.

Adam had risen so gradually that no one noticed his moving, but now he was standing beside Pierre.

"Does the *Übermensch* wish to speak?" Gabriel sneered at Adam. "Or act?"

From the doorway behind them came a stirring, a parting of those dark forms, a making way, and then another voice speaking, a soft Arabic voice, crinkled with age. Holding his twisty staff crowned with growing green, the bedouin walked through the men waiting in the hall and stepped just inside the library, still speaking. Very gently, he closed the door behind him.

"My father extends greetings to you," Pierre interpreted. "He quotes from the Psalms, albeit in Arabic. Allow me to translate: 'He preparest a table before me, in the presence of mine enemies.'"

All in an instant, their three pairs of eyes shifted to look at the beautifully appointed table, and the wrinkled old man took a red leather book from the shelf, opened it, and pressed the control. The bookcase revolved open. Pierre pushed Adam through it. I grabbed Arielle's wrist and pulled her with me. Shots were fired. Immediately I heard the satisfying click and lock of the bookcase behind us. Like spirits, we floated down the stairs to the netherworld.

# THE CHASE: LUCY

ONE AFTER ANOTHER, Pierre, carrying the French horn case, Arielle, Adam, and I ran across the basement, ducked, then squeezed our bodies between the stone lips. For one step inside the cavern, light followed us, but a dozen steps ahead was utter darkness. I extended my hands, as though the darkness were a series of curtains I must part.

"In my pocket, I always have a small torch," Pierre said, turning on the device. "Farther down the corridor, we will find my workshop."

"Matches?" Adam asked. "Perhaps spare flashlights?" I heard the quick edge in his voice that arose whenever the situation was urgent and in need of practical action.

"In the storeroom."

Light from Pierre's small flashlight bored into the darkness, and he began to move forward. "No doubt the gang will eventually force the door and follow us."

"Your father?" I asked.

"I have obeyed him," Pierre answered.

When Pierre seemed to disappear sideways, I knew he had stepped through a fissure in the wall and into the cavity he had used for a workshop.

Pierre's light illumined a rough wooden table, a pile of small stones, and flashlights. Red, yellow, and blue flashlights stood upright on the table.

"Will they have lights?" I asked.

"Perhaps they brought torches with them," Pierre answered. "Or they will find torches in the house. No doubt they will follow us. They want your flash drive, Lucy, as well as the codex."

A thud reverberated through the cave. "They've forced the door now. They see the darkness. But perhaps they've not found torches yet. Probably they're running down the stairs. Quickly, quickly—" He touched my arm. "You're trembling, Lucy."

"It's chilly. I'm not afraid."

"No," he agreed. "Not intrepid Lucy. Not bold Arielle." He touched his daughter's shoulder. When he took off his jacket and placed it over my shoulders, Adam immediately gave his jacket to Arielle. "And here are matches for your pockets."

"We have a great advantage," I said as I flicked on my flashlight, "having been here before." The beams from each of our flashlights were strong and bright, more powerful than Pierre's elegant pocket light.

"Follow me," he said.

As we stepped back into the passage, another low thud sounded.

"They went back for something."

With all the flashlights burning, the corridor seemed safer. When we came to the first crevasse, no one hesitated to step over it, though the clatter of the stone Pierre had dropped into the crack still echoed in my memory. We hurried on, Pierre in front and Adam in the rear. Ahead I saw the shadow of a bear, then realized that a rock shape had cast the image. In the corridor coated with calcite, the white mineral reflected and brightened our lights.

Here was the white-veiled panel depicting animal tenderness, but we passed it without pausing. The thought skipped through my mind that probably many other drawings and paintings had been totally obscured, sealed beneath the calcite, and I wondered if there might be some way to melt it away. Our footsteps echoed off the stone walls. We sounded confident and unafraid, but in my mind, Gabriel in his tweed jacket pointed the barrel of a handgun at me.

Because it was difficult to see anything lower than our knees, random rocks and shallow but unexpected depressions were more menacing. When we had earlier explored, we had moved slowly.

The corridor opened into the large arched room where aurochs, bison, and wedge-faced lions ran across the ceiling. When I directed a slash of light at the stampeding animals, the intention on their faces frightened me. The animals, too, were fleeing, their bodies jostling one another, and I felt the muscles of my own face tightening with the intention to survive. Pierre's light sought out the giant black cow, upside down, falling from the sky. She seemed awkward and disproportioned but also mythic and sinister.

Below her black bulk, Pierre stopped the group. "Perhaps you remember—here we have a choice of three arteries." Although he gestured with his light in three directions, shadows concealed the openings. In the distance, we heard the echoes of men's voices calling to one another.

"They are gaining on us," Pierre said. "I want Lucy and Arielle to go together the way we went before. But I think it might be wise, Adam, for our group to split."

"Which way shall I take?" Adam promptly asked, though I wanted to question the idea of dividing up.

"The middle way," Pierre answered Adam. "It empties near the panel where the animals are drawn in outline jumbled atop each other. The chaos panel. My corridor runs through the section with 'The Killed Man.' All three of the corridors come to the place of the spotted horses and the handprints, but we must not wait for one another. Each must exit into the countryside as quickly as possible. Go down the valley and across to one of the farmhouses."

"Your father—" I began, remembering the sound of gunshot as we rapidly descended the staircase. "I hope—"

"Go now," he interrupted. "I'll hide here. They will be confused when they reach this room. I will wait until they seem to arrive at a decision, then lure them after me. Along my corridor there are many crevasses and sudden drops. I know all the pitfalls and traps—very well. Should you hear screaming, know it will not be my voice."

Although we hesitated to part, we all heard reverberating footsteps.
"Godspeed," Adam said, and disappeared into the middle tunnel.

Arielle and I both embraced Pierre, then hurried on, with Arielle in the lead.

With only two flashlights, the darkness pressed more insistently. Our path began to descend steeply, and the continuous rock bed underfoot looked and felt slick. When one of my feet slid, I reached out to steady myself against a wet rock wall. Arielle was gliding on, sure-footed. I resolved to run faster to keep up with Arielle. I trailed my fingertips along the stone to give myself confidence, but moving with an extended arm both unbalanced and tired me. The wall I touched spoke its unforgiving hardness. As my light splashed the wall, I saw where two fingers, ancient ones, surely had stroked the surface when it was soft clay. Farther on in a small bulbous chamber, I saw high scratch marks of prehistoric bear claws in the rough, flat stone, and then an outline of a bear's head and neck frightened me.

The passage kinked, and turned, and descended still deeper. When Arielle passed the cunning little goat, drawn low and near the floor, she pointed her beam down to spotlight it and looked back to smile at me. Shadows mottled Arielle's face with a darkness like a mask. *My girl!* my heart insisted. When I had followed her through the bright, mazelike streets of the village of Nag Hammadi, Arielle had turned her head back to be sure she was followed, her sunglasses like a mask.

A sudden catch in my side, cruel as a hook, made me stop. As I pressed the pain in my side, I panted. My lungs disliked taking in the cave air so quickly. My mind whirled with tight dizziness, and I admitted to myself my need to move more slowly. "Arielle, Arielle," I called, as softly as I could. When she heard me, she promptly stopped. "Run on for help," I directed. "I'll find my way. I remember."

Rapidly Arielle sped back—the sound of her feet pattering on the stone—and put her hand on my shoulder. "Are you sure?"

I gasped for breath. I looked down at her good running shoes. In another world, Arielle was a runner of marathons.

"Do you want me to take your pendant?" she asked.

"No. I—I'm used to keeping it."

"Turn off, remember, before you come to that graffiti, the vulva, or you'll have to backtrack."

"Go."

While I caught my breath, I listened to the lonely retreat of Arielle's quick running till nothing but silence was left, and the sound of my own breathing. For a moment I knelt down to rest. I splashed the light again on the little goat, sweet with innocence, and strangely I thought of how Anne Frank had decorated her walls with pages torn from movie-star magazines.

So as not to waste its power, I turned off my light and sat down to rest in the darkness. The world was utterly and uniformly black. I thought of fear, though I myself was not afraid, and wondered if fear were not the original sin. Not disobedience. Every child knows that at some point it becomes wise to disobey. And every wise parent forgoes punishment for disobedience at some point.

Fear and violence, twin sins. Gabriel and his men feared the modification of ideas—the idea that a fatherlike God had literally created a first man and woman, the idea of the uniqueness of life on earth and our cosmic significance.

In the silent dark, I half fell in love with nimble-footed thought.

The friend of P, the Priest, had only written his own thoughts: the miracle of creation, for him, was the birth of new being, of children, and since that act required two, his ideas of creation were dualistic. The Strophe of his dance of ideas was Something, and the Antistrophe had been Nothing, and the synthesis had been Everything. The ground of being was Everywhere. I thought it a lovely idea, mystical and appropriately abstract. In his creation narrative, Thom would have written of matter and antimatter and the Big Bang.

P's friend had written a human-centered, a family-centered, procreational version of Creation. P's own version was one based on an idea of art: the lone Artist as Creator. It takes only one to create. One man, one woman, could create art. By himself, P's God fashioned Adam from the dust. For the first time in my adult life, I *liked* that version. Did I not believe in the sacredness of Art?

I rested till I could no longer hear rasping in my breath. How strange to be tucked in a pocket, deep in the earth, to dwell in the black blank of darkness, to be pursued by my fellow humans, and to feel no fear. After all, with Adam, I had dwelt in paradise. I felt fulfilled, safe from a certain kind of failure. The satisfaction made me fear death less. Shining the flashlight before me, I slowly made my way along.

From some other direction, from all directions, I heard a faint scream. Gabriel? I could not wish him dead. I had known him too long and well. His pistol seemed the toy of a child. Perhaps I was losing my mind in the darkness.

My light shone on the large image of a shaggy vulva. The strokes depicting a woman's hair were bold and angry. The man who had made them may have felt passion or mere insistence, but not tenderness. I had come too far, missed the turn.

Now I must backtrack. I pulled Pierre's jacket closer to my body as I reversed my direction and moved back through the dark tunnel.

## THE CHASE: ADAM

FOR ADAM, THE shriek sounded at his ear. The stone that separated his own body and the body of the man who fell was only a curtain, though Adam had assumed it was the surface of a great mass.

It was not Pierre whose body had sped down the crevasse, Adam told himself. He could not guess who had been swallowed by the crack in the earth, but it could not have been Pierre, who knew the pitfalls. Turning off his flashlight for a moment, Adam felt darkness enfold him like mourning. Now he was hidden even from himself.

Adam lifted his invisible hand toward what must be the proximity of his nose and sighed onto his hand. The ancient scribe, X or Q, the Quester, had breathed into his own hand when he tried to understand mysteries.

Deep in the earth, the fallen man's blood would have no brightness; his body would lie at the bottom of a shaft, his skull broken, his own bones piercing his flesh and clothes. Adam had seen such bodies. *"Move him into the sun," one of the army doctors had said. The doctor, a young fellow himself, was strained and pale with fatigue, near Damascus. "He wants to see the sun again before he dies. Move him."* Comrades in the desert—the doctor, the dying man, himself.

Adam had known them. They lived in the marrow of his own bones.

"The pure products of America go crazy," the poet-doctor William Carlos Williams had written.

Adam made himself draw slow, big breaths. His hands clenched the rigid flashlight in his right hand. Slowly and carefully, he moved his thumb onto the top of the sliding switch and pushed it on. Like a snake, the light sprang out, and a distant voice said, "Light!" The word echoed through the dead air trapped among the caves and corridors.

*Light!* Someone had seen him. He knew the voice of the Brit, Gabriel Plum, the one with the gun. Immediately Adam began to run, reserving nothing.

He ran and made the light scoop the ground in front of him and then dash up and into the distance as far as it could shine. A wet place glistened ahead, water oozing from the top of a wall and down onto the floor. He splashed through a shallow sheet of water, floored with mud, which sucked away one of his shoes as he crossed it. He cursed himself for wearing the thin, fashionable mahogany-gleaming shoes to dinner. Through his sock, the path over the rock felt hard and bruising as he ran. He wished for combat boots. Accidentally, he turned off his flashlight.

He stopped stock-still. In the stillness, he heard footsteps coming after him, not running but plodding steadily. Sheer fear engulfed him. He sank to his knees and wet himself as he had never done in combat. There was no instinct to survive, only abject terror. Though he was drowning in fear, the rock bit his knees as he knelt. He sobbed into his hands—for life, for life, for the life he was about to lose. There was nothing to do but pray, yet he could hardly speak to God through the chattering of his teeth. He gripped the tube of his flashlight.

His assailant would find him, inscribe him in light, point the gun at his head, and kill him. He wanted to sing into the darkness, "I know that my Redeemer liveth," but there was only the dull not-song of bones knocking. He could not move, not even his thumb. Without light, who would dare to move?

When the footsteps, cautious ones, came closer, Adam made himself open his eyes. Was light lapping near? Did he see something less than pure darkness, some gray contamination? He could feel the slab of wetness in his trouser leg pressing the flesh of his thigh.

Yes, slow footsteps on stone. And light. He knew his lips were moving, but no vibration emerged from his throat. When, with bowed head, he could see the whiteness of his shirt covering his chest, he knew he was in the light. Just so, long ago, the beam of his father's big box flashlight had found him, when he had tried to run away, and made his clothing flare in the woods.

Gabriel Plum said, "Well, I'll be a monkey's uncle."

Laying his flashlight on the stone, Adam pressed his hands together so God would see that he had tried. At the last moment, he had tried to sound a prayer. His hands shook uncontrollably, though he pressed them hard and harder together. His biceps bulged against the white fabric of his sleeve. He repented of his doubt, of his sins, of his life.

"Superman?" Gabriel said.

Adam could not reply.

"When you attacked me in the jungle," Gabriel went on, "you were a blur, but for a minute—your face—you were like Superman from the comics come to life."

Adam wilted and fell on his side, deadweight, but still in the posture of prayer, still in the center of Gabriel's circle of light. The side of his skull thunked against the stone floor. Through eyes fixed and open, he saw his own fingers pressed together like a church steeple, trembling.

"You seem so small," Gabriel said incredulously. "You seem to be only a foot tall or so."

Adam's bowels unloosed themselves.

"God, you stink," Gabriel said. "You've shat your pants, man."

Adam felt some flicker within himself rise up. A tiny flame in a stone lamp began to flare, like a campfire.

"Take off those filthy pants and shorts," Gabriel said. "And stand up."

Adam obeyed. He had to take off his other shoe to pull off the trousers. He left his soiled clothing in a pile on the cave floor, but arranged them to conceal the mess. Downcast, he stood slumped with shame, glad for the tails of his shirt hanging over his buttocks and front.

"Now you're going to run," Gabriel said. "Turn on your torch. That's right. Stand up. You're a man of stature," he said crisply. "Quite strong, actually. I'll count to three. You don't have anything I want, do you? When I say one, you run. I may shoot you. I may not."

Suddenly Adam looked at Gabriel, his sharp, smart face, his impeccably tailored tweed jacket.

"Like God," Adam said. "You are like God with the power of life and death."

"Not at all," Gabriel said. "Turn on your torch. Not much more than anybody else. Let's not have any blasphemy. *One!*"

Adam ran. His toes gripped the stone, and he dodged from side to side as he'd been trained, to make himself harder to shoot.

*"Two!"*

Ahead, Adam's flashlight plied the walls for a shadow that might be more than a shadow, that might be an opening in the stone. Yes, there! He ran harder straight toward the unreflecting shadow. No, an opening, a gap in the logic of the wall—

*"Three!"*

—and beyond the opening, in the floor he saw a huge hole, wide and deep, but there was momentum and no choice. With all his strength, Adam leaped. The gun resounded like the clap of doom, and Adam felt the shattering of his heel, but he had already pushed off. With all his strength he had leaped, desperation more insistent than the pain of his wound, and landed.

His flashlight showed an abrupt turn in the corridor before him, a bend, at right angles to the place where he stood. There was his salvation: a sharp bend in the passage. Glancing over his shoulder and down his back, he lifted his foot and shone the light on his heel. Blood poured from his injury. But he could use the front of his foot, or he could hop if he needed to. He could hear Gabriel's shoes moving faster and faster in the other corridor. Adam aimed his light back on the abyss he had leaped, found no bottom to it, and registered again the sounds of pursuit. Though bleeding, he saw that a pit nearly eight feet wide, with no discernible bottom, separated him from his assailant. Gabriel would have to fly to cross the hole. Quickly Adam hobbled forward, around the turn in the corridor, beyond the reach of any bullet.

Perhaps he was lucky enough to be in a tunnel that did not double back, but branched on and on. He hobbled forward faster. A little farther, a little safer, and he would tie up his wound. He would use the sleeves of his shirt for a tourniquet.

Even as the resounding impacts of senseless bullets ripped across the pit and ricocheted off the rock walls, he felt confident of his safety.

Adam smiled at Gabriel's fury.

"Thank you, Lord," Adam said in a barely audible voice.

The firing ceased.

"I hope you're dead, old chap," Gabriel called. His circle of light must surely inscribe Adam's blood on the stone beyond the hole. "Or dying."

Adam sat on the hard floor, cold against his bare flesh. He elevated his leg and foot on a stone. In the dark, he pulled off his shirt and ripped out both sleeves for a tourniquet around his ankle. By feel, he did everything that was necessary. From the remainder of the shirt, he folded a pad to press against his wound, but he knew the soft cotton fabric of his undershirt would serve better, so he pulled the undershirt over his head. He'd use the remainder of his dress shirt to sit on, to gain a bit of thin insulation against the cold hardness of the rock.

Someone would find him. After a while, when Gabriel had given up and gone away, Adam would use a rock to click against another rock, so someone could find his location. His savior would hesitate before the gaping pit—he would not choose to leap it any more than Gabriel had, but boards could be brought for a bridge. Adam thought soberly of the length of time his discovery and rescue might require. Now he would stop the bleeding. He would wait in the dark, saving the flashlight till he heard someone coming.

He hoped that when he was shot, some of his blood had sprayed backward into the main corridor to mark the place of his leap.

# THE CHASE: ARIELLE

WHEN ARIELLE BURST into the sunshine on the green hillside, she felt sheer joy. No sound of bullets or voices had reached her ears, and now it was she, she alone, who had come through the darkness into the open world. She alone would execute her father's plan to summon help. She imagined a small platoon of *gendarmes* or even military police arriving by helicopter. Perhaps a fleet of helicopters would drop down between the mountains.

Quickly she surveyed the sunny slope and its innocent grass. In case someone had followed through the cave close behind her, a stand of yew trees a fourth of the way down the mountainside would provide concealing cover. She would sprint for the grove. And there were other groups of trees dotting the long flank of the grassy mountain. Far away, across the bottom of the valley and the little creek, partway up the opposing slope, there was a stone farmhouse with a red tile roof. While she praised Allah and implored him to protect her father and friends, she freed her legs for running by unzipping her pants legs above her knees. Then she sprang forward as from a starting block.

Running downhill was almost like flying. With the help of gravity, her speed accelerated, and she had only to be sure her feet, well housed within her trusted shoes, kept up with her descent. Half leaping and springing, she felt as though she were moving with the ease of flight. Like a robin she skimmed close to the contours of the slope; sometimes she held out her arms to the sides, like wings.

When she got to the first grove of trees, she braked, slowed to a walk, and looked back. No one stood near the place she took to be the opening behind the holly shrubs. She wasn't sure she could tell where the opening was. *Arielle flew,* her inner voice sang. Not the least tired, she felt only exhilarated. She began again the controlled downhill mixture of giddy falling and running.

There should be a sport called "downhill running" to encourage such ecstasy. Had there really been danger? Of course there had; of course there had. How could she exult when those she loved most were inside a mountain? She could not remember the intruders distinctly, only the man who spoke British English, whom her father seemed to know.

And what of her grandfather? The sound of remembered gunfire tore through her brain. She gasped and leaped downward. She became a bird again, a goat; an ibex from the cave wall leaped within her legs. Finally, near the bottom of the slope, she tired. Her mood shifted utterly, and a terrible fear came upon her.

What of Adam? What of his perfect form? She imagined them living in Paris; she saw him sitting outdoors at a café with her, people slowing down to look, wondering if such handsomeness were a matter of misperception. Who would not lust for his beauty? Yet these were the thoughts of a fool, she knew. Her artist's eye had betrayed her into foolishness.

Here was the stream, and she would take care to keep her feet dry, would cross on that line of rocks arranged as though stepping-stones. A bird like an Egyptian ibis rose up from near the water. Progressing uphill would be harder and slower, but she was in splendid condition. *I flew, I flew.* Nonetheless, mounting the incline was much slower work, and she disliked getting hot and beginning to sweat. She unbuttoned the top button of her orange shirt as she tried to run uphill.

At the farmhouse a hunched old woman was in the yard, watering cornflowers with a large green plastic watering can. "Why, what's the matter, my dear?"

"I need help."

They spoke in rapid French.

Once inside, Arielle stood panting. Her explanation was quick, and the woman used an ancient dial telephone to call for help—the phone functioned—and then woke her husband from his nap.

They would all take café au lait at the table while they waited, the old man insisted. While they sipped the hot drink, cats emerged from hiding, more and more cats, as though there were dozens, maybe hundreds of all stripes and colors, brindled and spotted. One, the obvious favorite, with six toes, was bold enough to leap into the old woman's lap and purr like a contented motor. Arielle was surprised that this antique Frenchwoman called him "Calcifer," the name of a Japanese cartoon character.

Across from Arielle the old couple sat side by side on a bench, their brown faces like twin maps with wrinkles for roads and rivers. They communed. Sometimes they spoke. Yes, they, too, had seen the paintings and drawings, the incised animals hidden in the slope across the valley, the spotted horses wreathed by human handprints. No, they had never told. Well, a few cousins, close neighbors who could be trusted.

Arielle's vision of a helicopter proved prescient, for soon it hovered in a cloud of noise near the low stone barn.

Insisting that she ride back with the police, Arielle instructed them to look for the legs of her pants, which she had unzipped and discarded near the exit of the cave, but her explanation was unnecessary. From high in the air Arielle saw them coming down the mountain—her father and Lucy, hand in hand, her father carrying the codex in the black case. But where was Adam?

When Pierre and Lucy saw the copter and Arielle's smiling wave through its glass bubble (but not the tears that had filled her eyes), they reversed their direction and began to climb back toward the cave.

# ADAM'S HEEL

WITH CONSTANT PRESSURE from the pad of folded undershirt, the bleeding stopped. In the beam of his flashlight Adam saw the heel bone was shattered, the tendon torn. The pain was excruciating, and consciousness reeled and staggered.

Hunched over his leg, with infinite patience he gradually loosened, then removed the tourniquet made of shirtsleeves. All the while, he kept a steady pressure against the wound. With one hand, he folded a sleeve and placed it as a larger bandage over the bloody pad; the other sleeve he used to bind both pads against his heel. Now he could uncurl his spine and lie back.

When his skin first touched the cold stone, Adam recoiled, but he hoped the heat of his flesh would gradually warm the place where he lay. He turned off the flashlight again to conserve its battery. After he rested, he would begin the clinking of stone on stone as a signal he hoped would carry through the corridors. He would use the SOS code.

For now he would sleep in the bowels of the earth as though in the bosom of Abraham.

—

What woke him was his own shivering. Immediately he switched on the flashlight and checked his foot. The blood soaked into the fabric was brown and stiff; there was no bright blood. But it was dangerous to be this cold. Except for the wrapping around his foot, he wore nothing at all. He feared that he might go into shock, and he was grateful to his shivering and to his body for trying to warm itself. Slowly he rose and stood on one leg so as to put no weight on his injured foot. Feeling dizzy, he reached for the wall to steady himself, but his fingers found only air. He knew he must be very careful not to fall. To balance himself, he rested just the toes of his wounded foot on the stone floor. If he became unconscious, if no signaling noises were made, it might become impossible to find him. Would they bring in dogs? Yes, surely they would do that.

He pictured the tracking dogs passing by the images of prehistoric animals. With their noses to the stones, the dogs would have no awareness of the art. Adam mused on the fact that he had seen no dogs among the paintings. Art had begun before the domestication of animals.

Perhaps he should try to follow the corridor. Perhaps the effort required to move would warm him. Gingerly he placed a little weight on his hurt foot. Then a little more weight. Even before he saw the new blood, he felt a warm gush from his heel. As quickly as he could, he sat down again on the cold, stone floor, elevated the foot, yoga-lotus-style this time, and pressed hard against the bandage. He determined that he would not try to walk again for hours. Before he turned off the flashlight, he pressed three fingers across the lens to test the surface for warmth, but there was none, not even for the tips of his fingers.

For a moment, he stroked the cold stone. Almost he could hear someone singing, a tenor voice of pure beauty, *Speak ye comfortably to Jerusalem. Com-fort-ably*—there was a significant drop in the melody between the first and second syllables. He tried reversing it: the low note first, and then a spring upward. And then began a ringing in his ears.

It was a high-pitched, continuous ringing, and he knew it for what it was: the dreadful high mosquito whine of solitude. He had heard it in the hospital. When they placed him in isolation and removed him from all real sounds, then there was the ringing in his ears. A steady pitch, almost a hum except for its wiry, steely quality. He could hum now, on the same pitch, but he knew his humming could never overcome the whine inside his head. In the hospital, he had begun to shout against the sizzling silence, but he would not do that here.

Now his foot had stopped bleeding. He placed both palms over his ears and pressed in as hard as he could; then he could hear a roaring and also the sound of his own breathing, how the air rubbed in and out of his nostrils, but he could not obliterate the high-pitched ringing. If anything, it became louder while he pressed his ears. He thought of real ringing, of church bells and how he loved their clangor. When he married Arielle, he would have church bells ringing. Yes, he would marry Arielle—he was sure of it.

The bitter bile of his resentment against his father rose in his mouth. Why should he, Adam, not have drawn the private parts of girls and women? Adam pressed his hands together and thought of their strength. He was larger and stronger now than his father, perhaps more so than his father had ever been.

*Honor thy father and thy mother!* It was the voice of God reprimanding him, or the voice of Moses with his hated commandments. Adam had broken them all. Like ten lashes, the commandments seemed to smite Adam's bare back. From where he lay on the cold stone, he lifted a humped rock nearby and threw it crashing against a wall. Clenching his hands into fists, Adam made one fist beat the other for punishment. His heart pumped hard and warmingly, until finally he lay on his side in exhaustion, his hands bruised and sore from having reviled each other. Still the unremitting ringing in his ears.

*Adam! Adam!* God's voice cleft the rocks and found him where he lay. He opened his eyelids to utter blackness, but Adam felt happiness warm him as he lay in the cave. *Be still, and know that I am the Lord, your God,* so said the still quiet voice of his self.

*Adam!* Again the voice shouted his name, with fear and urgency—and why was that? He turned on the flashlight to search the darkness and heard the surprised joy of shuffling feet and startled voices. From the other side of the abyss, friends had seen the glow of his light.

And then the father voice barked command—to Adam? To someone else? "No! Don't!"

The authority in the fatherly roar was like a club knocking a man or boy to the ground, and it made Adam swoon into a moment of terrified oblivion. But as the cry echoed in his brain, Adam recognized there had been fear, even terror, resonating in that command. *Don't!*

When he opened his eyes, he sensed her presence. He picked up the flashlight and fixed her in light: there she stood, in all her beauty. She had leaped the abyss for him. Familiar, she was, in the splendor of her burnt orange blouse, tan shorts, bare legs. Tears glistening in her eyes as she gazed at his wounded nakedness.

"Eve?" he questioned.

"I'm here."

# EPILOGUE

## 2021—OLDUVAI GORGE AND SERENGETI PLAIN

WE ALL CONSIDERED it a sacred mission, even those of a rather secular disposition.

Certainly, we were solemn. I piloted the little craft, while Arielle sat beside me as copilot; she balanced the urn of ashes on the point of her knee. There was no room for the urn in her lap; her pregnancy occupied that territory. Even before the virulent infection set in and the amputation had occurred, an obliging priest had officiated at their bedroom marriage, and afterward the door had been closed. Despite the fever and Adam's delirium, she had told us, the marriage had been consummated.

The year 2020 had come and gone; whether the scientists had had their clear vision, I could not say. Soon I would give the legitimate astrophysicists Thom's flash drive. I would tell the secret of the red dot that became a heart. What of those images of the Lucys? I didn't care. I had my own reality, my own memory of my life with Thom.

Perhaps it would take a long time for people to develop a clear idea of our place in the cosmos. Decades or centuries might pass before people adjusted to the truth of Thom's discovery of extraterrestrial life. It was my faith that this truth would eventually help to free humans from the bonds of egotism.

The truth should make us humble: we are neither central nor unique in the universe. Values are not given; we must create our own. Certainly I now saw myself and my choices more clearly.

We had flown into the airport at Arundel on a commercial craft, then transferred to a light plane for the greater privacy it afforded. After takeoff, I had smiled when I piloted us past Mount Kilimanjaro; there had been no snow on it for over a decade.

I asked Arielle if she knew the Hemingway story set in the very Africa over which we were flying titled "The Snows of Kilimanjaro."

"No," she answered, "but I've heard the title."

"I can't remember what happens in it," I admitted. "Or who does it."

"Perhaps sometimes places are more important than people," Arielle observed. "You remembered Kilimanjaro."

From the backseat, Pierre Saad, suddenly awake, said, "I don't believe that."

I thought it no wonder that Pierre would be of a dissenting opinion about the relative value of places and people. Though I didn't say so, I certainly agreed that people mattered more than places. Individuals. Pierre had uprooted himself successfully from Egypt to become thoroughly French. When his mother was murdered, he had survived through the agency of another person, his Sufi stepfather. People were of crucial importance; let the places go. I said quietly to Pierre, "I wish your father were with us. I wish he had lived to know about the babies."

"He was glad to save us," Pierre replied. "I saw the look on his face, pleased and proud that he could command the gadget. He knew that Gabriel would kill him. He was at peace."

My body remembered that slow, gliding fall of the aircraft that had taken me to Adam's Eden, how I had passed the towering stand of redwoods, or what seemed to me to be California redwoods, though reason had told me that was impossible.

I looked down at Africa through this rented aircraft's window and saw a shattering of gold below.

"It's a yellow acacia tree," Pierre said. "Not much grows in the gorge."

The Great Rift Valley running down the eastern coast of Africa was the inverse, I thought, of the ancient Appalachian mountain range of the North American continent. The Appalachians thrusted upward, from Canada to north Alabama, along the Atlantic seaboard. Here it looked as though giant fingers had pulled the African continent apart. And out of that rift, something like human beings, precursors, had emerged. One might as well think of it mythically.

What in Eden had been real for Adam and for me? The animals, I hoped. The stray cow. And, sadly, Riley's loss was surely real, though we had saved him once. And the feral boy—did he still rage, unrelieved in his isolation and frustration, wordless, imprisoned in his own mind?

And what of my old life and how it defined me, of Thom? His body remained real to me. What could I ever know of his mind or his intentions?

I could look at the stars; I could believe in those so distant they could not be seen by the naked eye. I could believe, as Thom had, that round those stars, planets revolved, and on some chosen few something like people or animals lived. Everywhere throughout the universe. On Earth, some would lose their faith over the inevitable scientific news. For others, the idea of extraterrestrial life could only make God bigger, more mysterious, His wonders to behold. For still others, the idea of God would dissipate, thin as interstellar gas, become beautifully and utterly subjective. They might join the tribe of the mad English poet William Blake or Adam Black, of Idaho.

"I saw a photo, once," I said, "of ancient rock carvings—outdoors, on boulders in India, exposed to the sun and weather, at Mahabalipuram—a host of carved people and beasts seemed to emerge from the crevice. That, too, is a kind of book of Genesis."

Pierre's translations of the codex, along with other translations by experts in a variety of languages, would soon be published. Would it help to bring people closer together? Would the stranglehold of literalism on belief be loosened?

"We are of the Earth," Pierre said. "Perhaps that is the faith of all ancient peoples."

"My late husband, Thom, would have said we are of the stars. That atoms in our bodies were once forged by nuclear fusion in the hearts of stars." I thought but did not say, Bless him, whatever he was. I touched my own belly, bigger than Arielle's. My baby was a bit older.

I thought Thom would rejoice to know that I was pregnant now. He would be generous enough to rejoice—I felt sure of it, almost. I wondered for a moment if he might have been sterile, not I, and that was why he took so lightly our long postponement of having children. But we had been happy. At least I had been happy all those years.

"Would you like to visit India with me?" Pierre asked. "The president has given his new national director of parietal art an enormous travel budget."

"In time," I replied. "We'll be over the Olduvai soon. My pilgrimage."

"As a young child, I met Meave Leakey once," Arielle said. "Wonderful person, brilliant. She offered to meet me, if I ever came here, to talk about the discovery of Lucy while we stood near the spot."

"I'm a poor substitute, for sure," I said. I maneuvered the plane to fly lower and lower.

"Hold out your hand," Arielle said, "as we fly over."

"It's down there. Just here Lucy was found," I exclaimed, and I held out my hand as Arielle requested. To my surprise, Arielle placed in my palm a small, round stone. I glanced at it—a gray-white, fretted nodule, the size of a large marble.

"What is it?" I asked.

"It's a calcite formation, from the site, from Olduvai."

"Did Meave Leakey give it to you?"

"No." Arielle chuckled. "She would never have done that. I bought it recently on the black market."

I glanced down at the gray-white rock and then saw a similar color below, and a barren, grayish, sloping semicircle that appeared full of rubble. A large, cradlelike basin thought to be, by some, where the ancestors of humans had lived. There was the small upright monument marking the place where Lucy's fossilized bones had been found. I pulled back on the stick, and the plane ascended.

I made the airplane wings wave at the Olduvai Gorge as we flew away.

"We've seen it," I said quietly, "at least from the air. Now to the Serengeti." I added, "And Adam's ceremony."

The motor of the plane droned on, and for a while no one spoke. I glanced over at Arielle and noted her head was drooping and her eyes were closed. "I was so proud," Arielle said sleepily, "when Adam and I ran down the Champs-Elysées." Her eyes were closed, but she continued to hold the urn on her knee.

I pictured the moment that Arielle had mentioned, a moment photographed and used on a poster to encourage handicapped adults to participate in sporting events. Of course one quickly noticed Adam's leg, the shiny metal, but at first glance, anyone's gaze would be drawn to their youthful faces, bright and beautiful. Grinning happily, Adam had never looked more like Superman, and Arielle had never looked more like a beauty from the Arabian Nights. In the photo—the Arc de Triomphe in the background—their arms were curled up, and their hands closed. Anyone who looked closely would notice their matching golden wedding rings. Part of their happiness was that they both knew Arielle was pregnant.

"Pierre," I called softly, but he didn't answer. Asleep, I thought. Men doze so easily. And of course Arielle needed her sleep. I did not require conversation.

I listened to the drone of the engine. It was a nice little plane, shiny and new, called a Larkin. I watched our shadow move along beneath us on the ground. We wanted Adam's ashes to settle among the running herds. What better or more fitting place could there be to open the urn?

Were those lions below? I couldn't tell. Both Pierre and Arielle were dozing now. Below, I saw the shadows of giraffes, and then the giraffes themselves, three of them. Someday I would come back here with my own child. We would go on a photographic safari and be much closer than this to the animals. And was my child Adam's or Pierre's? I didn't know. I didn't need to know, nor did Pierre. He wanted me to marry him, but I saw no real need for that. We could be good companions, closest friends, parents, whether we married or not.

—

I thought of Arielle's child and mine sitting together on a donkey. One way or another, the babies were related. In the distance, I saw a grayish cloud and wondered if it had been stirred up from the plain by the running hooves of wildebeest. We had come to the vast Serengeti plain to see the migrating herds from the air.

I thought of the prehistoric cave paintings, of the glorious animals leaping across the dome of the large cavern. I thought, too, of the darling little goat drawing, curled down low on a wall where it seemed to wait happily. When we flew over the migrating wildebeest, we planned to open the plane door and scatter the ashes in the urn among the freely running animals of Africa. Like Arielle, Adam had become a runner.

"I smell dust," he said quietly from the backseat, awake at last.

"Dust to dust," I whispered so as not to wake the others.

"Are you feeling all right, Lucy?" Adam asked affectionately. "Not sleepy yourself?"

"Couldn't be better," I answered.

"Do you remember the night the zebras stampeded? How they ran around the bonfire and us?"

I did remember, and how he had held me close. There was no need to mention that. I knew he remembered, too, and treasured our togetherness in the past, as I did. Soon I would travel with Janet Stimson to Japan; Janet had suggested we go together to visit my parents at their mission.

"Look at this," I said to Adam, and reached back, handing him the nodule from Olduvai. "Arielle gave it to me, when we flew over the gorge. A calcite formation from the Lucy site."

"Did I miss it?"

"You were tired." I turned my head forward, then glanced down, at the vast undulations in the dark ocean of galloping animals—thousands and thousands of wildebeest, to be sure, and a few stray zebra and gazelle. I, too, could smell the rising dust of the Serengeti. Soon we would open the door and empty the urn, and the ashes of Adam's leg would meet the rising dust from the hooves of the animals. "On the way back to Arundel, I'll pass back over the Olduvai Gorge again, if you like."

"I'm very happy," he said, "that we've come here. The ashes of my leg are happy to become part of this."

"This? This what?" I asked gently. I heard Pierre stirring, and with a glance to the right saw Arielle opening her eyes. "Part of what, Adam?"

"This freedom, this authenticity."

*Finis*

# ACKNOWLEDGMENTS

As a writer, I am more grateful to my agent, my editors, and my publisher than it is possible to express. When the idea for this novel was hatched, it was nurtured and shaped by my agent, Joy Harris, and my editor, Marjorie Braman. I am grateful for the advice and support of my current editor, Jennifer Brehl, at William Morrow / HarperCollins, as well as for the entire team led by Michael Morrison. Sharyn Rosenblum has served as my inspired publicist since the beginning of my New York publishing career—for *Ahab's Wife, Four Spirits,* and *Abundance, A Novel of Marie Antoinette,* as well as for *Adam & Eve.*

Writer friends and relatives who have given me their time and expertise as wonderfully helpful readers of the manuscript in progress of *Adam & Eve* include Julie Brickman, Marcia Woodruff Dalton, Charles Gaines, Eleanor Hutchens, Nancy Jensen, John Sims Jeter, Robin Lippincott, Karen Mann, Nancy Brooks Moore, Eleanor Morse, Lucinda Dixon Sullivan, and Katy Yocom. My heartfelt gratitude to each of you. I also thank Katie Fraser Carpenter, my graduate assistant from the MFA brief-residency program at Spalding University, and Alan Naslund and our daughter, Flora, for conversations on the art of writing; and John C. Morrison for reading the early prospectus and chapters of *Adam & Eve.*

For conversations about various technical subjects addressed in *Adam & Eve,* including astrophysics, airplanes, and first aid, I thank John C. Morrison, Larry Dickinson, Marilyn Moss, and Herrick Fisher, though of course they should not be held responsible for my fictive use of their enthusiasm and knowledge. Likewise, I thank Christine Desdemaines-Hugon, author of *Stepping-Stones: A Journey Through the Ice Age Caves of the Dordogne,* for serving as Flora's and my wonderfully informed guide to cave art in the south of France. I also thank Jim and Mary Oppel for their hospitality in France to my daughter and me, and for Jim's guidance in my reading about parietal art—particularly Gregory Curtis's *The Cave Painters*. I also thank Jeanie Thompson for introducing me to Frederick Turner's *In the Land of Temple Caves: Notes on Art and the Human Spirit*. A lecture focusing on the fossil discovery of "Lucy" given by Meave Leakey to Flora and me and our fellow travelers with a National Geographic Society tour of Tanzania, including the Olduvai Gorge and the Serengeti Plain, was particularly inspiring. Also of crucial importance was my reading of the books on various religious topics by Elaine Pagels and Karen Armstrong.

For their love and encouragement and for being part of my family, I also wish to thank my daughter, Flora, and her husband, Ron Schildknecht; my brothers and sisters-in-law, Marvin D. and Charlotte Copeland Jeter, John and Derelene Jeter; and my extended family: my step-granddaughters, Lily and Ingrid Schildknecht, and my nieces and nephews, Lisa (Jeter) and Gregg Stucker, Amanda (Jeter) and Peter Brookmayer, Daniel Jeter, Kristina Jeter, and young Chase.

Other friends old and new for whom I am grateful in many ways but especially because of their affirmation of the creative life include Nana Lampton, Lynn Greenberg, David Messer, Charles and Patricia Gaines, Jonathan and Lucy Penner, Pamela Stein, Daly Walker, Janice Lewis Freeman, Bernard Moore, F. Elizabeth Sulzby, Luke Wallen, Jody Lisberger, Neela Vaswani, Elaine Orr, Suzette Henke and Jim Rooney, Deborah and David Stewart, Kay Gill, Ralph Raby, Maureen Morehead, and Pam Cox.

For my happy employment as teacher/administrator/writer, I thank the administrations and my colleagues at both the University of Louisville—President James Ramsay, Dean Blaine Hudson, and Thurston Morton Professor of English Suzette Henke; and Spalding University—President Tori

Murden McClure, Vice President Randy Strickland, and Administrative Director of the brief-residency MFA in writing program, Karen Mann. I also wish to thank all the staff, students, and alums of the Spalding University brief-residency MFA in writing, where I serve as program director, for their support of my writing, as well as my colleagues and students at the University of Louisville, where I am Writer in Residence. Parts of this manuscript were written during the time I served as Eminent Scholar in the spring of 2008 at the University of Alabama–Huntsville, and I thank for their hospitality President David Williams; the director of the Humanities Center, Dr. Brian Martine; and chair of the English department, Dr. Rose Norman; as well as Dr. Eleanor Hutchens, retired professor of English at UAH, and Agnes Scott, at whose historic home, Long Shadows, I resided.

Because *Adam & Eve* looks at beginnings and re-beginnings, I am remembering my own early stirrings as a writer. This novel is dedicated to the memory of James Michael Callaghan, student of philosophy, to whom I was married during most of my graduate school days in the Writers' Workshop at the University of Iowa. Michael encouraged my writing at every turn and believed in me as a writer and thinker; he also contributed to my education in literature, philosophy, music, political theory, and psychology. I am grateful for his support and that of his family, his parents, the late Dr. Nathan R. Callaghan and Helen Wolverton Callaghan, and his sister Kay Callaghan, my friend to this day.

I also wish to honor the memory of several other individuals. My love of literature and the critical analysis of it were affirmed and quickened by F. Dwight Isbell, as was my love of thought by Janice Kirkpatrick Entrekin, when I was an undergraduate student at Birmingham-Southern College. BSC professors, now deceased, who opened my mind, include Dean Cecil Abernethy, Dr. Leon Driskell, and Professor Richebourg Gaillard MacWilliams. Were it not for the influence of Leslie Moss Ainsworth, my beloved teacher of English and adviser to *The Mirror* of Phillips High School, Birmingham, Alabama, I would probably not have become a writer and teacher of writing and literature.

*—Sena Jeter Naslund*

*Long Shadows, Huntsville, Alabama*

*January 2010*

LYNBROOK PUBLIC LIBRARY
3 6646 00200 4339